Buried Deep
in Our Hearts

By Tracie Barton-Barrett

Buried Deep In Our Hearts
Copyright © 2016 by Tracie Barton-Barrett

ISBN 10: 0-9970259-0-5
ISBN 13: 978-0-9970259-0-3

Book Cover Design by Tugboat Design
Interior Formatting by Tugboat Design

This is a work of fiction. Names, characters, businesses, places, events and incidents are either the products of the author's imagination or used in a fictitious manner. Any resemblance to actual persons, living or dead, or actual events is purely coincidental.

For all the animals who have awakened my soul and changed me.
You, and your memories, are buried deep in my heart.

This is for you.

Acknowledgements

To Daniel: my sounding board, idea-generator, advocate, champion, and overall Love.

I also want to especially thank Madre, Shiela Braun, Robb, Ann, Emma & Rylan Sanner, Dr. Larue Coats, Leanna K. Murphy, and Deb Thompson. Sincere thanks to: Marilyn Brooks, Christine Ciecierski Berger, Allison and Jim Dickie, Anna Fuqua, Jason Grzegorek & Michael King, Jessica Henry, Julie and John Jarzabkowski, Chris Kometer, Dr. Teresa Lehnhardt, Sharon Meddaugh, Pamela Miller, Carole Gardner-Neurath, Bob & Cherie Nowak, Sylvie Hudgins Pleasant Parbus, Dr. Colleen Quinn, Mark & Jen Sansone, MJ Shannon, Sharon Shelton, Fr. Bill Sneck, Dr. Betsy Taylor, Dr. Gloria Vanderhorst, Lori Quinn Winkler, Aisling Winston, Sharon Elizabeth Wood, members of SSACP, and last but certainly not least, all the smart, savvy, supportive ladies at my book clubs. If your name isn't specifically mentioned and you were a part of my life during this process, please know that I thank you as well.

Thank you to Deborah Bradseth at Tugboat Design for your insights, patience, feedback, responsiveness and outstanding work.

A very, very special thanks to Mrs. Luana Russell. From day one, your unwavering and steadfast commitment, dedication, enthusiasm, feedback, and guidance to this process has been second to none. You were my teacher for high school English, and you continue to be my teacher in Life. But, now I can call you a friend. I am eternally grateful.

Characters

Bryn Troxell, Jacqueline's daughter, married to Julian Troxell
    Has two children: Megan and Ethan
    Has Tucker, a Gollie (Golden Retriever/Collie mix)
    Lauren Wright, Bryn's childhood best friend
    Taffy, Bryn's dog growing up
    Olaf/Pringle, Megan's kitty; Ace, a Boxer puppy
    Lawrence and Barbara Troxell, Julian's parents
    Madeline Waters, Megan's friend. Allison Waters is Madeline's mom.
    Doug and Janet, his wife, Julian's boss; Mike, Nate, and Sanjit,
        Julian's friends
    Reverend Owens, their pastor

Jacqueline Stanton, widow of Edmond, mother of Bryn Troxell
    Cocker Spaniel, Chloe
    Ranger, her beloved horse growing up
    Gladys Paisley, Jacqueline's neighbor. Roosevelt (dog), Piper &
        Petey (dogs) & Eleanor, (cat)
    Donna, Jacqueline's good friend. Lost her child in car accident.
    Ronni (Veronica), Jacqueline's good friend; Nivie's aunt
    Shirley, her housekeeper; Cynthia, her dog groomer
    Bill Langdon, Jacqueline's date/"friend"
    Fr. Kenneth, her priest

Nivie (Genevieve) Emerson married to Alex Emerson
 Had Minerva, the cat
 Kimball Kitty from Siobhan, Nivie's sister
 Sherlock and Watson, two kitties
 Brad, Nivie's friend from college and his partner, Esteban
 Chelsea, "problem student" of Nivie's
 John Porter, Nivie's principal; Anna Carlson, choir teacher

Dr. Tamika Carmichael, veterinarian

Part One: Loss

"Ever has it been known that love knows not its own
depth until the hour of separation."
~Kahlil Gibran~

"**I** REMEMBER WHEN YOU WERE JUST A TINY, PUFFY BALL OF FUR, fitting snugly in my hands," Nivie Emerson said, leaning down and whispering to her tortoiseshell cat, Minerva, or Mini, for short.

Mini's tiny stature, punctuated by her rabbit-like fur, endeared her to Nivie and her husband, Alex. The two-inch nub Mini had instead of a tail was an added bonus. Whenever Nivie or Alex lay down, Mini would leap up on them and begin kneading, or "making biscuits." Didn't matter where, or when; Mini was flexible. Nivie said Mini was so advanced in her skill, she could be employed at a fast food restaurant. Mini's habit of walking on her humans' hair, as well as directly upon sensitive anatomical areas, appeared almost deliberate. As a kitten, Mini enjoyed climbing up Nivie's jeans like a mountaineer and loved to pour her tiny body into boxes that, at first glance, appeared to be too small, but she made it work. Over the years, her meows morphed from a sweet kitten mew to a throaty warbled moan that seemed especially earsplitting in the early morning hours. Nivie and Alex almost lost their breath from laughing so hard when their laser pointer "chase" took Mini's attention to points on the wall previously unnoticed.

Nivie met Mini as an undergrad. Their strong bond cemented when Mini had been the mascot of the women's softball team. Although she never played any sports, Nivie eagerly agreed to house the team's stray kitten for a few nights when asked by a team member. Those "few nights" turned into weeks and she became more and more attached to Mini, despite the dorm's strict no-pet policy. Nivie eventually used her passion, charm, and humor to convince the team that Minerva was hers.

She and Mini were constant companions, surviving school, assorted jobs, relocations, and boyfriends. Five years ago, when Nivie married Alex, Mini initially was not a fan of these new living arrangements. Hissing was constant until one night when Nivie was away at a teaching conference. Mini unceremoniously climbed onto Alex's lap as he watched TV, silently acknowledging that she had accepted him. He could stay.

Twenty years had passed since college, and now Nivie and Alex were stroking a lifeless Mini on the sterile, cold veterinarian's examining table.

"I'm so sorry," Dr. Tamika Carmichael, their beloved veterinarian, whispered. "Mini was such a sweet kitty."

They had both dreaded this inevitable day. But, from the time she was a kitten, Nivie made a pact with Minerva: when the time came, Nivie would not let her suffer. Unfortunately, the suffering she had spared Minerva had now been transferred to her and Alex.

Dr. Carmichael brought out a clay paw print imprint keepsake kit. Gently pressing Mini's front paw into the clay, she wiped off Mini's paw and handed the circular tin holder to Nivie.

"I'll give you two some privacy. Take as much time as you need," Dr. Carmichael said, tip-toeing out of the room. "Please let me know if there is anything I can do."

Alex put his arm around his wife as she reached down for the bag of Minerva's toys, still clutching the paw print tin. "Here's your milk ring, sweetie. And, your mouse." Her voice cracked when she gently placed them in front of Mini's open eyes and still face. Nivie tenderly kissed the top of Mini's head as she pushed her own shoulder-length reddish-brown hair to the side. Due to her short stature, Nivie didn't need to bend too far over the examining table. Taking a pair of scissors and gently cutting a few swatches of Mini's fur, Nivie placed the strands in a Ziploc baggie. She slowly zipped it shut, illustrating the chapter of her life she was now closing.

After discussing all the options, they decided Mini would be cremated. They left her with Dr. Carmichael and Mini's ashes would be returned to them.

On a sunny, late spring day, walking silently out to their Toyota Prius, Alex put his arm around his wife again. "So, that's it? Years of love, and then, she's gone? Just like that?" Nivie asked, her green eyes filling up with tears. "This is it. Mini's really gone." She paused and shook her head, handing the Ziploc bag to Alex. "I need to go to The Gardens."

Alex stopped. "All right, Love. Do you want company?"

"Thanks. But, I think I need to go by myself."

He wiped his eyes. "I understand," he said, kissing the top of his wife's head.

"Hi, Mrs. Emerson," greeted the girl behind the register at the Visitor Center gift shop.

Despite her heavy heart and bloodshot eyes, Nivie smiled politely. She flashed her annual membership pass purely out of habit, not out of necessity, since she often frequented The Gardens. She found great solace here, visiting her favorite spots every few weeks, even though she wasn't a garden person, per se. But, as a painter, creativity and artistry coursed through her veins, and The Gardens had it in spades. She pulled out the paw print tin and examined Mini's paw impression. Placing the top back over the tin, she held it close as she walked.

Woodhaven Run Gardens, known locally as "The Gardens," was built by the original Woodhaven Run founders. The family home, built at the beginning of the 20th century, and then their son's home built forty years later, still stood on the one-hundred acre property. The son's modern architectural influences, inspired by Frank Lloyd Wright, were evident in various homes and churches throughout Woodhaven Run. At Christmas time, The Gardens became a winter wonderland, with luminous lights at every turn, sometimes combined with the melodic voices of the Woodhaven Run choir. As a rite of spring, most of the nervous Woodhaven Run high school students and their dates congregated in The Gardens for stunning landscape backdrops to endless Prom pictures. Nivie's own Prom photos were taken here. Many couples used The Gardens' wedding area to exchange "I do's," but Nivie's mother wouldn't hear of it. "The Catholic Church is the only place where your wedding will be held. Period." And so it was. Nivie and Alex married and honeymooned in Ireland, Nivie's family's homeland. However, not to be boxed in, shortly after returning home, Nivie got a tattoo of a heart on her upper thigh with her and Alex's name inside. Nivie never told her mother, and she certainly didn't ask permission.

She pushed open the Visitor Center double doors to The Gardens. The familiar winding path edged with fir, cypress, and pine trees guided her to an area where rock formations on either side of the path saluted her. She could continue straight, but she always enjoyed the waterfall tucked hard left. Because Nivie had spent her childhood years in Boston before moving to Michigan with her Mom and sister, water played an integral part in her favorite childhood memories. The rush of the water seemed louder than Niagara Falls, but never failed to soothe her.

I love my water fix. Just wish it were the ocean.

A steadily moving stream now ran parallel to her pathway, except for the occasional times it wove in and out under the path beneath her feet. The water trickled over interspersed rocks on the bank of the three-foot wide stream in a continuous and hypnotizing hum.

The path led her to the Sun Bridge, a cement arched bridge that, on the surface, appeared to be a sun rising over the horizon. The architect purposefully created it so one would have to look to the reflection in the water to see a complete circular sun. In the winter, the layer of ice covering the water created an especially stunning sight. However, Nivie much preferred the sunny, warmer days to the dreary, cold days of the north.

But, my Mini loved watching the snow fall through the window.

Drawing in a deep breath, she approached her favorite vibrant red bridge. The still water underneath and the trees, bushes, and rocks that cradled the bridge made Nivie's heart jump every time she came near. She looked for fish as she stood at the bridge's top, feeling that, for a moment, she was a small part of that beautiful scene. She normally delighted in seeing the frequent turtle visitors and often verbally greeted them, ignoring the other strollers' sideways glances. But, not today. Today, she would continue walking over, without taking in the view.

Although The Gardens were carpeted with countless plants, flowers, and a few bridges, many bronze statues were dispersed throughout. One of the art pieces that spoke to her was created by Marshall Fredericks. It was a gazelle, rearing, with his horns touching his back, leaving his neck exposed.

I feel like that gazelle.

The children's area was a definite "no" today. She found it odd that the body of water adjacent to the children's area was called "Snake River." And, her heavy heart couldn't handle the eruption of children's giggles and laughing from water randomly spurting from the concrete.

Someday, Alex and I will visit that area with our human babies.

She finally arrived at her favorite spot, in front of a majestic fountain. A large u-shaped flower bed greeted her with blooming lavender, red and yellow zinnias, tiny white sweet alyssum, and tall, thin purple salvia standing at attention in the middle. A vibrant thunbergia ivy laced the gateway leading to the flower beds. Just beyond the flower bed, she sank onto her favorite bench, donated by the Woodhaven Run Blooms Garden Council and closed her eyes. A male bluebird called, and she opened her eyes to see her favorite bird perched upon a branch. Facing the gushing fountain, with tears streaming down her cheeks, she whispered, "My precious mini Mini Minerva."

Bryn Troxell pulled her long, blondish hair back into a ponytail, and grabbed her Ray Bans in preparation for her regular morning jog. Jogging provided many benefits for her willowy figure and long legs, including some much cherished quiet time. However, she had to remain cognizant not to overdo it. A crushing fear of gaining weight, as well as a residual knee complication from a high school tennis injury, could both easily become inflamed again.

Bryn had loved her regular runs with her friend, Lauren Wright, since they met in Kindergarten. But, Lauren moved away a while ago and today, it was just Bryn and her dog, Tucker. Bryn's beloved mixed-breed leapt as she retrieved his leash from the drawer. Tucker's reddish fur and blondish belly highlighted his bulky body. His large tail, imitating a rudder, often did damage to a person's leg or any unsuspecting item on a table from the strength of his wagging. Julian, Bryn's husband of almost six years, worked as a marketing manager for Woodhurst Industries, the town's main employer. Julian and Bryn were both natives of Woodhaven Run with similar backgrounds. As former Prom and Homecoming King and Queen, they were also both actively involved in athletics and academics. Although Julian's job took him traveling out of town more than he was home, Bryn was beginning to anticipate the times he was away. She loved his tall, athletic build but his charming and charismatic personality often drowned her out. Bryn's mother, Jacqueline, lived a few miles from her and occasionally watched her two-year-old daughter, Megan. Although close in distance to her daughter, Jacqueline was not emotionally close to Bryn.

A small, Michigan city of about 40,000, Woodhaven Run benefited from a number of cultural and historical opportunities other cities its size rarely had. Bryn and Tucker, heading down the driveway of their five-bedroom, brick, Federal Colonial style house, ran past the Country Club. Her parents spent a great deal of time there when Bryn was growing up, and she was still a member. She continued past the Tridge, or three-way bridge, as well as the downtown area and the Woodhaven Run Center for the Arts, or The Art Center, as it was usually called.

Past The Gardens, and past Megan's school, through neighborhoods whose lawns were peppered with signs demonstrating U of M, Michigan State, Detroit Lions, and local high school support. Squirrels and chipmunks darted about, stopping only to see who was moving. Whereas they were fair game in their fenced backyard, Tucker ignored them on the run. As Bryn's constant companion, Tucker ran dutifully next to her, tongue dangling off the side of his smiling mouth.

With the anniversary of her dad's death, Edmond Stanton, looming, Bryn knew that today's run was imperative. She actively resisted any intrusion of painful memories so they wouldn't interrupt her jogging rhythm. Instead of turning around at the library or near the cemetery, she jogged past the place she and Julian first got Tucker six years ago.

Bryn and Julian shared a mutual love of dogs and knew their lives together would include at least one. They had thought about getting a dog through a breeder, but at that time, being recent college graduates, it was cost prohibitive. Despite both Julian's and Bryn's dads' positions of upper management at Woodhurst Industries, Julian thought it best that they not ask their parents for the money. For a house, yes, but not for a dog. They had looked at a few rescues, but never sincerely connected with any of the dogs they visited despite being prepared with a collar, food, toys, and bedding.

One Saturday, they were out shopping near the mall when they saw Woodhaven Run Humane Society advertising an adopt-a-thon a nearby pet store. Due to the sunny weather, some of the puppies and dogs were in carriers and shaded makeshift cages in front of the store. One dog, in particular, caught Bryn's eye.

"Oh, Julian. Look," Bryn said, pointing at a red and blonde puppy. "Can we please go over and see?"

Looking down at his phone, Julian sighed, "I guess."

As they approached the cages of adoptable animals, Bryn's heart beat faster. She crouched down next to the dog who was on a long leash, attached to an open crate. Patting the ground, she quietly said,

"Hi, sweetie, how are you?" Bryn continued to gush as Julian stood over her. "Come here. Aww. That's a good puppy. What a sweetie."

Although the dog's curly, fluffy tail was tucked between his legs, he edged over to Bryn. His head was down, ears back, welcoming a head-pat.

"What's his name?" Bryn asked, looking around.

"We've been calling him 'Spike,'" a voice said behind her.

"'Spike'?" Bryn asked, jerking her head around.

"Well, actually my son named him that." Bryn looked up and saw a short, portly woman walking towards them. "I personally don't think he's a 'Spike,' but you know how these things go. We've been fosterin' him for a few weeks now. Hi, I'm Linda, and you are—?"

"Julian Troxell. Nice to meet you," Julian interrupted, holding out his hand. "And this is my wife, Bryn. She's a little enthusiastic today."

Bryn looked up, waved and smiled, as she rubbed the dog's muzzle.

"Nice to meet you both," Linda said, looking down at Bryn and the dog. "Yeah, he's a good one. Poor thing was found neglected, with his ribs showing. Hair matted in different places, except for a few balding areas. And, two of his teeth rotted. Someone really neglected him."

"That's so sad. Poor sweetie," Bryn quietly added. Spike had settled down next to her on the concrete with his head on her lap. "So, how old is he? Like a few months?"

"Well, no. Actually, closer to a year," Linda said.

"Really? He looks like a puppy," Bryn said.

"Yeah, he was clearly the runt. And, with the neglect, lack of food, and probably bein' pushed around by his brothers and sisters. Well, the little guy never really grew. Didja buddy?" Linda stroked his side, as he wagged his tail.

"Great. A runt," Julian mumbled.

Linda continued, "After givin' him a good bath, and shaving out some of the mattin' of his long hair, and fattenin' him up, he's a new dog."

The dog swiped his tongue at Bryn's chin. "Awww. That's great."

Linda resumed, "He also gets along real nice with other dogs, and cats, and especially children. Loves children. But, he does get scared at loud noises, thunderstorms and the like. And, he can be submissive, even at times when he doesn't need to be."

Julian sighed and shook his head. "Great, a wuss."

"But, he's an extremely lovin', big-hearted dog, who will love anything that comes across his path. Wontcha, buddy?"

Bryn flashed a big smile up to Julian. "Well, you've done a great job with him," Bryn said to Linda. The dog moved even closer to Bryn, laid on his back with legs open. She began rubbing his belly, and he slowly blinked in enjoyment.

"Uh, he's not a pure Golden Retriever, is he?" Bryn queried.

Linda smiled, gently chuckling. "No, he's actually what they call a 'Gollie.'"

"What's a 'Gollie'?" Julian snapped, with a furrowed brow.

"A Collie-Golden Retriever Mix. A Gollie."

"Of course, he's a 'Gollie.' A mixed-breed. Not a Boxer. Not a Lab." Julian looked at Spike and sighed.

"But, Jay, he's just so sweet," Bryn quietly protested. "We haven't had a dog that has responded like this to us before."

"Well, let's see. Does he still have his...?" Julian crouched down to see.

Bryn gently touched his arm, trying to quiet her husband.

"Uh, no. He's already been neutered," Linda said. "Those things have been gone for a while!"

Julian grinned. "Well, you know. You can get implants."

"Jay," Bryn whispered, laughing nervously.

He smiled. "I'm just sayin'—"

"Did you say your name was Troxell?" Linda asked.

"Yeah," Julian flashed his bright smile. "Have you heard of Lawrence and Barbara Troxell?"

"Yeah, I have," Linda said, looking down at Bryn and the puppy. "Lookie there. He's really taken to ya. I think he'd be a good addition for you guys. We have an application, but I don't think it'll be a problem."

Julian bent down to pet Spike's head and asked, "Well, Gollie. What do you think?"

Julian looked over at his wife, whose eager eyes were waiting for confirmation.

"All right. Guess you'll do," Julian softened. "I guess we'll take him then."

"Yes!" Bryn embraced the dog. With his strong tail swishing back and forth, he licked her face again. "Let's take you home."

"What's the return policy again?" Julian asked.

Linda's eyebrows shot up. "Well...if he..."

"Julian!' Bryn interrupted, embarrassed. "Honestly."

Julian smirked. "Kidding. Just kidding."

"Spike" was now named "Tucker." Bryn had loved the name ever since she was in college, when she lived on Tucker Street. They completed the paperwork and persuaded a reluctant Tucker to jump into the backseat of their Infinity SUV with a treat. He silently watched Julian and Bryn the entire drive home, with a new squeaky Teddy toy by his feet. After a long walk around their neighborhood, they brought Tucker into their house, where for the rest of the day, he walked around with a lowered tail, smelling and investigating his new habitat. He watched with wide eyes when they prepared his food and showed him to his bed. When Julian or Bryn crouched down to talk to him, he lifted his paw and licked their hand. After any sudden noise, he cowered with his tail tucked between his legs. Although it was especially difficult for Julian, they tried to lower their voices as Tucker adjusted to his new home. But, Julian saw no need to change his habits. Especially not for a mixed-breed dog.

While Bryn and Julian prepared for bed on the first night, Tucker sat with his back hugging the wall near the bedroom door. His eyes studied their every move.

"It's OK, sweetie," Bryn reassured the pup as she got into bed. Julian climbed in next to her and turned out the light.

"'Night," Julian said.

"'Night, Tucker," Bryn said.

After a few minutes, a soft whimper and a loud, consistent thumping broke the quiet night.

Bryn dangled her hand over the side of the bed, quietly snapping her fingers. Almost immediately she felt warm air and a wet nose and was delighted once she felt the fervent licking of a coarse tongue. Her fingers moved to Tucker's soft, floppy ears.

"Oh, Jay. Can't he stay on the bed? Just this once?" Bryn pleaded.

"Hm. What?" Julian responded, dry-mouthed. "All right. I guess. Just this once."

Bryn sat up, patted the bed, and Tucker instantly jumped near her hand. Walking to the foot of the bed, he turned in a few tight circles, plopping his body down on the space between Bryn and Julian. Bryn leaned in, kissed the top of his head and almost inaudibly whispered, "This is your spot now." He licked her face in agreement. She pulled the sheets over herself as she fell asleep smiling. It wasn't long before Tucker was snoring. That was his spot from then on.

———⊱⊰———

"How many?"

Over the cacophony of restaurant patrons and clanging silverware, Jacqueline Stanton mouthed to the hostess, "One."

Halfway between Woodhaven Run and Traverse City, Jacqueline stopped to eat dinner at one of her favorite restaurants. Although Jacqueline had frequented it often with her husband, Edmond, it had been a while since she had returned. It was a bustling Friday evening, but she was disappointed none of the "regulars" were working. Jacqueline appeared younger than her 55 years. Her slim 5'7" stature complimented her styled, dark-brown hair, which sat just below her ears, accentuating her bright blue eyes.

"*How many?*" The hostess loudly repeated.

Jacqueline cleared her throat, leaned in slightly, holding up her index finger, and repeated, "One."

"Oh. There's room for you at the bar," the hostess pointed.

"I'd prefer to wait for a table."

"So, then, it might be a while," the hostess snapped. "What's the name?"

"Ed...I mean, Jacqueline."

"Ok, Jacqueline. We'll let you know when we're ready for you." The hostess flashed a quick, fake smile.

Jacqueline turned around to see people behind her lined up on either side of the dimly-lit foyer. Without an open spot to sit, she moved a few feet from the hostess desk, inadvertently standing in the path of guests headed to their seats, criss- crossed with harried waiters bearing full trays. People awkwardly squeezed by her to make reservations, while well-fed patrons made their way to the parking lot.

"Mike, party of four."

"Darcy, party of five."

"Jack?"

"Me?" Jacqueline pointed to her chest.

"No, the other," the hostess corrected, motioning to the people behind her.

The other Jack bumped into Jacqueline's elbow as he brushed by.

"Oh, pardon me," he said, looking behind him, while his wife and another couple proceeded to their table.

Jacqueline gently touched her elbow. Spotting a newly available seat on the bench, she sat down.

The veil of fog and numbness that plagued Jacqueline had begun to dissipate. That morning, ten months, twenty-three days, and nine hours ago, Jacqueline had been making their bed in preparation for a new day that included shopping for an important Master Gardener meeting. Their dog, Chloe, was outside doing her business when Edmond arrived home from early morning doubles at the Tennis Center with former colleagues. From the bedroom, Jacqueline heard the door slam and keys clinking on the kitchen counter.

"Eddy?" She yelled from the bedroom.

"Yeah," Edmond responded, slowly walking down the hall to their bedroom.

Glancing at her watch, she fluffed the pillow and straightened the sham as he walked in. "You're home early."

"Eh, this chest cold has really gotten a hold of me today," he said, rubbing his chest. He went into their bathroom and took an ibuprofen.

After straightening the other sham, the bed was now complete. "Why don't you lie down?" she said, patting the bed.

He lay down, and she adjusted his pillow. His brown eyes looked unusually distant against his pale face.

"Just rest your eyes," she said, lying down next to him. "That should help."

Just as she eased down, she felt his body violently jerk and fall over onto her. Stunned, she rolled him over onto his back. "C'mon now, Eddy. I'm not in the mood for joking. Especially today."

She looked up at his face and saw his eyes fixed and glazed, with a small amount of vomit oozing down the side of his mouth.

"Eddy? Eddy!" She screamed, shaking his shoulder.

No response.

Even though she immediately called 911, Jacqueline knew Edmond's soul left his body in their bedroom. An ambulance's siren could still send shivers down her spine.

Most of the years of their marriage were good. A few in the beginning were bumpy, since Edmond's job required extensive travel as he climbed the career ladder at Woodhurst Industries. But, he was the true love of her life. Their years of hosting work dinners, attending charity events, and entertaining were some of Jacqueline's favorite past times. To top it off, their dutiful daughter, Bryn, had given them a perfect granddaughter.

"Jacqueline, party of one."

Jacqueline quickly shook her head.

"Jacqueline, party of *one*," the hostess loudly repeated, looking straight at her. "Now you." The hostess' quick fake smile returned.

Following the hostess to the back, Jacqueline came upon Judy and Dave Hornbeck seated at a table.

"Why, hello, Judy. Dave. How are you?"

They looked up, their smiles falling slightly. "Oh. Hello, Jacqueline. How are you?"

"It's been a while. How have you been?"

"Yes, well, very busy," Judy said. "With AAUW. And, the book sale. Then, of course, there are the grandkids' games. Hardly a moment to myself."

"Yes, I'm sure you are quite busy." Jacqueline said. "Well, please give my best to your family. And, enjoy your meal. I hear the prime rib is delicious."

"Yes, it is."

Jacqueline smiled politely. Turning around she saw the hostess standing near a table in the middle of the floor.

"Here we are. Cameron will be with—," the hostess began, handing her the menu.

"—Excuse me, would it be possible to sit over there?" Jacqueline whispered, pointing to an adjacent booth, farther from Judy and Dave.

"Sorry ma'am. That is for a larger group."

"Oh, I see."

"But, that table is available." The hostess pointed to a table right next to the kitchen door.

"No, this will be fine. Thank you," Jacqueline acquiesced, pulling out her chair with her back to the Hornbecks.

Despite the eye contact she gave the waiter as he announced the specials, Jacqueline didn't remember any of them, nor was she interested. Behind her, occasional laughs from Judy sliced the hum of other diners' chatter. Slight relief took over her body when the waiter finally returned to take her order of lobster bisque, as she had tired of feigning reading the menu. Jacqueline had never before eaten so quickly, leaving half of it in the bowl. Thankfully, the Hornbecks were gone when she left.

After driving another hour back home to Woodhaven Run, Jacqueline turned down her maple-tree lined street. Planted every 15 feet in front lawns, the tops of the mature trees created a cozy canopy. No less than 3,000 square feet each, every house was built on at least half an acre. Most were built in the Frank Lloyd Wright tradition, giving them an angular appearance. Back walls of windows overlooked the spacious backyards, many adorned with pools and tennis courts. Clerestory windows accentuated long hallways, leading from the great rooms to the home's bedrooms and offices. Although the ceilings appeared low, the bedrooms were open and sizeable.

Jacqueline drove her Lexus sedan into her semi-circle driveway, cradled by lights ensconced in brick on either side. In her three-car garage, the Mercedes, as well as Edmond's BMW, were still under tarps.

A small, buff-colored Cocker Spaniel with deep, dark eyes and a wiggly nub greeted Jacqueline at the door, tags jingling. Jacqueline appreciated the welcome by this delightful companion she and Edmond brought home as a puppy "retirement gift" six years ago.

"Hi, Chloe," Jacqueline said. Chloe's furry body was bent in half with excitement, and she had her fuzzy lamb toy, Lammikins, gripped in her mouth. "OK, OK. Let me set this down." The metal keys clinked as Jacqueline placed them on the table. The sound echoed in the foyer.

Jaqueline sighed. "Happy Thirtieth Anniversary," she said, leaning down to pet Chloe's head.

Dame Edith Sitwell once said, "I'm not eccentric, I'm just more alive than most people." Thus was Gladys Paisley. A long-time resident of Woodhaven Run, Gladys was often the punchline of residents' jokes. In her 82 years, her diminutive height of barely five feet was a three or four inch reduction from her younger years. Dog and cat fur were constant passengers on her clothes, adorning the wool capes she wore nine months out of the year. To the casual observer, it appeared as though she purposely tried to include every color of the rainbow in her outfits. Rarely did her capes, hats, animal pendants, boots, and pants match; she loved colors, and any combination of them was fair game. In the warmer months, her shirts and blouses read "My best friend has whiskers" and "Wag more, bark less." Although she didn't say much, Gladys' high-pitched speaking voice accentuated her rounded, cherubic face. Plastic kitten and puppy barrettes and clips pulled her white hair back into a bun. When she dressed up to go out, usually to the Art Center, her face was never without heavy black eye liner along her eyelids, bright blue eye shadow, and dark outlining of her eyebrows. Gladys referred to people as "Dear," regardless of their ages.

Whenever one of her beloved animals died, Gladys submitted a full-page obituary to *Woodhaven Run Daily News* in honor of her pet, complete with pictures and details about how much she would miss him or her. She then dressed in all black for a few weeks after the pet's death. Although she rarely drove, her dark blue 1988 Oldsmobile Cutlass Supreme carried the expected amount of dings and scratches for a car that age. Some scratches were covered up with magnetic paw prints that read "Who rescued Who?" and "All My Children Have Paws."

Gladys' house was peppered with newspapers, books, and animal figurines, and the television was constantly tuned to reruns of *Lassie, Flipper, Mr. Ed,* or *Lawrence Welk*. On the front of her house she hung a flag of two tuxedo cats, and her mailbox was in the shape of a white Maltese dog. The garden flag by the mailbox displayed either a cat or dog in a scene reflective of the current month or season. Under an enormous pine tree in the backyard, headstones marked the loss of beloved animals. Pine needles surrounded the graves during the year, except when the snow blanketed the stones.

On her regular walks around the neighborhood, Gladys pushed her two Maltese dogs, Piper and Petey, in a stroller specifically designed for dogs. Their little white bodies looked like two Tic-Tacs inside the mesh enclosure. The neighbors always knew when they were coming, for the barking could be heard a half-mile before they appeared. Around Gladys' wrist was a leash attached to an old black Labrador Retriever, Roosevelt, who dutifully lumbered alongside. With cloudy eyes and a tongue hanging from his white-tipped snout, he tuned out the Malteses' noise to focus on his family time.

Living down the street from Gladys for many years, Jacqueline had encountered numerous members from Gladys' entourage, either those in picture frames on the wall, or residents beneath the pine tree in the backyard. Although Jacqueline couldn't escape the fact that today was her birthday, only a week after her anniversary, she knew some fresh air would divert her attention. At least momentarily. She and Chloe heard the barking before Gladys' stroller turned the corner. Jacqueline was relieved to see Gladys wearing a yellow top, blue puppy socks, with a bright green full length skirt, swishing the ground as she walked. No black clothes today.

"Why hello, Ms. Paisley. How are little Petey and Piper today?" Jacqueline's question almost drowned out by the ear-piercing barking.

"Oh, hello, Jacqueline, dear. We are just enjoying our walk on this lovely day. Aren't you, dears?" Petey and Piper's eager faces pushed up against the mesh, their twitching noses sniffing the air.

"They certainly are appreciating it," Jacqueline said, discretely rubbing her ear closest to the stroller, trying to dull the piercing barks. Chloe quietly stood by her side, watching a chipmunk dart across the street.

"And, how are you, Chloe, dear?" Gladys asked, leaning over and tapping her on the head, shaking Chloe out of her focus. "What a lovely dog, she is."

"Thank you, Ms. Paisley."

"We purchased a new stroller. Isn't it nice? It has four strong wheels, and a new pocket for carrying items. Piper and Petey really like it, and Rosie likes to have a new stroller to walk by, too."

Jacqueline leaned down and looked over at Roosevelt, his cheeks pulled back revealing a permanent smile. "That's a dapper bandana you have."

Jacqueline looked back up at Gladys, who continued to smile at her.

"Roosevelt is looking dapper in his new bandana," Jacqueline repeated slower, with increased volume.

"Oh, yes!" Gladys exclaimed. "Yes, he just went to the cleaners. He got his bath, and his nails trimmed up real nice. All the trimmins, didn't you, Rosie?" She stroked his head, making his tongue wag from side to side.

"Yes, yes," Jacqueline affirmed.

"And, today is a big day, I presume, dear?" Gladys asked.

"Why, yes. How kind of you to remember. Yes, it's the big 5-6."

"Oh, my. You're still so young," Gladys chuckled.

"Yes. But, no need to make a big ordeal."

"And, how is our Bryn-dear?" Gladys asked.

"She's doing quite well. She's got her hands full with the little one."

"Indeed."

"Yes, Megan is now thirty months and loves to dance. She adores her princess dress and her tiara."

Gladys giggled, her eyes almost disappearing.

"I have a picture, if you are interested," Jacqueline said.

"Oh, goodness, yes."

Jacqueline pulled out her phone. "Let's see here. Oh, this is a good one. This is a picture of her a few weeks ago."

"Oh." Gladys blinked deliberately, adjusting her head and stretching out her arm. "Eyes aren't what they used to be!" she quipped.

Jacqueline smiled, thinking about the new unused reading glasses sitting next to her chaise lounge in the living room.

The barking inside the stroller resumed with increased intensity, while Chloe began to whimper.

"Well, you take care, Ms. Paisley. It was lovely to see you."

"Oh, you, too, dear." Gladys began pushing the stroller past Jacqueline and then stopped.

"Oh, Jacqueline?"

"Yes?"

Gladys gently pushed her cart aside and took Jacqueline's hand.

"Again, I am so sorry about Edmond. He was a wonderful man."

"Oh, yes. Yes, he was." A lump began to form in Jacqueline's throat, which she was able to stave off. "Thank you, Ms. Paisley. I truly appreciate that."

Gladys quickly tapped Jacqueline's hand with her fingers and gave a tight smile. Putting both of her hands back on the stroller, Gladys commanded, "All right, dears, onward and upward!"

"Onward and upward," Jacqueline quietly echoed, as Gladys walked away. She stared at the top of her hand, rubbing her finger over her wedding ring.

"All right, Chloe. Let's go," Jacqueline said, as the distant barking finally subsided.

"You're moving? Where? When?" Nivie queried, never knowing where her younger sister, Siobhan, was going next. She had a wanderlust that exceeded even Nivie's.

"Korea! To teach English."

"Korea? Really? When are you leaving? How long'll you be gone?"

"Not sure. At least a year. It's an awesome opportunity to see the world. And also, you know, to give back and stuff."

"True," Nivie said, then paused. "Uh, what are you going to do with Mr. Kimball Kitty?"

"So… funny you should ask. Not exactly sure. But, I was thinking, maybe….you and Alex could take him?"

Silence.

Siobhan spoke faster. "I really can't take him. He'd hate the long flight, and then I'd have to find a place with him. Just too much."

More silence.

"And, with what just happened with Minerva, and all. Thought you guys might, you know, be really good for him."

"Well… let me talk to Alex. He's working late tonight on a new software program."

"You know, you guys, like, loved him so much at Christmas and stuff," Siobhan repeated, with even more speed.

Sighing, Nivie said, "Shiv, you really don't know anybody else who can take him?"

"Not really. You know, Alyssa has young children. Brandi's pregnant, and Carrie has too many dogs. And, you know, Ma sure as hell won't take him. He's still young, so he can adapt. Please, please, please?"

"Um, just not sure. I'll need to check with Alex. But, I'll let you know."

"So—well. It's just, um, not a lot of time here. And, I'd hate to take him to the shelter."

"Well, we know *that's* not happening," Nivie admonished. "Again, I'll need to check with Alex. I'll let you know."

"Thanks, Niv. I know you guys will love him! He couldn't have a better home!"

"Hey! Not a done deal!" Nivie snapped.

"Yeah, just playing with ya."

Nivie sighed. "It would be nice to have him around, since you're right: it sucks without Minerva. Like, really sucks."

"Yeah, I'll bet," Siobhan said.

"Thanks so much for your sympathy card, Shiv."

"You're welcome."

"But, it's like, there is no more energy in the house. Just…blah. But, at least our vet is awesome. She even, like, called to see how we were doing. Ma did, too."

"Really?" Siobhan asked. "Our Ma?"

"I know, right? Could hardly believe it. Oh, and, Brad and Esteban sent flowers and a card with their kitty Roxie signing it too," Nivie added, talking about her friend from college and his partner.

"Love those guys," Siobhan said.

"Yeah, they're the best."

"Well, it's been great talking to you, but I need to get going," Siobhan said. "The clothes won't pack themselves, and time is tickin'!"

"Oh, OK."

"Just let me know about sweet little Kimball Kitty! Love ya, Niv!"

"Love ya too, Shiv."

Nivie knew in her heart that Kimball Kitty would do best with them. Still, she wasn't sure. But, she knew that to know Kimball Kitty was to love him.

After replaying the conversation about Kimball with Siobhan in her head for the next hour, Nivie knew she needed to call Ma.

"Well, look who's callin'!"

"How's Boston today, Ma?" Nivie asked.

"Wicked good! No city betta, *Aednat!*"

"It's 'Nivie,' Ma," she interrupted. "You know. Genevieve. Nivie. Has been for years. Not '*Aednat.*' We really have to go through this every time?"

"Ug, what kind of name is 'Nivie'?" Ma fussed. "'*Aednat.*' Now that's a good solid Irish name."

"Yeah, but really, Ma? *Aednat?*"

"Yes, means 'little fire.' Sure fits!" Ma added.

"—But, really, Ma? Ay-nit. Sounds like 'ain't it.' Like 'Ain't it right, *Aednat?*' If I hear that one more time… Maybe that's why I became an English teacher."

"Well, we sure know it wasn't your grades!"

"Yeah, I made my poor teachers work for their money," Nivie chuckled. "But, Genevieve is a 'good solid' Catholic name."

"Maybe. But, you haven't been to mass anytime lately, have ya?"

"Ding, ding, ding. We have a winner."

"You loved your time at St. Joe's," Ma reminded.

Nivie sighed. "Yes, but things seemed to have changed so much since I was in college. With all the scandals and stuff. And it seemed like the church has just become, I don't know, different. And, not in a good way."

"Yes, well, the church is full of people, and people change."

"Whoa, that's really deep, Ma. Proud of ya."

"Well, it's true."

"But think about this," Nivie said, "You know who doesn't change? The ushers! Think about the power they have! Oh my god! What if you decided not to wait until they told when to go up for communion. Huh? What if you made a bee-line for the J.C. wafer without their permission?"

"Now, now…"

"I mean, I love the Billy Joel song, 'Only The Good'—"

"—Not the same thing," Ma snapped.

Nivie giggled and continued. "And another thing. With ushers: they tell you where to sit, or they make others sit next to you. Trying to squeeze a family of five in the pew, with a crying baby, when there's only room for three. That can make a mass a living Hell. Literally!"

"All right! That's enough."

Nivie laughed. "Now, I'm a child of the world, devoid of any religion!"

"If you say so," Ma said.

"But, I will say," Nivie added, "this Pope does give me hope."

"Well, that's good to hear at least," Ma said.

"Guess I'm 'Popeful'!"

They both laughed.

"Oh, before I forget to ask you, do ya need a recipe for corned beef?"

"No, Ma. Can you be any more of a stereotype?"

"Wicked proud of where I come from. You could be proud too, ya know!"

"Hey, we went to the Homeland, didn't we?"

"Yeah, but..."

"So, what's the problem?"

"Being proud of who ya are is more than jus' cartin' off to Ireland for a wedding!" Ma said.

"Hey, our time there was extraordinary. There's just more to me, that's all," Nivie stopped. "You're looking at your JFK picture on the wall now, aren't cha?"

"Yeah! And, would it kill ya to show it a little more respect? Your Pops and I had such hopes for ya. May he rest in peace 'til I get there."

"OK, Ma," Nivie said. "But, no. I don't need the recipe for corned beef, since I haven't eaten meat in, oh, I don't know, fifteen years."

"What kind of person doesn't eat meat?"

"The kind that changes her name!" Nivie joked.

"Hmp," Ma mumbled.

"Anyway, you heard about Kimball."

"Yeah. I told Siobhan to call you," Ma said. "You've been so grumpy since Minerva. I told her you guys would be great."

"Well, thanks, but..."

"Kimball's a good cat, as far as cats go. And, your sista needs you. That boyfriend of hers isn't the best to him."

"Asshole."

"And, growin' up, ya know, ya always wanted to be a veterinarian," Ma added.

"Yeah, until I figured out what they actually did. I realized animals like to go to the doctor as much as people do," Nivie said.

"True. Do you still 'boo hoo' when ya see lobsters in the aquariums at the store or restaurants?"

"Yep. Still do."

"Well, you could never live hear! But, it's nice to know *some* things haven't changed!" Ma snickered. "I remember when you were young, and we had mice in the house. Rememba?"

"Oh, yeah. Actually they were voles."

"And you—"

"—spent that one lunch period trying to get him out of that damn sticky chikawaka."

"Chick-a-waka? What is that?"

"*Cheek*-a-waka," Nivie corrected. "Like the word 'cheek.' You know I use that word when I don't want to search for the real word. I mean mousetrap."

"You and your words," Ma muttered.

"Yep, another reason I became an English teacher!" Nivie laughed. "Anyway, I thought I was being so secretive, taking the poor vole who was stuck in the mousetrap into my big bedroom closet. That gooey stuff gave me away!"

"'Cuz you had it all over your hands."

"But, seeing that little guy on his side, struggling to breathe. Just too much. And to make it worse, I spent my entire lunch period trying to get him out. For nothing. Couldn't even get him free. Just had to leave him there," Nivie lamented.

"We knew what you were doing. Didn't have the heart to tell ya."

"Yeah, well. I tried, anyway."

"That ya did."

"All right. Well, I gotta scoot," Nivie said.

"Give a big bear hug to Alex."

"OK, Ma. Will do."

"Do think about taking Kimball," Ma said.

"I will. I have to still talk to Alex about it."

"And, maybe…just maybe someday soon—" Ma said.

"Don't say it."

"I'll be hearing the pitta patta of little feet."

Nivie groaned.

"Time is a 'tickin'. Not gettin' any younger, ya know!"

"All right, Ma," Nivie interrupted.

"And neither are you…"

"All right, Ma!"

Ma chuckled.

"Love ya," Nivie said.

"You know I love ya, *a leanbh*," Ma said, the Gaelic endearment for her children.

Jacqueline's beloved housekeeper, Shirley, a sturdy woman in her 50s, had been a permanent fixture in Jacqueline's house and life for many years. Driving her 1992 Nissan up Jacqueline's semi-circular driveway, she parked and carried her supplies to the front door. She was about to use her key when the door opened.

"Oh. Hi, Ms. Stanton!" Shirley exclaimed.

"Good morning, Shirley. Come on in," Jacqueline said, standing back to let her inside.

"You're here! What a nice surprise!"

Jacqueline closed the door behind Shirley, and Chloe trotted over, Lammikins in tow.

"Hi, Chloe-girl," Shirley said, reaching down to pat her head.

"Can I get you anything?" Jacqueline asked. "Something to drink? Or a snack, perhaps?"

"What?" Shirley quickly furrowed her brow. "Uh, no, no. I'm fine. Thank you, though, Ms. Stanton."

"Well, I'll be in the living room, if you need me," Jacqueline said.

"OK. I've been cleanin' your house for about twenty-seven years but, yeah, I'll be sure to call ya if I have any questions!" Shirley laughed.

Jacqueline smiled and walked into the living room. She picked up her book for book club and today's newspaper and sat in her chaise lounge. Chloe turned in tight circles and lay down in front of the chair.

A few hours later, Jacqueline realized she had dozed off. The newspaper formed a tent over the book.

"OK, Ms. Stanton. I'm on my way out," Shirley called from the kitchen.

"Oh, OK," Jacqueline said. Bleary-eyed, she pushed herself off the chaise and walked toward Shirley's voice. Chloe followed her, and Lammikins came, too.

"Oh good. You got your check," Jacqueline said.

Shirley had always received her payment the same way: from the kitchen counter. "Yes, I did. Thank you. Won't let it burn a hole in my pocket!"

Somewhat confused, Shirley looked at Jacqueline. "How ya doin' today, Ms. Stanton?"

Jacqueline cleared her throat. "I'm fine. Thank you, Shirley."

Shirley pursed her lips. "Just that, I know today's another anniversary. I know it's hard. When I lost my Dale, it was like a knife to my heart."

Jacqueline was relieved. The awkwardness had finally abated.

"I understand," Jacqueline paused. "Shirley, if you don't mind me asking. How did you do it?"

She thought a minute, placing the check and her keys in her pocket.

"Well, God, of course. I don't know how anyone can make it through somethin' like this and not believe in God. If His eye is on the sparrow, I know it's on me! Plus, I know my Dale is up there waitin' for me, whenever the Good Lord sees fit," she said looking up, pointing to the ceiling. "And, my church family was there for me, too. Comin' over. Bringin' food and such."

Jacqueline smiled and nodded.

"And, couldn't have done nothin' without my family. My babies. Brothers, sisters, nieces, nephews. My Dale was a big person to all of them. And they all looked up to him. Really did! He was a big man!" Shirley chuckled. "Ya know, he loved havin' everyone around. We always had pig roasts, corn hole, euchre tournaments. Oh, and potlucks. He loved celebratin' with everyone around. Those are my favorite memories. The grandkids would go up on his shoulders, and he'd gallop around like some fool horse."

"I'm sorry I can't think of the specific date, but when did Dale...?" Jacqueline asked.

"Oh, it's been ten years now."

"It's been that long?"

"Yeah, remember I asked for that week off? So we could, ya know, have the funeral, and get everythin' ready," Shirley said.

"You really should have asked me for more time off than that."

"I know, but, don't cha remember? It was right before your big fundraiser. Not a great time."

Jacqueline remembered her frustration during that time.

"But, gettin' back to work helped me a whole bunch. And, I'm glad to be workin' for ya. You're family."

Jacqueline forced a smile, trying to attend to Shirley's compliment.

Shirley continued, "My kids said, 'Ma, get back to work. Ya gotta get outta the house.' Ya know, they do landscaping, snow removal and such, so they know. So, they said, 'Ma, you gotta get outta the house. Get back in the game.'" Shirley chuckled. "My family. We're all a little nuts. But, I love them. Nothin' like family. And, I'm glad that I had your house to come back to." She looked at her watch. "But, I gotta go. Didn't mean to talk your ear off."

"I thank you, Shirley."

"No problem. Anyway, I'm still real sorry about Mr. Stanton," Shirley pulled her purse strap over her shoulder. "He was a very good man."

"Yes, thank you," Jacqueline said, barely gathering enough energy to answer.

"Well, I'll be here next week. Same time, same place!"

Jacqueline watched Shirley leave the kitchen, hearing the hollow echo of the front door closing behind her.

In preparation for their "Date Night," Julian and Bryn dropped off an excited Megan at Grandma Stanton's house.

"How's the most beautiful mother-in-law in the world?" Julian asked, walking through the front door.

"I'm doing well, Julian," Jacqueline blushed.

"Gamma!" Megan yelled. "Horsie!"

"No, Megan. Horses are dangerous," Jacqueline corrected.

"Thanks for watching her, Mom," Bryn said. "Here's her bag. Her bedtime is 7:30. If she wants some of her animal crackers, she can have them—"

"Believe it or not, I have done this before," Jacqueline smiled.

"No kitten," Megan said.

"That's right," Bryn affirmed. "We don't have a kitten."

Although she was the consummate greeter, Chloe usually made sure there was a healthy distance between herself and any small humans with unpredictable behaviors.

Megan saw Chloe and said. "Tucko scayed. Bacoom."

"Oh, Tucker was scared of the vacuum?" Jacqueline clarified.

"Yes, well, some of the old issues are popping up again," Bryn said. "No biggie. Anyway, so—"

"—Oh, Brynnie," Jacqueline tsked. "I still wonder why you had to get a mongrel."

Bryn sighed. "He's a designer dog, Mom."

"Goodness, 'a designer dog'? In my day, we called them mutts!"

"I'm not a breed snob, Mom."

"I'm not a 'breed snob' either, Brynnie. But, as I have mentioned to you before, I had the contact information of a few reputable breeders that I fully intended to pass onto you. With a purebred, you know exactly what you're getting."

"I know, I tried telling her!" Julian said, shaking his head.

"We're still having this conversation," Bryn said through a tightened mouth. "He's a wonderful family dog, and we love him. Anyway, even purebreds aren't perfect," she said, motioning down to Chloe.

They all looked down to see Chloe scooting her rump across the carpet with legs outspread and front paws pulling her body along.

"Chloe, stop!" Jacqueline's face blushed.

Bryn turned her head to the side to hide a grin.

After picking Megan up from Jacqueline's house later that evening, Bryn completed her last-minute packing for the visit to her in-laws' lake house Up North. Barbara and Lawrence Troxell's five-bedroom, four-bath lakefront property was a second home for Julian and his family, filled with childhood and recent memories of happy times. When Bryn was growing up, her family vacationed in different cities, but there wasn't one location to which they returned regularly.

Bryn especially looked forward to having her morning coffee on the deck, watching the sun rise over her in-laws' personal boat dock. Although the living room's wall of windows showcased a breathtaking scene, the deck offered an even clearer view. All of the bedrooms were on the first floor, and a spiral staircase wound up to a loft overlooking a wide open-floor plan.

Simply breathing in the warm summer air at the lake house was Bryn's idea of nirvana. Although she never felt completely comfortable with her in-laws, spending time with them was a small price to pay for paradise.

Her in-laws' speedboat was the icing on a very beautiful cake because Tucker cherished it too. He jumped at the chance to plant his front legs on the side of the boat, observing anyone who was waterskiing or tubing move from the left side of the boat to the right, then back to the left, then the right. Watching Tucker's head was like watching a tennis match. One time, Bryn wiped out waterskiing and, without hesitation, her faithful dog jumped overboard into the water, doggie paddling all the way to his fallen human. After that, no more boat rides without a dog life preserver. His was even monogrammed: "Tucker, the Wonder Dog."

Shortly after they arrived at the lake house, Julian, Bryn and Tucker took the boat out for a sun-drenched time on the water while Megan enjoyed Grandma and Grandpa Troxell time running errands in town. As their boat approached the dock, Tucker jumped into the shallows and sprinted over to something lying on the bank twenty feet away.

Julian, fumbling to tie up the boat, shouted, "Tucker, come back here! Leave that alone!" Turning to Bryn, he yelled, "I thought you had him!"

"Oh, my gosh, Tucker!" Bryn said. "Please stay away from that!"

Tucker reveled in his new found toy, a decaying lake trout. Jamming his nose deep into the gills, he licked the fish's side. After he yanked up on the side fin, the carcass flopped down on the sand about a foot away. He proceeded to roll his damp, fluffy body over the fish's scaly, rancid carcass. The fish's bulging eyes seemed to grow larger after each of Tucker's rolls. Julian rushed over to his dog, grabbed Tucker's collar, and pulled him off.

"Holy crap!" he exclaimed, coughing at the rotting smell.

Bryn caught up to them. "Oh, my gosh!" She buried her nose in her arm in an attempt to shield herself from the stench. "Oh my gosh! What are we going to do? Your parents will be back, like, any minute!"

Taking Tucker by the collar, they walked his wet, smelly, sandy body up the hill to the side of the house.

"Um…OK. I got it. Here, hold onto him. I'll be right back," Julian said, running into the house.

"Hurry!" she yelled after Julian. "Oh, Tucker." Bryn buried her nose back into her elbow pit, trying to hold onto a leaping Tucker, who yearned to return to his new toy.

Inside the house, Julian ran straight for the refrigerator. "OK. Now, where is it?" he said, dancing around the kitchen. He turned the corner to the pantry and opened the door.

"Nope, not there either. Crap!"

Scanning the room, he spotted the wet bar. "Ah, here it is! Thank God for Bloody Marys!"

After running to the linen closet, Julian ran back outside with two cans and his hand full of towels.

"Tomato juice?" Bryn asked incredulously. "Really?"

"Yeah," Julian walked to the outside tap and turned on a hose. Startled, Tucker jumped from the hose, then lapped at the arch of water coming toward him.

Julian laughed. "Tuck, that's not for you to drink!"

"Oh, man," Bryn worried. "Tucker. C'mon."

Once they contained him, Julian took a deep breath and poured one of the cans of tomato juice over Tucker's back. The red juice flowed, causing his reddish hair to momentarily turn a more vibrant hue.

Tucker playfully ran in circles with droplets of juice splattering on Bryn and Julian. "Tucker, stop!" Bryn yelled. "Oh my gosh. What a mess," she said wiping her face with her hand.

"You have to leave it on for a few minutes," Julian advised, wiping his brow with his arm. "Next time, hold onto him," he added.

"Sorry," Bryn whispered.

"Tuck, you big goof!" Julian chuckled. "Leave those dead fish alone! Now you're just a marinara pup!" After what Tucker thought was a reprimand, he looked up at Julian with big brown eyes, his head down, tail tucked between his legs.

"Aw, you're OK," Julian consoled, petting Tucker's head.

After a few minutes, Julian poured another can over Tucker's back. And again, Tucker danced around in an attempt to avoid this strange liquid.

"Poor thing! Poor Tucker sweetie," Bryn cooed. "It's OK. You're OK."

Trying to keep Tucker still, time slowed to a painful rate. Bryn kept both ears and eyes out for the others to return as Julian rinsed Tucker off.

While Julian took out the towel to dry Tucker off, the playful puppy jumped around; play-time had returned. Balling up the red-stained towels and tossing them into the outside garbage bin, Julian said,

"Well, these won't be used any time soon! Or, ever again!"

"Julian! Bryn!"

"Your parents," Bryn whispered.

"We're back!"

"Hi, Mommy!" Megan yelled from the kitchen.

"Having a good time out there?" Barbara asked, setting the grocery bags down on the kitchen counter.

"Oh yeah," Bryn said.

"Tucker, too?"

"The best!" Julian quipped, in response to Bryn's eye roll at his mother's question.

Nivie stood looking out at the summer morning through her dining room window. "Where is she?" she asked, checking her phone. "She should be here by now."

"She'll be here soon," Alex said from the living room. "C'mere and sit down."

Pacing back and forth between the dining room and living room windows, Nivie exclaimed, "There she is!"

Nivie flew out the front door before Siobhan put the car in park. Craning her neck to see the passenger seat, Nivie saw a black mesh cat carrier with a whitish mass inside.

"Oh my god. There he is!" she exclaimed. "My Kimball Kitty."

Siobhan stepped out of the car, giving Nivie a quick hug. Walking around to the passenger side, Nivie opened the door and in a high-pitched tone asked, "Hi, honey. How are you?" Nivie whistled. "Whoa, what the hell is that?"

"So, he had a little accident on the way over," Siobhan said.

"Little?" Nivie coughed. "Oh, poor guy," she said, seeing Kimball's face smooshed against the side of the carrier. "Let's get him inside."

"So good to see you! I've missed you! Ready to do this overseas thing?" With one hand, Nivie carried Kimball's carrier and the other she wrapped around Siobhan, who was carrying a bag of food, dishes, and other necessities.

"Yeah! I'm super stoked. Only thing is, my flight leaves in about four hours."

"Really? This is a quick trip."

"Yeah, sorry, it's the only way this could work."

"No worries. We're good. Aren't we, Kimball Kitty? Well, except he needs to be cleaned up before that smell burns my nose hairs."

Nivie thought it best if she bathed Kimball upstairs alone, so Alex and Siobhan could set up his food and water downstairs in the kitchen. Plopping Kimball's piles into the toilet, Nivie gently placed him in the bathtub, cleaning off the residual feces. Using a cup to pour the water over him, Kimball's body shrunk to half its size. His soaked paws squeaked trying to escape along the side of the tub, but the water afforded him no grip. Nivie scrubbed him down, the dirt leaving his body and circling the drain. Discovering a particularly difficult spot on his back leg, Nivie scrubbed and scrubbed, to no avail. She then realized it wasn't a poop stain, but one of his darker markings.

"I'm so sorry, Kimball Kitty!" The drenched cat longingly looked up at her with big green eyes.

Nivie wrapped him in a towel, cradling him like a baby, and kissed his head. "Are you ready for this? You're such a good boy."

She opened the bathroom door to see Alex and Siobhan standing there.

"Oh, so much better!" Alex said. "And, wetter!"

"Wait a minute. This might be the first time he's ever been on steps," Nivie pointed out.

"Yeah, I never had them in my apartments," Siobhan said.

Nivie set him down, gently removing the towel. Kimball's damp body walked over to the railing.

All three humans walked downstairs and turned around to see Kimball's face peeking out from one of the railing spindles. He sat down and began to clean himself, returning his fur to its original scent: his.

"C'mon Kimball. C'mon, boy," Alex coaxed.

"He's thinkin': 'I'm no dog'!" Nivie said.

After his self-induced bath, Kimball peeked out from the railing spindles again and acknowledged the humans at bottom of the steps. Curious and outgoing by nature, crossing this new threshold was not particularly challenging for him. With his bottom in the air, and his front legs on the step below him, he lumbered down each step.

"Good boy!" Alex praised.

Each with their respective phones in hand, all the humans took pictures of this new accomplishment.

"I better slow down!" Nivie said, shaking her phone. "There *is* a limit on this thing!'

Siobhan looked over at his designated food and water area. "You'll be happy to know he has a very good appetite," she said.

"Well, that's good," Nivie said.

"And, although that's a really nice fountain you got for him, he's not going to use it."

"Really? Why not?" Nivie asked.

"He likes to put his paw in the water bowl and lick the water off his paw."

"Really?" Nivie laughed. "That's awesome!"

"And, he also likes ice chips, but only in this specific bowl." Siobhan pointed to an empty blue bowl next to his water and food bowls.

During the inspection of his new home, Kimball sniffed around, ending up at the back porch door.

"No, no. No kitties on the back porch," Nivie said, gently moving him along backwards with her foot.

The curious cat moseyed into the living room where he stretched up onto a rocking chair seat, sniffing around. Approving its scent, he hopped up. With the chair still moving, he curled himself into a ball and looked up at the humans.

"Looks like he found his spot," Alex laughed.

"Aww, so sweet," Siobhan said, looking at the sympathy card next to Mini's paw print.

"Yeah. That's from our vet, Dr. Carmichael," Nivie said. "She's the best. She even like, called to see how we were doing after Mini died. You'll be going to see her, Kimball Kitty. Yes, you will. And, you'll love her, too," Nivie said, looking down at him.

Siobhan looked down at her phone. "Dang, I gotta scoot. Bye, bye, Kimball Kitty. You be good." Scooping him up for a quick hug, she choked back tears.

"Gonna miss you so much, Shiv," Nivie said, as she gave her sister a hug.

"Oh, me, too," Siobhan said, wiping away a few tears. "Thanks again, you guys. You're really gonna love him."

From inside the house, Nivie and Alex waved good-bye to Siobhan. Kimball jumped down from the rocker and joined them near the front door, tail wrapped neatly around his paws. Nivie turned and said to him, "Welcome to the family, Kimball Kitty."

"So, big question: do we let Kimball sleep with us, or not?" Nivie asked right before bed.

"Well, I can't really sleep if he walks all over me. Especially if he ruins the family jewels," Alex said.

"I know! Thanks to Minerva, I'm going to have to bottle feed!"

"What do you say, we keep the door closed?" Alex asked.

"It makes me sad, but we gotta get our sleep," Nivie agreed.

They shut the door, apologizing to Kimball as they shut it, and climbed into bed.

A few moments later, the gentle meowing morphed into loud howling. Suddenly, the door rattled in its frame.

"What the hell was that?" Alex looked over and saw a white paw shoot out from under the door. "Oh man. He's having a hard time with this."

The cries intensified. The paw made another appearance under the door, this time flailing around, as if reaching for something. The door banged even louder in its frame.

"OK. That's it." Nivie threw off the covers and opened the door.

Kimball chirped and walked in. "Hello, little creamsicle Kimball Kitty."

Nivie plopped back into bed, pulling the covers over her.

Kimball walked around the bed, into the closet, and then inspected the bathroom. A minute later, they heard him running back downstairs.

"Well, that was worth it," Nivie said, underneath the covers.

Poke, poke, poke.

Alex groaned.

Poke, poke, poke.

Alex groaned again.

Poke poke, poke.

"Love?"

"Yeah," Nivie grumbled.

"Kimball's poking me."

"*Facebook*?" she yawned.

"No. Literally poking me."

Kimball's paw, with a hint of claw, stretched up over the edge of the bed to tap Alex's arm. The cat stared at Alex, cocking his head and meowing softly. Since he didn't receive the response he needed, Kimball jumped up onto the bed, walked across their pillows, stepping on Nivie's hair.

"Ow! Man, Kimball. C'mon, let us sleep. You apparently don't know what a weekend is," Nivie said, curling herself in a ball, covering her head with the heavy comforter.

A few seconds later, Alex exclaimed, "Ow!"

"What happened?" She threw off the comforter to see Alex rubbing his head and Kimball sitting on Alex's pillow.

"Little booger bit me."

"Kimball Kitty!" Nivie said, chuckling. "Just like our Mini when she wanted something."

"All right. You win, Kimball. Let's get you some breakfast," Alex said, reluctantly getting out of bed. He stopped to give Nivie a quick kiss. "Just like our Mini."

Kimball jumped down from the bed and looked up at Alex. He rubbed against Alex's leg in approval and meowed again as Alex closed the bedroom door behind them.

"Thanks, Love." Nivie yanked the comforter back over her head, pulling herself into a tight ball, and went back to sleep.

The July book club meeting just ended at Donna's house. While the rest of the members left into the night, Jacqueline and Ronni stayed behind. The hostess, Donna, a warm, earthy woman in her mid-50s with shiny gray hair, was Jacqueline's friend of almost thirty years. Twenty-five years ago, Donna lost her daughter, Rachel, in a tragic car accident. Rachel, an stellar student, involved in many community projects as well as her synagogue, was returning home from college on Spring Break when her car swerved across the dotted line, instantly killing her and her German Shepherd mix, Kano. No definitive cause of the accident was ever determined. After this excruciating and life-changing loss for Donna and her husband, Donna went back to college to become a therapist. It was a way for her to resurrect the portion of her soul that died with Rachel. She often traveled around the country with her husband, William, in their large RV with their Boston Terrier, Winnebago, or Winnie, as their co-pilot.

Ronni was another member of Jacqueline's book club and long-time friend. Known as the "fun friend" of the group, Veronica, or Ronni, as she preferred to be called, was always dressed to the nines; her charisma, infectious. Short, spiky, highlighted hair accentuated her loud, gravelly voice. Although she often complained about her Yorkshire terrier, Corky, Ronni's grumblings merely matched the strong love she had for her pup. Now retired, Ronni and her husband, Jerry, were "snowbirds" who enjoyed living six months in Florida, where Ronni worked part-time at Disney World. She delighted in making jokes about the changes that often accompany growing older. "I would never get a white car. Why would I ever get a car that matches my real hair color?" And, "If I stand up and a noise comes out, I turn around and point down at the chair, saying, 'Bad seat cushion'!" Jacqueline could rely on Ronni to brighten her mood— if only for a fleeting moment.

Donna's and Ronni's husbands had known Edmond well, for both had worked for Woodhurst Industries too before they retired. Although it was still a blur to Jacqueline, both of her friends Ronni stayed overnight at Jacqueline's house the day Edmond died. In the following days and weeks, they organized meals and helped with other arrangements like shepherding Jacqueline through the agonizing and surreal task of writing Edmond's obituary, picking out an outfit for Edmond's burial, and removing his name from bank accounts.

Jacqueline and Donna chatted in the living room, picking up dishes when Ronni walked back into the room from the bathroom. She leaned in and gave Jacqueline a big bear hug. "How are you, my friend?"

"Doing OK," Jacqueline said, slowly bobbing her head.

Vigorously tapping Jacqueline's hand, Ronni said, "Whatever you need to feel is fine. Don't let the bastards tell you any differently."

Jacqueline smiled.

"Well, ladies, I'm off like a prom dress," Ronni joked. "Time to feed 'Her Canine Highness.' Then, we're both getting our 'Poodle Treatment'," she said, stroking the top of her head. "You know, once you see the roots, you're already too late! Gotta scoot."

"Bye, Ronni," Jacqueline and Donna said.

"Ciao, ladies!" Ronni stopped, holding the door open and pointed at Jacqueline. "And remember what I said."

Jacqueline gave her a quick nod and smile as Ronni left. Turning to Donna, she said, "Thank you again, The only reason I came this month was because I knew you were hosting."

"I'm so glad you came, Jacquie. It's been a while." Pausing, Donna added, "I was wondering. Have you given any thought to talking to someone about Edmond."

"Oh, Donna. I'm fine. Really."

"It would be completely understandable if you did."

"Well, some days are better than others. But, sometimes the grief can be so intense, I can hardly—" tears welled up in her eyes.

"—breathe," Donna said.

She reached out and gave Jacqueline a hug. "I wanted to share some information with you about a group that meets for widows and widowers."

Jacqueline cringed. "That dreadful word. 'Widow.' Thank you, but I just don't know. This is your area. I'm not quite sure that it would be a good fit for me."

"Jacquie, there is no need to do this alone," Donna urged, looking into Jacqueline's eyes with care and understanding.

Jacqueline sat down. "Other than you and Ronni, every conversation I have is simply a derivation of 'Have you moved on?' or 'Are you done ruminating yet?' or 'Will you stop thinking about him, so we don't have to tip-toe around you?' Some are kinder than others. But, it seems as though they are afraid to 'catch' what I 'have.'"

Donna nodded, sitting at the table across from Jacqueline.

"That's not to mention the others who stop including you in invitations. Or, who avoid you altogether. I try my best not to let it get to me. Sometimes I think I should receive an Oscar for my acting ability. But, I know I'm not the only one who has gone through a loss like this. But, it's impossible not to think about him. Everywhere I look. Every piece of furniture. His closet, his clothes, his valet."

Donna nodded again.

"When I see one of his shirts hanging in his closet, I still see him walking around in it. I see him with Chloe. Or, I see a car on the road that reminds me of his, or a conversation we had in that car. Then there are the holidays, birthdays. It seems as though there is literally no escape." Jacqueline paused again. "I've gone on and on. I'm truly sorry," she said standing up.

"No need to apologize." Donna said, standing and handing Jacqueline a tissue. "This might sound strange. But have you had any dreams?"

"Dreams?" Jacqueline quietly blew her nose. "No. Why?"

"Well, sometimes our grief can manifest itself through our dreams. It's one way of trying to work through the grief."

"It's strange, but there are times I can....almost....feel him. But, I know that's just wishful thinking. And, sometimes I do catch myself talking to him."

"Yes, both of those are common," Donna reassured.

"But, dreams? Not that I can recall."

Donna retrieved her purse and pulled out a card with the support group information on it. Handing it to Jacqueline, she said, "Here, I think this will be helpful. Just try one meeting. See how it goes."

"OK. Well. We'll see." Jacqueline paused, staring down at the card. "But, thank you for your thoughtfulness. And also, I appreciate it if you wouldn't share this with anyone."

"There is no shame, Jacquie."

Jacqueline stared down at the card, without looking up. "I know. Thank you, Donna."

A few days later, with a rosary from her Italy trip three years ago firmly in her grasp, Jacqueline walked into the sanctuary of St. Agnes Catholic Church. Returning after the beautiful funeral mass they celebrated for

Edmond, St. Agnes had been too painful for Jacqueline. Her absence had been lengthy. As members of the community for three decades, not only had Jacqueline and Edmond been married there, but Bryn was baptized and confirmed as well. Since Julian and his family were Methodist, Bryn converted and now attended Julian's home church. Jacqueline's footsteps echoed in the empty house of worship. She sat down at a pew in the back row and raised her eyes to the stately statues of Jesus, Mary, and Joseph.

She heard a voice ask, "Is that Jacqueline Stanton?"

She looked to the right in the sacristy and saw Father Kenneth walking toward her. He was the parish priest, in his 60s with a warm smile and a soft voice.

"What a pleasure it is to see you, Jacqueline. How are you?" he asked, sitting down next to her.

"Good to see you, Father. I'm doing fine. Some days are better than others."

"That's perfectly understandable. Death is one of God's mysteries. I heard from a very wise man that we are here on earth on loan from God. When He's ready, He calls us home."

"Interesting."

"We certainly miss your presence around here. If there is anything we can do, please let us know," he said, standing up and squeezing her hand.

"Thank you, Father, and everyone at St. Agnes. You were all so supportive and loving."

Fr. Kenneth smiled. "Well, you and Edmond have been an important part of our church family for many years."

"I was considering returning as a Eucharistic minister at some time."

"I'm so pleased to hear. If you get in contact with the front desk, they can help get you back on schedule. They will be pleased, too."

"Thank you."

"These things take time, so no rush. God is always there. Whenever you need Him," Fr. Kenneth said.

Jacqueline smiled, finding some relief in his words.

The sun was beginning to set when Jacqueline arrived home from St. Agnes. Walking into the house, there was an unusual stillness. No jingling of tags. No Lammikins. No Chloe. Heart pounding and darting from room to room, Jacqueline called out for her, searching all the rooms. No answer.

Returning to the kitchen, she saw the sliding glass door ajar and felt her heart drop. Jacqueline dashed out to the backyard. Surveying the landscape, she quietly called Chloe's name, so as not to disturb the silence of the neighborhood. Still no Chloe. Rushing into the house, she located her phone and called Bryn. No answer. She left messages for Donna and Ronni asking for help. Frantically, she searched for the number to the Woodhaven Run animal shelter and called them. No, they hadn't seen Chloe but would let her know if they did.

Grabbing her keys, Jacqueline dashed back into her car. Driving slowly down the street, she leaned forward in the driver's seat, hands tightly clutching the wheel. Circling the Woodhaven Run neighborhoods, she continued to wrack her brain, while looking for a glimpse of the buff-colored fur. Then, it came to her—there was another place Chloe might have gone.

As she turned into the main gate, the large pine and maple trees created a tunnel of darkness. Jacqueline could hear her pulse pounding as she drove down the long, dark main drive past the Woodhaven Run Cemetery sign. Gravel crackled beneath her tires as she drove slowly, scanning for Chloe amidst the headstones lined up like soldiers. She took a deep breath and followed the path around a sweeping corner. Straining her eyes to see, she looked straight ahead. Her beloved dog lay on her side in front of Edmond's grave. Hearing the car slip into park, Chloe raised her head. Jacqueline choked back tears of sadness, coupled with relief.

The last time Chloe was here was the day Edmond was buried.

Jacqueline's visits to the grave had been spotty, at best, because when Edmond went into the ground, she wanted to go with him.

"Oh my goodness, Chloe-girl. Come here," Jacqueline said, quietly walking toward the grave. Chloe stood up, wiggled her bottom, yet remained in front of his stone.

With Edmond's photograph etched into the solid, dark grey granite, Jacqueline read the words she chose fourteen months ago. "In Loving Memory, Edmond James Stanton."

She bent down and attached a leash to Chloe's collar. "I know. You miss him, too."

As Jacqueline turned back to the car, Chloe initially resisted the leash, then relented.

"C'mon, Chloe. Time to get moving."

Bryn gently laid a sleeping Megan into her Disney-sheeted bed. She tried to contain her excitement: Megan taking a nap on a summer afternoon without a fuss was a luxury. For Bryn, anyway. As she shut Megan's door, Tucker jumped up on Bryn, pawing at her. Looking closer at Tucker, Bryn saw Megan's Disney stickers adorning his fur.

"Shhhh, Tucker. Don't want to wake her," Bryn said, walking down the hallway, and removing a *Frozen* and *Bambi* sticker off his head and back.

Making her way downstairs, with Tucker directly underfoot, Bryn clutched the handrail to prevent herself from tripping. Once Bryn got to the ground floor, she walked into the kitchen, with the canine weaving in and out of her footsteps.

"Tucker. Geez. Do you want a treat? Why don't you go play with squeaky Teddy toy?"

Bryn grabbed a dog treat for him, and he scarfed it down. She laid down on the living room couch, basking in these few, quiet moments. Tucker trotted over to her, smelling around, and pawing at her.

Bryn groaned. "No, you're not getting another treat. You've probably gained five pounds this week alone from all the extra ones you've gotten."

She gently nudged his muzzle away. He exhaled and groaned, laying down in front of the couch.

After a short nap in the stillness of the afternoon, Bryn opened her eyes and sat up, yawning and stretching. Tucker, hearing her rousing, also stood up, aiming his long front paw at her again.

"What is goin' on? Good grief. What's so interesting about my bel—?"

Bryn stopped cold.

"Laur, I'm pregnant again," Bryn said to her childhood friend on the phone a few hours later.

"Oh my gosh! That's gr—." Lauren stopped. "Wait a minute. How are you doing?"

"Um—." Tears began to well.

"Aww, Bryn," Lauren said.

"Just don't know if I can do this again, Laur."

"Listen, you did this before, and you can do it again."

Bryn blew her nose. "I miss my dad."

"But, now you know when things aren't going well, you're better prepared. Plus, you have me."

"Yeah, but you just *had* to go and move," Bryn lamented.

"I know, it's been hard for me, too. But, I'm only a few hours away. And, you have me, you have Julian…your mom…"

"Well, Julian—he's never here," Bryn said. "And, mom. Well, you know. She won't even mention my dad."

"Well, you have Tucker."

"Yeah, I do," Bryn chuckled through tears. "You'll never know how much he helped me with Meggie."

"Actually, I do," Lauren interjected.

Bryn continued, "When all I could do was sleep, nurse, and maybe eat, he'd lie down next to me and set his nose on my leg." She looked down at Tucker, whose muzzle was resting on her thigh.

"I get that," Lauren said. "I know I told you how much my Rufus-pup really helped me. Fur and all, even though it was short Doberman fur. But, he was there. Actually what really helped me was talking to my doctor and taking something for it."

"Well, mine's not bad enough to take something," Bryn said, then tilting her head asked, "Really? I didn't know you felt that way after Gavin was born?"

"Yeah, that's why we only had one child," Lauren said.

"Wow. I thought that was what you guys decided."

"Well, we did. Eventually. I mean, we had planned on having more. But, I got so bad. Hubby even asked me if we wanted to go through it again."

"Wow."

"So, after a lot of praying and crying, I realized that I couldn't," Lauren said. "Everyone's got to make their own decision. And, it was best for me, and for us, really, not to go through that again."

"Oh, I'm so sorry," Bryn said. "I mean, I knew that it was hard for you. But, I never knew it was *that* bad. Why didn't you tell me?"

"Well, it's kind of embarrassing saying, 'Yeah, I just had this beautiful baby. And you know what, I really wish I hadn't.' And thinking that I wish I could have my old life back with Hubby and my dog. Wishing I had my old body back. Plus, all the poopy diapers. The nursing. The lack of sleep. Everyone seemed so excited. Except me."

"Yes! Oh my gosh…"

"And, the crying. Oh, the crying. All I wanted was to be left alone, when everyone needed things from me. It never ended."

"Yeah, some days were like that for me, too," Bryn said.

"And frankly. Well, at times, not knowing if I really, you know, felt love for my baby," Lauren quietly added.

"Wow. I had no idea it got that rough for you. Fortunately, I never felt that. But, I'm so, so sorry that I wasn't there for you."

"Oh, don't worry about it. It's not your fault. I never really let you know. But, since Hubby saw me and how bad it got, he suggested I look into getting help."

"That was nice of him," Bryn pined, wishing Julian had shown her support like that when Megan was born.

"And, there are online support communities," Lauren said. "Who knows, there might even be a group in Woodhaven Run."

"It wasn't *that* bad that I'd have to go to a group," Bryn said. "Just wish Jay were around more. Plus, spilling my guts online to someone I don't know scares me. I mean, I could be talking with some 60-year-old man, posing as someone else, who is 'catfishing'."

At either end of the phone, they both crinkled their noses.

"Gross! But, again. You've done this once," Lauren said. "And, you can do it again."

Bryn exhaled. "Yeah, I guess."

"Have you told your mom yet?"

"Not yet. She's always busy with her appointments, book club, gardening, yada, yada. And, as you know, Megan still just wants a kitten."

Lauren chuckled. "And, Julian?"

Bryn rolled her eyes. "You mean 'Invisible Man?' Don't ask. Plus, I know he will say, 'Come on, Brynnie. Shake the lead out and smile! It'll be fun! Another blessing. God has blessed us.' I just don't want to bring him down." Bryn groaned. "Oh, man, that's another thing, his mom, Barbara, will just be ecstatic. Don't get me wrong. I'm not saying we're not blessed, and that I'm not grateful…It's just I miss my dad so much."

"I know," Lauren consoled.

"He would have been so great with all this."

"I know, Bryn. It's a lot."

"It's just," Bryn continued. "It seems like I just got Meggie out of diapers. And, like everything else you said. The late nights.

Hemorrhoids. Constipation. Getting all fat again. Then, there is paying for their college. Then, of course, huge boobs."

"Bet Julian loves that," Lauren laughed.

"Yeah," Bryn gaffawed, "Plus, I'll tell Julian something, and he's like, 'Babe, you never told me that.' And I *know* I told him. And now, with two children? It's going to be so much worse."

"You're overwhelming yourself. But, you can do this," Lauren affirmed. "Plus, you always have me. We've been buddies since kindergarten. I'm not going anywhere now!"

Bryn smiled, rubbing her belly.

"But, after this one, no more. Right?" Lauren asked.

"Right!" Bryn affirmed "Two and I'm done."

Bryn pet the tiny hairs along Tucker's nose, adding, "Well, this one will really be my third, since Tucker's still a bit of a child. But after this, I'm done!"

Jacqueline walks to the entrance of the forest where she used to ride her bike. The tiny hill into the woods is now flattened. The trail used to come out the other side, but now withered trees with brown leaves grow over the trail. Through the murky fog, she sees movement. Adjusting her eyes, she sees a horse, underfed, ribs protruding, walking slowly, head hung low. The snow falls quickly, and she has an impending feeling that the flowers will all die in Woodhaven Run. Trying to get out, she sees her bed in the snow. Edmond is lying dead in it.

"Eddy!"

Dead silence.

"Eddy!" Jacqueline's deafening screams from her nightmare tore through the silent November night like a knife.

Gasping, she opened her eyes, and stretched her arm out, desperately grabbing the sheets. All she found was a pile of pillows that lay where her beloved Edmond had once slept. This bed, which had once been such a warm and welcoming place, was now cold and lonely. This was supposed to be *their* bed, not hers.

Chloe crawled up from the bottom of the bed. She startled Jacqueline, but nudged her with a warm snout. The clock said 2:16 AM.

"Oh, Chloe." Jacqueline leaned on her elbow in an effort to move her face away from Chloe's muzzle. "Thank you, Chloe." Jacqueline's head slowly fell back onto her pillows as she looked up at the ceiling in the dark room, and pulled the sheets to her chin. "Eddy," she lamented.

After turning in a few tight circles, Chloe plopped herself down next to Jacqueline's head, slightly groaning. Jacqueline reached out to stroke her dog's warm head and back.

"*Why* did you have to go? Why did *you* have to go?" Jacqueline whispered. Repeating the rhetorical question didn't make the reality any easier. She turned on her side, her white knuckles clutching the sheets while her teardrops formed a damp spot on the pillow.

Her words trailed off into the night. Sleep had been found again, if only for a short time.

───•✦•───

Jacqueline eyes flittered open. "Eddy?" Quickly turning over, her hand feeling the other side of the bedsheets. They were cold; reality hit once again. For the past eighteen months, each morning had arrived in almost the same way.

Another day without you.

Naps weren't sufficient; Jacqueline was weary to her core. Eventually she was able to muster energy to slowly sit up in bed, allowing her feet to dangle over the side. Chloe sat up and cocked her head, staring at Jacqueline. Grabbing her Lammikins, she jumped down and spun in circles on the floor. Jacqueline noticed how the originally pure-white Lammikins was now a beige brown, like an old pillow without a cover. She didn't want to wash it for fear it wouldn't survive. She couldn't bear any more losses.

"Good morning, Chloe-girl," Jacqueline said, her voice as soothing as she could make it. Her knees and joints cracked as she put on her robe. Chloe led the way down the long hallway to the kitchen, occasionally glancing back. Jacqueline opened the sliding glass door to let her dog out, using her whole body strength to shut it. Chloe visited her usual spots, jumping over them, in an effort to avoid stepping in her work. She quickly returned to the door, barking with eager eyes.

"Good job, Chloe-girl," Jacqueline praised, opening the sliding glass door. "Now, sit. Stay."

Holding the can opener, Jacqueline struggled to twist the knob. She looked down at her hand, slowly making fists, gently stretching her fingers out again.

How did this become so difficult?

Although the content fell like a lump in the dish, Chloe licked her lips and pranced at Jacqueline's heels as though she was expecting steak tartare. Jacqueline pretended to eat the food before giving it to a very excited, yet disciplined, Chloe.

Gazing out the window to the backyard, Jacqueline lost herself in the view, without allowing Chloe's slurping noises to divert her thoughts. She stared at the hill that opened directly to the park, the brick patio, the outside kitchen, the fountain and hardscaping, where flowers used to frame the sides of her property. The pristine, manicured backyard had now mutated to drooping stems and brown sticks emerging from the dirt as frost had arrived last week. Weeds choked out other areas where clusters of flowers had once bloomed.

The neighbors are not appreciating this. How could you let it get this bad? This is disgraceful.

"Get it together, Jacquie. Pull yourself together," she said aloud, allowing her gaze to settle on a nondescript pine tree. Chloe stopped eating for a moment, cocked her head, soft brown eyes glancing up at her beloved human. She gave Chloe a quick smile, who resumed eating after a gentle pat on the head.

Jacqueline walked into the living room, where the wall of windows allowed even the cloudiest of days to brighten the area. Luckily, Shirley would be here in a few days to help tidy up inside; she had begun to anticipated Shirley's visits more. Sighing loudly, Jacqueline sunk down on her chaise lounge and grabbed the previous day's newspaper from the floor. Announcements page. A lump formed in her throat. Silver and Golden anniversaries.

Must be nice.

She set the newspaper down and looked out the window at a male cardinal fluffing its feathers.

After devouring her breakfast, Chloe trotted to the back door, snagging her monogrammed leash off a hook that housed various jackets and hats. She made a beeline to Jacqueline and dropped the soggy leash into her lap. Chloe paced around, spun in a few circles, whimpering. The "after breakfast walk" had always been Edmond's time with Chloe, with Jacqueline occasionally joining them.

"Oh, Chloe," she replied, snapping out of her daze. Chloe's nub wiggled fiercely, eyes darting from Jacqueline, to the leash, back to Jacqueline, back to the leash, and back to Jacqueline. "Here," she said, reaching for Chloe's collar, and fastening the leash to it. Jacqueline garnered more energy, forcing herself up out of the chair. She walked over to the door to the garage to put her tennis shoes on and zipped up her winter coat. She looked down at Chloe.

I know what I need to do.

"You're such a good girl. But, it's just so much. This is all so much," she said, walking into the garage, steering Chloe toward the car.

Although this was a departure from her usual routine, Chloe jumped right in. She had always loved car rides and was thrilled at the prospect of going on another. Driving down her street, Jacqueline gave a perfunctory wave to Ms. Paisley, Petey, Piper, and Roosevelt, and a few other neighbors along the way. In her rear-view mirror, she saw Chloe sitting in the back seat, face relaxed, tongue out, watching the world go by.

After about an hour of semi-conscious highway driving, Jacqueline parked the car in the gravel parking lot. She walked around to the back of the car and opened Chloe's door.

"C'mon, Chloe-girl. Let's go."

Chloe extended her neck, her head making tiny, quick "figure eights" in the air.

"C'mon Chloe. Let's go," Jacqueline commanded a little louder, pulling the leash.

Chloe gave a quick exhale, scuttled toward the opposite car door, leaning away from Jacqueline.

With her frustration building, Jacqueline yanked on the leash. "C'mon. Let's. Go."

Chloe pressed her body against the door, while averting her eyes from Jacqueline.

"Come on. I do not have time for this." Jacqueline's tears returned, this time in frustration.

"Come on! Get *out* of this car. *Right now!*" Jacqueline used what little physical and emotional strength in her reserves to drag Chloe by the collar to the edge of the backseat. Chloe resisted, her toenails grinding against the leather seats.

Jacqueline's eyes locked onto Chloe's mournful eyes. Her body melted as she threw her arms around her beloved dog and buried her face into the soft blonde fur. She sobbed with such intensity, tears and saliva landed on Chloe's neck fur.

Cradling Chloe's face in her hands, Jacqueline said, "I am so sorry. This will never happen again. You sweet, sweet soul." Jacqueline looked up at the sky. "Dear God, you sent me an angel." She cuddled Chloe's shaking body, feeling Chloe's rapid heartbeat.

Jacqueline shut the backdoor and climbed back into the driver's seat. Gazing out the front windshield, she repeated, "I am in the driver's seat now. I really am in the driver's seat now," each affirmation stated with stronger conviction. Turning her body around to see Chloe in the back seat, she saw a dog sitting tall, head slightly cocked, mouth closed, focused directly on her human.

Reaching into her purse, Jacqueline pulled out the card that Donna gave her. She exhaled loudly, blew her nose, and turned the car around for home.

Chloe, sensing the shift in Jacqueline, gave a small groan as she slid down in the back seat, tucking one front paw under her body. Her eyes eventually relaxed looking out the window, enjoying whatever came across her visual field.

Pulling out of the parking lot, Jacqueline looked out her rear view mirror. Beyond Chloe was the sign for the Greenville Humane Society. She shuddered, thinking about what she had almost done.

"You know what today is?" Nivie asked Alex, standing up on her toes in their kitchen.

"Um, Tuesday?"

"Yeah, and…."

"The day before Wednesday?"

"No! Time for Santa to arrive!" Nivie jumped up and down.

"Oh, OK," Alex grinned.

Today was the first Tuesday after Thanksgiving; the kickoff to Nivie's favorite season, Christmas. Every year on this day, Santa Claus arrived at the Tridge and was the guest of honor to light the Courthouse for Christmas. After that, hundreds of families followed him to the nearby Santa House, where children of all ages sat on his lap, telling him what they wanted for Christmas. After consecutive years of waiting in line, Alex let Nivie know this was the year to stop.

In October, two months prior to the lighting of the Courthouse, Woodhaven Run's well-known Santa House also hosted a yearly Santa School. Portly men from around the world with white beards and big hearts gathered to hone their Santa skills. Mrs. Clauses accompanied their husbands, too. The classes, purposely held during the school year, helped to prevent any "run-ins" with Woodhaven Run children.

However, should that occur, the man in the red suit would simply say he is a representative of the real Santa Claus.

Nivie giggled to herself when she was downtown and saw two or three Santas walking in red herds down the sidewalk.

Ho, ho, ho, ho, ho, ho, she thought to herself.

In December, The Gardens' Christmas celebration consisted of local choirs singing along luminaria-lit pathways. Nivie enjoyed visiting during their Christmas celebration, but "as soon as her boogers froze," it was time to head home.

In addition to the festivities, visiting the Bronner's store at Christmas was equivalent to visiting New Orleans for Mardi Gras. About an hour away, the world's largest Christmas store was open all year, except for Christmas Day. For Nivie visiting was "coming home to the Mothership." She relished the endless aisles of moving displays, ornaments, and decorations. Regardless of the time of year, the piped-in Christmas music made it feel as if it were always December 25. Tour buses stopped and unloaded scores of people from various parts of the globe. The small chapel on the other side of the parking lot played continuous and various forms of "Silent Night," providing a reverent side to Christmas.

The Santa House, Santa School, and Bronner's emboldened Nivie's strong vindication of her deeply embedded love of Christmas. "It's literally in my genes," she would say.

When Nivie and Alex returned home from Santa's arrival festivities at the Courthouse, Nivie walked straight to the basement.

After Alex finished in the bathroom, he almost tripped over three large red and green plastic bins in the living room. Kimball found a rogue ornament and tapped it across the floor.

"So, it's starting," Alex said.

"You know how it is, Love. With everything we saw tonight and not decorate? Sacrilege!"

Alex smiled.

"And, Kimball Kitty had his wellness check today with Dr.

Carmichael. Didn't ja, Kimball?" she said, picking him up, massaging his head. Alex walked over and joined her. "And, everything looked good, didn't it? Yes, it did. Dr. Carmichael loves our baby Kimball, and she's always so good to you. Isn't she?"

Placing a squiggly Kimball down, she said, "So, it's time to celebrate! Hey, can you help me carry the tree up?"

"We already keep one up all year," Alex said, motioning to the tree upstairs.

"That's just a small one as a reminder of Christmas cheer all year! I meant the big one. Downstairs. It's time for it to join us and unleash its beauty everywhere!" Nivie declared.

Alex looked over at Kimball, who hopped on a bin to inspect the lid.

"Hang on little buddy. You've never seen anything like this before." Alex said. "I can guarantee it."

Alex braced himself for the yearly barrage of rhetorical Christmas questions and comments from Nivie: "Do you notice that the bird can fly at the end of *Rudolph*? Santa fixed him!" And, "What's wrong with the little doll? Why is she on the Island?" And, "I love when Yukon Cornelius throws up his ax, licks it, and says: 'Nothing.' That's the best," with Nivie reenacting the scene.

Kimball jumped off the closed bin, walked up to an open one, sniffed around and hopped inside. Locating another orphan ornament in the corner of the bin, he batted at it, his paws pushing out the plastic sides. After fun with the ornament, he sat down and curled his tail around himself, watching his humans decorate.

Their lawn should have been entered into contests. All the mangers, snowmen, Rudolphs, polar bears, Grinches, and *Peanuts* characters mirrored a wing at Bronner's. Nivie delighted seeing cars slow down in front of their house to appreciate their lawn.

"You know. We could give the neighbors a break this year," Alex pointed out.

"But, look! We can't deprive these people of Christmas cheer!"

"Could deprive them a little," Alex quipped, handing over another box of decorations to Nivie.

"This is so much fun!" she said, dancing around the living room, head adorned with a Santa hat, and neck donned with a necklace of blinking lights. Turning on Bing Crosby's Christmas CD, Nivie said, "I'm so glad that when we were growing up, Ma played Johnny Mathis, Bing Crosby, and Andy Williams' Christmas albums. We used to turn off all the lights in the living room and light candles. You know, the real kind. Then, we'd listen to the albums over and over." Every year Nivie reminded Alex of past joys.

Alex scanned the room full of plastic bins with Santas, snowmen, stuffed animals, and ornaments spilling out of them. He hauled the larger Christmas tree from downstairs, and organized it into three different sections on the floor.

"We aren't going to end up on one of those TV Christmas light shows, are we?" he asked.

"One can only dream!" Nivie said. "Look at this, Kimball!" She lowered his new monogrammed bright red stocking so he could smell it. The smiling cat face on the front almost matched Kimball's coloring.

"Your very own stocking, and it's going right here," she said, hanging it up on the mantle. Alex got a small lump in his throat when he noticed Minerva's stocking next to Kimball's. He secretly appreciated the exciting and festive ambience Nivie created at Christmas. But, he would never tell her that.

Standing in her unused basement, Jacqueline walked over to a wall full of red plastic bins and tightly closed boxes. Wiping a year and a half's worth of dust off, she peeked inside one of bins to see her Christopher Radko box of ornaments nestled next to her Beyer statuettes. Chloe' body wiggled, moving from container to container, Lammikins still in her mouth.

"Come on, Chloe-girl. This year, these are going upstairs."

This December, Bryn mustered the courage to invite her in-laws to their home for Christmas Eve dinner. Hosting Julian's entire extended family consisting of two older brothers and two older sisters and their families would have been too much, but Barbara and Lawrence alone was doable. When Bryn was growing up, Jacqueline adored cooking, so she either took over the kitchen at the holidays, or for the extremely extravagant gatherings and parties, she hired caterers. Barbara, too, was an outstanding cook and delighted in preparing large family meals. Labeling herself as a novice cook would be generous, Bryn mused. But, she was determined to take on the Christmas dinner this year.

"All right, guys. Wish me luck," Bryn said out loud, her shaking hand turning the oven dials to preheat. "Going to use the good china tonight. We're going all out!"

Tucker pranced at her enthusiasm, and Megan followed suit. Bryn crouched down in front of the dining room china cabinet and dug out many of their wedding gifts only used a handful of times.

"Arg, big belly," she groaned, positioning herself in a squat in front of the open cabinet door. "Ok, dishes. Check. Flatware, check. Linen napkins, check. Those will need to be folded later." After ransacking the china cabinet, she stood up. "Megan, no touch. Leave these alone, please."

"OK, Mommy," Megan said, agreeably.

After retrieving the stepstool from the kitchen, Bryn took Megan's hand and walked to the guest room. Putting her finger to her lips, Bryn asked aloud, "Now, where are those wine glasses and flutes? C'mon Meggie," she said, opening the closet door and climbing on the stepstool to reach the top shelf. "Let's look in here." She continued to search, leaving open boxes spread over the bed and on the floor. "Now where could they be?"

Megan delighted in all the "new toys," plopping down on the carpet and tossing some of the tissue pieces in the air. Tucker, outside the guest room, paced between the kitchen and the bedroom, whimpering.

"What's wrong, Tuck—?" Bryn asked. A pungent smell caught her nose, and the smoke alarm shrieked in her ear.

Struggling over the boxes, Bryn grabbed Megan and waddled to the kitchen to find black and gray smoke billowing out of her closed stove.

"Oh, my gosh!" she said, randomly punching at the oven dials. "Meggie, stand back!"

She opened the stove, and waves of smoke rolled out. She coughed so hard, she barely heard Julian rush into the kitchen after work.

"Merry Christ—! Holy crap! What's going on?" he asked, trying to talk over the blaring alarm.

Bryn reached into the smoking oven to pull out the charred remains and threw them in the sink. "I forgot about the plastic containers—All I did was preheat it, and—well, it didn't go very well," Bryn said, turning on the stove fan and waving her arm around to air out the kitchen.

"Mommy bone!" Megan said, hands covering her ears.

"I can see that! Mommy did burn!" Julian burst out laughing. "Only thing I *can* see!"

Bryn reached to open the kitchen window to dissipate the fog engulfing them all.

"Meggie, just stay in the living room," Julian said, turning on the vent fan and stretching up to turn off the smoke alarm. He was only able to make out the outline of the uncooked dishes ready to be placed in the oven.

"Food didn't even make it in, huh? Wow, you won't be a professional chef anytime soon!"

Tears welled in Bryn's eyes. Without looking at Julian, she asked, "What do we do, Jay? I just wanted it to go perfectly."

Tucker returned to the kitchen to "help" in any way he could. "Tucker, move!" Bryn commanded.

"Well, I'll call Mom and Dad and tell them we need to go out instead," Julian decided. "Unless they don't mind a raw Christmas dinner!"

Bryn tightened her mouth and frowned.

"Don't worry, babe. I got it covered," Julian said, in a failed attempt to contain his laughter.

He pulled out his phone and walked into the other room. Bryn continued to fan air and smoke toward any possible exit route. Megan joined Bryn in the kitchen, copying her mother's actions.

"Hey, Mom," Julian said. "Well, it's going OK. Except that…Well, let's go out to eat instead. Everyone's fine, but the stove was smoking and not fit to use…Yeah, yeah…we're fine…We're all fine. Yeah…I know. She'll learn…I guess someday. Who knows! I'll just call and see if some place has availability."

Julian returned to the kitchen, walking through the lingering veil of smoke, while Megan and Bryn continued to move the air along. "I know, Mom. Well, that's what you get from trying. I really think the oven was rebelling from insufficient use!" Julian laughed. "Love you, too, Mom. See you guys soon."

"OK, Meggie. We're going to go out for Christmas dinner with Grandma and Grandpa Troxell soon," he said, taking Megan's hand and walking into the living room.

Bryn silently wiped her tears, running more water over the charred plastic in the sink. Tucker, sitting by her side, watched quietly.

Jacqueline stepped into the warmly lit room with trepidation. The grief counselor's meeting space was more inviting than she had anticipated on the cold January night. Glancing around the room, she saw five other people sitting on chairs and a couch, positioned in a circular formation. An older woman at a check-in table greeted her with a gentle smile. "Welcome. Come in, please. And, you are—?"

"Jacqueline."

"Hi, Jacqueline. Thank you for coming tonight. So glad you could make it. I'm Bonnie. Please fill out a nametag and have a seat. There is coffee if you would like."

"Thank you."

With a shaky hand, Jacqueline tried to write her name on the sticky nametag. She pressed it to her chest a few times, although the sides never fully laid flat. Spotting an empty seat, she sat down and smiled politely at the woman to her left. She struggled to take off her coat.

To Jacqueline's right, a man in his early 60s with salt and pepper hair, glasses, and blue eyes said, "Oh, let me help you with that."

"Oh, no, thank you. I'm fine," she said, hanging her coat on the back of the chair.

"Hi, Jacqueline, I'm Bill Langdon," he said, extending his hand, reading her nametag.

"Hi, Bill. Nice to see you."

"I'm sorry for your loss."

"Thank you. I am sorry for yours, as well," she said.

"If you don't mind me asking, what brings you—?"

"My husband died of a heart attack," she answered, surprised at the emptiness of the words. "And, how about you?"

"Oh, my beloved wife, Betty, died after a courageous battle with cancer. We were married for forty-two wonderful years."

"I'm so sorry."

"Thank you."

Jacqueline looked at him. "By any chance, was your wife Betty Langdon, who was a Master Gardener?"

"Yes. Yes, she is," he replied. "Or was."

"Oh, my goodness. We were Master Gardeners together."

"Is that right? She really enjoyed gardening, especially after I retired from Woodhurst."

"She was a lovely woman."

"Thank you. And your husband—?"

"Edmond," Jacqueline added.

"Edmond. Yes, what did Edmond—?"

"—Good evening, everyone," the counselor interrupted. "I want to thank each of you for coming tonight. I know it might be difficult to be here, but my intention is to create a place of support for you."

Jacqueline's initial apprehension waned. Although most of the details from what others shared was a blur, she felt deeply comforted by hearing others' stories and experiences.

At the end of the meeting, she stood up and gathered her belongings.

Bill asked, "Listen, Jacqueline. I was wondering. Might you be interested in getting a cup of coffee sometime?" Briefly taken aback, she looked around to see if anyone else could hear. "I enjoyed talking with you and thought you might like to continue our conversation," Bill continued.

Jacqueline sighed. "Thank you, Bill. I, too, have enjoyed our conversation. However, I don't think it will work at this time. I'm sorry."

"I am, too," Bill said, looking down. "Well, let me know if you change your mind. Or, if you'd like company for the symphony sometime."

"Thanks, Bill. Have a good evening," Jacqueline said, dashing out the door to her car.

"Just look at it snow," Nivie eagerly exclaimed, pulling back the curtain. "As much as I hate the cold and gray, I do love the first major snow-fall. At the beginning of January, no less! It's like a nice, white blanket slowly floating down on us all. Makes me all warm and cozy," she said, wrapping her arms around herself.

"You know, they are saying that people will be snowed in. Businesses and schools closed," Alex said. "We're even going in later tomorrow."

Nivie snapped her head around, a smile forming across her face. "Really? Well..now. Let's have a look-see. Wouldn't that be awesome?" she said, picking up her phone, swiping to the local weather app.

"Let's see, of course, all the surrounding counties are closed. Except, wait a minute. Woodhaven Run Public Schools, CLOSED!"

Nivie stood up and danced as Alex toasted her with his pre-dinner glass of wine.

Rushing to the television for confirmation, she anxiously read the crawler of closed schools.

"Where is it...where is it? T.....U.....V....W...Woodhaven Run Public Schools! Let the fun begin! I know students are excited, but that doesn't come anywhere close to the loving relationship between a teacher and her snow day!"

She nestled next to Alex on the couch. "You know, honey, now that we have tomorrow off..." She flashed him a coy smile, which Alex reciprocated.

He stood up and outstretched his hand. They almost tripped running up the steps.

As they were about to enjoy the benefits of holy matrimony, Nivie was dismayed to see Kimball lying in the middle of their bed. Alex continued, as if Kimball weren't even there, kissing Nivie with her back on the bed. Her legs dangled over the side and Kimball's balled body sat inches away from their heads.

Nivie hoped the bouncing motion would be enough to move Kimball's sleepy body. Rather, his outstretched paw touched her nose, and the feline gently closed his eyes.

"Um...Kimball...Kitty," Nivie murmured with Alex's lips on hers. "You're going to have to move," she said, nudging his side with her head.

After being awakened from his slumber, Kimball stretched out, with his back haunches now directly on Nivie's forehead, as Alex continued.

"Oh, screw it..." she said.

"Good idea," he whispered into her ear.

Three weeks later, the day had arrived when Nivie practically skipped into the grocery store to purchase pregnancy tests. It just so happened it was the same time they needed beer.

Let them think what they want.

In the days prior, Nivie repeatedly Googled, "How do you know when you're pregnant?" What interested her was the range of answers the women gave: "My boobs hurt; my boobs didn't hurt at all; sometimes the test was negative when I really was pregnant; smells really got to me; I didn't even know; I was *so* tired; I knew within three days; I had my period for three months before I even knew." Ironically, she found solace in the varied responses. She also spent more time on Facebook, smiling and liking her friends' pictures and posts about their children. The prospect of posting her sonogram picture especially excited her. "The baby book starts early," she joked.

After returning from the store, Nivie met Alex at the door as he arrived home from work.

"Today's the day, honey!"

"For what?" he asked, smirking, as he laid his keys on the kitchen counter.

Nivie flashed him a smile, holding up the small box that held so much weight. She tried to open it, hands fumbling.

"Dammit! Can you open this?" she asked, flinging it to him.

Alex took the package and began gingerly opening it with a big smile on his face.

"Are you friggin' kidding me?" Nivie tried to swipe it from his hands.

He pulled away and held the package out of her arm's reach. He leaned in and kissed his wife. "Oh, Love. So sweet of you to want to kiss me."

"Come on!"

"Ok, here you go," he chuckled, handing her the open box. His heart pounded, too.

Stepping into the bathroom, Nivie looked at her reflection in the mirror.

Just one question: Do I pass or fail?

She completed the test and laid the stick on the side of the sink and stepped out.

"Ok, honey. Here we go." She set her phone's timer for two minutes and hugged her husband tightly.

One hundred and twenty seconds was an eternity. All the chatter on the TV was inane.

"Honey, whatever it is, it'll be OK," Alex said. "We'll keep trying."

"I know."

"But wouldn't it be awesome if it were positive?" he said, touching her belly. "Man, that'd be so sweet." He hugged her tighter.

Nivie's phone went off. She looked up at him, giving him a quick kiss on the nose. She took a deep breath and walked back into the bathroom.

A few moments later, the door slowly opened. Alex's face fell as he saw Nivie's distant stare. He embraced her and they stood in the hallway, swaying as she sobbed.

It was a death every month, and this was the fifteenth month. When people would ask them, "Do you have children?" Nivie understood it was a way of connecting. But the days Nivie could remain optimistic and answer "Not yet," were fading. They had gone in for testing but at Nivie's age of 42 and Alex at 45, coupled with their combined physiological issues, it would take strong fertility interventions with slim chances,for pregnancy to occur. Adoption was the next question brought up by well-intentioned people, but Nivie and Alex decided it would involve too much time, money, and energy for them at this point to embark on that journey.

She went to her Facebook page, hiding most of her friends' posts about their children and even unfollowing others. The constant reminder of what they had and what she would never have was too much to bear. Over the next few weeks, she cried on the drive to school and on the drive home, making an earnest attempt to dry her tears before Alex got home. Nivie knew he was hurting, too.

"Well, we can keep trying, Love," Alex consoled.

"I guess," Nivie said.

"But," Alex pointed out, "I mean, do we really want kids? I mean, really, really, really want to be parents? Kids are loud, expensive... messy. You know, crap everywhere."

"But, they're also loving and sweet," Nivie protested. "And when they wrap their little arms around your neck, can't beat it. I babysat enough times to remember. There's nothing like it. And, Christmas, and other holidays. And, you can teach them. And, also the fact that they are a part of you and me."

Alex nodded.

"And, who will take care of us when we're older? As much as Kimball Kitty loves us, he won't be picking out the best nursing home," Nivie said.

"Not a good reason to have kids."

"I know. But, like, everyone is having kids, or has kids now."

"But, do we really need to have them, just because others are?" Alex asked.

"Well, Ma would be ecstatic!" Nivie said.

"Well, OK, then. We'll have the baby, and then she can raise him or her!" Alex got quiet. "I do have to admit: there is this inexplicable primal, biological desire to be a dad. You know?"

"Yeah, I get that," Nivie paused. "But, you know what. From now on, none of our news will ever be interesting."

"What do you mean?"

"I mean, for other people. Kids and their schedules will always take precedence. And, if we have something to do, it'll never be as important as 'the kids'."

"Nah, it won't be that bad."

"You'll see. None of our news will ever be 'as good'," Nivie said, using air-quotes. "Like, we'll do something to the house. Or, we'll travel somewhere. Or, we'll get a something new. Those things will always pale in comparison."

"Well, just not a good enough reason to have a baby," Alex said.

"I know. Just sayin' that's how it's going to be."

"Well, those things will be important to us. That's all that really matters."

Kimball Kitty jumped down from his rocking chair and sat at their feet in the kitchen. Alex picked him up and moved him near Nivie's face. "Kimball Kitty knows that."

Nivie gave Kimball a kiss on the head. "You're such a good boy," she said, nuzzling her face in his side, tears falling into his fur.

Embracing each other, Alex and Nivie stood in the kitchen, holding Kimball Kitty close to their hearts.

"Please stop crying," Bryn said, on a cold January afternoon. Through her own tears, she paced the living room, rocking her newborn baby boy, Ethan. Megan was already down for her nap; one more child to go.

"I just changed you. Fed you. Burped you."

Ethan's cries intensified.

"Tucker, move!" Bryn said, almost tripping over him, "Baby, please stop for mommy. Please. Please, stop baby." Bryn's need to use the bathroom was reaching epic proportions.

After five more agonizing minutes of pacing and rocking, Ethan's screams finally quieted to whimpers. Bryn slowly peeled the calmer baby off her shoulder and onto a blanket on the floor.

Rushing out of the room to the bathroom, she said, "Be right back."

When Bryn returned to the living room, she saw Tucker's head nestled next to Ethan's side. A sleeping Ethan's arm rested on the dog's head.

"You're such a good brother, Tucker," Bryn cooed.

Poke, poke, poke.

"Mumph."

Poke, poke, poke.

"Yeah, I'm up, Kimball Kitty," Nivie yawned, purposefully avoiding eye contact with the green eyes staring up at her from the floor.

Nivie stretched and stumbled to put on her robe. Kimball chirped, rubbing his quivering tail against her leg. Taking the lead, he ran downstairs. From the first floor, he looked up at a sluggish Nivie plodding down each step.

When she saw an empty coffee pot left in the machine, she said, "Uh, oh. Daddy forgot to make coffee. How's Mommy gonna make it through the day without?" Kimball brushed his tail against her leg once more. "Don't wanna see what could happen there. No one would be safe."

Glancing out at the back porch, she saw the winter wind had opened the back porch storm door. "Oh, man. Need to shut that. No, no, no," she said to Kimball, nudging him away with her foot. "This is not a place for Kimball." She opened the entry door and pulled the storm door shut.

Returning to the kitchen to fill Kimball's food bowl and prepare her own breakfast, she slathered cream cheese across a bagel. "There, breakfast of champions," she muttered.

Plunking down in front of the television, Nivie took a bite. Kimball jumped up on the couch, sniffing the air around the breakfast food.

"Uh, no. You already got your food," Nivie said, using her elbow to nudge him away. "Don't need Kimball Kitty fur on my bagel as an 'extra goodie'."

Kimball sat down on the couch cushion next to her, never diverting his gaze from her delicious treat. "Wow. This isn't uncomfortable at all," Nivie joked. "Why don't you go over to your favorite rocking chair? You know, so Mommy can eat?"

Once Nivie finished her bagel, she patted her leg. As was the case each morning, Kimball stepped into her lap, plopping down and curling his puffy tail around himself.

"Oh, what a good Kimball Kitty. You know, your cousin Mini, the matriarch, used to do this. So glad you do, too."

Nivie studied his white body, marbled with orange spots. "Do you know you have one little, random snip of a spot on your face? And two long spots on your butt and legs?" Nivie said, moving her fingers over his soft fur. "You also look very dapper in your collar and your 'Kimball Kitty' tag and tiny chikawaka," she said, flicking at the collar's jingle bell. "Hey, maybe we'll see a bluebird today?" she asked, looking out the window. "Not likely with the weather, but wouldn't that be fun? You know Mommy loves bluebirds. Yes, I do, and I'm sure you would, too." She paused. "You know, you are a very special little boy. Daddy and I are so glad you're here, little guy."

She gently closed her eyes, reveling in the soft vibration of Kimball's purr and the warmth of his body on her legs. After about twenty minutes, Nivie looked over at the clock.

"Man, Kimball Kitty. Gotta scoot! Mommy's got to go to work. You know, make the big bucks." She contorted her hips and butt muscles to get a noncompliant Kimball to move. He responded by stretching in an upside down "U" on her legs, and then curled back into a ball on her lap again.

"Oh, man. Every morning? Please don't make this harder than it already is. I would love to stay here all day with you. Believe me," she said, setting him down on the couch cushion next to her. His ears pulled back into a display of "Owl Ears": a true look of annoyance.

With a little more energy from her breakfast, Nivie headed upstairs to finish getting ready for work. Leaving the bathroom door open, she stepped into the shower and began singing her morning tunes. Turning around on a sustained note, she saw a small orange and white mass through the frosted glass shower door.

Her singing ceased, and she slid open the shower door. Sitting on the toilet, with his tail wrapped neatly around his front paws in a cat statue pose, was her very attentive feline audience. He would have applauded if he could.

"Oh, my god, Kimball! You are just too cute! But, no. You cannot come in."

She shut the door, making his body blurry again.

Giggling, she opened the shower door again, to get a clearer view. He was bent over licking his back paw but snapped his head around to look at her. She closed the door again, laughing harder this time. "This just never gets old," she said.

Stepping out of the shower, she left the shower door open as thoughts of work began to muddle her mind. Brushing her teeth at the sink, she looked through the frosted glass door. There was the orange and white mass again, licking water puddled by the drain.

"Really, Kimball? That's nasty. C'mere." She picked him up, wiped down his paws and placed him on the floor by the toilet. "Now it's time for Mommy to put on a little bit of makeup. You don't need it because you already have your markings. And well, besides the fact you're a cat!"

As Nivie pulled out her mascara, Kimball's butt wiggled, looking up at the toilet, ready to leap.

"Whoa! Wait a minute," she said, flipping the lid down. "Let me put this down, or you're gonna get a nice little bath. Remember last time?"

The sound of a trickling water faucet coupled with the toilet lid lowering were obvious signs to Kimball Kitty to jump into the sink. At first, he stuck out his paw, trying to catch the water droplets. Then, he stuck his nose under the faucet, lapping at the drips.

"Silly, Kimball Kitty."

Nivie picked out two different sweaters from her closet and held them up in front of a damp Kimball. "Which do you think Mommy should wear today?" He walked toward the one she held in her left hand. "Yeah, you're right. This one is better."

After blow drying her hair and putting earrings on, she looked over at the clock. "Oh, man. Gotta scoot!"

On the way downstairs to the car, Kimball shot by Nivie on the steps. Since it was clear to him that this was, indeed, a race, he arrived in the kitchen first.

"Bye, Kimball Kitty," she said, picking him up and kissing his head. "Have a great Kimball Kitty day!"

Nivie grabbed her purse, school bag and laptop, and stepped into the garage. As she opened her car door, she glanced back through the window into the kitchen. Although the rule was "No Kimball Kitty on kitchen counters," she smiled, catching a glimpse of him sitting on the granite surface, seeing her off to work.

Later that night, Nivie finished up her dinner sitting on the couch next to Kimball Kitty, getting their nightly *Golden Girls* fix. Hearing her phone beep, she read a text from Alex: "Hurt my leg at work. Slipped on ice. Hard to walk. Going to Dr."

Nivie called him immediately, but no answer. She texted: "OMG. Where r u now? Need me?" She called and texted several more times. No answer. After an hour of pacing and biting her nails down to the quick, she heard the garage door open. Running to the door, she saw Alex struggling to get out of the car, hobbling on crutches.

"Oh my god, honey! What happened? I've been calling and texting you! Are you OK?" Nivie ran behind him to carry his bag and close the car door.

"I had to turn my phone off in that medical place."

"What did they say? This doesn't look good," she said, placing her hand at the small of his back.

"Let me... get up...these steps," he said, trying to catch his breath.

"What can I do?" Nivie was unsure where to stand, so as not to be in the way, but to be there in case he fell.

"Nah, I just need to sit down."

Nivie hovered as he struggled through the kitchen to the living room couch.

"Oh, Love. What did they say?"

"Well, they said," Alex paused to catch his breath. "They said I have a small lateral hairline fracture near the kneecap and a sprained MCL."

"Oh my god, what does that mean?" Nivie asked.

"It means I'm not going to work for a few days," he said falling back onto the couch. He reached down, pulled up the recliner footstool under his leg, and sighed deeply. Kimball jumped off his rocking chair and onto the couch, cautiously sniffing Alex's wrapped leg.

"Yeah, it's going to be that way for a while, Kimball Kitty," he said.

"So, do you need me to stay home with you tomorrow?" Nivie asked.

"Nah, I'll be fine. I do need to pee, though. Wish I'd thought of that before," he grumbled.

"What can I do? Do you need any help?"

Alex gave her a coy smile. "Nah, I should be fine in there, too." Hoisting himself up off the couch, he hitched one crutch under his right arm, and placed the other crutch under his left. Standing a second to gain his balance, he hobbled forward. In spite of his assurance and seemingly good technique, Nivie kept her hand close to his back the entire journey. Kimball joined in the parade to the powder room.

"Yep, this is my litterbox for a while, big guy," Alex said, as Nivie shut the door behind him. She and Kimball waited outside and escorted him back to the couch.

"Still don't need any help?" Nivie asked again.

"Nah."

"All right. Just let me know."

"Yeah. Just need some water for these pills they gave me. Oh, and a protein bar," he said.

"Absolutely," she said, heading into the kitchen.

After handing Alex his glass of water, the remote, and his

insignificant dinner, Nivie said, "Sorry, Love, but unfortunately, I need to get to bed here. Early meeting tomorrow."

"It's OK," Alex squirmed, moving a few pillows around to get comfortable.

Nivie darted over to help him. "You want Kimball in the bedroom with me?"

"Nah, he can stay down here."

"You sure? You might not sleep very well."

"Well," Alex looked down at his elevated leg. "I don't think quality sleep will be around for a while."

"Well, let me get you a bell, or something. Ring it anytime you need me, OK?"

"OK," he said, as Nivie rushed to find the bell from their trip to Mackinac Island.

"Let me know if you need anything. Anything at all." Nivie kissed Alex's head, gave him a big hug, and leaned down to kiss Kimball's head. "Have a good night, boys."

"You too, Love."

Joining Alex on the couch, Kimball circled tightly next to Alex's leg, throwing his body against Alex's hip. His bell collar jingled.

"Thanks, big guy," Alex said, turning on the television. "Just you and me here for a while."

Alex opened his eyes. He was surprised Nivie had already left for work, succeeding in not waking him. It was time to use the bathroom, but he hesitated to upset Kimball, who was snuggled warmly against him. Alex wiggled his leg, and Kimball reluctantly jumped off the couch. Placing one crutch under one arm, and another crutch under the other arm, Alex tried to lift himself up. Still wobbly, he took a step and tumbled to the floor.

"Shit!" he yelled, punching a couch cushion. Kimball jumped up on the couch and licked Alex's head.

"Thanks, Kimball Kitty. Gotta try this again."

Throwing his torso onto the couch, Alex struggled and pushed himself back to a standing position. Regaining his balance and control of the crutches, he slowly hobbled to the bathroom. Since getting there had been such a task, he decided to hop back to the couch, holding the crutches in his hand. Framed photographs of Phoenix, Blue Ridge Parkway, Boston, San Francisco, Mackinac Island, National Parks, and wedding pictures rattled on the entertainment center and piano with each lurching hop.

After getting comfortable in a reclining position, he texted Nivie at school: "Fell down. Kimball licked my hair. Fine now."

An hour later, Nivie texted back. "OMG. R U OK? Glad Kimball Kitty there to take care of you. Be home soon. Cook your favorite dinner. Love you. XOXO."

"Thanx. Love u 2," Alex replied. Kimball resumed his position on the couch, tucking his balled body next to Alex's side.

"Love, are you all right?" Nivie called out from the kitchen, arriving home from work a few hours later. She walked into the living room and saw Kimball Kitty snuggled against the side of a bleary-eyed Alex.

"Oh, sorry. Didn't know you were sleeping," she said, kneeling down next to Alex, giving him a kiss.

"Oh, yeah. We're fine," he yawned. "Just us men-folk."

"Hungry?"

"Yeah, for some strange reason the breakfast bar just didn't seem to sustain me."

"Yeah," Nivie looked around the living room. "Hey, did Kimball knock those three pictures over?"

"Nah, that was me hopping around. But, I'm getting the hang of it now."

"Honey...." Nivie started to give advice but caught herself. "Anyway, gonna get started on dinner," she said, straightening up the frames and walking into the kitchen.

The bell rang.

Nivie walked back into the living room. "Yes? What do you need?"

"Love you, honey," Alex said.

"Love you, too," Nivie melted.

For the next several weeks, Nivie's weekday schedule was the same: return home from work, fix dinner, clean up, help Alex change his clothes, grade papers, and off to bed. Her weekends were also filled with litterboxes, laundry, snow shoveling, garbage, and on and on it seemed. Making his temporary bed the couch downstairs, Alex crawled up the stairs every few days to take a shower, but to avoid this ordeal, Nivie usually washed his hair in the kitchen sink. Although Nivie was beginning to tire, Alex routinely thanked her for all her efforts. Slowly, he gained more stability on the crutches, relying on them less and less. Nivie was glad when the bell ringing died down. Through it all, Kimball Kitty was Alex's constant sidekick.

The door creaked as Chloe followed Jacqueline into the stuffy air. Edmond's office hadn't been opened since that fateful day. Jacqueline saw his large mahogany desk, two pens still in the pen well, and his black leather chair. The notes and papers were meaningless at this point, but she took comfort in seeing his handwriting again. Taking a deep breath, she walked over to the closet and jiggled the door open. Three work shirts and a suit hung on the rod, still in plastic dry-cleaning bags. On the floor were two pairs of work shoes with socks balled inside. She spotted a small, but familiar box on the top shelf. Stretching to reach it, she coughed when some of the dust was disturbed. Like opening a buried treasure, she pried off the top. Inside the musty smelling box she found a stack of loose pictures. Intrigued, she sat down in the leather chair to peruse them, and Chloe settled down next to her.

"My goodness, I haven't seen these in years," Jacqueline said.

"Oh, my gosh. Me and Edmond in Traverse City...... Brynnie's graduation...Salutatorian....her school play.....her swim meet... tennis games... class president...Homecoming Queen...Prom Queen...vacation with the Hornbecks... cheerleading...Woodhaven Blooms charity event..."

Jacqueline thumbed through and found a few pictures of a golden retriever. "Taffy," she exclaimed. "Oh my goodness. What a pleasant dog she was." She browsed through several more pictures of Taffy, most which featured a younger Bryn.

Shuffling through the pile, she came across three pictures she couldn't immediately identify. Pulling them closer to focus, she swallowed hard.

That's me. So long ago.

In one photo, a young Jacqueline with short, curly brown locks stood with her arms wrapped around the neck of a large horse. Even gazing at a well-worn black and white photograph, with the top right corner bent, she distinctly remembered his deep chestnut color. His soulful dark brown eyes accentuated by long lashes, a chestnut mane, and a white star on his forehead. On the bottom of the picture the smudged ink pen caption read: "Me and Ranger. Best Friends Forever." A lump formed in her throat. For much of her life she had successfully pushed the memories of Ranger out of her head. But, in this moment, they rushed back like a tidal wave.

As a young girl, loneliness was one of Jacqueline's closest companions, but when Ranger entered her life, he dissipated the darkness like a candle in the night. Ranger was a quarter horse-thoroughbred mix, about fifteen years old and had belonged to one of her parents' friends before they fell on hard times. Nothing made Jacqueline happier than being with her beloved horse, riding him, brushing him, talking to him.

The hours that Jacqueline and her dad rode Ranger bareback

together were even more significant. She remembered her dad's strong, loving arms keeping her close as they rode around their farm together. Her mom thought this was dangerous, but Jacqueline cherished these moments. Her dad not only taught her how to ride but also to appreciate nature and its beauty.

Jacqueline fondly recalled that, when she was doing chores in the barn, Ranger was never far behind. On special occasions and holidays, Ranger would patiently stand still while she neatly braided his forelock, the mane between his ears. She smiled, remembering some of the "designs" she created and Ranger sported.

Chloe lifted her head to look up at Jacqueline, immediately getting a head pat. The contented dog stretched out, readjusting her body into a comfortable position as Jacqueline shuffled through the photos.

The next picture, smudged on the top left corner, was of Jacqueline sitting on Ranger bareback, leaning forward, hugging his large neck. The picture didn't do justice to this gentle giant who stood almost sixteen hands.

Shifting to the third picture, she gasped.

It was a stunning close-up side view of Ranger's magnificent head and strong neck with his ears pricked forward.

What an incredibly stunning animal.

Closing her eyes, she could still feel his velvety muzzle against her cheek and the tickling sensation from his tiny coarse whiskers. It was always paradoxical; these fine, tender features seemed incongruent in such a majestic and powerful creature.

Eyes still closed, the pleasure of seeing her old best friend dissolved as she dove into sadness. *No one prepared me. I understand money was really tight. But, as an 11-year-old girl, no one prepared me.* She covered her eyes as more of the memories she had tried so hard to suppress gushed back to the surface.

Eleven-year-old Jacqueline skipped home from school, celebrating the early release that day. She turned the corner, surprised to see the truck belonging to their vet, Dr. Bradford, an old family friend, parked near their barn. Defying the rule never to run near or in the barn, she scurried to the wide open door. No one. And, Ranger's stall door was open. Dropping her book bag, she looked to her left and heard the muffled male voices coming from an area behind the barn. Following the sounds, she saw her dad holding Ranger on a lead rein and Dr. Bradford standing next to Ranger with two syringes in his hands. Without warning, he drove both syringes into Ranger's neck, one immediately after the other.

Ranger's head dropped and he lunged forward. Collapsing to the ground, he landed on his side. His hooves kicked grooves into the dirt as his legs convulsed.

"Ranger!" Jacqueline ran to her dad, stunned. "Daddy? Daddy? What happened?"

She attempted to run to her beloved Ranger when her dad, caught her around the waist, stopping her. "Daddy? What's wrong with Ranger?"

Her dad avoiding eye contact, held onto her tightly.

Jacqueline's eyes locked onto the frightening scene. "No, Daddy! Ranger!" she repeated, until her voice was almost a whisper. Ranger's jerking legs began to slow. And eventually stopped.

Dr. Bradford touched Ranger's open eyes. No response. He took out his stethoscope, slowly nodded to Jacqueline's dad and wiped his forehead and eyes with his handkerchief.

"Ranger?" Jacqueline twisted out of her dad's embrace and knelt down next to the stilled body. She lifted Ranger's heavy head onto her lap. It was still warm. Stroking his forehead, she repeated, "Ranger! Wake up! Wake up!" Her tears landed on his cheek. "C'mon. Please get up. C'mon. Please stand up," she said, pulling on his neck. "Please come back. Please come back. I'll take good care of you," she whimpered, twisting his forelock.

"I love you, my Ranger." She leaned down, resting her cheek against his muzzle, trying to hug him one last time.

Her dad's hand on her shoulder made her flinch. He leaned down and said, "OK, Jacquie. That's enough. Pull yourself together. It was Ranger's time. Let's go." He grabbed her hand, forcefully pulling her away. Ranger's head plopped back on the ground. Jacqueline tried to stand, but her shaky legs wouldn't carry her small frame. Her dad picked up her limp body and carried her into the house. Her inconsolable weeping was muffled by her dad's shoulder, as Dr. Bradford slowly packed up his bag and left to make arrangements with the county landfill next to the motionless Ranger.

Carrying her into the house upstairs to her bedroom, Jacqueline's dad hoped she would get some rest. When he opened her bedroom door, she scanned her empty room, letting out an anguished gasp.

"Daddy? Where are? Where are?" she asked, sliding out of his arms.

"Your mother thought it best —," her dad said, shaking his head.

Exhausted and out of breath, Jacqueline ran past her dad, mustering all the energy she could and tore back down the stairs to find her mother in the kitchen. "Mommy, where are my pictures of Ranger? And, Black Beauty and the Black Stallion posters? Where are they? What did you do?" she asked angrily, trembling with emotion.

Jacqueline's mom pursed her lips, dried her hands on her apron, and wiped her brow.

"And, my horse statues?" Jacqueline frantically added. "And, stuffed animals?"

Her mom opened her mouth to answer, but Jacqueline ran past her to the back door, tears welling in her eyes. "And, my riding clothes and boots?"

"Oh, Jacquie," her mom said, walking up behind her and reaching out to stroke her hair. "We didn't want you to be even sadder after Ranger passed. So, I took them into town while you were at school. The horse statues, posters, and the like."

Jacqueline snapped her head around to look at her mom, and

crossed her arms over her chest.

"It's much better not to remind yourself over and over," her mom continued. "Ranger was a great horse, and you had some great times together. But, he's gone now. It's time to move on. Pull yourself together."

Her mom leaned over and gently kissed her forehead. Jacqueline could hardly breathe, standing immobilized.

"Now, wash up. Dinner's almost ready," her mom said.

Numbed, she turned and slowly walked upstairs to wash her hands, dry her tears and catch her breath.

The only thing Jacqueline remembered from dinner was that everything sounded as if it were under water. Her mom's endless chatter about neighbors and friends, and her dad, although quieter than usual, emitted noncommittal grunts to her mother's commentary.

After eating a few bites of noodles and corn, Jacqueline asked to be excused and plodded up the steps, returning to her barren room. Although her dog and cat posters and other stuffed animals were still there, no sign of horses. And, no Ranger. Flinging herself on her bed, Jacqueline covered her ears, trying to erase Ranger's deafening thud. She wept and rocked herself to sleep.

A few hours later, she opened her eyes and looked at the clock: 2:16 AM. Easing herself out of bed, she cautiously opened her door and peeked down the hall. Her parents' light was off. Making a concerted effort to control each movement to mitigate any creaks from the steps, she tiptoed downstairs into the kitchen.

Wondering if they had thrown some of her things away, she dug through the kitchen garbage can, swallowing hard at the smell of the mush and feel of noodles and corn remains on her hands and arms. Towards the bottom of the trash, her efforts paid off. Jacqueline pulled out three pictures of her and Ranger slightly bent and stained by the remains of dinner. Wiping the pictures clean with her smudged fingers, she clutched them to her chest and silently tiptoed back upstairs. Kneeling next to her bed, she pulled out her "memory box" and added the three pictures to her collection. She relocated the box to a new place in her closet and it remained hidden from not only her parents, but ultimately herself, even as it moved from one house to another. And Ranger, nor his death, was ever mentioned again.

Sitting on the couch in the living room with his leg elevated, Alex yelled, "It's about to start, honey!"

"Be right there! I've got a bag of cat poop in my hand!" Nivie yelled from the kitchen on her way to deposit the litterbox deposits. After washing her hands, she grabbed two beers from the refrigerator, a steaming bag of microwave popcorn, and headed into the living room.

"Alright, Kitten Bowl. Come to Mama!" Nivie said, setting down the beers. She handed the popcorn to Alex and nestled her head on his shoulder. Kimball took his usual spot on the rocker.

"So, what is this again?" Alex asked, looking at the two "teams" of kittens on the screen, each wearing matching collars.

"Well, all these sweet babies are up for adoption. Whichever kitten gets one of the mice or balls past the plastic goalpost gets a point for their team." Nivie and Alex "oohed" and "ahhed" as the teams were announced: Terrell Snuggs, Ryan Fitzcatrick, Beau Catson, Aaron Pawgers, to name a few.

"This is just too much! It's almost wrong," Nivie said, leaning over the couch, pretending to pick something up from the floor.

"What are you doing?" Alex asked.

"That was my heart popping out of my chest!" she exclaimed. "Just putting it back!"

They laughed. Nivie glanced down and saw Kimball had hopped down from the rocker and walked over to them, a jingle ball firmly gripped in his teeth. He dropped the ball at the foot of the couch, right next to their feet.

Nivie leaned over and grabbed it. "Check this out. Alright, Kimball Kitty! Go get it!"

She chucked the ball across the living room and Kimball sprinted after it. Once it stopped rolling, Kimball delicately sunk his teeth into one of the spaces in the ball and trotted back to them, jingle ball in tow. They looked at each other in amazement.

"So, that just happened!" Alex said, smiling at Nivie and Kimball.

"That's what I was telling you!" Nivie gave him the ball. "Here, you do it!"

"Alright, Kimball," Alex said to the fixated feline, who was poised, ready to retrieve. He flung the ball across the living room and Kimball galloped after it, barely missing the television. As before, Kimball bit into one of the holes and carried the ball back to his humans. Although this time, he dropped the ball further away from the couch, and walked over to the living room chair, rubbing against it.

"What did I tell ya?" Nivie said.

"That's crazy! We have a cog dat!" Alex said. "Yeah, Kimball Kitty, you could have your own Kitten Bowl!"

They both laughed. Meanwhile Kimball resumed the crouching position, staring at the ball, patiently waiting for it to be thrown again.

Part Two: Adapting to Loss

"Until one has loved an animal,
a part of one's soul remains unawakened."
~ *Anatole France~*

"Mourning is love with no place to go."
~Anonymous~

"**G**ET OVER THERE, ETHAN!" JULIAN YELLED AT HIS TWO-AND-a-half year-old son. "Man, he's wide open! C'mon now!"

Spring was in full bloom at Woodhaven Run. Front and backyards displayed yellow and white daffodils bursting from the earth, alongside a rich assortment of tulips. The Gardens boasted light blue squill, yellow witch hazel, red cyclamen, and pink rhododendron along the paths.

Despite all this, what really mattered to Julian were the Saturday mornings in May and June when Ethan's soccer team competed at Woodhaven Run's well-known soccer complex. Although Julian wasn't the head coach, his ubiquitous sideline commentaries made him seem as though he were. His outbursts garnered sideways glances from other parents, especially since the field was much smaller for the younger players. And, the purpose of playing was to instill coordination and confidence. Two things that Ethan had in short supply.

"Crap! He had it," Julian said, throwing his fist into his open palm. "He had it, and that other kid took it from him. He had it."

After Ethan returned to the sideline to talk to his coach, he walked up to his Dad, head lowered. "That's OK. That's OK. Keep your eye on the ball, not on us. Stay focused," Julian told him with thinly-veiled disappointment.

Scrawny for his age, Ethan didn't share his father's enthusiasm nor interest in kicking around a black and white checkered object. And, Bryn knew this. Although she had to run errands, Bryn had an idea.

After picking up an energetic Megan from the five-year-olds dance class, she gathered Megan and Tucker into the car and drove over to the complex.

Walking toward the field, Bryn whispered, "Now, Meggie, we have to be really quiet." Locating Ethan's field, she purposefully stopped behind Julian, but far enough back that they were barely visible to the players.

"There's Daddy!" Megan shouted.

"Yes, honey," Bryn whispered again. "But we have to be quiet because Tucker's not supposed to be here."

During his ongoing scanning of the crowd, Ethan spotted his beloved dog. He also saw his mom and sister, jumping up and down, giving thumbs up.

"Tucko!" he said, waving wildly.

Confused, Julian weakly waved back saying, "Yeah, I'm still here. All right, bud. You can do this!"

Ethan's grin grew, running after the ball.

"Look, Julian," said another parent, pointing to the field. "Look at Ethan now!"

"That's my boy!" Julian said.

Ethan, stole the ball from the opponent, handed it off to a team member, who in turn, made a goal.

"That's it, bud!" Julian shouted, pumping his fist in the air. "Now we're talkin'!"

"All right, Meggie. C'mon, Tucker. Let's go," Bryn said, dashing everyone to the car. The whistle blew, and a herd of little boys ran to their coach.

"Great job, Ethan!" his coach yelled.

Ethan looked over and saw his dad waving, pumping his fist in the air. Galloping to his dad, he heard, "Great job, bud. Now, I want you to keep playing like that. Go gettum!"

Beaming from ear to ear, Ethan ran back out onto the field, practically hopping.

Jacqueline walks to the entrance of the forest where she used to ride her bike. A Chihuahua she had never seen before approaches her, moaning. A bright, beautiful horse appears, but she realizes that horses aren't supposed to be here. It begins walking toward her, and she runs away.

The arrival of the Fourth of July meant one thing: the annual Troxell family baseball game at The Stadium. Although dark, ominous clouds were as common as the games themselves, everyone hoped the weather would hold out. The highlight was the magnificent fireworks at the end, even though on the way to The Stadium, their neighbors had already previewed their own.

"This'll be fun!" Julian said, repeating his famous line on the way there. After getting their tickets, Julian looked down at Ethan and said, "Hey, bud! Let's go see if you can run the bases. See if you can be a part of that."

"No, Daddy. Don't wanna," Ethan said, his left hand dangling limp, covered by his catcher's mitt.

"Daddy, I wanna run the bases!" Megan looked up at Bryn. "How come he gets to?"

"Jay—" Bryn said.

"—C'mon, Ethan. It'll be fun. We'll be right back, babe!"

Julian took Ethan by the hand and walked him over to the information booth. "Hi, I'm Julian Troxell and this is my son, Ethan. He wants to run the bases."

"Daddy, no," Ethan mumbled, looking at the ground. "No wanna."

"Are you sure, Mr. Troxell?" the gentleman asked. "Looks to me he's not that interested."

"Oh, he will be. Don't worry," Julian assured. "C'mon, Ethan," he grabbed his son's hand, pulling him away from the worker. Crouching down in front of Ethan's face, he took hold of his son's shoulders. "Now you listen to me: this is going to be fun. So, quit whining. Now."

Julian sprung up, "All right. So where do we sign up?"

Julian located Bryn and Megan in the stands, and Ethan crumpled into Bryn's lap, "No wanna."

"Babe, don't baby him. He's fine," Julian said.

"Julian! Julian! Hey! Up here!" He looked around and saw his friend Mike and his family sitting five rows up.

"Hey! How are ya?" Julian yelled up. "Be right back, Babe."

Bryn looked over at her two disappointed children and then up at the dark clouds.

This was supposed to be fun.

The third inning came and went without Ethan or Megan running the bases. Although Ethan was relieved, his slumped shoulders and dangling mitted hand reflected Julian's weight of disappointment. Megan's shoulders slumped for different reasons. The dark clouds finally spoke, releasing a deluge of rain. Lightning illuminated the sky followed by loud claps of thunder. No Stadium fireworks this year. The disappointed family ran through the rain back to the car and returned home.

As the first one into the house, Bryn surveyed the scene. She gasped.

Innards from the living room couch cushion and chunks from a windowsill littered the kitchen floor. A blanket that had been draped over the couch lay tattered. And, Tucker was nowhere to be seen.

"Oh, my gosh. What happened here? Tucker! Tucker!" she yelled.

"Crap! Where is that dog?" Julian asked, right behind Bryn.

Bryn found shoes without their mates strewn down the hallway and into the kitchen.

"What a mess," she said.

Julian went out to the garage, calling for Tucker, both kids right on his heels. He opened the door to the backyard, calling for him. No Tucker.

Running upstairs to their bedroom, Bryn found a shoe, a tie, and more pillow remnants scattered across the bedroom floor. Turning on the bathroom light, she found Tucker in the shower, trembling.

"Oh, sweetie," Bryn said, opening the shower door further. "Poor sweetie. C'mere," she said, crouching down. His tail thumped against the tiled wall. "Oh, it's OK."

"Babe, you upstairs?" Julian yelled.

"Yeah. Found him."

The kids ran upstairs, Julian right behind, taking two steps at a time.

"Tucker! Why is Tucker there?" Megan asked. "Was he dirty?"

"No, just scared," Bryn said.

"What a mess. And, what a wuss," Julian muttered, walking out of the bathroom. Bryn shot him a look.

"Oh, Tucker," Megan said, kneeling next to him and petting his head.

Ethan threw his arms around a damp Tucker who nestled his nose into Ethan's lap. "It's OK, Tucko. No be scaoed."

"Merry Christmas, Love!" Nivie exclaimed.

"Uh, honey, thought we decided this was just going to be Kimball's birthday party," Alex said.

"It is! Only this time with an added bonus!" Nivie said.

"It's July."

"I know! What a perfect time to have a Christmas-birthday party!"

The table was adorned with red and green table cloths and Christmas plates and napkins. A cat cake made from chicken, sweet potatoes and peas displayed a "4" flameless birthday candle. The Christmas tree was lit up with four presents underneath it. Two presents wrapped in birthday wrapping paper, two presents in Christmas wrapping paper. One must be balanced, Nivie would say.

"So, the Bing Crosby CD playing in the background. That's staying?" Alex asked.

"Yeah, adds to the mood!" Nivie said, handing Alex a pointed birthday hat that matched the one she was wearing.

Sporting his own birthday hat, Kimball jumped up on the couch, sitting next to Alex. With a faint pout on his face, his green eyes looked up at Alex.

"Oh, big guy," he said. "So sorry, man."

"Meggie, go get your sandals on," Bryn said, fastening Ethan's sneakers on him. "Mommy has to run a few quick errands."

"Can Tucker go?" Megan asked.

"I guess," Bryn relented. "But, we have to be really fast because it's not good for Tucker to be in the car for very long."

"C'mon, Tucker!" The kids squealed, running to the SUV.

In the grocery store, Bryn reminded herself, "OK, just need a few things. Now, which aisle for the...? Ok, there it is. C'mon, Megan. We need to hurry."

"Mommeeeeeeeeee..." Megan said, walking alongside her mother. "I want Cap'n Crunch!"

"I told you, 'No.' Just eggs, milk, yogurt, and snack bars for Ethan's soccer team."

"Yum!" Ethan chimed in from the front of the cart.

"That's *all* I'm getting," Bryn asserted.

Megan whined, dragging the tips of her toes. "But, Mommmeeeeeee....why can't I have....?"

"Because. C'mon Meggie, let's go. Tucker's waiting for us."

When they arrived back at the SUV, they were greeted with strong tail thumps against the seat.

"C'mon, Tucker. Let me get these things in here. Meggie, please hang onto him," Bryn said, buckling Ethan into his seat.

"Why does he get to have what *he* wants?" Megan griped, pointing at her brother.

Ethan shot Megan a huge smile.

"Don't do that!" Megan's eyebrows furrowed, her arm swinging, yet missing, her brother. "Mommeee!"

"Meggie stop it." She lightly touched Megan's arm as she buckled her in.

"C'mon. Time to get home. Starting to get dark."

Megan's relentless whining prompted Bryn to turn the corners rougher than usual. Once safely inside the garage, Bryn opened up the side car door. Tucker jumped out, standing under her feet as she unbuckled the kids.

"Tucker, move." Bryn sighed looking at the splattered groceries on the car's floor. "Meggie, take your brother's hand and take him inside. I need to clean up this mess."

Bryn filled her arms with bags of broken eggs and punctured yogurt containers seeping over a milk carton, and left the house door open behind her.

"Megan, please unhook yourself from my leg," she said, hobbling into the house.

Inside the kitchen, Megan continued. "But, Mommeee..."

"Megan, stop!" Bryn's eyes darted around. "Wait a minute. Where is your br—?"

A loud noise outside, then a piercing yelp followed by loud crying, startled Bryn.

Dropping the bags on the kitchen floor, she sprinted out the door through the garage. Ethan was running toward her from the end of the driveway, shrieking at the top of his lungs.

"Ethan!" Bryn screamed, Megan running right behind her. The mother and son met half-way down the driveway. Bryn grabbed him, squeezing him tightly. His little arms clung to his mother. "Don't you *ever* do that again! Do you hear me? *Ever!*" His head nestled snuggly on her shoulder, tears running down his cheeks. "Always stay with Mommy!" She stood up, rocking back and forth on her return to the garage, with one hand cradling Ethan's head to her shoulder.

Megan ran past Bryn and Ethan toward the end of the driveway. "Mommy! Look! Tucker!"

Bryn turned around, rushing toward Megan. In the middle of the street, Tucker's shaky front paws slowly dragged his right rear leg. The right side of his body was cut in several places, funneling down to a trail of blood. He softly whimpered, with a still tail and shallow breathing.

"Tucker!" Megan screamed, standing frozen.

"Oh, my gosh," Bryn muttered. "Megan! *STOP!* Come here."

Ethan lifted his head, "Tucko?"

"Megan—come here!" Bryn reached out her left hand, keeping her right arm wrapped around Ethan. "Bud, I need to set you down."

Bryn wrapped her other arm around Megan, as Megan buried her sobbing face into Bryn's shoulder. "It's OK, Meggie. It's OK." She grabbed her phone from her pocket and said, "I need to make a call. It's OK," she said, trying to quiet her weeping children.

Bryn asked Siri for the number to Dr. Carmichael's office. Tucker collapsed onto the driveway. From a crouching position, Bryn averted her eyes and kept them on her children to focus her racing thoughts. Trying to stabilize her quivering voice, she said, "Yes, this is Bryn Troxell. My dog, Tucker, has been....has been hit by a car."

"OK, is he conscious?"

Bryn looked up. "Yes, but he's on his side now. He's not breathing very well."

"Find a blanket and carefully lift him. Be careful though. Some dogs will bite out of fear and pain."

"OK."

"We'll be waiting for you."

Bryn ran to the car and snatched a blanket from the emergency kit. She wrapped it around Tucker's leg, desperately trying to ignore his heavy panting. "OK, guys. Please get back into the car." She drew in a breath. "Mommy has to get Tucker."

The adrenalin coursing through her veins allowed her to lift Tucker into the back of the SUV. He yelped.

Bryn didn't remember any of the drive to the vet, except for incessant queries by Megan and Ethan about their beloved dog's status. The stench of spilled yogurt, broken eggs, and blood hung thick in the air.

"Oh, please, God," Bryn quietly prayed. "Please."

The hospital staff swiftly retrieved Tucker from the car. As they took him inside, Bryn picked up the phone and called Jacqueline. "Mom, can you please come pick up the kids?"

"Why, what's wrong?" Jacqueline asked.

"Well, Tucker was hit by a car, and—."

"Oh, my goodness! Whatever possessed him to do such a thing?"

"He was protecting Ethan from running into the road," Bryn sternly said.

"I see."

"Anyway, I'm at the vet's now. I'm not sure how long I'll be here. Can you please come take the kids?"

"Sure. My pottery class is just finishing up, but I will be there as soon as I can."

"Thanks."

Bryn texted Julian in Texas on another business trip: "Tucker hit by a car. We're at Drs now. Will let you know how things go."

Julian responded to Bryn's text: "Wow. Hope he pulls through."

"Mommy, what's going to happen to Tucker?" Megan asked.

"We'll see, Meggie."

"Put on band aid?" Ethan said.

"We'll see, bud."

Time slowed to a snail's pace. Bryn's face softened when she finally saw her mom come through the doors.

"Gramma!" the kids said.

"How is he?" Jacqueline asked. "Have they given you any more information?"

"Not anything specific. But, at least he made it over here. They said that was the biggest hurdle. Now, we just wait and see."

"OK. Have the kids eaten?" Jacqueline asked.

She shook her head.

"Come on. Let's go get some dinner," Jacqueline said, corralling the wearied kids out the door.

"Thanks, Mom," she said, waving goodbye.

Sitting in the waiting room, Bryn overheard another client say, "But, I can't afford that."

"We understand. But, we have a payment plan," the receptionist offered.

"But, I can't afford that," the woman gulped, choking back her tears. "I hardly have money for...I just can't do that."

Bryn closed her eyes, resting her head against the wall. Time moved both quickly and slowly simultaneously.

"Mrs. Troxell?"

"Yes?" Bryn jerked awake to see a veterinarian standing next to her.

"Dr. Ansbaugh," she said, quickly shaking Bryn's hand. "Dr. Carmichael is away at a conference. It's good you got Tucker here as soon as you could. He's out of shock now—"

"Oh, good—"

"—Yes, it is because his capillary refill time was about three to four seconds, which is long," she said, at a quickened pace. "His breathing was shallow and rapid. Temperature was about 99.4 degrees, which is lower than we like. But, things have improved. His spleen is not ruptured but he has been catheterized. We treated the few lacerations he had."

"Ok, so..."

"His lungs were auscultated and fortunately we found no signs of fluid. But, his back right femur has sustained a closed fracture. We have stabilized the leg and he is receiving fluids and pain meds. If everything looks good, which we anticipate it will, surgery using a plate and screws will be done tomorrow morning."

"Ok," Bryn shook her head and frowned. "So...?"

"He's stabilized now. He just needs some rest."

"So—"

"Go home," Dr. Ansbaugh said, turning around, heading toward the back room. "Come back tomorrow and you can see him. He should be out of surgery by noon. I'll pass his chart onto Dr. Carmichael. She'll tell you about his progress and devise a treatment plan." She rushed back through the swinging doors to the surgery room.

Bryn looked at the receptionist, who returned a tiny shrug and a forced smile. Shenhanded over her credit card and signed the treatment authorization for a preliminary estimate of $1,500 to $2,000.

After signing the receipt, she folded it and put it into her purse. Looking around the dimly lit, empty waiting area, she walked over to the exit and pushed out through the double doors toward home.

The next morning after Bryn dropped the kids off at school, her phone rang. She was happy to see Dr. Carmichael's phone number appear.

"Dr. Carmichael?"

"Hi, Bryn."

"So glad to hear from you."

"Well, he pulled through surgery like a champ," Dr. Carmichael reassured.

"Oh, good," Bryn said, truly exhaling for the first time in 24 hours.

"Yes, he's resting now. And, he should be good to go home tomorrow."

"Would it be OK for me and the kids to visit later?"

"Of course. I'm sure he would love that," Dr. Carmichael said.

"I'll bring them after school. It was just so much yesterday," Bryn said.

"I'm sure."

"They told me all these things about cap....cap—"

"Capillary refill time."

"And, something about his spleen," Bryn added. "And, his lung."

"His spleen was not ruptured," Dr. Carmichael said. "They checked his lungs and there wasn't any fluid. Those are good things."

"Oh, good. I just wasn't sure what was happening."

"I understand. Looks as though you had quite a night. It's important to know he'll need to be kept very quiet, or as quiet as possible for about six to eight weeks. No running around, jumping, chasing squirrels."

"Wow, OK," Bryn gulped. "Well, the kids' school year is ending next week."

"And, he'll need to be on a leash when his does his business. We'll have him back in about 8-10 days to get his sutures removed, but just make sure you do the proper aftercare."

"OK, sounds good," Bryn said. "Just so glad to hear from you and that everything went well."

"Me too," Dr. Carmichael said. "He's a real sweetie."

After school, Bryn gathered the kids and drove to see Tucker. Walking into the waiting room, Ethan asked, "Mommy, where Tucko?"

"Shh, Brother," Megan said.

"Hi, we're here to see Tucker Troxell," Bryn said to Kelly, the daytime receptionist.

"Yes, of course. He'll be so happy to see you!"

"Yay!" Megan and Ethan jumped.

"Ok, kids. We need to be quiet, and not get Tucker too excited. He's still healing," Bryn said. One of the kids stopped jumping.

Kelly led the three of them to the recovery room in back. Lying next to a small stuffed animal, Tucker was resting on his side in his cage. He jerked his head up when he heard his loving family's voices.

"Tucko!" Ethan exclaimed.

"Shhhh, bud," Bryn shushed. "We need to be quiet for him."

His tail thumped against the side of the cage, and he struggled to stand. Quietly whining, he lifted his front paw and grabbed the cage door.

"What's wrong with him?" Megan asked.

"Well, his leg is broken. But, he should be fine in a few hours," Bryn said.

"Hello, Troxell family," Dr. Carmichael said, joining the others in the recovery room and leaning over Tucker's cage. "Thanks, Kelly," she said, as Kelly left the room.

"Hi, Dr. Carmichael," Bryn said.

"Mr. Tucker, how are we doing?" Dr. Carmichael said, opening his cage. "There are some people here to see you."

"Oh, my sweetie," Bryn said, kneeling down. She accidentally squeaked his squeaky toy as she tossed it to the side.

Ethan leaned in and gave him a hug.

"Ok, bud," Bryn intervened. "Gentle."

Dr. Carmichael towered over the Troxell family doting on their recuperating family member. "You have a very lucky dog there. But, you need to be as quiet as you can with him. Give us a call if you see anything wrong, or something comes up. But, we should be good."

"He's OK, though?" Megan asked, looking up at Dr. Carmichael.

"Yes, with the proper after care, he should be fine, Megan."

"Thanks, Dr. Carmichael," Bryn said, stroking Tucker's head and kissing his snout.

"Thanks Docto Cahmahyco!" Ethan said.

"Thanks for trying to protect my son," Bryn whispered into the ear of her recovering and loving dog. His tail didn't stop thumping against the cage wall the entire time his family was there.

"Hey, honey," Nivie called to Alex from the kitchen, "Have you noticed that Kimball's not eating as much since we got back from Mackinac Island. Usually can't feed him enough."

"Well, he seems fine. He's acting normal," Alex replied.

"Well, it just looks as though there's been more food left in the bowl than usual the past few days."

"We've only been home about a week. Plus, it could be the unusual heat. It is early July after all. I wouldn't worry about it too much."

"Hm, OK. It's just that it's been a few days. Just concerned about that fatty liver thing they can get if they don't eat."

"Well, if you want, call Dr. Carmichael's office again. We just had him Kimball there a few weeks ago for his rabies shot. Don't want to take him in again if we don't need to."

"I know, but I think I'll call."

Nivie arranged a same-day appointment. But, since Dr. Carmichael was on vacation, they would see Dr. Robinson. With Kimball in his mesh carrier, they drove to the veterinarian's office.

On the examining table, Kimball pulled in his front paws to make himself smaller.

"Hi, I'm Dr. Robinson. Hi, Kimball," she said, placing her stethoscope on his chest. "Well, it's usually cars or kidneys that do them in." Nivie wasn't amused with her attempt to lighten the mood. After the examination, Dr. Robinson recommended taking a blood sample to look at his levels. She also recommended a Feline Leukemia-Feline AIDS blood test, saying although it is rare, it could be what was causing his lack of appetite. Nivie was reluctant to do it again since Siobhan had the test done when Kimball was a kitten. They agreed to the test, nonetheless, and would get the results the next day.

When Nivie found out they would draw the blood from Kimball's neck, she was more than happy to let them take him to the backroom. In the meantime, Dr. Robinson prescribed medication to stimulate Kimball's appetite and showed Nivie and Alex how to give subQ fluids for his dehydration. She even suggested buying baby food until his appetite returned. After dropping Kimball off back home, Nivie and Alex went to the store.

"Wow, it's weird being in this aisle. For a kitty, no less," Nivie said.

"But, look, Love," Alex said. "Look at all the different types of foods. What do we get? Meat? Pureed meat? And, maybe beans? How many jars?"

Nivie looked to see about twenty of them in the cart. Alex studied her face.

"Well, maybe we can put a few of these back," he said.

For a few days, they gave him the appetite-stimulating medicine that garnered modest success, at best. Nivie's level of anxiety and disappointment mounted as Kimball didn't improve. He only picked at the baby food, avoiding his dry food entirely. Nivie and Alex worked together to give him fluids, which temporarily gave him more energy. But, soon he was lethargic again.

One night after dinner, Alex said, "Hey, honey. Tonight is the Music by the River. We should go."

"I don't know. Who's playing?"

"Not sure, but I can look it up."

"I don't know, Love," Nivie said, looking down at Kimball resting on the front door rug.

"He should be OK for a little while."

"But, what if...?"

"He ate a little bit before."

"Yeah, but..."

"We can even leave early, if you want."

"I don't know. This summer vacation is starting out terrible."

"Honey," Alex asserted. "We really need to go."

They gathered their belongings and drove to the Tridge. Locating a spot, they made sure their blanket was opened in front of their chairs, preventing others from sitting too close. The area by the Tridge was expansive, since the town demolished the old buildings, leaving even more open space. It was a welcome contrast to how constricted Nivie's life felt.

She looked around at the sea of people tapping their feet, clapping, eating, chatting. Kids dancing, spinning, twirling to the music. Even a few dogs on leashes rested quietly next to their humans.

None of these people know how sick our baby Kimball Kitty is.

For a few moments, Nivie allowed herself to get lost in the music. She looked over at Alex, and gently took his hand. He smiled, gave her hand a squeeze, and kissed it.

"Do you wanna walk around?" Alex asked, interrupting Nivie's stream of thought. "Our stuff should be fine."

They walked past the downtown Farmer's Market. Although it wasn't open on this day, visiting was always a treat, especially when there was fresh kettle corn. During certain days of the week in the summer, people sold their fresh fruits and vegetables, as well as other homemade goodies. The season was shorter in Woodhaven Run than other areas of the country, but Nivie was grateful for the turnout. Anything to support local businesses, she said.

Holding hands, they strolled onto the Tridge, behind the musician's stage. This vantage point provided a delayed reaction to the music, but the warped sounds weren't unwelcome to Nivie.

The three legs of the Tridge converged to form a Y at the confluence of the Chippewa and Tittabawasee Rivers. She took a few steps on the first leg, feeling the suspension give, just enough for her stomach to drop. Like a small roller coaster. Standing in the apex of the three legs, it seemed to Nivie each side was calling to her. The second leg led to Chippawassee Park with a skateboarding area in the distance and a dog park in an open area. She chuckled thinking about a cat park. A small reprieve.

"The Family" statue stood at the top of a hill near the dog park. The piece elicited a peaceful feeling— two children flanked by two adults, all holding hands. It always interested her that they all seemed to be in bathing suits, except for the mother, who appeared to be in a night-gown. Even if the rivers weren't perfectly clear, the Tridge's reflection in the water, punctuated by canoers, calmed her. Behind the Tridge was downtown Woodhaven Run. Past Christmas seasons were called to mind when the lights on the Tridge were even more magical.

The third leg led to Chippewa Trail, which ran to the Chippewa Nature Center. She fondly remembered visiting as a child. Kids loved tapping the trees for sap. Or, syrup. She could never remember. All she remembered is that it was a fun, but freezing field trip.

Returning back to their chairs and blanket, they passed the Rail-Trail, a former railroad track turned biking and walking trail. It went on for miles and miles.

What would happen if I started walking, and just kept walking…?

Squeezing Alex's hand, she nodded. Time to go back home.

As they pulled into the garage, they saw Kimball sitting on the counter, watching them through the window.

Nivie barely waited for the car to be placed into park before running into the house. "Look at that, Love! He's feeling better!" she exclaimed. "Poor thing, he was waiting for us to come home."

"Oh, Kimball Kitty! How are you?" She gently picked him off the counter, cradling him. Arriving in the kitchen, Alex scratched Kimball's head. "Hey, big guy." They both talked quietly and smiled at him, as if talking to an infant. Nivie gently placed him down and he slowly walked to the front door rug. He balled up his body, facing the door.

Nivie and Alex looked over and saw that neither the food nor water had been touched. Their stomachs fell. Again.

⚬⚬⚬

Donning her sunhat, Jacqueline stepped into the garage. She scanned the wall until she found what she needed: a hoe, gloves, trimming shears, and a plastic bag. Chloe spun in circles in anticipation before they both walked to the backyard. Jacqueline stood with hands on her hips over an area that was once lush with blooms. Now, it was a sea of withered sticks. She knelt down and tugged on one crispy stem until the roots released its hold on the earth. Shaking the dirt off, she placed it in the bag. Chloe, momentarily interested in this adventure, laid down a few feet away, rolling around on her back. Jacqueline grabbed another stem, shook the dirt remnants off, and bagged it. She continued as the once dense, unkempt flower beds slowly became ripe for replanting.

After following the treatment plan for a few days, Kimball continued to decline. His once smooth coat was now reduced to dull tufts on a more skeletal Kimball.

They returned to the clinic to see Dr. Robinson where they took X-rays, finding a large amount of stool in his colon, but no foreign bodies. His lungs and heart were normal but interestingly enough, he showed traces of hip dysplasia.

Alex asked Dr. Robinson many questions. But, without a definitive diagnosis, or solid answers, the questions became repetitive, followed by her almost seemingly evasive responses.

"It could be pancreatitis," Dr. Robinson said. "There are places you can send bloodwork to know for sure, but time is a concern now. I'm not sure if that's the route you want to take, but that is a resource for you."

At home, feeling even more exhausted by the process, Nivie and Alex collapsed into bed to go to sleep. They left the door open for Kimball, but he didn't join them in bed or even make a nightly visit.

In the middle of the night, Nivie sat up in bed, tears streaming down her cheeks.

Oh, my god. He's really not going to make it. He's really going to die from this.

Trying not to wake Alex, she balled up her pillow and pushed her face down deep into it.

Early the next morning, Nivie walked downstairs to see Kimball lying on his favorite rocking chair. Alex sat in front of him, a can of baby food and plastic spoon in hand. He placed a spoonful of food in front of Kimball.

"C'mon, Kimball Kitty," Alex coaxed. "C'mon, big guy. Just need to eat for us. Can you do that? Just eat for us?"

Without Alex noticing, Nivie rushed back upstairs to the bedroom. She didn't want him to see her tears flowing again. She called the vet, pressing for more answers.

"When will Dr. Carmichael be back?" she asked.

"Not for another day or two. Sorry," the new receptionist said.

"Dammit! Our kitty is not doing well. Not at all!" Nivie yelled.

"I'm so sorry, Mrs. Emerson. I can get you in to see Dr. Robinson again. But, not until tomorrow afternoon."

"That's not gonna work!"

"Maybe take him to the emergency vet?"

"Thanks."

About 45 minutes later, Nivie dried her tears and returned to the kitchen with Kimball's litterbox in hand. Alex was cleaning off the spoon and said, "He ate about three spoonfuls."

Nivie said, "Thank you, honey. Thank you for taking care of our baby." She paused. "Alex?"

"I know. We need to take him in."

After almost an hour drive, Nivie and Alex arrived at the emergency vet's office. Dr. Lin carried Kimball and his carrier to the back.

After about a half hour, Dr. Lin returned with Kimball in the carrier. "You have a very sick little kitty here," he said.

No shit. "So, what *is* it?" Nivie asked.

"Well, we're still working on that. We have all his test results from the other doctors you've seen. They've ruled out Feline Leukemia. His kidneys and liver functions, all within normal limits. X-rays look normal."

"We know. So….."

"We could also keep him overnight…"

"Overnight? Why?" Nivie said. "Poor thing."

"We would be able to get more information and keep a closer watch on him."

"I hate to ask this to put a price tag on our baby. But, how much would that be?" Nivie asked.

"About $500."

"What?" Nivie shrieked.

"Per night."

"Oh, my god."

"We'd have to insert a feeding tube."

Nivie grimaced.

"Through his nose."

"Oh, my god! That's barbaric!" she yelled.

"Well, he isn't eating, and that's a way to get the nutrients into him quickly. He needs energy," Dr. Lin paused. "Or, we could start thinking about whether to go on."

"—Oh, my god. This is just too much…" Nivie cried.

"There is a test we could do that measures sodium, potassium, and other parts of his blood," Dr. Lin said. "It could give us some information and tell us which direction to go in."

"I just don't know what to do." Nivie looked at a pensive Alex for direction, but his eyes reflected as much uncertainty as hers.

"I'll give you some time, and I'll check back to see what you decide," Dr. Lin said, walking out the door.

Through their emotional fog, they decided to have the test. It showed low calcium and low potassium, but didn't offer any more information.

Nivie picked up her phone to call her sister. She had texted her a few times during the week, letting her know about Kimball, but she needed to talk to her now.

"Hey, Niv," Siobhan answered.

"Shiv, Kimball Kitty is really sick now. And they are saying...they are saying..." Nivie gasped for breath, squeezed her eyes shut, quickly shaking her head.

Alex took the phone from her. He cleared his throat, and said, "They are saying that his chances are very, very slim. It's not looking good. Actually, they said we could euthanize him here, or take him home. So, we decided to take him home."

Nivie motioned to Alex for the phone. "I'm so sorry. I'm just so sorry, Shiv. We tried...we...."

"I know, Niv. It's OK," Siobhan said. "I know you guys did the best you could. Nobody could have loved him more."

"Love you, Shiv," Nivie said, barely getting out the words as she ended the call.

Returning Kimball to the room, Dr. Lin said, "I will send home some more fluids, just to make him more comfortable. I will also give you a script for pain-killers. If he shows any symptoms that he's in pain, please don't hesitate to give it to him."

On his discharge papers, it showed low calcium and low potassium explained his low heart rate and weakness. Nivie read, "Unfortunately, we don't have an underlying cause for these symptoms at this time. Please monitor for seizure activity, as that can be the result of the low calcium level, and recheck immediately if this occurs. Kimball was a good patient. I am so sorry for the struggle he has been through. Sincerely, Dr. Lin."

After a silent ride home, they stared at the door to the back porch. Looking at each other, they opened the door, setting Kimball's carrier down and unzipping the top of his mesh carrier.

"You think....we'll have to do this soon then?" Nivie asked Alex.

"Yeah, we don't want him to go on suffering," Alex said.

After a few minutes of allowing Kimball to roam the back porch, Dr. Carmichael called.

"Nivie? This is Dr. Carm—"

"Yes. Thank you for calling so fast," Nivie said. "Our baby's not doing well."

"I'm so sorry."

"Can you….can you just come here? I know you don't usually do that. But, we've had to haul him everywhere lately."

"Sure. I can do that for you," Dr. Carmichael asked. "When would be good?"

Nivie put her hand over her face in an attempt to stop the tears. "We were thinking later this evening, maybe?" she said, looking at Alex for confirmation. He nodded.

"OK. I can come back earlier than planned and be back in Woodhaven Run later today. Would 7:00 tonight work for you?" Dr. Carmichael asked.

"Thanks. Yeah, I guess that would work."

"Ok. You take care. I'll see you then."

Nivie and Alex spent all day on the porch with Kimball Kitty, reading books, surfing online while John Rutter's *Gloria* CD played in a loop in the background. When they spoke in quiet tones, it was reminiscing about their kitty.

Midafternoon, Nivie said, "Love, do you think he seems a little better? He seems, like, perkier than before."

"Huh. You're right," Alex said, looking at him from afar. "How can that be?"

"Don't know."

"But, you know, he's still…."

"—Yeah, I know. Just weird that he's responding to the birds more, and stuff."

"Yeah," Alex said. "How 'bout we take a quick walk. Just for a few minutes."

Nivie twisted her face.

"Just to get some fresh air."

"Alright. Just for a few minutes."

Walking around their neighborhood, Nivie asked, "Do you think that we could wait a bit?"

"I don't know, Niv."

"I'm going to call Dr. Carmichael to see. What about tomorrow?"

"Niv, honey. I have to work."

"Then, after you get home."

Alex looked into Nivie's eyes. "I guess. But, again, if he shows any signs of—"

"I know, I know. Thanks, Love!" Nivie said, jumping a little.

When they returned home, Nivie called Dr. Carmichael explaining why they were considering rescheduling. She was surprised when the vet said that sometimes animals will seemingly improve, but that they needed to keep monitoring Kimball. With slight relief, Nivie and Alex basked in the extra time they just bought.

After spending all day on the porch and with the arrival of darkness, Nivie said, "I'm not ready to leave him."

"What do you say we stay out here?" Alex proposed.

"You mean overnight?"

"Yeah. We get our old blowup mattress and stay out here?"

"Really?"

"Yeah, why not?" Alex said.

Nivie felt an odd, but welcome, twinge of excitement as she reached under the bed for the mattress and air pump. The clamor of filling up the air mattress didn't seem to bother Kimball. Nivie and Alex enjoyed camping and the sounds of the crickets were a soothing contrast to the inevitability they faced.

During the night, Nivie woke up every few hours, locating Kimball. She tried not to wake Alex, although the squeaks and movements of the air mattress made it difficult. She stroked Kimball's thin body to ascertain he was still breathing. Her heart sunk again when she saw no paw prints in the litterbox, nor less food or water in the respective bowls.

The next day, when Alex went to work, Nivie stayed out on the screened porch with Kimball all day. She talked to him quietly, cried, pet him, cried, watched him watch the birds. Cried some more. With Kimball still resting on the porch, she gathered some of his toys, and placed them on his favorite rocking chair beside a pillow embroidered with the words: "Cats are Children in Furry Clothes."

A few hours later, Nivie was relieved to see Alex come home. The reality of their situation had sunk in. The predicted thunderstorm was also in full force, so she brought Kimball inside. "It's really coming down out there," Alex said. "How are you doing, big guy?" he asked. Nivie wanted Kimball to stay in the living room with her, but he did his best to hide in the corner of the bathroom.

Dr. Carmichael called saying she would be there as soon as the torrential rains let up.

About fifteen minutes later, the rain stopped. Alex said, "She's here, Love," as he opened the door for Dr. Carmichael.

"Already?" Nivie's heart began to race. "Could we? Could we, do this on the porch?"

"Sure," Dr. Carmichael said.

Alex held the back porch door open as Nivie carried Kimball's frail body and gently placed him on the floor.

"I know this is the right thing to do, but..." Nivie's voice trailed off.

"I know this is hard. This is your baby," Dr. Carmichael consoled. "I just need to tell you a few things: animals do not close their eyes when they die. That's just in movies."

"Ok," Nivie sniffed.

"And, first, I'm going to give him a sedative, something to put him in a deep sleep. Then, I will give him the second, and final, injection. Afterward, I will leave you two and let myself out."

Nivie and Alex sat next to their Kimball, quietly talking and stroking his fur. Dr. Carmichael administered the first injection. After a minute, she whispered, "He's asleep now."

"We love you Kimball Kitty. We love you, Kimball Kitty. Be at peace. We love you," Nivie and Alex each repeated, petting him.

Dr. Carmichael signaled to them, asking if they were ready. She then delivered the final injection.

"Is he gone?" Alex asked, voice cracking.

She took her stethoscope and gently placed it on his heart.

She slowly nodded.

Nivie erupted into uncontrollable sobbing. Neither one noticed Dr. Carmichael's departure.

After a few minutes, Nivie slowly lifted Kimball's limp body, holding him to her chest. She asked Alex to take pictures and even snipped off some tufts of fur. His markings were so striking, they both wanted samples to keep his memory alive.

"You know, some people might think it's weird we're doing this," Nivie said. "But, to hell with them. He's our cat."

They had called the pet crematorium before Dr. Carmichael came over, and now called again. They had purchased a simple urn, light colored wood reminiscent of Kimball's orangish color.

After the owner of the crematorium left with Kimball, Nivie and Alex slowly walked up the steps at the same slow rate Kimball walked down them when he first arrived. They walked into the bedroom and Nivie lay down on their bed facing the headboard, her legs on the wall. Alex did the same and took her hand.

After an inordinate amount of time without words exchanged, Nivie looked over at the clock. "The Gardens are closed. Dammit."

"But, we can go tomorrow, if you like," Alex added quietly. "Yeah, I'll take tomorrow off."

Nivie squeezed Alex's hand. "You know what's weird?"

"What?"

"I feel a little more at peace now than I did 24 hours ago," she said. "It's like I'm all cried out."

"Yeah, I cried more tonight than I did at my grandma's funeral," Alex said.

Nivie turned to him with puffy eyes. "It's like, it's done. Nothing more we can do."

"Yeah."

"Thank you, Honey. There's *no way* I could have gone through this by myself."

"Me either," he said, squeezing her hand again.

After ten minutes of staring at the wall in silence, Nivie leaned over onto her side and fell asleep, feet on her pillow. Alex curled up next to her and did the same.

Twenty-four hours had passed since Kimball Kitty left the earth. Walking hand in hand with Alex through The Gardens, Nivie was eerily quiet. Sitting on the bench facing the fountain, she hardly paid attention to the water splashing out to the sides and the birds chirping in the background.

"Just doesn't seem right," she said, her voice breaking, clutching a Kleenex. "All this beauty and our Kimball Kitty— Gone."

"Yeah," Alex exhaled. "Really sucks."

"Sometimes it feels like I can't breathe. Like a huge weight is sitting right on my chest. Like if I lie down, it will swallow me whole."

Alex furrowed his brow. "I thought you were OK. Especially with what you said last night."

"I know. But, I don't know. It just really hit me again this morning. No poking. No Kimball Kitty. He's really gone."

"I know."

"I had to take down the Christmas trees this year. Like all of them," Nivie said.

"I noticed you had."

"I couldn't have them around all year like we usually do. Way too cheerful." Nivie paused. "He was my baby, Alex. He was my baby."

"*Our* baby," Alex whispered, almost inaudibly.

"Did we do the right thing?"

Alex sighed. "Well, we did the best we could under the circumstances."

"I hope we did the right thing." Nivie sat up, shifting her weight on the bench. "People talk about the most ridiculous things. Who cares?

Don't they know that my baby died? Don't they know that I lost part of my heart? He was not *just* a cat. He was my family."

"*Our* family," Alex gently added.

Nivie's eyes met Alex's, but her mind was miles away. "I mean, what a cruel thing we do to ourselves. We get an animal and invite them into our hearts and lives. But we know, on some level, that they are going to die." Her voice cracked as it got louder. "We don't say it out loud, or talk about it at parties. But, they are actually going to die. It's like, 'Come right in—come be a part of family. Let us love you, and hold you and be there for you, just so we can just see you die in 15 or 20 years.' Or, less."

Alex looked down.

"I can't go through this again," Nivie added.

Alex shifted his gaze to the fountain.

"I'm sorry. I just can't do this again," Nivie continued. "Scares the hell out of me. No more animals. It's like the world's gone dark. Sorry, honey."

Alex cleared his throat, wiped his eyes, and looked over at Nivie, squeezing her hand.

"Honey, I think you should do it now."

Nivie sighed as she blew her nose. "Oh, Alex. I don't think so. Not now. Way too much."

"I know you think that. And this really sucks now. But, you're so creative, you've wanted to do it for a long time. It would help a lot of people. Just think about it."

Slowly shaking her head, Nivie's staring eyes locked onto the tower of the fountain. "Thanks. But, no. I can't even begin to imagine creating and building that. Not now." She focused on a white pine tree branch towering above them. "And, I really don't want to talk about it now. Even though you're the only one I've told."

"All right. I just think it would be incredible. And, you would be amazing," Alex said, wiping another tear and gently pulling his wife closer.

Bryn opened her eyes, her body curled in a fetal position. Her previously crisp, clean comforter had been worn into a Tucker-sized imprint, covering about a third of the bed. Knowing his human was awake, Tucker lifted his head and sneezed. Jumping onto the floor, he stretched out, yawning; his back quivered. In the last seven weeks, his leg continued to improve, despite the challenges of following his recovery plan.

Taking his usual position, he rested his damp nose on the mattress right by Bryn's face. She reached her hand over the bed and rolled his velvety ears between her fingers. As much as she loved the texture of them, Tucker's malodorous breath wilted the enjoyable moment. Bryn stretched up, grabbed a hair tie and pulled her hair back into a ponytail. Despite some residual stiffness Tucker had, he grabbed his squeaky Teddy and pranced in victory: Time for breakfast.

Julian was away for work again, but Bryn was accustomed to the three of them at home. Four, really.

Both kids moaned at being awakened. Megan was still clothed in her princess dress and Ethan in his Superman onesie from the night before. Bryn prepared breakfast for her little princess and superhero.

Ethan, eating his scrambled eggs, asked, "Mommy, what is Weptile fun shun?"

"What is what?"

"Weptile fun shun? TV," he said.

Bryn looked over at the screen where Ethan was pointing.

"Oh, erectile dysfunction," she whispered to herself. "Well, that's just for when boys get old."

"Like Daddy?"

"Well…kinda. But, definitely *not* Daddy," Bryn said, suppressing a smile. Walking into the laundry room next to the kitchen, she groaned when she opened the dryer door. A heap of wet clothes.

"Mommy, no shirt?" Ethan asked.

"No, the laundry was still dirty, so we had to put it through again," she said, grabbing an unclaimed t-shirt resting on the dryer, hiding the fact she forgot to press the start button.

"Just put this on," she said, pulling a bright pink "I Love To Dance" t-shirt over him.

Megan was busy coloring at the art table in the living room. Her pudgy hands clumsily held the stocky crayons, yet still colored within the lines.

"Brother, c'mere," Megan said to Ethan who had joined her at the table. "Here's a crayon for you, and....Mommy! Why is he wearing—?"

"It's only for a little bit, Meggie."

"But…"

"But, you are such a good sister to help Mommy now. Oh, and you colored so well, too."

"I wanna dooah," Ethan said.

"You want to draw?" Bryn asked. "OK, here. Use the crayon and piece of paper Meggie gave you."

"Wanna dooah Tucko."

"OK. Sounds good. Here, use this brown crayon."

"No. Wanna use boo."

"Balllooo, Brother. Blue. Blue. Not 'boo'," Megan corrected.

"That's OK," Bryn said.

Ethan used the blue crayon to draw what Bryn could only deduce was a dog. If a person looked and strained their eyes hard enough, the random long strokes could be perceived as a living thing.

"You're doing such a great job!" Bryn said.

Megan's face beamed. "Mommy, can we do it now? It's been forever."

"You don't want to keep coloring?"

"No, I'm pretty exhausted," Megan said.

"Ok, then. Sure," Bryn chuckled.

"Yay! Time for the Bubble Parade!" the kids rejoiced.

"We still need to be careful with Tucker, though," Bryn advised.

"OK, Mommy," Ethan said.

"Run and get your cape, bud. Meggie, don't forget your tiara."

The sound of children's squealing quieted as each approached their respective rooms, and strengthened on their approach back down the steps to Bryn in the kitchen. The Doppler Effect in full force.

"Brother, you go here with Tucker," Megan directed. "Mommy, you be in back. I'll be in front."

"Tucko cape?" Ethan asked.

"Oh, yeah!" Bryn said, running over to the half-emptied pet store bag near the kitchen.

After Bryn tied the cape on Tucker, Ethan wrapped his arms around his dressed-up dog. "Tucko have yo cape. I have my cape."

"Ready?" Megan asked from the front.

"Ready!" Ethan and Bryn said.

Turning on *Thomas the Tank Engine* on TV, Megan blew bubbles, while Ethan held onto Tucker. Bryn was the caboose. They marched as a train throughout the house, making a grand circuit of the first floor.

Next order of business: playing outside. They all splashed around in their backyard pool. Even though he couldn't play with his usual fervor, Tucker enjoyed being near water again. Bryn retrieved the Radio Flyer wagon from the garage and Tucker jumped in. He patiently allowed the kids to pull him around the backyard before he hopped out. For a minute, anyway. After everyone dried off, the humans took a bike ride. Ethan was pulled in a plastic bike trailer behind Bryn's bike while Megan rode her "big girl's bike." Bryn didn't have the heart to tell her that most "big girls" don't use training wheels. The smell of freshly cut grass against of the backdrop of the green maple and evergreen trees delighted their senses as they rode to The Gardens and the library.

When they returned home, Tucker greeted them with a bark, clumsily turning in circles. For him, they might as well have been gone a week rather than a few hours.

"Tucker, sweetie," Bryn said. "Still need you to take it easy."

"Tucko!" Ethan said, running to the piano. He pounded on the keys singing, "Tucko is bestest Tucko in the ho wide wod! Tucko is the bestest—"

"Stop, Brother!" Megan yelled.

"Ok, kids," Bryn intervened. "Let's wash up and think about what we want for dinner. How about yummy chicken?"

"Mommy, I want pizza," Megan said.

"Honey, pizza's not really good for you."

"But, my mouth is set on pizza," Megan quipped.

"Ok," Bryn chuckled. "Just this one time, we can have pizza."

"Yay!" Megan said, taking her brother's hands and dancing in a circle.

"You can even have silly bread if you want," Bryn added. "It comes in a basket."

"Can we keep the basket?" Megan asked.

Bryn chuckled. "We'll have to ask!"

Once the pizza arrived, Bryn cut each kid's pizza slices into bite-size pieces. Tucker's tongue licked up at Ethan's plate, snatching and scarfing down four pizza bites.

"Tucko eats pawt of the samich," Ethan said.

"You mean pizza, Brother! Not sandwich!" Megan laughed. "Pizza!"

After dinner, the Troxell Bubble Parade commenced once again until it slowed because two children started yawning and slowly blinking. Bryn joined in.

"C'mere guys," Bryn said, sitting down on the couch, opening her arms. The three of them watched an episode of *Bubble Guppies* and *Peppa Pig*. Tucker slept, gently snoring at their feet.

All in all, a good day, Bryn thought, kissing the tops of her sleeping children's heads.

With packed bags, Jacqueline drives past a flower garden on the way to the airport. In the parking lot, she knows it will be the last time she'll

see her car. To get to the terminal, she grabs onto a railing to walk over a creaky bridge. Barely making it across, she briefly steps onto a broken elevator, then steps off. Running to her gate, the temperature in the terminal gets colder with each step.

Jacqueline blinked her eyes open, heart racing. Chloe stared down at her, only a few inches from her face. Throwing her left arm to the other side of the bed, Jacqueline yanked it back. The bed was cold. Again.

It stood alone on the cold, hard kitchen table. Nivie could hardly believe her Kimball Kitty's ashes rested in the urn. Lightly touching the polished wooden side, she sighed, placing it next to Minerva's urn in the living room. She hesitated.

Should I call?

Nivie picked up her phone and dialed the number she found online. "Hi, yes. My name is Nivie Emerson, and I would like to make an appointment…Great…Yes, next Tuesday at 2pm? That should work… Do you accept credit cards?…Awesome….I'll talk to you then."

Julian, Bryn and the kids geared up for Labor Day's "Summer's Last Hurrah Up North." Although Tucker needed a little more "oomph" to stand, his excitement was nonetheless palpable. Feeling the enthusiasm of the kids, he assumed his favorite place in the car: his long snout poking out of the window, jowls flapping in the wind, with his squeaky Teddy toy firmly in his grip.

Watching him in the rearview mirror, Bryn saw Tucker's great joy. However, her mind jumped anxiously to images of what would happen if a truck passed too closely. Fortunately no disaster ever occurred. As they exited off the interstate and drove down the street to Barbara and

Lawrence's lake house, Tucker paced back and forth in the far back seat, whining in excitement.

"We're almost there, guys!" Julian said. "This'll be fun!"

"Yay!" The kids cheered. Tucker's barks echoed in unison.

They pulled into the driveway and unstrapped themselves for the usual greetings from Barbara and Lawrence. After the hugs and asking about the car trip, the kids and their dog raced to the backyard where Tucker's golden retriever heritage rejoiced. Splashing around in the lake and retrieving a thrown stick, toy, ball, no matter, was his idea of Heaven. He didn't have a schedule and could have done it all day and night. If they let him.

"Yeah, we got the Chris Craft fixed," Lawrence said, standing next to his son and grandchildren on the private dock. "Again."

"Yeah, you know what 'boat' means— 'Bust Out Another Thousand'," Julian said.

"Or, two. Or, six….," Lawrence chuckled.

"Daddy, can we go out?" Megan asked, tugging on her father's elbow.

"Yeah, we go out?" Ethan parroted.

"Absolutely, kids. C'mon, Grandpa—let's take her out for a spin. This is gonna be fun!" Julian said.

The kids jumped up and down, making the dock's natural rocking motion even more pronounced.

"Careful, now," Lawrence said, as he steadied the boat tied to the dock.

"Hey, babe! Wake up!" Julian yelled up to the house. "You wanna go out with us?"

Resting in the antigravity chair, she cringed looking out over the lake with Tucker alert at her feet.

I've never liked that term of endearment.

"Thanks, but I'm just going to enjoy the view here," she shouted down, sitting up. "You guys go on without me."

"Ok, later!" Julian said. "Tucker. Boat!"

Hearing Julian, Tucker looked up at Bryn. "Go on. Boat!" she repeated. He leapt up and rushed down the hill to the dock, moving at a quicker pace than he had in weeks.

Waving goodbye as her family departed with revving engines, Bryn sighed in relief. She closed her eyes, delighting in the silence, feeling the warm, late-August sunshine on her face.

"How are you doing, Bryn?"

Startled, Bryn opened her eyes to see Barbara in a large sunhat and sunglasses standing over her.

"We are so pleased you guys could come this weekend. So, when can we expect our next Troxell baby?" Barbara asked, a large grin splashed across her face.

"Oh, hello, Barbara. Well, we'll just have to see how things go."

"Splendid!" Barbara said, "A large family is a blessing, indeed. I know that God, in all His goodness, has blessed us so. Our big family is a blessing. We would have even had more children, if we could."

Bryn gave a tight smile, looking out at the lake.

Barbara continued, "I simply cannot imagine my life without children. What is life without family? Especially children. God is good. All the time." She patted Bryn's arm and walked away, opening the screen door to the kitchen, letting it snap shut behind her.

Bryn, now fully awake, tried to match her feelings with Barbara's sentiments.

Worn out from the day's activities, Ethan laid down in the living room, resting his head on Tucker's belly.

"Time to go to bed now, kids," Bryn said.

"Aw, Mommy…" Megan protested from the corner table where she was putting together a puzzle with her grandparents.

"I know, I know. It's been a really fun day. And, tomorrow will be another fun day. But, only after we sleep! OK, goodnight hugs."

"Mommy, Tucko limp," Ethan said, pointing at Tucker.

Looking down at him, Bryn said, "Well, he's getting older, bud. He had a lot of fun running and playing today, but he's just plain worn out. OK, you two, let's go," Bryn said, ushering the kids off to brush their teeth.

"Hi, this is Althea from Pets From Beyond," a gentle, slow voice spoke on the other end of the phone.

"Hi, Althea," Nivie said. "So glad we could set up a time to talk."

"Yes, as am I. Just a reminder— our conversation will be recorded, and I will send you a copy of the CD. Then, you will have it to go back and listen to."

"Yes, that's great."

"Now, as I say 'we,' I'm talking about Quan Yin, the goddess energy. I'd like to start with the name of your animal and your first question."

"His name is Kimball. And, I'm not really sure where to start. I've never done this before."

"That's fine. As we tune into the energy of Kimball, he's very laid-back, very loving, and very attentive, like your shadow. When you were working, he would be lying close by. Like a good buddy. Is that Kimball?"

"Yes. Uh, huh."

"When they go across, the soul leaves the vehicle and a family member comes to get them. We get a woman who…a very strong woman, she passed away, but not that old. We're sensing a reconnection to your family. Kimball was once one of your beloved. Pets will be there because they are part of our family."

"Yeah, they are."

"The animals don't have a fear of crossing over. They just lay and relax into it. They come and go, and come and go back to the source energy. No different than us. They go back to a place they recognize. Their soul regenerates. It may take a day, week, month, year but they reincarnate into new vehicles."

"So, is Kimball reincarnated?" Nivie asked.

"Um…let's see…We sense that he has. Have you recently gotten another animal?"

"No. Would he come back as another animal?"

"Yes. You know, we sometimes have the urge to create the same kind of energy around them, or a past life connection. We'll say, 'I intend to find Kimball again.' But he may be a different color."

"Is his soul still in the house? Does he say anything about how he passed? He was euthanized here."

"In what way?"

"Well, it wasn't 100% clear about what took his life," Nivie clarified.

"Oh, indeed. Let's just look into that. They're taking me to the head. Something like…Did he have a stroke? We're sensing around here. Did he have some sort of kidney problem?"

"No, it wasn't his kidneys. We did a lot of tests. But, they still weren't sure."

"Feels like the head…like a stroke…like blood bursting. Were his eyes bulging?"

"No, but at the very end he stopped eating. We couldn't figure it out. The doctors said that we could try this and that, but that there are no guarantees."

"He wasted away. Stopped eating. It could have been really painful for him," Althea said.

"He *did* stop eating," Nivie repeated. "But, I wanted to know what precipitated all this. We tried tests and getting him to eat and everything. He was relatively young. So, it was surprising he died before he should have. Obviously his work here was done on his journey."

"You're right, his journey was done. He was of service. He did what he came to do. He didn't leave you because he *wanted* to leave you. It was just because it was his time, you see?"

"I guess."

"Things just shut down. You gave him the gift of release and helped him. It was right. No feeding tubes."

"Yeah."

"We don't sense this could have changed. You miss him deeply and your heart goes out to him. He knows that. He says, 'I'm always there. I'm always with you.' His energy always remains, you see?"

"Is he there with other animals?" Nivie asked. "Or, other family members?"

"Was there a black cat? With white on chin and chest?"

"No. Probably a tortoiseshell, though."

"Torties are usually different colors. Could have been quite a while ago. Um, we see a small dog too."

"What kind of dog?"

"Like..a wiener dog...longer back. Could be a smaller breed," Althea said.

"IIIıııııı..."

"Did you have a bird?"

"No."

"We see a bird on your shoulder. Could be a guardian angel. We see it blue. Beautiful blue."

Nivie laughed, "That's interesting because bluebirds are my favorites."

"Ahh...OK. Well, we see this bluebird on your shoulder, just being very special."

Nivie changed the topic. "Are you seeing Kimball in our house?"

"His energy is there. He sometimes cuddles on the back of a chair or sofa. He comes to bed with you and cuddles next to you."

"Would other animals sense his energy?"

"They can, and often do."

"How would they show that?" Nivie asked.

"They will look up into the corner of the room. They don't see energy, they sense it. If they're lying next to you on the couch and get up and walk to the other side of couch, they are making room for another's energy. If we walked around more with our eyes shut, we would sense more. Our eyes distort what's going on. But, the other animals know he's there."

"Oh, ok."

"Sometimes they'll go look for them. They can't see them, but they know they're there. It can frustrate them a little."

Nivie chuckled. "Right. Do you get a sense of a tortoiseshell kitty with Kimball?"

"Yes, there are more cats with Kimball. Quite a few, actually. I see one of them, a female, rubbing on him."

"Really?"

"We see her trying to be friends with Kimball. And he's like, 'Yeah, yeah. I know you're there.'"

"Hmm," Nivie thought. "That's different from what happened on earth."

"Well, on the other side, there are no physical agendas. What was her name?"

"Minerva. Mini, actually. We would talk, or 'burble,' back and forth to each other. She'd 'burble,' then I'd 'burble,' and we'd go back and forth."

"How nice. Could she retrieve things?"

"Yes, she loved the plastic tops on gallon milk containers. 'Milk rings' we called them."

"Was she part Siamese in some way?"

"No, don't think so."

"Siamese are usually big on talking and retrieving. Coming when they're called. Acting more like a dog than a cat. She ruled the roost though. She chose who she would allow. Very opinionated."

"Well, she was very sweet."

"She had a strong personality," Althea repeated.

"Well, we went through a lot together," Nivie said "She needed a strong personality to get through everything. But, definitely my cat and eventually my husband's cat. She wasn't really open to others."

"She didn't acquiesce to a lot. Kimball was more laid back. More of a basic cat, you see?"

"I guess. Are animals ever scared when they cross over?" Nivie asked.

"Not usually, no, unless maybe if it's not their time to cross over and they don't want to leave. But, usually animals go with the flow. Maybe not in the first day or two, but they adjust to a new situation."

"Good to know." Nivie furrowed her brow. "Just to clarify, is his energy still in the house? And, Mini's, too?"

"Yes. Absolutely. Both are still there."

"Ok. Will they always live in the house?"

"Yes. Yes. Or they'll follow a family. Sometimes a family will say, 'We moved,' yet they still follow you. They know their energy. They came back to be of service and stay with you. Like anything else in energy, just because it's no longer in a physical form, that doesn't mean the energy doesn't still exist. It's still there."

"Yeah. Hmm. I'm still a little confused, though," Nivie said. "So, are they still in the house or reincarnated?"

"It's both. How do I explain that? I don't know. I don't know 100% how this all works. They show me bits and pieces. The soul goes across and that soul reincarnates into another vehicle and generates another soul print, as it were."

"Ok."

"How long has it been since he crossed over?"

Without answering, Nivie asked, "Is it different if he's been gone a while versus last week?"

"No. Sometimes I talk to people about animals who crossed over years ago. Sometimes ten years. But they are still stuck in the middle of this terrible trauma of losing their animal."

"Yes, it is hard."

"I'm thinking it's been two or three weeks," Althea said.

"Actually, it's been two months."

"Ok, got the two. So, it's been a few months. Indeed."

"Still—"

"But, still you miss him a lot. Because there is a past-life connection," Althea said.

"Really? Did we know each other in another life?"

"Oh, yes."

"How?"

"That's what we're looking for. We're seeing a young girl, about five or six years old. We don't always reincarnate in the same gender, by the way. Like animals. But, we see a young girl and we see a very large house. Like a plantation."

"Like in the south?"

"Perhaps. Your special friend was a kitty. It was Kimball. You didn't put him in a baby buggy, you would walk and talk with him, and carry him in your arms. He was your best friend. You were kind of alone. People cared for you, but your parents were distant. Didn't give warm love and affection. From Kimball you got that."

"Wow. Interesting."

"Does this ring true for you? Sometimes past lives bleed through. Maybe this area had bluebirds you liked to watch. Feels like a correlation there."

"Well, not—"

"He was your best friend. So when your best friend returned again it was like, you felt loved. You don't feel like you've had enough time with him."

Nivie shook her head. "Just amazing creatures, animals are."

"Aren't they? Just come to serve. Cats are emotional healers and dogs are physical healers."

"Interesting."

"Yes, people say, 'Isn't it funny, my dog has the same ailment as I do.' That's because he took it on but can't slough it off. They do it out of love, not out of martyrdom. In the wild, people are not around, so they don't take the ailment on."

"Interesting."

"Yes, indeed." Althea took in a breath. "Well, if we're complete, then we will sign off."

"Thanks, Althea. I really appreciate this."

"You're welcome. Enjoyed talking with you and am happy to help."

"Looking forward to the getting the CD."

Nivie hung up, sighing with a heavy heart, unsure how to process everything.

A hint of crispness in the air and scarlet-tipped leaves signaled the first day of school. Megan and Ethan squealed in anticipation, each wearing new back-to-school outfits, put on only after Bryn had a long conversation about why the tiara and superhero cape would remain at home.

Bryn directed her excited children to their front porch to take pictures while their tiny hands were fastened securely to their backpack straps. "Meggie, look over here! Bud, thumb out! Tucker, move... Actually, Meggie, call Tucker to you. Wait a minute, let me get his squeaky Teddy from him...Have him sit in front. That's right. Good... No, bud, look over here! Meggie, can you back up, just a bit?"

It's easier to herd cats.

"OK. Say cheese!" Bryn said.

"Eeze!" The kids said in unison, with large, mostly toothy smiles plastered to their faces. Tucker sat in front of them, his tongue handing to the side.

"OK, one more. Meggie, please fix your headband. Thanks. Bud, thumb! Eh, just leave it," Bryn relented, taking two more pictures.

"Great job, kids! Grandma will love these," Bryn said.

"Daddy too!" Megan added.

"Yeah, him too," Bryn agreed. "Ok, let's go have fun at school!" She loaded the two frenetic kids and a restless Tucker into the SUV and began the short drive to St. Agnes Elementary School.

"Look, Mommy!" Megan said, looking outside her window.

Gaggles of children, parents, and teachers streamed in and out of the school building, some chatting in groups outside the front doors. Many more people than when Bryn was here for "Meet the Teacher" night.

"I know," Bryn said, choking on her words.

As Bryn unbuckled a squiggling Megan and Ethan and snapped Tucker's leash onto his collar, all three exited the SUV. Reaching back for Megan's lunch, Bryn wrapped Tucker's leash around her wrist.

"Got everything? Ok, let's go!" Bryn led the kids and dog single file through the parking lot.

Walking up to the entrance door, Bryn stopped and crouched down next to Megan while Tucker and Ethan huddled around. "Ok, Meggie. You have a great day. Mommy loves you very much. This is as far as I can go with Tucker." Bryn hugged her daughter close and released her.

Megan turned and ran toward her new teacher. "Hi, Mrs. Sanner! Bye, Mom! Bye, Brother! Bye, Tucker!"

Bryn watched her daughter race to the threshold, focusing on her tiny legs and the kitten backpack swishing across her back. Across the sidewalk she spotted Madeline Waters, Megan's long-time friend. "M&Ms" they were called. Waving and smiling at Madeline and her mom, Allison, Bryn took comfort in the thought that Madeline was going to be in the same classroom as Megan.

Glancing down at her hand, Bryn saw Megan's lunch. She called out, "Oh, Meggie! Don't forget your lunch!" Megan ran back to Bryn, grabbed the bag, giving her mom a quick hug. She ran back to the school entrance again where a welcoming Mrs. Sanner stood. Tucker watched and whimpered, pulling the leash taut. Still holding onto Ethan's hand, Bryn looked down and wiped a tear. "Alright, bud. Your turn."

Driving a few miles away, they arrived at Woodhaven Run United Methodist Church Preschool. She unbuckled Ethan from his seat and handed him his backpack and snack. In her peripheral vision, she saw Ethan's teacher walking towards them.

"Good morning, Mrs. Russell."

"Good morning, Mrs. Troxell." Leaning down to a thumb-sucking Ethan, she said, "Hi, Ethan, I'm Mrs. Russell. We are happy you're here."

Bryn crouched down next to Ethan to give him a hug. "You have a wonderful first day. Mommy loves you very much." Tucker's frenetic body almost knocked Bryn over as he tried to give Ethan a kiss.

"Wuv oo, too, Mommy," Ethan whispered, with his left thumb planted firmly in his mouth. Mrs. Russell held out her left hand. The start of the symbolic shift from one hand to another. Tucker tugged even harder on his leash, unable to comprehend why he couldn't follow his Ethan into the church.

Bryn took a deep breath. "I know, sweetie. Time to let 'em go."

Bryn caught herself watching the clock all day and was relieved to return to the school and church for pickups. Tucker, sensing Bryn's excitement, squirmed even more than usual in the car, running between the two windows, watching the houses go by on familiar streets. After picking Megan and Ethan up, Bryn asked each child about their first day. She was pleased when she heard that it went well and was fun. For both of them.

As they drove away from school, Bryn steered the SUV toward the center of town. Megan asked from the back car seat, "Where are we going, Mommy?"

"Yeah, waw we goin'?" Ethan added, looking out the window.

"Have to wait and see…" Bryn smiled, glancing at them in the rearview mirror.

"Ice cream!" the kids squealed.

"Yes," Bryn said, pulling into the City Dairy's parking lot.

"I want Blue Moon!" Megan yelled.

"Me want Supaman!" Ethan said.

Getting out of the car, letting Tucker out first, Bryn snapped the leash on his collar. She then pulled out a sign hidden in the far backseat and gently placed it over Tucker's neck. It read: "Today is my sister's first day of school at St. Agnes School and my brother's first day at Woodhaven Run United Methodist Church Preschool." Unbuckling themselves, the kids hopped out and ran to the ice cream shop.

Sitting outside, eating the delicious dairy treats and basking in the sun, the family chatted about the day.

"Today is your first day at St. Agnes?" one nearby lady asked, reading Tucker's sign with a smile.

"Yes!" Megan exclaimed.

"That's a terrific school."

"The preschool at Woodhaven Run United Methodist Church? My grandson went there, too!" said another. "And your 'brother' here is proud of you both," another lady commented, petting Tucker's head.

"Yeah," Ethan said, wrapping his short, sticky arms around Tucker's neck, and swinging his face in front of a doggie snout. "Love Tucko."

Tucker licked some lingering remnants of Superman ice-cream off Ethan's face, turning his sign askew.

For Nivie, nothing was more mind-numbing than a beginning-of-the-school-year afterschool faculty meeting in the large, double classroom. The countless administrators talking about the "latest and greatest ideas" in education, while simultaneously being out of touch about what actually happens inside a classroom, infuriated her. Adding to the mix were fellow teachers, many of whom were on their phones, not the least bit interested. It was the last place Nivie wanted to be. She found a little solace that the choir teacher, Anna Carlson, with whom she was friendly, sat in front of her.

After endless droning, the meeting finally ended. Most teachers and even administrators made a quick exit.

"You doing OK, Niv?" Anna turned around to ask.

"Yeah. Hangin' in. Thanks," Nivie said.

"Been able to play lately?"

"Nah, my poor piano at home is lonely. Sometime soon, I will. I hope."

"Yeah, it'll help. Take care, Niv." Leaving the room, Anna gave an anemic smile to Melissa and Heather, two fellow English teachers who had been sitting near Nivie.

They approached Nivie, who was lost in her thoughts, as she gently touched Kimball's collar and Minerva's paw print tin on the bottom of her school bag.

"Hi, there," Heather said. Melissa smiled.

"Hi," Nivie said, quickly placing her notebook over the collar and tin.

"Um, Nivie, you heard that Angela is pregnant, right?

"Yeah, I did. Congrats," she replied flatly, gathering her belongings.

"Well, anyway," Melissa said, "We wanted to throw a *spectacular* and *fantastic* baby shower bash for her. So, since you had such fabulous ideas for Gayle's shower, we wanted to have a meeting to pick your brain for Angela's!"

Nivie sighed. "Sorry. Just can't do it right now. Thanks anyway."

"Oh. Ok," Melissa said, her face falling.

"I mean, I can give some money for a gift, but that's about it right now."

"Oh, OK."

Nivie continued, "It's the two month and two-week anniversary since my Kimball Kitty died." She rubbed her eyes. "So, I'm just not up for participating in any big project right now. Sorry."

Melissa looked at Heather, raised her eyebrows, and said, in a slightly sing-song voice, "Um, well. OK. Thanks, anyway."

Nivie watched them silently walk out the door. Chucking her pens into her purse, she heard their voices echoing down the long, empty hallway.

"I know...I know....'anniversary'." Then, snickering. "'I mean... it's a cat." More laughing. "...Get a grip...Real problems...Give me a break..."

Nivie marched to the door, leaving her belongings back on the table. To her right, Melissa and Heather were half-way down the hall, giggling.

"Um, excuse me!" Nivie shouted down the hall.

Melissa and Heather stopped abruptly and turned around to face Nivie.

"You *know* I can hear you, right?" Nivie said, walking directly at them. "You know—those things called echoes?" she said, waving her arms at the walls.

Melissa's and Heather's eyes met each other's.

"I just don't feel like being a part of that right now. I mean, is that OK with you two?" Nivie said, pointing at them.

"Yes. Yes. That's fine," Heather said, putting up her hands trying to calm Nivie. "We got it. No problem."

"Thank you," Nivie firmly answered, shaking her head. Turning on her heel, she heard the whispering and giggling resume behind her.

"Oh, and by the way," Nivie said, twisting back around to face them.

Melissa and Heather caught themselves in a mid-laugh, threw their heads back in exasperation, and slowly turned around to face Nivie.

"You just don't get it, do you?" Nivie sai.

"Well, we were just trying to ask for a little help," Melissa said.

"Yeah, right," Nivie snorted. "Oh, and, as far as 'just a cat' is concerned. Well, we took him to the vet, stayed up with him, had sleepless nights, many tears. And, after he died in our house, we held his lifeless little body in our arms." Nivie's throat tightened, as tears threatened to spill over. "So, maybe to you he was 'just a cat,' but to me, he was my baby boy."

"All right. Fine. We get it," Melissa said. Both of them slowly and deliberately nodded their heads.

"So shut your pie-holes, and mind your own damn business!" Nivie snapped, swinging herself around and storming back down the hallway to fetch her things. She didn't look back.

As she pulled into her driveway from this terrible afternoon, Nivie saw she had a voicemail message from her principal, John. It said she needed to meet with him in his office at 7:15 a.m. tomorrow morning.

An hour later, Alex arrived home from work. As the garage door closed behind him, he mumbled, "Dammit. I keep forgetting to get that thing to HR. Well…guess just have to do it tomorrow."

Walking into the living room, Alex found his wife curled up on the couch, blanket over her. *The Ellen DeGeneres Show* was on the television, and an empty carton of Ben and Jerry's sat on the end table.

"Hey, Love. How was your day?" he asked.

"Don't ask," Nivie responded flatly. "How was yours?"

"Good. Hey, did you hear that they demolished another old building by the Tridge? Loved that place. Going to be so empty down there now."

"Yeah, someone mentioned it before our meeting today."

Alex studied her. Looking up at the television, he said, "This is a good show. I know you've missed Oprah since she stopped hers. I'm just glad to see you decided to stop the *Old Yeller, Marley & Me, Charlotte's Web* marathon."

Nivie's eyes remained on the screen.

"Before I forget, did you call—?" Alex asked.

"No, not yet," She shifted her weight, readjusting the blanket. "It's still on my list."

"So, uh, when do you think you'll get to it?" Alex gingerly asked.

"I. Don't. Know," Nivie answered, aggravated, her eyes still fixed to the screen.

Alex stopped, stared at Nivie and said, "You know, you seem to think you have a monopoly on grief."

"What?" Nivie's head snapped around to look at Alex, who was shaking his head. "What do you mean? C'mon now, Love. That's not it."

"Oh really? It's like…it's like, you think you're the only one having a hard time here?"

"That is so not true!" She sat up on the couch, muting the television, and turned to face him.

"Well, you know what, Niv? You're not. I miss him, too!" With his voice cracking, Alex turned away and strode into the kitchen.

Nivie tightened her mouth. With a furrowed brow, she stood up, wrapping the blanket around her, and followed him.

"What's wrong, Alex?"

He thumbed through the mail on the kitchen island. "You know, Kimball was always there, by my side," he said, his eyes remaining down. "I mean, especially with my leg. When I was like a damned cripple." He stopped and looked out the window. "Yeah, and he, he would jump up on my lap."

Nivie's face softened. She wrapped the blanket tighter around herself.

"And you know what, when I nudged him off, he wouldn't give up," Alex quietly chuckled. "He really wouldn't. 'Come on guy. Not the leg.' I said."

They both smiled.

Alex continued, rubbing the side of his leg. "He would, he would smoosh his fuzzy little body right next to my side, and then look up at me with those green eyes."

Nivie swallowed hard.

"And it was like…I know it sounds crazy, but, but … it was like he

was saying, 'I got your back. I'm right here for ya.' It's like he knew."
Alex looked down at the mail on the island again. Wiping his eyes
with the back of his hand, he shook his head. "God, I must sound like
a friggin' crazy person."

"No. No. Honey." Nivie looked up at the ceiling and quickly
exhaled. "I'm so sorry." She rubbed her head. "You know, I forgot. I
forgot that you spent a lot of time with him too. I guess, I just thought
since he was my sister's cat and all...that...." She saw Alex's eyes fill
with tears. "Well, he was your cat, too."

"Yeah," Alex continued, his frustration growing. "And also, how
easy would it be for me to say to my bosses, 'Yeah, I had to take the day
off because my cat died'. Imagine me saying that, huh?"

"I know," Nivie said, rolling her eyes. "Because today at work—."

"—I mean, if he were like, I don't know, some dog for hunting.
Maybe," Alex interrupted. "Or some other, like big dog. Some big
manly dog. Ya know?"

Nivie nodded.

"But, because he was a cat, and being a guy and all," his voice
cracked. "Who gives a shit?"

"I know," Nivie rubbed his back.

"And, I know you don't want another pet. But, it's so hard. I like
having them around. I mean, it won't be Kimball. But the house is so
quiet. No jingle collars. No nothing."

Nivie stopped rubbing his back and looked aimlessly out the back
window.

Alex moved away from her hand. "And you know what kills me
even more," he continued. "I mean, when Minerva died. God, that was
hard. Really hard. But, ya know, she lived a nice long life."

Nivie nodded.

"But that little guy, I don't know, that little guy. He didn't get to live
very long. Not long at all."

Nivie began to tear up.

"He didn't deserve it, Niv. He didn't deserve to be harassed by your sister's ex-boyfriend. He didn't deserve all the suffering before he died." He paused, tears building in his eyes. "Didn't deserve any of the crap he got."

"I know." She outstretched her arms with the blanket still clutched in her grasp. Alex leaned down into her, and she wrapped her arms and the blanket around him, holding him up, as he had done for her numerous times before.

"Morning, Debbie," Nivie said, clutching her bags tightly. "I have a 7:15 appointment with John."

"He'll be right with you," the friendly administrative assistant smiled back. "Have a seat."

"Thank you," Nivie said, slowly sliding into the chair.

"So, how is it going in your neck of the woods?" Debbie asked.

"Well, it's been better."

The principal's door opened. John Porter, a short man in his 50s with almost a completely bald head and small, black-rimmed glasses, had been the principal of Woodhaven Run High School for ten years. Despite his deep voice, he had an approachable demeanor.

"Good morning, Genevieve. Come on in," he said.

Nivie took a deep breath as she stood up and walked into his office. Shutting the door behind her, John asked, "Can I get you something to drink?"

"Whiskey, if you got it," she said, sitting down.

John tried to hide a smile and slowly eased into the large leather chair behind his desk. Taking off his glasses, he rested his chin on his hand. "I understand there was a bit of an incident yesterday."

"Yes," Nivie's voice fell.

"So, tell me what happened," he asked kindly.

"Well, it was after the meeting yesterday. I mean, I so did not want to be there. No offense."

"None taken."

"And, Melissa and Heather asked me to help out with Angela's baby shower. I said that I couldn't because it's only been a little over two months since my Kimball died." Nivie paused. "My cat."

John nodded.

"Anyway, everyone had left except for me, and I heard Melissa and Heather talking and laughing out in the hallway about my Kimball Kitty. I heard them say things like 'Just a cat' and 'Give me a break.'"

"OK—.' John said.

"—I mean, I meant what I said, but…"

"OK, Nivie."

"I could hear them giggling…made me so mad…and…."

"Nivie," John said again.

She looked down, exhaled loudly and shook her head. "All right, I said a few things that I shouldn't have. Sorry."

"'Shut your pie-holes?'"

"I know." Nivie quickly shook her head. "Not the best thing to say."

John tried to hide a small grin and cleared his throat. "Absolutely. Not acceptable. Not acceptable."

"I know, John. This whole thing has been a mess. Losing Kimball Kitty, and everything with him. And, then this whole debacle yesterday."

She sighed and looked back up at John. "It won't happen again."

He studied her face, put his glasses back on, and pointed to several pictures on top of a handmade bookcase along the wall.

"You see those pictures?"

Nivie looked to her right to see a variety of framed photographs of his wife, children, and several animals.

"Yeah, wow! Look at all the animals. Oh, and your children, too," Nivie joked.

"Yes. I, too, have had a few pets in my life that were extremely important to me." He walked over to the bookshelf and, using the back of his hand, dusted one of the pictures off. Carrying it over to Nivie, he said,

"This was Trixie, my Beagle-mix. We grew up together, and she even lived with me in college. She was literally the best dog I've ever had."

"Oh, that's awesome. All this time I've known you, and I never knew," Nivie said, looking at a much younger John with long frizzy hair, arms wrapped around Trixie's neck.

He stared at the picture.

"So, you get it," Nivie quietly said.

John cleared his throat, placing the picture back on the shelf.

"I understand what it's like to lose a trusted friend. However, one needs to act professionally when..."

"Yes, I know," Nivie interrupted. "And, those are beautiful, too." She motioned to the handmade wooden shelves on which the pictures rested.

"Thank you, I enjoy woodworking from time to time." John cleared his throat again. "So, if there is nothing more. That's all for today, Genevieve."

"Thank you," she said, standing up, shaking his hand. "And, again, I'm sorry."

He held on for a moment and looked her in the eye. "Not acceptable," he gently emphasized, pointing at her with his other hand and smiling.

"Yes, I understand," Nivie smiled, casting her eyes downward. "Thanks again, John!"

He nodded and walked over to the door, opening it.

"Bye, Debbie!" Nivie said, walking by her desk and out into the hallway.

"Well, that's a change," Debbie said after Nivie left.

"She's going to be all right," John said, closing his office door.

Every September, for as long as she could remember, Bryn eagerly awaited Woodhaven Run's annual Hot Air Balloon Festival weekend.

Early that Friday morning, before the kids awoke, she pressed her face to the glass door and looked upward to catch a glimpse of the rainbow gliding across the sky. Rich blues, radiant reds, and vibrant yellows, in assorted checkered and unique patterns, painted the ethers. An occasional burner noise pierced the hush of the soaring balloons. Bryn stepped outside on the deck to get an even clearer view; steam arose from her coffee mug. Watching the balloons glide across the heavens offered her a rare tranquil moment.

In contrast, Tucker had his own reasons for enjoying the Festival. The balloons' unpredictable movements, as well as sheer numbers, offered him a novel way to play. He sprang through the air, in hopes of bringing one down to earth. His determined attempts, however, always proved fruitless.

On the first night of the Festival, residents could go to the fairgrounds for "Glow," when some of the balloons remained tethered to the earth, blasting their burners to light up the unique designs. In previous years, Megan and Ethan spent a majority of the time covering their ears to block out the noise, so Bryn and Julian decided not to go this time.

Saturday was the Big Balloon launch at the fairgrounds, another chance for people to gather for a mass ascension. The sights, smells, and sounds of fried foods and cotton candy energized two already enthusiastic children, as well as two enthusiastic adults.

Holding Ethan's hand and scanning the crowd for friends, Julian announced, "Hey, there's Doug and Janet! Be right back, babe." He dropped Ethan's hand.

"But, Jay—oh, OK," Bryn smiled politely, waving to Julian's boss and wife as she took Ethan's hand.

"Mommy, can I have a pretzel?" Megan asked, jumping up and down.

"Yeah, Mommy have petzo?" Ethan asked, mirroring his sister.

"Um, OK. Sure," Bryn said, watching Julian make his way across the fairgrounds to greet his boss.

After about ten minutes, Julian returned, much to Bryn's relief. She was now juggling a half-eaten pretzel and two drink cups, while the kids ran in circles around her playing tag.

Walking up to her, out of breath, Julian said, "Doug and Janet say 'Hi.'"

"Daddy! You're back!" The kids rejoiced, touching Julian with salty fingers.

"Yeah, I'm here!" Julian said, taking a cup from the crook of Bryn's elbow. "Doug was saying how nice Texas is this time of year."

"We had petzo!" Ethan exclaimed.

"I see that, bud. Careful with the mustard," he reminded Ethan.

"Daddy, one of the balloons came to our school yesterday!" Megan told her father, hugging his arm. "We didn't go up, but we got to stand in 'em. And, we even got to help carry it!"

"Wow! That's great!" Julian bent down, hoisting Ethan onto his shoulders, who squealed in delight.

"Let's go guys! Look! Look at the pumpkin balloon!" he said, pointing to the sky.

"Yeah!" Ethan said, tilting his head to the direction of his father's finger.

"I want to be on Daddy's shoulders," Megan said to Bryn.

"In a bit, Meggie," Julian called back.

Julian pointed upward again. "Look at that one, bud." He walked away from Bryn and Megan.

Bryn sighed and took the hand of a crestfallen Megan. "Tell you what. Let's you and me go and see the Kids' Zone!" she said, walking toward the trash can to empty her hands.

"OK, Mommy," Megan said, a spring returning to her step.

"Meet you both at the Kids' Zone," Bryn yelled over the music to the departing Julian and Ethan.

"OK, babe," Julian waved, not looking back.

Taking Megan's hand, Bryn tried to keep her daughter moving forward. Megan who kept looking back at Julian and Ethan. She hoped her own frustrations weren't traveling from her hand to Megan's heart.

In her bathrobe, Nivie chugged down the second round of her September Saturday morning coffee. Loading a *Friends* episode on Netflix, she heard the text indicator on her phone.

Looking down, she read: "Get ready! Chicos from Chicagoland are coming in for the day," Brad texted.

"Really? Here? Today?" she immediately texted back.

"Yes. But only 2day. Taking you out."

"Fun! Where?"

"Not telling. ☺ Have to trust us," Brad said.

Nivie smiled and typed, "Love you guys, but still kinda rough here."

"We know. But we love you. BTW: Alex thinks it's a good idea. Wanted him to come, but couldn't. Work."

Although Nivie wasn't completely ready for a "day on the town," she didn't often get to see her college friends, Brad and Esteban. Since they moved to Chicago a few years ago and rented an apartment there, her visits with them were few and far between. Flickers of excitement grew as Nivie rose from the couch to get dressed.

"Brad! Esteban!" Nivie ran out to their car.

"How are you, darling?" Brad asked, hugging her.

"Good morning, gorgeous," Esteban said, kissing her on the cheek.

"So, let's see it," Brad said.

Nivie smiled. She pulled down the shirt around her shoulder to show them a tattoo of a paw print with wings and a "K & M" in the middle.

"Very nice. Tasteful," Brad said. Esteban agreed.

"Thanks. Alex likes it too," Nivie said, pulling her sleeve back up.

"So, what's going on?"

"You'll see," Brad smiled, with a glint in his eye.

"Not even a little hint?" Nivie held her thumb and forefinger close together.

"Not even a little bit," Brad said. "Ready?"

"Oh yeah!"

"Your limo awaits," he said, pointing to their Honda hybrid and opening the backseat door.

Without diverting her gaze from the car window, Nivie pelted them with questions for a majority of the forty-five minute drive. To their credit, Brad and Esteban remained steadfast in their resolve not to provide any clues about their destination. As they turned the corner into the parking lot of a large building, the words "Cat Show" blinked brightly on the marquee.

A lump began to form in Nivie's throat. "Really?" she asked.

"Yes. It's time to immerse yourself in the feline world again," Brad said, parking the car. "It's a fantastic world. We know—we live there with our little Roxie girl."

Linking arms with Nivie, Brad and Esteban escorted her to the entrance of the arena. She was met by the familiar smells of pine kitty litter and sights of booths selling treats, kitty magnets, food, and other mementos. Whirling dervishes of kitty hair rolled by on the arena floor while a steady stream of "mews" and "meows" filled the air. Nivie caught her breath as she stood in awe. And "awww."

They took their time strolling down the countless aisles. Surveying the rows upon rows of various cat breeds in cages almost made Nivie's head swim. Peering into the cages to greet the kitties, they saw breeds ranging from the petite, but athletic, Abyssinians to the smiling face of the Chartreux; from the long, svelte body of the Cornish Rex to the shimmering silver-tipped blue fur of the Korats; from the massive Maine Coons to the stubby-legged Munchkin; from the long, fluffy flat-faced Persians to the playful and social Tonkinese. And, petting the kittens was simply magical. Any kitten would do.

They stopped at a cage with American Bobtail kittens. "May I hold her?" Nivie asked the lady brushing one of the kittens.

"Sure. This one is really special," she said, handing her to Nivie.

Nivie cuddled the kitten as she would a human infant, kissing her on the head. "I remember when my Mini was tiny. My baby girl," Nivie said, brushing the soft kitten fur against her cheek. "She even has the nub that Mini had. Oh, man. My heart. I need to give her back to you. Thank you."

Nivie handed the kitten back to the breeder and scanned the room. "This is unbelievable," she said. "The number of kitty breeds has grown. Exponentially! And, all of them don't even have to have fur!" she said, looking at the Sphinx. "Aww, they can't help it. Still so adorable."

Judging tables lined the periphery of the arena, and the three of them paused to watch. Mesmerized by the ballet-like choreography of each exam, Nivie watched the judges hold up each cat, stretching them out, like playing an accordion. After setting the cats down on the table, they used a feather fishing rod on the side of a vertical scratching pole to get the cat to stretch up. Placed back in the cages, some cats sat at the front and meowed, while others sat in the back, curling their tails around themselves, protecting them from such uncivilized exercises. Some batted at the top of the cages while others batted at the ribbons in front of the cages. Nivie could not stop staring. She vacillated between feeling as though her heart would burst from cuteness overload and bursting into tears from the waves of grief that threatened to overtake her.

"We actually got our little Roxie from the Ragdoll breeder back there. Why not talk to them?" Brad suggested.

"Well, we'll see," Nivie said. "Ya know, still just taking all of this in. But, I appreciate it."

"Niv, you must see this," Esteban said. Nivie turned to see a large, mesh enclosure housing the cats' agility trials. She could hardly contain her giggles. An owner, using a feathered fishing rod, led the cats along a feline version of an obstacle course—up the steps, over tiny fences, and through the fun run, a plastic tunnel where they emerged on the other side. The trio stood watching one after another, adding commentary as scores and times were announced. Many of the trials took much longer than the dog agility trials.

After several felines ran the course to their delight, Brad looked down at his phone. "Well, Niv...,"

"Awww, is it really time?" she asked.

"Afraid so," Brad said, retrieving the car keys from his pocket.

"Thanks, guys," Nivie said, wrapping her arms around Brad and Esteban. "I really needed this." Nivie spun around and said, "And, good bye, little kittens. Thank you for lighting up my life."

Nivie was a chatterbox driving home from the arena and stopping for a quick bite to eat. She endlessly shared her highlights and encouraged Brad and Esteban to do the same. Once they returned to Nivie's house, they all stood in her driveway to say goodbye.

"Thank you both for doing this. You are just the *best*," she said.

Esteban hugged her back. "You're welcome, Niv. We knew you've had a hard time lately. And, we haven't seen you in eons. So, we cooked up this idea, and voila!"

Nivie laughed and shook her head. "Guess I needed to get out of the house more than I thought. It's just sucked. Miss my Kimball Kitty and Mini so much."

"We get that. When our beloved Velma passed, we did the opposite and made a beeline for the cat show. That's when our little Roxie entered the scene. Sometimes getting out of the house is the first step," Brad said.

"Yeah, I know. Can you guys come inside for a minute?" Nivie asked.

"Unfortunately, no. We must be off," Esteban answered.

"Damn," Nivie shuffled her feet.

"Yes, long drive back home. But, we love ya, darling." Brad outstretched his arms again.

"Love you guys." Nivie initiated another group hug, wrapping her arms around her friends.

Sliding into the driver's seat, Brad said, "You need a cat, Niv!"

"Thanks," Nivie said, rolling her eyes, smiling, and waving goodbye. Brad's words echoed in her mind.

Maybe he's right. Maybe everyone was right.

As strictly dog lovers, Julian and Bryn never quite understood Megan's adoration of cats. Although she loved dogs too, Megan's incessant pleas for a kitten seemed to intensify after she discovered the "Adopt-A-Kitten" enclosure right outside Dr. Carmichael's clinic. The wooden and screened octagonal structure, 10 feet by 8 feet, encircled one large maple tree, on which the adoptable kittens could climb. Three other large logs formed a "z" inside the enclosure providing even more climbing opportunities. The top of the structure was screened in to prevent fallen leaves from entering. The screened sides allowed the kitties to bask in the fresh air, and a passerby could stick his or her finger in to pet them. Fresh wood chips carpeted the bottom of the enclosure. The "Adopt-A-Kitten" sign, visible from the road, rested by the door on top of the padlock that kept the felines safe inside. Every time the Troxell family drove by, Megan craned her neck to look and report on how many cats she saw inside.

One morning, as Bryn pulled into the parking lot of Dr. Carmichael's office, Megan audibly gasped, squealing and clasping her hands.

Jumping out of the car, Megan sprinted directly to the kitty corral with her little brother following behind.

Looking in, they saw one cat, four little kittens, and a staff member.

"How come she gets to be in there?" Megan asked.

"Shhh, Megan," Bryn said. "She works here. Hi, Lea. How are you today?"

"Good, thanks," Lea said, smiling at Megan. "The kitties are excited to see you."

"Meggie, I have something I want to tell you," Bryn said, crouching down in front of her. "Daddy and I were talking, and we decided you could have a kitty."

"Really?" Megan hopped up and down. "Yay, Mommeee," she said, throwing her arms around Bryn's neck.

"So, we can look today, or come back and—."

"—I want that one!" Megan said, pointing to a small, white ball of fluff.

"OK, today then," Bryn said. "That is a cute kitten."

The kitten Megan chose had a large faint beige marking on its head and even fainter beige splotches on each side of its head. It jumped around, twisting its tiny body at the stick Ethan ran against the screened side.

"And, his name is Olaf," Megan stated.

"Looks like Pwingo," Ethan said, pointing to his head.

"No, Brother! Olaf, not Pringle," Megan corrected.

"Well, actually. 'He's' a 'her,'" Lea said.

"See? Pwingo!" Ethan said.

"That's OK, still Olaf." Megan reaffirmed.

"Pwingo!"

"Olaf!"

"Pwingo!"

"Olaf! Mommeee!" Megan howled.

"OK, kids," Bryn looked up at Lea, widening her eyes. "Let's go in and sign the papers to take Olaf home."

"Yay!" Megan said, quickly sticking her tongue out at Ethan before skipping up the sidewalk to the entrance.

"Pwingo, Pwingo, Pwingo," Ethan repeated, running behind her.

"Olaf!" Megan stopped, turning around to remind him.

Bryn sighed, but chuckled. *What have we started?*

"Tucker, look what we have!" Megan said, walking into the house.

"Yeah, Tucko!" Ethan said.

Bryn placed the kitten carrier in the middle of the living room. With his tail up, Tucker sniffed it as Olaf slowly crept out of the opening on her belly, observing all sets of eyes on her. Tucker stuck his snout on her tiny, triangular nose and the two exchanged messages that only felines and canines could understand. Making the infinity sign with her body, Olaf walked under Tucker's belly, up across his front paws, back behind his tail, and under his belly again, each time sweeping her tail against his fur. Tucker sat down. Not understanding his change of position, Olaf twitched her back and licked her front shoulder. She playfully swiped up at Tucker's muzzle with her white paw, then jump-hopped to the living room coffee table, allowing Tucker a moment to glean more information about this diminutive creature.

Once he got his fill, Tucker laid down, watching the white kitten closely for her next move. Olaf flattened her body and wiggled her bottom with an eagle eye on Tucker's fluffy tail. She pounced. He jerked his head around, as she caught his tail, lightly touching his nose to Olaf's belly. She scrambled on her back, ears flat against her head, and darted off to the side. Returning, she grabbed his front paws, flopping and contorting her body over them. He watched patiently for the demon to be exorcised.

Standing, he yawned and licked his lips, walking over to Bryn. His big brown eyes conveyed one message:

"Help me."

The never ending cat items in the pet store made Bryn's head swim. It didn't help that Megan, who was walking next to the cart, fired off relentless questions of, "What about this, Mommy? Can we get this?" Ethan, sitting in the cart, held onto an anti-anxiety shirt for Tucker, keenly observing and smiling at people and their dogs as they walked up and down the aisles.

Bryn picked up a cat collar and exhaled loudly. "Where to start?"

In her peripheral vision, she saw a woman standing next to her, also looking at the collars.

"There really is a ginormous amount of stuff, isn't there?" the woman asked.

"Yeah," Bryn exhaled. "Too much, almost. We just got a kitten for our daughter, Megan here, and there is so much. My husband and I are more dog people."

"Here, let me help you," the woman offered, setting her basket down.

She looked down at Megan. "So, I understand you just got a kitten. What's his name?"

"*Her* name is Olaf," Megan corrected.

"Pwingo!" Ethan chimed in, sucking on his thumb.

"No—Olaf!" Megan angrily replied.

The woman laughed. "Olaf! What a great a name! So, she's a white kitten."

"Yeah, she's got white all over her body," Megan's arms spread out. "And she has one big spot on her head. Oh! And, two spots on her ears." Megan's hands landed on her head. "And when she goes to sleep, she goes like this." Megan pulled her arms in and gave herself a hug. "…And, then she runs around the tree and on the branches and jumps up at toys like this." Megan outstretched her body.

The woman laughed. "Kittens really are awesome. How old is she?"

Megan looked at Bryn.

"The vet says she's about eight weeks old."

"Did you get her here? Woodhaven Run Humane Society adopts out some of their cats here. They're really good."

"No, we got her at the "Adopt-A-Kitten," near Dr. Carmichael's office."

"Oh, I know that place! That's a cat-lover's dream. And, Dr. Carmichael is my vet too. She's great."

"Meggie gots a new titty," Ethan added.

The woman chuckled. "Well, probably not for a more few years."

Bryn smiled politely, "My son, Ethan."

His eyes darted around. "We gots Tucko, too," he added.

"He's our dog," Bryn clarified.

"Oh, so Olaf isn't an 'only child,'" the woman asked.

"He wikes it when I pway piano," Ethan added.

"Oh, you play the piano, too? I do too, a little. Isn't it fun? Bet you're really good at it."

Ethan smiled a thumb-filled smile.

"So, what do you know about Olaf's history?" the woman asked.

"The only thing we know is that she was one of a litter they found abandoned in the woods," Bryn answered.

"Oh, that is sad because mama cats are the best mothers around," the woman said. "Yeah, they'll go to their deaths, literally, to take care of their kittens. There are mama cats who will save their kittens from burning houses. Sometimes they come out with burns on them, and sometimes....well, it doesn't end very well."

Bryn's face grimaced, and the woman cleared her throat. "Anyway. So glad you were able to save one of them."

Changing the subject, the woman continued, clapping her hands together. "So, first we need a litter box. They aren't a big fan of having a cover over it, but I say, if you want it, get it."

She turned to Bryn, stopped, and said, "I'm sorry, but...you just look so familiar to me."

Relieved, Bryn replied. "I was thinking the same thing."

"I'm Nivie Emerson. Nice to meet you," she said, extending her hand.

"Oh, I'm Bryn Troxell. Nice to see you," she said, taking Nivie's hand, gently shaking it.

"I'm Megan!" Megan said, jumping up and down, holding onto the sides of the cart.

"Yes, you are!" Nivie said, then turned to Bryn. "So, where would I have seen you before? Let's see..."

"Do you know Julian Troxell? He's my husband."

"Hm. Doesn't ring any bells."

"Or, Jacqueline Stanton, maybe? She's my mom."

"Jaqueline Stanton....Jacqueline Stanton....."

"That's my Gramma Stanton!" Meggie chimed in, still jumping up and down.

"Yes, she is!" Nivie said to Megan. "Wow, that name sounds familiar. Jacqueline Stanton....Oh wait, do you know Ronni Gillespie?"

"Yes, Ronni's one of my mom's best friends."

"Awesome! That's it! Oh, thank God," Nivie said.

Bryn smiled in confusion.

"Ronni's my aunt! God, my brain was starting to hurt."

Bryn sighed in relief.

"Yeah, I think they're in a book club together. Oh, and of course, Red Hat. Yeah, I've seen the pics."

"Oh yeah. She has a great time with the other ladies," Bryn said.

"They are crazy, but good for them! I hope I have that much energy and excitement when I'm older, too!" Nivie said.

"Gramma has lots of red hats. I get to wear 'em! But, we haven't done it in a long time," Megan added, her face falling.

"Well, it's been hard for Grandma Stanton since Gramp-E died," Bryn said, looking down at Megan.

"Yeah, I'm so sorry," Nivie added. "I understand. It's hard to lose your dad."

Bryn cleared her throat. "Thanks. But, your aunt has been so good to Mom."

"Aunt Ronni was just happy to be there for her. She's rarely in Michigan anymore. She's hither and yon!"

"Mommeee, can we get things for Olaf?" Megan asked, swaying

from the side of the cart.

"Yes! Might as well, since we're here!" Nivie said.

Nivie escorted them up and down the aisles, helping them to pick out cat necessities, while giving an in-depth tutorial on food, litter, toys, and brushing teeth and fur.

Standing in front of the store with a cart full of bags, Bryn said, "Thank you again, Nivie, for all your invaluable information. It really helped."

"Oh, no problem. Now that we have each other's number, just let me know any time you have questions. Glad to help!"

"Meggie, thank Mrs. Emerson for all her help," Bryn reminded.

"Thanks, Mrs. Emerson!" Megan said, impulsively hugging Nivie's leg.

"You're welcome!" Nivie said, side-hugging her and then bending down in front of her. "Maybe sometime I can meet your Prin....Olaf, I mean."

"Yeah!" Megan said, twirling around the cart.

"And, we can play the piano," Nivie added, looking at Ethan.

"Yeah." Ethan smiled.

"That would be great," Bryn said.

"Nice to finally meet you!" Nivie said.

"Thanks, you too, Nivie."

"Bye, Mrs. Emerson," Megan said, still bouncing up and down.

Ethan waved good-bye with the fingers attached to his weathered thumb.

A few days passed since Olaf joined the Troxell family. The furry kitten slowly tip-toed across a sleeping Tucker's paw. Tucker woke, jerking his head up to get a closer look at this frenetic fluff. After smelling the tiny, white creature, he rolled over onto his back, splaying out. The kitten patted his dangling jowls, then sprinted into the other room, returning almost as quickly as she left. Cocking her head, she tapped his face.

Tucker blinked and buried his long muzzle into her side. Her body closed around his nose, gently bunny-kicking it. He turned his head away and she sprinted off into the other room, returning as a puffy, side-walking, upside down "U." Once he stood up and moved over to the other side of the room, Olaf looked confused, like a younger sister whose older brother had left her behind. He groaned as he lay down, tucking one paw under his chest. She trotted over to him, "marking" his face with her tail and nestled herself into his thick neck fur. As she kneaded on his neck, her relaxed eyes mirrored Tucker's. His personal cat masseuse. The two quadruped, non-human mammals had started to understand one another. Or, at least give it more of a shot.

After submitting the midterm grades, student learning outcomes, and paperwork, Nivie couldn't be more relieved to be home on a Friday night. It was already getting dark, typical October weather, so she changed into her pajamas, plopped on the couch, and pulled a blanket over her legs. She brought a warm mug of tea to her lips when she heard Alex arrive home.

"Hey, honey!" Alex said.

"Hey," Nivie said, slurping her tea, her eyes half-open.

"Hey, guess what?" Alex asked playfully.

"What?"

"I have two brothers I want you to meet."

Nivie turned her head, twisting her body to face Alex. "What? 'Two brothers'?"

"Yeah," he said.

"You mean you, like, just picked up two little children. Like on the side of the road?"

Alex laughed. "No. Two little brothers." He gestured with his hands. "You know. Kitties. Brothers."

"You mean on Petfinder? You've been there a lot lately," she noted.

"I'm not the only one," he replied, smiling coyly. "But, no, at the pet store. You know, shelter animals are there for adoption."

"I'm familiar," Nivie said.

"Wanna go see?"

"Oh, honey," Nivie said, throwing her head back on the couch. "I am really, really tired tonight. Some other time?"

"Well...we could. But they might not be there. They were really cute," he coaxed.

"Honey. I....I just don't know..."

She looked at Alex's disappointed face and deeply exhaled.

"Oh, all right," Nivie pulled the blanket off. "Let's go see these 'brothers'."

Passing cat and kitten-filled cages, Nivie tried to keep up with a quick-paced Alex.

Stopping in front of the last cage, he pointed down and said, "Here. Aren't they cute?"

Nivie knelt down and chuckled. "Um, honey. These aren't brothers."

Inside the cage was a lean, all-gray kitten with green eyes, playing with a mouse toy while the other kitten, white with large and random shaped tabby splotches, rested.

"Well, close enough. Their eyes are the same color," Alex repeated, kneeling down to see. "So cute."

"Aw, yeah," Nivie studied the cards attached to their cage. "They really are. And, oh, good, they've had their shots and been fixed. Two little boys. A little older, though, about four or five months."

"That's fine," Alex said.

"They weren't here a few days ago," Nivie added, poking Alex on his thigh.

They smiled at each other.

Alex looked around for someone to help so they could properly meet these "brothers." One of the employees opened the door to the cage, along with a few other cages.

Watching all the kittens running and jumping as they enjoyed their freedom delighted Nivie and Alex. They learned that the two "brothers" had originally been placed in adjacent cages, but the gray kitten kept reaching his paw under the door to play with the other kitten. Then, due to a lack of space, the volunteers decided to put them together in the same cage. They were "brothers" ever since.

"Well, whatddya think?" Alex repeatedly asked, as Nivie sat on the floor, cuddling the gray brother in her lap.

"I don't know. I just can't make that decision right now," Nivie repeated back, stroking the purring kitten with a smile on her face.

After about fifteen minutes of playing, a lady and her daughter entered the area with the scampering kittens. She picked up the white cat with patchy tabby spots, cradling him in her arms. Once Nivie saw this, she pointed right at the kitten and said, "We'll take him." The gray kitten was already a given.

Pointing at the gray kitten, Nivie said, "This one is Sherlock and…" pointing at the cow kitty "…he's Watson."

The only sound heard on the ride home was the soft classical music playing on the radio. Not a peep from the felines huddled in the corners of their separate carriers in the backseat.

Since they weren't completely prepared for two cats to join their family that night, once they got home, Nivie and Alex scurried around, setting up the newly purchased litter and food, while scattering jingle balls and plastic mice in various areas of the house. Soft classical music played in the background again, in hopes to counteract the humans' bustling movements.

The kittens slowly crept out of open carriers onto the kitchen floor. Alex and Nivie spoke softly and avoided making sudden moves so as not to startle the uncertain kittens.

The first night, Nivie and Alex slept in their sleeping bags and pillows on the living room floor in an effort to be present for their new family members. However, Sherlock and Watson hid underneath the couch, with only the reflections of their eyes visible. Books, binders, and textbooks were later placed under the couch to block this hiding spot.

"Poor things. They're so scared," Nivie said. "Good thing we kept them together."

———✦———

Nivie awoke at 3:00am. Lifting up the couch skirt, she found a snoozing Sherlock. But, no Watson. Whispering his name throughout the house, yet knowing he wouldn't come to her, she finally located him under the base of the dining room pedestal table. He had rolled himself in as tight a ball as possible.

"Awww. It's OK. I know you're scared, but you're going to like it here," Nivie said to his bottom. She gently stroked his back. He flinched from her touch. "Ok. Well, this'll take a while," she said returning to her sleeping bag in the living room.

I really miss my Kimball Kitty. And, my baby girl, Mini.

Saturday morning arrived, and the kittens finally emerged from their hiding places. Nivie and Alex were relieved when they saw the previously untouched food being eaten by two hungry kittens. Alex pulled out a fishing rod feather toy and ran throughout the house, dragging it behind. Sherlock took the lead, investigating this feathery, unpredictable moving thing. Watson remained on the sidelines, watching his brother chase after it. Yet, the reluctant kitten batted his paw when the feathery toy dangled in front of him.

The doorbell rang, disturbing their newfound playtime. Watson scurried away, running low to the ground, burying as much of himself under the couch as he could. However, only his face was hidden since his back haunches and tail remained visible.

"Mean mailman," Nivie said.

Over the next couple days, Sherlock investigated more of the house, sticking his gray nose into any nook or cranny he could find. He sniffed around the back porch door, but Nivie shooed him away.

"No, no, no. The back porch and the rocking chair are sacred spaces."

Watson's progress was limited to observing his brother from afar, yet spending less and less time under the table and couch. It pleased Nivie and Alex when they were able to pick each kitten up for a solid five seconds without them squiggling in protest.

Baby steps.

The multi-colored maple trees glistened in the sun, red tips contrasted against the yellow leaves. Those that had fallen to their destiny formed a carpet surrounding the solid trunks. Fall flowers coordinated with the orange pumpkins and yellow mums on the town's porches.

A few birch trees had shed their bark, at times peeling off in whole sheets. The apple trees released their fruits, forming an apple paste on the ground, as the other apples stayed up in the tree, awaiting their fate. Not to be overlooked, the evergreens had shed some of their needles, too.

After a rain, the leaf-blanketed sidewalks created an aroma indicative of the season. Even the wildlife reflected the time of year. Due to their size, the black squirrels could easily have been mistaken for black cats, adding to the Halloween feeling in the air. The chubby fox squirrels chased each other with their tender, orangish underbellies mirroring the leaves on the trees. Chipmunks with their natural Halloween markings gave the "eye" to anyone who might impede their ability to create a nest.

Walking into the living room, Bryn saw Olaf snuggled next to Tucker's head. Smiling at the sight, Bryn asked if Tucker wanted to go "O-u-t-s-i-d-e"? He unsteadily pulled himself up, rolling Olaf to her side. Once he got his footing, Tucker's large tail swished against the kitchen island as he barked excitedly and spun in circles.

"C'mon, kids! Tucker and I are ready to go!" Bryn said, opening the door for everyone to head outside.

Grabbing their toy rakes from the garage, the kids ran out to the backyard. An excited dog followed but his stops and turns weren't as clean and quick as before.

Bryn raked leaves into a pile and yelled, "Ok, kids! One at a time!"

Megan, getting a head start, jumped into the pile of leaves with such force that a couple of them landed in her mouth and in her hair. Ethan rushed the pile, landing on his belly with the leaves absorbing his fall. Tucker didn't follow the "one-at-a-time" instructions as he ran and jumped in after each child that headed to the mound. Obviously, they were there to play with him. Even if Tucker didn't keep up with every dash toward the pile, he barked in merriment, with crinkled orange and yellow leaves clinging to his reddish fur. Bryn laughed, snapped a few pictures on her phone, and raked the displaced leaves into a pile for another run.

"Come on, answer the phone. Answer the damn phone," Nivie muttered from her kitchen, quickly shifting her weight from side to side. The consecutive days of cloudy, gray skies and spitty rain added to Nivie's frustration.

"Hey, Love," Alex answered.

"Honey! Oh my god! Oh my god! Oh my god!" Nivie yelled through her tears.

"What's wrong?"

"I just got home, took off my shoes, and was walking around the kitchen. And I stepped on something and I thought it was kitty litter. And I'm like, what is kitty litter doing down here? I mean it really hurt. Like, I thought I was bleeding or something!"

"Nivie..."

"So, OK. I look at the bottom of my foot. And there, implanted in it, is a tiny tooth!"

"What?" Alex's voice broke with chuckles.

"Yeah! A tiny kitty tooth. One of the babies lost a tooth!"

"Honey…"

"It's looking at me right now on the counter!" she continued, ignoring the laughter on the other end of the phone. "I don't know whose it is! How can we tell? They hardly even let us touch them. Oh my god, honey. I don't want to have to, like, pin them down to look in their mouths. What do we do?"

"Honey…deep breath…deep breath."

"Alex! Come on! What the hell do we *do*?"

Alex replied, matter-of-factly, "Honey, if human babies lose their teeth, I think it's OK for baby cats to also lose their teeth."

Silence.

"You know, losing baby teeth? I'm thinkin' that's OK."

Nivie chuckled. "Oh, my god. You're right. Of course. If children do it, so do kittens!"

"Yeah. So just keep it. Put it in a little baggy, or box, and put the date on it. Ya know, like you did with Minerva and Kimball's fur."

"Yeah, OK," Nivie said, tears welling up.

"Or, put it under your pillow tonight," Alex chuckled. "Or, under theirs!"

Nivie sniffed.

"Niv?"

"Yeah," her voice cracked.

"It's OK. It's OK," Alex gently responded.

"It's just. Honey, I just got so scared."

"I know."

"Dammit. Still hurts so much. I just didn't want to go back to the vet right now. I just can't go through that again. Not right away. They're just babies."

"But, it's OK. Everyone's fine. Kitties are fine. In fact, they even played together this morning. And, they ate really well."

Nivie loudly exhaled, shaking herself out of it. "It's OK. Everything's OK," she repeated to herself, blowing her nose.

"So, you good?"

"Yeah," she said, wiping away the tears. "Thanks, honey."

"You're welcome. I'll be home in about an hour. Just need to finish up these programs."

"Thanks, honey. Love you."

"Love you, too."

Locating a permanent marker and a baggie, Nivie gently placed the tooth inside. Drawing a smiley face on the outside, she tucked it away in the drawer, next to two other baggies. One contained some tufts of Minvera's fur and whiskers, and the other some of Kimball's fur and whiskers. Looking down, she saw Sherlock gazing up at her, blinking slowly.

Trick-or-treating in Grandma Stanton's neighborhood was a requirement as it meant a second round of goodie gathering. After visiting most of Jacqueline's neighbors, Megan and Ethan sprinted up Gladys Paisley's driveway. Bryn and Jacqueline trailed behind accompanied by a costumed Tucker. Chloe stayed home, finding the entire Trick-or-Treating tradition too overwhelming and frankly, undignified.

The milder evening allowed for the children's costumes to be in full-view, rather than buried beneath layers of clothes. Adorned in her cat and dog Halloween sweater, Gladys stood on her front porch holding a large bowl of candy. A Halloween wreath comprised of lights and small plastic cat and dog figurines hung on the door. Roosevelt's face peered outside behind the closed storm door, while Piper and Petey took turns barking and jumping into view. Eleanor, Gladys' cat, sat in the front windowsill, watching all the action.

"Trick or Treat!" Megan and Ethan yelled.

"Oh, dear!" Gladys giggled.

She waved to the adults bringing up the rear and lowered the bowl in front of Ethan and Megan.

"Wow!" The kids exclaimed, wrappers crinkling as they reached to grab full-sized candy bars.

"Thank you, Ms. Paisley," Megan said.

"Yeah, tank oo," Ethan parroted.

"Hello, Dears," Gladys said to Bryn and Jacqueline on their approach. Tucker, donned in a brown suit with a small saddle, still walked with a slight limp. But, he was determined to do his best to keep up with the two eager children.

"Happy Halloween, Ms. Paisley," Jacqueline said. "A lovely evening tonight, isn't it?"

"Yes, indeed," Gladys said, eyes fixed on Tucker. "Oh, dear. My goodness, Tucker. Whatever happened to you?"

"Tucko hit by cah," Ethan said.

"Yes, Tucker was hit by a car last summer," Bryn clarified.

"Oh, dear!" Gladys said.

"In front of our house, one evening, about like, I don't know, about five months ago," Bryn said, looking at Jacqueline for confirmation. "It was scary. But, he's actually doing better now."

Gladys' eyes widened in shock. "Oh, dear." For a split second, she remembered a soft thud and a brown spot in her peripheral vision while driving by Bryn's house around that time.

Quickly shaking her head, Gladys shifted her gaze to the children. She set the bowl down on the front stoop and put her hand on her hips.

"So, who do we have here?" she asked.

"I'm Elsa," Megan said, spinning around.

"Oh?" Gladys prompted.

"Yeah. From *Frozen.*" Megan said.

"'*Frozen*'?" Gladys asked.

"I'm Woody!" Ethan jumped in. "Tucko is Bullseye!"

"Oh, dear. Bullseye?"

"From *Toy Story,*" Ethan said.

"Toy? Story?" Gladys repeated, perplexed.

"Yes, with Woody! And Buzz Lightyear!" Megan said.

"Woody Lightyear?"

"No! Buzz Lightyear," Megan laughed.

"Alright kids," Bryn said, tapping Megan's arm. "Ms. Paisley probably hasn't heard of these movies."

"I'm afraid I haven't," Gladys said.

"It's OK," Bryn smiled. She looked at the kids and asked, "Did you thank Ms. Paisley for the candy?"

"Thank you, Ms. Paisley!" Megan said as Ethan waved goodbye, spinning his candy bag in his hand, hopping down the porch steps.

"You are more than welcome, dears."

"Thank you. Happy Halloween," Bryn said. "Kids, hold my hands."

"Have a good night, Ms. Paisley. It's been good to see you," Jacqueline said, smiling.

Bryn, Jacqueline, and the kids made their way down the driveway. With bags of candy flapping, Megan and Ethan yanked on Bryn's arms, pulling her forward.

"You do the same, dears," Gladys whispered, staring at Tucker's slow and limping progress down the walk. She closed the door behind her, and stood with her hand on the knob.

"Oh, Rosie. My Piper. Petey. Eleanor," she said, covering her mouth as she walked in the living room. The three dogs followed her, cocking their heads. "Mommy didn't know it at the time, but she did something unforgiveable," she said, choking on her words.

Armed with a large cup of coffee, Nivie sat at her home desk. These tests *had* to be graded. Today. Sherlock, who was becoming even more comfortable with his new home, stretched up on his hind legs and craned his neck to see what his human was up to. Watson sat quietly in the doorway, allowing Sherlock to be the scout.

"Hey, there. No. I don't need your help. Thank you," Nivie said, gently nudging him over with her arm.

The kitten sat next to Nivie's chair, blinked up at her, and released a grand meow.

Without turning her head, Nivie replied, "Yes, I see you. And, I hear you."

Sherlock stretched up again with his front paws on the side of Nivie's chair, back twitching. "No..no...no. Come on now! I've got to get these done. I put this off way too long," she said, nudging him down with her elbow.

She started adding up the number of missed responses. "2, 3, 5, 6…"

The kitten extended his paws up again, back twitching and bottom swaying back and forth. Noticing this movement in her peripheral vision, Nivie threw out her leg to block his attempt.

"Ah, ah, ah. No, no, no."

Nivie smiled, watching him walk away with his "Owl Ears" pulled back.

"OK, now. Where was I?"

Focusing intently on her tests, she felt pointy little teeth gently wrapping around her big toe.

"What the…?"

Nivie looked down to see Sherlock stretched out on his back with mouth agape.

"No!" she yelled, sending him running out of the room.

"Man, are these ever going to get done?" she said, looking over the numerous tests splayed on her desk.

"OK ..2, 3, 4….7 wrong. Hmm. Not her best exam," she sighed, writing the grade in her gradebook.

Suddenly, a gray feline mass flew directly in front of her face, landing on her desk.

"Oh, my god! No!" Nivie exclaimed.

Sherlock shot off the table, sending most of the tests airborne in all directions and the coffee cup remains spattering a few. Watson tore down the stairs, trying to disassociate himself from his brother feline.

"Dammit, Sherlock! Really?"

Sherlock ran down the hall, stopped, turned around, and peeked around the corner to watch Nivie's rant.

"What are you? Half monkey or something?"

Disgusted at the mess, Nivie grabbed a nearby Kleenex and wiped off the brown liquid on the tests still on the desk. She gathered even more off the floor, Alex's desk, and the windowsill. Reaching into the bookshelf, she repeated a plethora of expletives.

She turned around to find the little gray kitten had returned, sitting intently in the doorway. Nivie looked down at him and took a deep breath.

"Yeah, you think because you're so damn cute that you can get whatever you want. Not gonna happen," she said, shutting the door with her foot. She pulled out her earphones to drown out the incessant meowing on the other side of the door.

After an hour of organizing her tests and thoughts, Nivie felt the rumble of the garage door open as Alex arrived home.

"Man," Alex mumbled to himself entering the kitchen. "Can't forget to email—"

Nivie ran to greet him, spouting, "Sherlock was all over the place today. I tried to grade my tests. I told him 'no.' Pushed him away. Told him 'no' again. Even friggin' used my leg to block him. Then, he flies out of nowhere and lands on my desk right in front of me! Scared me to death! I jumped and yelled. He went running. The papers friggin' flew all over the place. Coffee all over. One even landed stuck on the bookshelf. The bookshelf!"

Alex sighed, sliding his heavy bag off his shoulder onto the floor. "Oh man, honey. He is part monkey you know."

"That's what I said! So friggin' frustrating because now most of them are wrinkled. Some even got ripped. And ruined. They were all over the friggin' place! Like all over."

Sherlock entered the kitchen, wondering what all the fuss was about. Nivie turned to him and pointed. "And I told you 'no' so many times."

Using the heels of his palms, Alex rubbed his eyes. He turned to Nivie and opened his arms, motioning to her. She reluctantly walked over to him, and he wrapped his arms around her.

"Honey," Alex said.

"What?"

"Remember Minerva?"

"What do you mean?"

"Remember how she was?"

"Yeah…" she said.

"Remember her amazing vertical jump?"

"Yes, but…."

"And the endless jumping at the curtains?"

"Yeah…but…"

"And, the Christmas tree? Or better yet, the lack thereof for many years after the Incident of 2007?"

"I know, but honey…"

"And the jumping on top of the fridge. And, batting at our heads as we walked by?"

"Yeah," she resigned. "But, she wasn't *that* bad."

Alex let out a loud gaffaw. "Are you kidding me? We couldn't set our drinks down on tables until she was like friggin' twelve years old!"

"I know, but…."

Nivie continued to roll her eyes as she swayed in Alex's arms. Alex stopped her and said, "Honey, I miss him, too. But, remember, Kimball was a kitten once, too. We just weren't there when he was."

"I know but…" Nivie stated indignantly. "I just wish they'd just grow up already."

She looked at Alex, then scrunched her face. "I know. We don't always have that luxury." She sighed. "I just really miss my creamsicle Kimball Kitty."

Alex gently brushed away the hair on Nivie's forehead to kiss it. "I know. I do, too," he added. "But, this won't last forever. This is what healthy kittens do."

"I know. But, it's still frustrating," she stated, taking a step back and glaring at Sherlock.

"Yeah. This whole thing really is," he said, shaking his head, walking upstairs.

A few days after Halloween, Bryn heard her phone's text alarm go off as she folded laundry.

"Hey! I have extra food and treats that our boys don't like. Maybe Olaf would like them? Can drop off now, if want," the text from Nivie read.

Bryn called her back, giving her directions to her house, and a few minutes later, Nivie arrived, cat food in hand.

"Hi, c'mon in. Thank you so much for thinking of us," Bryn said, opening the door.

"No problem! Glad to help." Nivie said, handing the food off to Bryn.

Ethan and Tucker ran to see who was at the door. "Oh, who's this? Olaf's sibling?" Nivie asked.

"Yeah, this Tucko!" Ethan squealed. Tucker's tail wagged, smelling this new person, who would, of course, become his friend.

"There he is, thumb and all!" Nivie said to Ethan. Turning to Tucker said, "What a beautiful dog. Where did you get him? He probably smells our boys."

"Thank you. He's a sweetie. We got Tucker years ago at the adopt-a-thon. He was found neglected with his ribs showing."

Nivie looked at Tucker. "Poor thing. People who treat animals like that should be euthanized."

"Yeah," Bryn chuckled. "And, he's still limping from his accident several months ago."

"What accident?"

"He was hit by a car in front of our house."

Nivie audibly gasped. "Oh, poor thing." She leaned over and scratched his bottom, causing him to lean into her. "Do you know who did it?"

"Not sure. I was inside and didn't see it. But, we were lucky. It could have been a whole lot worse."

"Poor Mr. Tucker. You're a survivor!"

Megan walked into the foyer cradling Olaf.

"Megan, do you remember Mrs. Emerson?" Bryn asked.

"Yes, Mommy. Hi, Mrs. Emerson! Here's Olaf!" Megan said, handing her to Nivie.

"Hi, Megan! So, this is the famous Olaf. Oh, she's so adorable," Nivie said, bending down on her knees. "Can I hold her?"

"Yes, but be sure to hold her bottom," Megan commanded.

"Oh, she is precious," Nivie gushed. The wiggly kitten patted up at Nivie's face. "Did you know that when kitties slowly blink, it's like they're giving you little hugs and kisses?"

Megan giggled.

"Her butt sometimes in ow face!" Ethan drew out his words, clasping his hands and giggling. "Her butt!"

"Yes, sometimes they do that, too," Nivie giggled.

"And, she goes like this at the curtains," Megan said, jumping up.

"Kitties are so funny, aren't they?" Nivie sighed. "It's kinda hard because my cat, Kimball Kitty, just died."

"Oh, I'm sorry," Bryn said.

"Thanks. We only had him a couple years. It's hard. Special little guy," she said, clearing her throat. "But, we have two adorable little kitties now. And, you have such a sweet, adorable kitty here," Nivie said, handing her back to Megan.

"Oh, who plays the piano?" Nivie asked, seeing the Steinway baby grand in the living room.

"Me!" Ethan squealed.

"That would be Ethan," Bryn answered.

"Good for you. I took lessons and used to play, but it's been a while. Be sure to keep it up!"

"We wiv heeo," Ethan said, pointing to the middle of his open hand.

"That's right! We live in the middle of the Michigan Mitten," Nivie affirmed.

"OK, kids," Bryn said, apologetically. "Let's not overwhelm Mrs. Emerson."

"Oh, they're fine," Nivie reassured.

"Come on in," Bryn said. Walking by Bryn's office, Nivie saw a bulletin board with thumb-tacked papers and a dry erase board with words splashed across. "You're really organized."

"Thanks. I try," Bryn said. "Those piles are for organizing my college's big Spring Fling. It's going to be held at The Stadium."

"Wow, that's a nice place," Nivie said.

"It's been busy with that and school holiday celebrations, dance recitals, and I made the kids' Halloween costumes this year. But, I enjoy it."

"Well, it looks as though you really have good systems in place." Looking around the house, Nivie added, "And, I'm impressed with how clean your house is, especially with two little ones." Spotting Olaf and Tucker, she added, "And, then two more little ones!"

"Thanks," Bryn blushed.

"Our house is full of books, bookshelves, and my neglected painting supplies!" Nivie said.

"Mommy?" Megan interrupted, tugging on Bryn's leg. "Can Mrs. Emerson stay for dinner?"

Bryn's mouth opened to speak, and Nivie interrupted, "No, that's fine. But thank you, Megan. I really appreciate the invitation."

"Oh, OK. Maybe some other time," Bryn said.

"Yeah, I also have some great recipes I can share with you," Nivie added.

"That would be nice," Bryn said. "Always looking for those."

"Well, better scoot! Thank you all for introducing me to adorable

Olaf and sweet Tucker. Oh, and for also reminding me where we live," Nivie said, looking down at Ethan and pointing to her open hand.

"Say goodbye to Mrs. Emerson, kids," Bryn said.

"Bye, Mrs. Emosin!" Meggie and Ethan ran to hug her.

Shutting the door behind Nivie, Megan said, "Mommy, can Mrs. Emosin come over again? She's nice."

"And pwetty," Ethan added.

Since the beginning of the semester, Chelsea, one of Nivie's students in her last class of the day, had been a daily thorn in Nivie's side. Nivie had given Chelsea many opportunities to redeem herself, repeatedly reminding her of the school's detention and demerit policies. But her student's eye-rolling, disruptive talking, and snippy remarks were starting to wear thin. Nivie walked around the class as she taught, keeping the students engaged as much as possible. For many teachers and presenters, lecturing behind a podium was security; for Nivie, it was confining and restricting.

During a lesson on Shakespeare, Nivie noticed Chelsea sitting in the back of the room, incredibly focused on the right side of her body. Making her way to Chelsea's desk, she leaned over as Chelsea fumbled to hide her phone back in her pocket. Nivie whispered, "Need to talk to you after class."

Chelsea glared at Nivie. Her neighbors laughed.

When the bell rang, all the students quickly emptied out of the classroom, talking a mile a minute.

Chelsea slammed her books together and gathered them in her backpack. Walking straight up to Nivie, she said, "What?" cocking her head to the side, pursing her lips.

Nivie took a deep breath, confusing Chelsea. "I just need to know. Is there something going on with you? Something that's bothering you?"

"You mean, besides this class?" Chelsea smirked.

Nivie ignored the comment and continued probing. "I need your help here. I know you can do really well in this class. I know you can."

"Um, not really."

"You play it like you're not very smart, when I know that you are," Nivie reminded her.

"You don't know that," Chelsea muttered.

"Oh, yes I do." Nivie chuckled. "More than you know. So, what's really goin' on?"

Chelsea rolled her eyes, looked around the room, and adjusted her backpack.

"So, OK," she said, her jaw jutting to the side. "If you *must* know. My dog Gracie was really sick, for like, a really long time."

"I'm sorry to hear that."

"Yeah, so she just, like..." Chelsea paused. "You know, died, and stuff."

"Oh, no. I'm so sorry."

"Whatever," Chelsea said, shaking her head.

"What kind of dog is she?" Nivie asked.

"So, actually, she *was* a Cairn Terrier," Chelsea corrected.

"So sweet."

"You know. Like, Toto? *The Wizard of Oz?*"

"Yeah," Nivie said. "Did you know that Toto was really named Terry and was a girl?"

"So, anyway," Chelsea sniffed. "My parents. *So* ridiculously clueless about all this."

"Oh, man."

"Just sucks. 'Cuz she was my BFF. She came with us everywhere. Slept with me, and stuff. And, now she's like..." Chelsea's voice trailed.

"I totally get that. Our pets are important people," Nivie affirmed.

"Anyway. So, that's what's going on. That's the big mystery in Chelsea's life," she added sarcastically.

"I'm really sorry about Gracie. I know, personally, I couldn't live without my little fur balls."

Chelsea looked around, tears welling up. "So, anyway..."

"Sorry again about Gracie. I just want to see you do well here. Because I know you can."

"Thanks," Chelsea said, walking out the door.

Nivie gave her a quick nod. "You're welcome, Chelsea."

When Nivie returned home, she found Sherlock lying on the transition between the living room and the kitchen, awaiting her arrival. With Christmas music playing in the background, and decorations in the house, she looked down at her Sherlock. Leaning over, she sat down next to the grey kitten, kissing his furry head.

She sighed. "I'm sorry I haven't been a great mommy to you and your brother. You deserve better."

Sherlock stretched out on his side, exposing his soft, white-patched belly.

"You don't ask for much. All you want is to be near us, food, water, toys. Occasional head-butts. You really are good babies. You too, Lotsa Watson," she said, looking at Watson straddling the back of the couch in his "Monorail Kitty" position. His new favorite place.

"Ya know. You would have liked Kimball Kitty. Minerva, not so much. No offense. But, she only liked Daddy and me."

Sherlock stood up. He leaned in, gave Nivie a head-butt, his tail grazing across her face. "Thank you for letting us be a part of your pride." She walked over to the back porch door. Despite the cool weather, she held it open for both cats to follow her out and explore.

Jacqueline finished cleaning up the Eucharistic chalices after the Christmas Morning mass. She exited St. Agnes Church into the cold December morning when she felt a gentle touch on her shoulder. Turning around, she was surprised to see who it was.

"Bill!" she exclaimed.

"Hi, Jacqueline. How have you been?" he asked, standing just outside the vestibule.

In the three years since they first met, she had seen Bill a few times at mass, but did not approach him. She even entered his phone number into her phone but never pressed the send button.

"I'm doing well, thanks. And you?"

"Doing well. Was a beautiful mass today, wasn't it?" Bill said.

"Yes, Fr. Kenneth always gives meaningful homilies."

"And, the church looked really nice, too, with the trees and lights."

"Thank you. Some ladies and I decorated it."

"I know," Bill smiled.

Jacqueline blushed.

"Listen, Jacqueline. I know it's not the first time I've asked. But, would you be interested in going out for a cup of coffee?"

All the reasons to say "No" bubbled to the surface, but Jacqueline surprised herself when she answered, "Yes, Bill. I would like that."

"Great! I'm glad to hear. Well, I don't want to keep you outside here in the cold too long. I'll call you soon," Bill said.

"Thanks. I look forward to it," Jacqueline smiled.

"Merry Christmas, Jacqueline," he waved, as he headed toward his car.

"Merry Christmas, Bill," she waved back. The cold December morning had just become a little warmer.

This Christmas morning was special: Julian was home. Megan played with her new *Frozen* Elsa doll, singing the theme song while Ethan sang "Jingle Bells," jumping around the house with his new Superman and Batman figurines. The night before on Christmas Eve gifts they received their gifts from Grandma Stanton. They had already been played with; therefore, they were now defunct. One sheet of wrapping paper formed a small tent over Tucker's behind as he played with his squeaky Teddy toy. Olaf pounced on the paper, as any ferocious predator would do.

"Well, I think that's about it," Bryn said, scanning the living room floor to see even more wrapping paper pieces strewn about.

"No, it's not," Julian said, with a smirk.

Bryn furrowed her brow. "It's not? I thought that we gave all our gifts?"

"Yes, *we* did. But, Santa didn't! Come here, kids. Come open this!"

"What is it, Daddy?" The children rushed over to their father.

Julian reached into his pocket and pulled out a sheet of paper and read.

"It says:

'Dear Ethan and Megan,

Because you have been so good this year, you are going to get a new puppy. Don't forget to have fun!

Love, Santa.'"

Bryn slowly closed her eyes.

Megan's mouth dropped open, and her brother watched her reaction. When Megan began jumping up and down, he did the same, and then scurried around the house. "New puppy? Where?" He looked under the couch, in the pantry, even opening the oven.

Tucker struggled to hoist himself to his feet, wanting to participate in the excitement. Olaf dashed off out of the room in the opposite direction.

Julian laughed. "Well, he's not here."

"Awwwww," both kids moaned.

"We need to go to Grandma and Grandpa Troxell's house now. They might know something about it," Julian said.

"I thought we were going later?" Bryn mouthed to Julian. He grinned while their two hopping and squealing kids grabbed their coats off the hooks.

"Jay," Bryn whispered to her husband. "You just sprung this on me now? Without even a discussion?"

"See how excited the kids are?" Julian redirected her attention.

"I mean, for Tucker."

"He's getting older," Julian said. "Plus, it'll be good for him to have a buddy!"

"You mean other than Olaf?" Bryn corrected.

"Pfft. I mean a *real* buddy. Come on, babe! It's Christmas! Lighten up!"

Bryn's eyes narrowed.

"Can we go now? Can we pleeezzzz," the kids pleaded, looking up at Bryn, necks extended back, leaning over to the side, so their heads were nearly parallel to the floor.

Bryn shot Julian a long stare.

"Only if it's OK with your mother," Julian said.

"Pleezzze, Mommy!" the two kids begged.

Bryn unlocked her stare and smiled down at her children. "I guess, but Mommy's going to stay here. You guys go have fun. Just make sure to put on your hats, gloves, and—"

Julian opened the door to the garage and Megan and Ethan rushed out to the car.

"Here we go!" Julian yelled, pressing the garage door opener and texting his parents to let them know they were on their way.

Bryn shot him another look and knelt down next to Tucker, petting his head. He struggled to stand amid all the commotion, a piece of wrapping paper still stuck to his tail. "I'm so sorry, sweetie," she said, as he licked her face.

The doorbell rang repeatedly.

"Coming! Coming!"

Barbara and Lawrence opened their front door to see Julian with two bouncing children, still in their pajamas, coats unzipped, wearing one glove, and feet not completely inserted into their boots.

"My, my! What do we have here? May we help you?" Barbara said.

"Grandma, Grandpa! Puppy! Puppy! Santa left a puppy here!" Megan exclaimed.

Julian entered the foyer as Lawrence walked towards the closed bathroom door. Plentiful puppy whines and barks reverberated through the closed door.

"Come on in! It's cold out there!" Lawrence said.

"Where's Bryn?" Barbara asked, craning her neck out the front door.

"She's staying behind, getting things ready for the puppy!" Julian explained.

"Santa weft us a puppy!" Ethan repeated, echoing in the foyer.

"Well, let's see here. Grandpa, did you hear anything about a puppy?" Barbara drew out her words, looking up at Lawrence, with a finger over her mouth.

"Hmm. Let me think." Lawrence feigned deep thought.

"Puppy! Puppy! Puppy!" Ethan squealed, springing around in front of them.

"Why, yes, Grandma," Lawrence said, smiling back. "I do believe that Santa left a puppy around here somewhere. But, only for two little children who have been very good this year."

"Ooooooo, I hear him!" Megan squealed, cupping her hands together, looking over at her grandparents and father.

"OK, now. I need you two to stand still," Lawrence said. The kids stopped jumping up and down, but the energy diverted to swaying.

"He's right in here…"Lawrence slowly opened the door to the bathroom. A chubby, fawn-colored purebred Boxer puppy with floppy ears clumsily galloped over to the kids. His tiny tail wagged so hard it appeared it would fly off.

"Oh! He's so cute!" Megan said. She picked him up, holding him under his front paws, his rounded belly protruding. He turned his face around and licked her.

"Ewwwwwoooo. He licked me on the mouth," she said, whacking

her lips, tongue extended. The puppy slid out of her hands.

"Me next!" Ethan joined in.

"Wait a second, Ethan," Barbara said. "Be sure to hold his bottom."

The squiggly puppy licked Ethan's face with even more fervor. Ethan emitted a loud giggle.

Barbara went into the laundry room and brought out a large basket full of squeaky toys, including a Kong and a small puppy jacket.

Ethan set the cuddly canine down, and the puppy rushed to Julian's shoelaces, yanking on them with such force he nearly knocked himself over.

Megan laughed. "Look, the puppy almost fell over! Come here, little puppy," she said, kneeling down. "What's his name?"

"Yeah, what name?" Ethan asked.

"How about Jagermeister?" Julian quipped.

"Or, Khalua?" Lawrence added. "Or, cognac? Or, Baileys?"

Julian and Lawrence emitted a hearty laugh, and Ethan's eyes darted around, trying to make sense of the adults' ideas.

"Now, boys," Barbara chuckled. "What do you think?" she asked, leaning down next to Ethan.

"How about Ace?" Julian offered, leaning over to Lawrence. "As in, Ace-in-the-hole."

"Ace," Ethan repeated.

"Yeah, Ace! Ace!" Megan said, dancing around.

"Do you think Tucker will like him?" Barbara asked.

"Yeah! Tucko has new fwend!" Ethan said.

"It's a doggie-dog world!" Megan shouted.

Flanked by two bundled-up, squealing kids, Julian carried Ace into their backyard. The puppy, sporting his new parka, was plopped into two inches of snow. He looked around, then sprang to the side, with his tiny ears accentuating his jerky movements. Bryn stood inside with

Tucker as they both watched Ace through the door window. She was surprised at how cute this clumsy canine was. Julian motioned to Bryn for them to join the family in the backyard.

"Alright. Let's go, sweetie," Bryn said to Tucker, opening the door.

Tucker bounded through the snow to meet this springy pup.

With his tail up, he sniffed the top of Ace's head. Ace rolled over, yielding to Tucker's meeting ritual.

"Ace's new coat is all wet!" Megan exclaimed.

"No problem," Julian said. "I think it can handle a little snow."

Ace hopped to the left side, then to the right side of Tucker. With a closed mouth, Tucker's eyes focused on this intriguing new, younger version of himself. Tucker walked past Ace over to his favorite tree. Ace bounded after him, following in his tracks and jumping around in circles. The puppy leapt up near Tucker's face; Tucker's sniffing nose smelled Ace's head, causing the puppy to roll over onto his back. After a few more sniffs, Tucker decided that this thing could stay. He shot his bottom into the air, front paws down on the ground. The universal dog language for "Let's play." Running together, Ace initially took the lead, looking back at Tucker as he ran, weaving his little body through Tucker's running legs.

The two dogs ran circles around the crabapple trees, by the pool, across the backyard, around Bryn, and around Megan.

"Ace and Tucker!" Megan squealed.

Tucker stopped to smell another tree. Bounding to the side, he nicked Ace's paw, dropping the puppy to the ground. But, Ace bounced up, no worse for the wear. When Tucker stopped to smell the air, Ace never took his eyes off him, like watching an elder statesman. Tucker's bottom shot up in the air again, and the two formed figure eights around a giggling, running Ethan.

"Wow. Tucker hasn't been that active in a long time," Bryn commented.

"See? What did I tell ya, babe? Ace is good for him! And, Boxers have one of the longest tongues of any dog," he boasted.

"Great," Bryn moaned. "Just great."

"Can Olaf come out too?" Megan asked.

"Nah, she's gotta stay inside," Julian said.

"Why?" Megan pleaded.

"Because. We wouldn't be able to find her in all this snow," Bryn quipped.

Julian looked at Bryn. "That's funny, babe!"

Taking in this moment and and appreciating the smiles and laughs, Bryn remembered the time she ran up to Tucker at the adopt-a-thon. Her resentment faded. A little.

Olaf observed this canine commotion from the kitchen window. Ace, noticing the interested feline, bound directly toward the window. She flinched, tail puffed out. Julian opened the door and placed Ace in front of a slow-walking, hesitant Olaf. The feline observed this little puppy jumping in tight, tiny circles, throwing his head back, and snorting through his flat nose. He darted under the kitchen table, flopping around, and returned to Olaf. He ran around the table, again returning to a less-puffy Olaf. Touching his nose to Olaf's, she recoiled, sitting upon her haunches, front paws extended. Wiggling his bottom, Ace jumped toward the cat. She rolled over on her back and tapped his head, as if saying: "I dub thee…"

With his moist nose in her belly, Olaf's back legs balled up around his face. They wrestled, Ace's tail wiggling as he scooted Olaf's back across the floor. She grabbed onto his neck, giving it a small nip. He yelped, and she released, racing into the living room. Ace followed her, but she stopped and rolled over onto her back, "dubbing" him again. On her back, Olaf splayed out her paws in a Y formation, and then sprang to her feet, sprinting into the other room. Tucker watched from the sideline, allowing these two youngsters to figure it out.

"Bill has asked me to dinner and the symphony tonight," Jacqueline told Ronni on the phone, staring at her packed walk-in bedroom closet.

"Oh, Jacquie! That's mag-nifi-cent!" Ronni rejoiced. "He's still single?"

"Apparently so," Jacqueline snickered. "We've met for coffee twice already, but I haven't done anything remotely like this in ages. What shall I wear?"

"Something you can pull off easily!" Ronni laughed.

"Ronni! Honestly."

"Jacquie, it's just dinner and the The Art Center. I mean, it's not as though he's inviting you to the Bahamas or anything. Is he?"

"No."

"Because, if he were, at least you wouldn't have to worry about what you wore!" Ronni laughed.

Jacqueline chuckled and put Ronni on speaker phone. Scanning her numerous shirts, skirts, and dresses from Neiman-Marcus, Talbots, and Nordstrom, Jacqueline asked, "Where does one begin?"

"Well, how about wearing that dress you wore for Edmond's retirement party? Bill wouldn't be able to keep his eyes off you!"

"You mean the—"

"—yeah, the dress that—"

"Yes! Now where did I put that?" Hangers slid along the clothes rod as Jacqueline shuffled blouses and dresses. Chloe walked into the bedroom to investigate all this unusual commotion.

"Ah, here it is," Jacqueline said, as she pulled the dress out of the far corner of the closet. She held it up to examine. "Yes, it really is lovely, isn't it?"

"Of course!" Ronni said, "You'll look stunning. Oh, be sure to wear those diamond earrings that—."

"—oh, yes, the ones that—?"

"Yeah, those."

"Now, where could they be hiding?" she asked, moving over to the dresser to rummage through her jewelry box.

Just as she located them, Jacqueline heard barking through the phone.

"Corky!" Ronni said, "Jacquie, so sorry....Corky is....Now you stop that right now! Corky! Jacquie, so sorry, but I need to take care of this. My apologies. Gotta scoot!"

"Thanks, Ronni," she said, fastening the back of the earrings.

"Have so much fun! And, be sure to tell me how it goes! Don't leave out a single detail."

"Certainly."

With her hands on her hips, Jacqueline sighed, looking at the Neiman Marcus v-neck, short-sleeved black dress spread out on the bed. Unzipping the dress, she stepped into it, pulled it up, and looked in the mirror. She turned to examine the small slit at the back hem. A smile emerged.

"It still fits," she said, sliding her hands down her sides and landing on her belly. "Just need to get rid of these ten pounds." In the mirror, Chloe's reflection was right behind hers, peeking around her knees.

Reaching behind to zip up the dress, Jacqueline struggled to reach the top. Bending her arms, her fingers slowly crept up her back. The tips of her fingers grazed the top of the zipper. No luck. Glancing over at the clock, her nervousness returned.

More determined, she twisted her arms back, with elbows in the air, even rubbing her back against the wall, hoping the zipper would catch. To no avail.

Taking a big sigh, she plopped down on the side of the bed. Chloe eased over to nudge her knee.

I guess not tonight. She patted Chloe's head, stood up and pulled the dress down past her hips, letting it fall around her feet. Walking over to the closet, she removed a long-sleeved white blouse, black sweater, and black slacks. She picked out a pair of black flats from her adjacent shoe closet, where the footwear lined up like soldiers. Comfortable, yet familiar, as many "Old Reliables" are.

She replaced her diamond earrings with pearls. Glancing down at her hands, she rolled her fingers over her wedding ring. Slowly sliding the ring off, she tucked it into her jewelry box next to her black pearls and diamond tennis bracelet.

Looking down at Chloe, she said, "Here we go."

After an enjoyable evening of dinner, symphony, and comfortable conversation, Bill pulled into Jacqueline's driveway, putting his BMW into park.

"Thank you again, Jacqueline, for a lovely evening."

Jacqueline saw Chloe peering through the front window with Lammikins gripped in her mouth. She paused. "Bill, would you like to come in for a nightcap?"

Bill smiled. "I'd love to." He followed her into the foyer where Chloe greeted them. The canine dropped her soggy Lammikins, sniffing the air around this new man.

"What a beautiful dog," Bill said.

"Why, thank you. This is my Chloe," Jacqueline said, patting Chloe's head. "Chloe, this is Bill." She didn't budge from Jacqueline's side, eyeing Bill without response. "Do you have any animals?" Jacqueline asked, filling the silence.

"Not at the moment. Growing up, I had dogs, and a few horses. Betty and I also had dogs when the kids were growing up. But, not a Cocker Spaniel. Mutts, mostly."

"Oh, she's been my rock since…. Well, she's been my rock."

"Hello, Chloe," Bill said, crouching down, slowly extending his hand for her to smell.

Chloe emitted a low growl. Quickly grabbing Lammikins in her teeth, she stood in front of Jacqueline in a perfect "sit."

Jacqueline snapped her head down. "Chloe! My word! I'm so sorry, Bill. That's not happened before."

"No worries. I said we had dogs. I didn't say all of them liked me!" he said, smiling.

Trying to change the subject, Jacqueline motioned to the living room, and asked, "How about that drink? What can I get for you?"

"A Manhattan would be great."

Behind the wet bar, Jacqueline prepared Bill's Manhattan and her gin and tonic. Making their way to the living room, Chloe and Lammikins remained directly under Jaqueline's heels.

"This is a beautiful room," Bill said. "You have some excellent landscape art. It seems you like realistic nature scenes as much as I do."

"Yes, thank you. Edmond and I both enjoyed collecting art, and supporting local artists, especially."

Noticing the fireplace mantle with family photographs and baseball memorabilia, Bill asked, "Is this a signed baseball from the 1984 Tigers team?"

"Yes, Eddy loved the Tigers. He was thrilled when they won the World Series that year."

"I'm sure he was," Bill said. "We all were!"

"Yes, he even participated in the...what is it called? Where you go, and you're with the team...?"

"The Fantasy Camp?" Bill said.

"Yes, that's it."

"Is that right? A couple of guys I worked with have talked about doing that. We're adding it to our 'Bucket List'."

Jacqueline smiled, motioning to the couch. Chloe laid down by Jacqueline's leg, keeping an eye on Bill at the other end.

"How about a toast?" he proposed. "To friendship."

Jacqueline smiled. "To friendship," she said, clinking their glasses. After about a half-hour of even more pleasant conversation about traveling, art, and children, Bill asked, "So, how are things going for you?"

"Well, a little better. Although some days are better than others," she said, glancing at Chloe sitting directly in front of her.

"I understand," Bill nodded.

"As was said by others in the group, I know it's hard. It's hard to see those your daughter hurt too. It's hard for everyone," Jacqueline continued.

"Yes," Bill nodded. "Seeing my children hurt is difficult." He paused. "Do you mind if I ask? Did you ever go back to the group after that first night?"

"No, did you?"

"Yes, once or twice. I'll tell you, though, it wasn't the same without you," Bill said.

Jacqueline blushed. The gin and tonic helped. "The moments that still get to me are when I notice others wince or glance away when I mention Eddy's name. As if saying 'Edmond' will somehow reduce me to tears. I'm not sure they truly realize he's always in the forefront of my mind. Even three and a half years later."

Bill nodded.

"I understand people are trying to be helpful. But, it seems as though those who do talk about him are often trying to console themselves. It rarely provides me comfort," she angrily continued. Chloe stood up and rested her head on Jacqueline's knee.

"Yes," he said, rubbing his fingers over his glass. "For me, with Betty, I often heard, 'She's in a better place' or 'Everything happens for a reason.' But, I found the platitudes quite unhelpful. I am slowly realizing they are said with the best of intentions. Slowly."

"They never tell you that when you lose a spouse, the losses extend past the physical death of the person," Jacqueline added.

"Yes, the tendrils of death seep into other areas of your life and strangle them too. It can be very difficult to find one's footing," Bill said. "I even had a well-meaning buddy say, 'I went through a divorce, so I understand.' But, it's not the same. No one chose to leave. Betty died. I certainly did not choose this."

Petting Chloe's soft head, Jacqueline shared, "Yes, Eddy and I were just starting our retired life together. We were gathering ideas to build a house Up North when…" Jacqueline stopped petting Chloe and cleared her throat.

"Perhaps we should go back to wearing black mourning arm bands, as they did in the Victorian era," Bill joked. "At least then we wouldn't have to explain anything."

"Well, it's getting late," Jacqueline said, abruptly. Standing up from the couch, she smoothed her hands down her thighs.

Bill glanced down at his watch and said, "Yes. I probably do need to think about heading home."

Chloe followed right behind Jacqueline and Bill as they walked to the foyer, keeping her body wedged between their feet.

"Thank you, Jacqueline, for the wonderful evening and company," he said, standing at the door.

"Thank you," she smiled up at him.

Leaning over, he kissed her gently on the cheek.

"Have a good night. We'll talk soon," he said, with one hand on the doorknob.

"Yes, have a good night," she said, holding onto Chloe's collar.

She shut the door behind him, smiling and gently touching her cheek.

"Well, Chloe-girl? We did it." Jacqueline exhaled and walked back to the living room. With Chloe on her heels, Jacqueline's eyes landed on her wedding picture on the mantle. A picture Bill had not mentioned.

Two days later, while Jacqueline prepared Chloe's dinner, the phone rang.

"Hi, Bill. How are you this evening?" Jacqueline asked, placing the bowl in front of an eager Chloe.

"Hi, Jacqueline. Would you be interested in going to see *Fiddler on the Roof* at The Center Friday night?"

Jacqueline paused. "Um, I'm sorry, Bill. I don't think that's going to work."

"Well, perhaps another time then."

"I mean, well, I just don't think it's going to work out," she repeated, covering her eyes with her hand.

"You mean Friday night?" he asked, puzzled.

"Well, yes and also…."

"Oh, I see."

"I'm so sorry, Bill. I thought I was ready. I really did." Jacqueline shifted her weight and leaned against the kitchen counter. Chloe slurped, unaware of the difficult conversation occurring above her. "I didn't mean to mislead you in any way," she continued. "I do hope you can forgive me."

"I'm very sorry to hear this," Bill said. "But, I do understand. You are a lovely woman, Jacqueline, and I've enjoyed your company."

"Thank you."

"Well, please give me a ring if you feel like getting together again. Even just for coffee. You have my number."

"Thank you. I will do that. Again, I am sorry," Jacqueline looked down at Chloe, who had stopped eating and gazed at her quizzically.

"Yes. Me too. Take care, Jacqueline," Bill said.

"You too. Goodbye, Bill." She pressed the button to end the call, setting the phone on the counter. With Chloe as her shadow, she walked back to her bedroom. Standing in front of her jewelry box, she slowly slid her wedding ring back onto her finger. Looking into the mirror, she thought, *Am I truly alone now? Will anyone ever think I'm beautiful again? Jacquie, pull yourself together.* Kneeling down next to Chloe, she wrapped her arms around her furry rock.

Finishing some of her leftovers from Christmas dinner, Nivie grabbed some frozen blueberries from the freezer as part of her dessert. One of them tumbled onto the floor.

"Grrr...Really?"

Sherlock trotted over to inspect this new thing when Nivie yelled, "Locky, stay away from that!"

But rather than leaving, Sherlock lightly touched the side of the blueberry, watching it roll across the floor. As Nivie poured the rest of the blueberries in a bowl, she became enthralled when he continued to bat at the blueberry, jumping around, twisting his body in the air, and falling back to a standing position. He was engrossed. As was she.

Nivie decided to join him in his game. Picking up the blueberry, she held it in front of him and said, "Hey, Locky!" His eyes immediately locked onto it.

"Go get it!" she said, tossing it across the kitchen. He leapt up, racing after it, twisting his body again, swatting it along the way.

Nivie walked over to him, rubbed the top of his head, and picked up the blueberry again. His eyes never left the piece of fruit, which had begun to lose its round shape.

"Go get it," she said, tossing it down the hallway to the front door.

Sherlock gallivanted down the hallway but missed it, almost running head-first into the front door.

Nivie laughed. She was surprised by her own reaction. It had been a while.

As Nivie walked back down the hallway toward the front door, Sherlock ran in the other direction into the living room. She inspected the remnants of the blueberry, which now consisted of a warped, cracked skin with some insides smeared on the floor.

"That's OK, Locky! No problem. No problem." She grabbed the demolished blueberry and threw all of its innards in the trash. Running to the freezer, she snatched a handful more.

Nivie knelt down in the kitchen facing the hallway. She flung a new blueberry down the hallway with no cats in sight. Sherlock shot out of the adjacent dining room, running past Nivie's field of vision and into the living room, out of sight again.

Nivie walked toward the front door where the blueberry rested.

Curious about all the hullabaloo, Watson padded over to the hallway, as Sherlock again ran past the dented blueberry.

"Come on, Watty Watson!" Nivie exclaimed. "Join us!"

Nivie tossed a new blueberry toward the kitchen. Watson joined Sherlock in the pursuit, causing a small collision.

Nivie laughed so hard she snorted.

Sherlock licked his neck, creating an unnatural upward tilt of his head. Watson quickly shook his head, locating the contorted blueberry. He patted it with his paw, pushing it under the kitchen table.

"Good boy, Lotsa Watty Watson!" Nivie said. He rubbed up against Nivie's leg in agreement.

"Alright boys," she said. Both cats concentrated intently on the fruit she held.

"Go get it!" she exclaimed, lobbing it toward the front door.

Both cats galloped down the hallway with a thunderous echo.

Nivie laughed even harder. *It can't be this easy!*

She walked toward them, and, in a flurry, they disappeared into opposite rooms. Taking another blueberry from her hand, she chucked it toward the kitchen table.

Watson sprinted after it, while Sherlock remained in a crouching position, hugging the side of the wall.

"Oh, Locky. What's the matter? Did Lotsa Watty Watson take over your game? Well, we can share."

Nivie was pleased that she found something that brought Watson out of his shell, especially this close to the front door and doorbell.

When Alex arrived home from work, Nivie jumped up in excitement.

"Honey, check this out!" she exclaimed.

"OK. Look, Locky!" Sherlock trotted after Nivie with a blueberry in her hand. "Go get it!" she said, throwing the blueberry down the hall toward the front door. Sherlock tore after the bouncing berry, frantically swatting at it. Nivie ran to the front door, lobbing it back toward the kitchen again.

Alex laughed and added, "Maybe it would be better if I stood by the front door, and you just stay in the kitchen."

"Yeah! That's much easier!"

Alex smiled, happy to see some joy in his wife again.

Watson returned from the dining room and sat down. Licking his back, he snapped his head around to follow the motion of the fruit down the hallway.

Once Sherlock ran past him, Watson crouched down, his side touching the wall. Facing away from Nivie, he waited, back twitching in anticipation. When a blueberry flew by his head, he shot off toward it, watching it land and batting it away from the front door.

A different blueberry rolled down the hallway back and forth a few more times. Sherlock watched from the sidelines as Watson took over chasing the little blue sphere. After his time was done, Watson signaled that he was getting bored by rubbing his puffy tail against the wall. He sat down, simply observing the blueberry fly from Nivie to Alex and back again.

"You do realize," Alex pointed out, "it's just us throwing a piece of maimed fruit down the hallway to each other."

Nivie laughed. "Yeah, I guess the famous Blueberry Time is over."

Watson followed Sherlock into the living room. Using his front paw, Sherlock groomed his face, while Watson plunked down on his side. Indeed, Blueberry Time was over. For now.

The two dogs and one cat had finally arrived at a truce, deciding to live harmoniously under one roof. The hissing, batting, jumping, squealing, and chasing had finally subsided. It narrowed down to an occasional tussle between Olaf and Ace, while Tucker watched the two young ones burn off their energy.

Brushing Tucker had become one of Megan's favorite things. She went to the drawer and approached a sleeping Tucker in the living room. She enjoyed running the comb through his long fur, and he gladly obliged her. However, he was coughing more than usual, ending their brushing session earlier than Megan hoped. He stood up and walked into the other room. Megan said, "Mommy, Tucker's really coughing. And, he's limping," she reenacted for Bryn.

"Oh, Meggie," she said. "You know, he's still getting over his injury. And, he's getting older."

Bryn's heart fell when she realized it was his other leg.

Returning from carpool the next day, Bryn found the three furry ones sleeping in a mound together. Tucker was on his side, while Ace was curled up on Tucker's back, front paw over his older brother's neck. Olaf found warmth snuggled in his usual place: in Tucker's fluffy neck fur. Bryn hated to disrupt these siblings, but Dr. Carmichael's office awaited.

Once they arrived, Bryn and Tucker were led to an examining room. A minute later, and after a quick knock on the door, Dr. Carmichael entered. "Hi, Bryn." Bending down, she petted Tucker's head and asked, "So, what's going on, Mr. Tucker?" He licked her face as she pulled out her stethoscope. "Thanks. Such a sweetie." After listening for a moment, she said, "Breathing's a little labored." Feeling Tucker's back left leg, the dog flinched. "Yeah, that's a little tender. With the limping you told Kelly, the receptionist, I'd like to take x-rays." She examined his eyes, nose, and ears.

"What do you think it is?" Bryn asked.

"Well, could be a few things. But, bloodwork and x-rays will give us more information." Dr. Carmichael attached Tucker's leash to his collar and took him back.

After giving Tucker a kiss, Bryn waited in the examining room, happy the kids were in school.

A half-hour later, Dr. Carmichael and Tucker returned to the room. Her countenance had changed.

"Well, we have our results," she said. "I'm very sorry to say. It looks as though Tucker has Osteosarcoma."

Bryn shook her head. "What is that?"

"Bone cancer."

Bryn slowly closed her eyes.

"We could do a bone biopsy, just to make sure, but based on his symptoms and the X-ray results, we are confident of this diagnosis. I'm so sorry."

"So, what does that mean? Like, radiation and chemo?"

"Well, there are few options: chemo is one of them. But, removing the leg and chemo are more standard."

"OK...." Bryn said, struggling to take it all in.

"But, I must tell you, most dogs, even with this treatment, usually live maybe another year. Without either of those it's usually only a few months."

"Oh, my gosh," Bryn's voice cracked.

"And, with Tucker's age, it puts him at a disadvantage."

Bryn looked down at Tucker's big, brown eyes staring back up at her and crouched down next to him.

"Discuss it with your family. If you decide not to amputate and skip chemo, we can give you something to help relieve his discomfort. But, you'll need to keep an eye on him for any progression of symptoms. If, actually when, the symptoms get worse, we'll have to think about making some hard choices." Dr. Carmichael leaned down and hugged Tucker. "I'm so sorry, Bryn."

Bryn sighed. Through a slight pant, Tucker's face relaxed when she massaged his velvety ears.

Alex grabbed two beers from the fridge in preparation for the Kitten Bowl. As Nivie poured chips and dip into bowls, she asked, "Is it wrong that I can't get the theme song from *I Dream of Jeannie* out of my head?"

"Um, yeah," Alex smiled. "It is."

"I mean, really. Me! Having a theme song of a repressed woman as an earworm. 'Yes, Master.' Give me a break!"

Alex smiled, walked over to her and wrapped his arms around her. "It wouldn't be all that bad."

"Yeah, you wish!" Nivie smiled, nudging him with her side.

"All right boys. Time to watch your cousins play on TV again," Alex said, watching them watch their humans.

"We know Lotsa Watty Watson loves it. C'mon Locky, get in on the fun this year!" Nivie said. "But first, I've gotta empty what's full so I can fill what's empty!" Nivie said, making her way to the bathroom.

When she returned, Alex said, "Your phone went off."

Nivie found her phone on the counter. "Oh, awesome. It's Bryn!"

"Who's 'Bryn'?" Alex asked.

"She's someone I keep running into at the pet store. Like a million times now. And, I've taken some kitty things over to her house for her. She has two dogs, too and her mom is one of Aunt Ronni's best friends. Oh! And, she has these two little kids, Megan and Ethan. So, so cute."

"That's cool," Alex said, taking a swig of his beer.

"Yeah, so we kept saying we need to get together again. So cool she actually did it!" Nivie said. Dialing Bryn's number, she said, "Hey, so glad you called! What's up?"

"Hi, Nivie," Bryn answered. "We're doing well. We were wondering. Well…we were wondering if…"

"Spit it out!"

"We were wondering if Meggie could watch the Kitten Bowl with you."

Nivie laughed. "Of course! You know we'll be watching. We'd love to have her here. I've given you directions to my house before, right?"

"Yes, thanks. We'll be right over. Thanks, Nivie."

"Don't mention it."

"There she is!" Nivie said, opening her front door. "C'mon in, Megan. We've been waiting for ya. Hi, Bryn!"

"Thanks again, Niv."

"How are you, Meggie? Excited?" Nivie asked, standing in the foyer.

"Yeah! I wanted to see Kitten Bowl, but Daddy wanted Super Bowl football. I wanted kittens everywhere!" she said, opening her arms.

"Hi, I'm Alex. Nice to meet you," Alex said, walking in from the living room.

"Bryn Troxell, nice to see you." Bryn extended her hand.

"Megan, this is my husband. Mr. Emerson."

Megan stood next to Bryn, looking up at Alex with her chin tilted down.

"What do you say, Meggie?" Bryn asked.

"Nice to see you, Mr. Emerson. Thank you for watching Kitten Bowl."

Alex laughed. "No problem. I understand you have a kitten."

"Yes, Olaf."

"Well, we have two, Sherlock and Watson. Let's go see if we can find them," Alex said. "Nice to meet you, Bryn."

"Thanks, you too."

"Bye, Mommy!" Megan hugged her mother good-bye.

"Bye, Meggie," Bryn said, turning to Nivie standing in the foyer. "Thanks, Niv. I really appreciate it."

"You OK?" Nivie asked.

"Yeah. Just tired."

"Yeah, I get that. Well, we'll let you know when it's over," Nivie said.

"Thanks again, Nivie." Nivie shut the door behind her and walked back into the living room. She joined Alex and Megan, who were watching the screen.

"That's my favorite!" Megan said, pointing to a tiny black and white kitten.

"Who's that?" Nivie asked.

"I don't know, but she's my favorite!" Megan said.

Nivie and Alex chuckled. Watson returned to join the humans and his feline brother in the living room. Megan sat on the couch next to Nivie and Alex, as they announced the kitten antics. Nivie shared various pieces of cat trivia and Megan topped off the afternoon by sharing her "Kitty Dance" for Nivie and Alex. The movements consisted of starting on all fours, then leaping up and spinning around. Laughter ensued.

"I need to go to the bathroom," Megan said, shifting her weight.

"Sure, c'mere," Nivie said, taking Megan's hand and leading her to the powder room. "Just come on out when you're done."

"OK, Mrs. Emerson."

Nivie walked back to the living room and sat down next to Alex.

"We would have been good parents," he said.

"Yeah, and she would have been a great daughter."

Megan emerged from the bathroom. "Hands washed?" Nivie asked. Megan showed Nivie flatted palms.

"Great, c'mere!" Nivie said, walking over to the freezer. She grabbed a handful of frozen blueberries. "You're going to love this!"

Although Bryn had attended college a few hours away from Woodhaven Run, her alumni board decided to have their mid-March Spring Fling dinner and dance in The Stadium's special event room. Calling it a "Spring Fling" in Michigan was optimistic, but it was the The Stadium's only available date before June. Bryn was one of the main organizers of the fete, a repeat of duties from college because organizing events was one of her pleasures. And holding the event there was even more important, since she had loved attending games with her father there.

Talking to her friend Lauren on the phone, Bryn said, "It's only a few more days until the big event, Laur."

"It's one night," Lauren reassured. "You'll go out, come back. Should be fine."

"But, Laur, Julian will be out of town. And, Tucker's really not doing well now."

"So, so, sorry, Bryn. So much for you to juggle right now."

"Yeah, so I went ahead and actually made *the* appointment with Dr. Carmichael for the day after the Spring Fling. Really didn't want to have to make that decision, but really needed to at this point."

"Oh, man. I didn't know it was that bad. Is the vet coming to the house?" Lauren asked.

"No. That would be too weird. We're going there."

"Have you told the kids yet?"

"No. They don't need to know," Bryn said. "They know he's been sick and is moving slower. But, they're so excited about the school carnival the same night as Spring Fling. One thing at a time."

"I guess. Does Julian know?"

"Yeah, he does. But, he made it clear before he left that he didn't want to do it. So that 'fun task' was delegated to me."

"Geez, Bryn. So sorry. Poor Tucker. I know it's hard. But, try to focus on Friday night. You've organized a great party. I wish I had a fraction of your ability to do that. But, you do need to take a break," Lauren asserted.

Bryn nodded. "I do, but I don't see one coming any time soon."

"Then, you definitely need to have fun," Lauren said. "We're driving up to Woodhaven Run for Spring Fling, but then we have to go back home that night. Visiting the in-laws early the next morning."

"Boo," Bryn said. "Well, at least you can make it. Wouldn't be the same without you."

"Thanks! How much fun is it going to be to see everyone again? Can't believe it's been ten years!"

After all the planning, Bryn felt her excitement grow as she put the finishing touches to her hair. Megan and Ethan were ready to stay overnight at Madeline's house, their backpacks packed. Although Megan was fascinated by Madeline's new cockatiel, Fred, "Fred Time" would need to wait. Tonight was all about the school carnival. Bryn told Allison, Madeline's mother, about Tucker's declining condition when they made sleepover plans the week before. She also told Allison about Tucker's appointment the next day, stressing that the kids didn't know about it.

"You look great. I love your updo and dress! That deep blue looks great on you!" Allison said, as Bryn dropped off the kids.

"Oh, thanks," Bryn said, touching the top of her head.

"Have a great time tonight."

"I might text you. You know, to see how they're doing."

"Text as many times as you need. We will see you tomorrow morning. Just have a wonderful time!" Allison said, waving goodbye.

At the Spring Fling, Bryn delighted in seeing her college friends— Mark and Jen, Sara and Andy, Christine and Scott, Brian, Jennifer, Lori, and Jessica. It was as though no time had passed. They laughed about the time they had too much to drink and ended up sleeping in the wrong dorm, about coming back from an away game when the bus broke down and singing at the top of their lungs until it was fixed, about the snowball fights in shorts, about going to the leadership conference and writing their speeches the night before, about pushing each other into the pond and taking a test in wet clothes. Bryn's face hurt from laughing; however, her feet simply hurt. Not only was she wearing heels, a footwear choice she hadn't made in years, but she also danced to songs she hadn't heard in years.

Despite her exhaustion after Spring Fling, Bryn felt more alive on the drive home than she had in years. Although she hadn't imbibed too much, staying up past 2:00AM was not a usual occurrence. However, when she pulled into her driveway, her mood changed, knowing what awaited her.

With her heart racing, she opened the door to the mudroom.

Tucker's eyes opened and he struggled to lift his head. His tail thumped on the ground in a puddle of urine.

"Oh, Tucker. Sweetie." She bent down and he gently licked her hand. "Oh, I know. I know."

She stroked the top of his head, rubbing his soft ears between her fingers again. His head plopped back down and his eyes gently blinked as she pet him.

"Oh, Tucker. My sweetie."

Hiking up her gown, she cleaned up his wet tail and back legs, as well as the floor underneath.

"Good night, Tucker. See you in the morning. Unfortunately, tomorrow's a big day." Holding her heels in her hand, she quietly shut the door, trying to leave before Tucker struggled to lift his head again.

The howling and whimpering from downstairs awakened a deep-sleeping Bryn. She yawned, licked her lips, and cleared her throat. The time said 8:06AM.

Suddenly remembering the day's activities, Bryn jolted awake. Dashing out of bed, she sprinted down the hallway and down the steps. Turning the corner, she saw Olaf running away from the mud room, and Ace scratching and howling at the closed door.

"Acey, let me get in here," Bryn said, gently nudging him to the side.

Opening the door, she saw Tucker, lying on his side.

He was gone.

Cupping her hand over her mouth, she quickly shut the door.

"Oh, no. Oh, Tucker. My poor Tucker. So, so, sorry, sweetie." The urine stench that had filled the room made its way to her nose. She coughed a few times.

Olaf returned to investigate. Both she and Ace paced back and forth in front of the door. Ace pawed at the door, still whimpering. Bryn took him by the collar and pulled him into the basement. Olaf rand and hid under the couch in an attempt to avoid the turmoil.

For a second, Bryn was discombobulated before she switched into high gear. She texted Lauren: "Tucker passed away last night. Knew shouldn't have waited."

Almost immediately, Lauren responded. "So sorry!!!!!!!!! ☹ ☹ U OK? Should have stayed in WHR last night."

Bryn answered: "Kids still at Madeline's house. Guess gotta do this."

Lauren replied: "I'm sure Allison can keep kids longer. Don't forget 2 call the vet."

Bryn was grateful for the reminder.

"Let me know if you need anything, Bryn. Keep me posted. Love you. (((((Hugs)))))"

From the basement, Ace's whimpering served as background noise. Bryn shuffled through the layers of Ethan and Megan's works of art on the fridge for Dr. Carmiachel's number. After dialing, she realized she could have used Siri.

"Good morning, Carmichael Clinic. This is Kelly. How may I help you?" a cheery voice answered.

"Um, yes. This is Bryn Troxell. We had an appointment for Tucker today for...for....."

"Yes, Mrs. Troxell," Kelly gently said.

"Well, unfortunately, he didn't make it through the night," Bryn's voice cracked.

"Oh, I am so, so sorry."

Bryn cleared her throat. "Thank you. I'm just concerned about my children. They weren't here because they stayed overnight at a friend's house. And...well, don't want them to see him like this. And, um...he relieved himself, and there is a very strong smell."

"Yes, sometimes that can happen," Kelly consoled.

"Oh, OK. I wasn't sure. Just wasn't expecting that," she said. "Wasn't expecting any of this."

"So sorry, but I have to ask: would you like to bury or cremate Tucker?"

Bryn thought a second. "Well, I think I'll bury him before my kids come back. I don't want this to be their last memory of him."

"OK. Well, thanks for calling. And I will tell Dr. Carmichael. Let us know if there is anything we can do to help."

"OK. Thank you," Bryn hurried.

Staring off into the distance for a second, Bryn tried to harness her whirling thoughts. She texted Allison, telling her what happened, asking if it would be OK if she kept the kids a little longer. Allison generously agreed by text and asked if there was anything she could do.

Bryn called Julian; no answer. She didn't leave a voicemail message, but texted: "Tucker didn't make it through the night. Passed away in the house. Very sad. Going to bury him in backyard now. Don't want the kids to see him like this."

Almost immediately, Julian texted back, "That sucks, babe. How are the kids? In meeting now. I'll be home in a few days."

Bryn answered: "The kids are still at Madeline's house. I'll get them when I'm done."

"Thanks, babe. Things are going well here."

Bryn ran to the garage and found a large black garbage bag. She also located some garden gloves and a mask to cover her nose and mouth. Pulling out the kid's wagon, she grabbed a shovel, knocking over some toys and a garden hoe.

With the mask and gloves on and a garbage bag in hand, Bryn returned inside the house. Holding her breath, she slowly opened the mudroom door. The depth of her sadness mirrored the stench in the room. She stared at Tucker's body and tears formed.

"Oh, Tucker. Sweetie," she said, closing the door behind her. Removing the mask, she kneeled down. The smell overtook her for a minute; she coughed harder and put the mask back on. Walking over to the window, she opened it in an attempt to circulate the air. For a split-second, she secretly hoped her coughing would rouse Tucker, causing his big tail to thump again. She bent down and placed her ear directly above his chest. Her stomach fell. His chest remained still.

Gently lifting his tail, she cleaned up the urine puddle on the floor. Unhooking his collar, she set it on the shelf behind some coats. Kneeling back down, she opened the garbage bag, placed it underneath his back legs, and pulled it up over his back. Tucker's body had started to stiffen, ironically making this process easier. She tucked his front legs in and brought it over his reddish-brown chest. Peering into Tucker's open big brown eyes, Bryn took one last mental picture of his face. She had to look away as she closed the bag on her beloved companion.

She opened the mudroom door into the kitchen. Olaf sprinted away from the intimidating sight of Bryn dragging the black bag behind her. Trying to ignore Ace's unrelenting whimpering and barking from the basement, Bryn lugged the heavy bag through the kitchen and into the garage, hoisting it onto the wagon. The squeaky front wheel emitted a strangely soothing rhythm rolling into the backyard. Even though the mild winter had allowed the ground to be more forgiving, for almost an hour, she repeatedly stabbed at the dirt to create a large enough hole for Tucker's body—one that reflected the hole in her heart. Beads of sweat formed. With all her might, she lifted the bag, setting her beloved Tucker in the ground. Replacing the dirt as quickly as she could, she patted it down with the other side of the shovel.

Bryan scanned the backyard for some sort of marker. A small rock nearby would have to suffice.

"Bye, my Tucker, sweetie," she whispered, wiping her brow.

Walking into the kitchen to text Allison, she saw a text:

"I'm so sorry to hear about sweet Tucker. He was such a good boy and well-loved by all of you. Take care, Dr. Carmichael and everyone at Carmichael Clinic."

Bryn choked up, texting back: "Thank you for being so good to him."

With shaking arms and legs, Bryn finished cleaning up the

mudroom and staggered upstairs. She took a quick shower and finished getting ready. In the car ride to Madeline's house, she exclaimed, "Oh, no! Ace!" when she remembered he was still in the basement.

Bryn hurried to Allison's front door, noticing a few flecks of residual dirt still beneath her fingernails.

Allison opened her front door, whispering, "So sorry, Bryn."

"It's OK. Thanks again for keeping the—"

"Mommeeee!" Ethan ran to Bryn, throwing his arms around her legs. Megan and Madeline held hands, skipping behind.

Bryn cleared her throat. "Hey, guys. Did you have fun?"

"Yeah, we got to go to the cake walk! And play the ducky game! Mommy, I almost won," Megan added.

"Oh, that's great," Bryn said, looking up at Allison.

"What wong, Mommy?" Ethan asked.

"Oh, nothing, bud." Bryn looked at Megan and Ethan. "Have everything?"

"Yes," they answered.

"OK. Did you thank Mrs. Waters?"

"Thank you!"

"Thanks again," Bryn mouthed to Allison.

"You're welcome. Please let me know if I can help."

On the drive home, the endless talk of the school carnival and Fred the cockatiel ricocheted off of Bryn's consciousness. Her occasional nods and smiles kept the non-stop talking going. That's what she wanted.

"Tucko!" Ethan said, running to the mudroom.

"Oh, bud. Wait!" Bryn yelled.

Hearing Ace's barking from the basement, Ethan turned and asked, "Why Ace down dere?"

"Oh, Mommy forgot. Please let him out." Ethan ran over and opened the door to find Ace standing at the top of the steps, holding Tucker's squeaky Teddy toy in his mouth.

Megan ran over to the mudroom and reached for the knob.

"Meggie!" Bryn yelled after her. "C'mere. You, too, bud."

Bryn gently took them by the hands and walked them over to the couch.

Taking a deep breath, she said, "Now, I need to tell you kids about Tucker. He passed away last night."

"'Passed away'?" Megan asked.

"I mean, God took Tucker to live with him last night."

Megan wrinkled her face. "Why did God take Tucker?" she asked.

"Tucko bad?" Ethan asked.

Bryn sighed. "No. No, he wasn't bad. You know that Tucker was sick. And so, now God's taking care of him."

"You mean—?" Megan ran to the mudroom, tears forming.

"Meggie!" Bryn yelled after her.

Megan opened the door to an empty room, cold from the still open window.

"Where's Tucker?" she cried out. Ethan ran over to her.

Bryn followed them and shut the door. "C'mon, guys. Tucker's not here anymore. Mommy buried him, but he's with God in Heaven."

"Buried him? Where is he?" Megan asked, sobbing.

"In the backyard."

"Wanna see," Ethan said, running to the door.

Bryn herded him back to a motionless Megan and said, "We don't have time now. Mommy picked you up later than we planned. But, let's be happy that Tucker is not hurting anymore." She hugged Megan and Ethan, wiping Megan's tears. "OK?"

"Want to see Tucko," Ethan declared.

"Maybe later, bud," Bryn said.

"Yeah, I wanna see him too," Megan said.

"Later. OK?" Bryn firmly repeated. "We don't have time right now. We need to get Meggie to her dance rehearsal."

"Wanna put on my Supaman suit," Ethan mumbled.

Bryn shook her head, surprised. "Um, sure, bud. Absolutely. And, you know what? You can even wear it tonight for your jammies."

"Thanks, Mommy," he said, trudging up to his room, tears in his eyes.

"Now," Bryn said, looking down at Megan, "I know it's hard, but we've got to get going in a little bit, and we're bringing the treat. Don't forget, we need to make cookies for your school party next week. Easter is so early this year."

Megan's bottom lip still protruded.

"So, let's wash our hands and get working on these treats," Bryn added. "C'mon, we need to get moving."

"OK," Megan said, slowly turning with her head down.

The day after Tucker left the earth, Jacqueline took Chloe on a morning walk. As many times before, she heard a cacophony of barking before actually seeing anyone.

"Good morning, Jacqueline, dear," Gladys greeted, turning the corner. "How are you this fine morning?"

"Oh, we're doing fine, Ms. Paisley," she said.

Gladys furrowed her brow. "Is that right? Could have fooled me," she said, over Piper and Petey's barking.

"I apologize if I seem a little preoccupied." Jacqueline paused, then said, "Bryn's dog Tucker passed away yesterday."

"Oh, dear," Gladys said, covering her mouth with her hand.

"Yes, so I've been thinking a lot about her and the kids."

"Oh, no. Oh, no. I'm so sorry to hear this," Gladys said.

"Thank you."

"How are Bryn and the children doing?"

"I think they are hanging in there," Jacqueline said, leaning down to pet Chloe, who was pulling on the leash. "It's hard to see your children hurt."

"I imagine it would be. And, it's always painful to lose a beloved. Tucker was a very, very special boy," Gladys said, as her voice cracked.

Jacqueline nodded.

"Please give my most sincere condolences to Bryn and the children," Gladys said, taking Jacqueline's hands, slightly shaking them. "Again, I'm just so very sorry."

"Thank you, Ms. Paisley, for your concern. I will pass on your sentiments to them."

"Thank you, Jacqueline, dear," Gladys sighed, and gently tugged on Roosevelt's leash. Jacqueline turned around and watched Gladys walk down the sidewalk, at a slower pace, with her head hanging lower than before.

A few days later, Bryn swung by Jacqueline's to pick up the kids after finishing some errands. Time with Grandma Stanton included watching another of their favorite shows, *Spongebob Squarepants,* a treat not allowed at home. More special at Grandma's, their fixed eyes stared at the flat screen television.

With only a few more minutes of the show remaining, Jacqueline gently touched Bryn's elbow and motioned to her in the foyer.

"I know it's been hard without Tucker, Brynnie. So sorry," Jacqueline said, leaning in and giving her daughter a hug.

"Thanks, Mom. It is hard. But, at least he's not in pain anymore."

"That's true, but it still can be difficult."

"Yes. Even though I know you weren't a big fan of his," Bryn pointed out.

Jacqueline gulped. "Well, he was a wonderful dog for your family. And, he really loved you."

Bryn felt her throat tighten.

"Here, I wanted to give you a couple things." Jacqueline said, gently tapping her daughter's hand.

"OK?" Bryn questioned.

She handed Bryn two envelopes.

"What's this?"

"Just open them," Jacqueline said.

Bryn opened the first envelope. On the front was a picture of a dog inside of a heart. It read: "No longer by my side, but always in my heart." Opening the card, Bryn read, "I'm so sorry to hear about Tucker, dear. Please accept my condolences. Fondly, Mrs. Gladys Paisley."

Bryn's tears began to fall.

"She stopped by earlier and wanted to be sure I gave it to you."

"Oh, my goodness," Bryn said, wiping a tear. "Please thank her for me, when you see her."

"And, now, open the second card," Jacqueline said.

On the front was a heart with paw prints running through it. Bryn read: "With deepest sympathies for the loss of your beloved dog. Remember that the special bond will always live in your heart." On the inside of the card was handwritten: "I'm so sorry about Tucker, Brynnie. Love, Mom."

Bryn swallowed.

"I know it's been hard. And, I had no idea they had pet sympathy cards. I hadn't any idea such a thing existed. That is, until Ms. Paisley told me."

"Wow," Bryn said, exhaling and wiping her eyes.

"One more thing. I wanted to give you this," Jacqueline said, reaching into the foyer table's drawer.

Bryn focused her eyes on a framed 5 x 7 picture of her as a six-year-old sleeping on the floor of their home. Her head was resting on the belly of a sleeping reddish-brown Golden Retriever.

"Taffy! Oh my gosh," she gasped. "Where did you find this?"

"It was buried," Jacqueline answered.

"I cannot believe this. Taffy! What a good girl."

Looking up at Jacqueline, Bryn said, "Thank you, Mom."

"You know, your father and I got her for you right before the big flood in 1986. Remember?"

"Yeah, I remember," Bryn said quietly, without taking her eyes off the picture.

"He wanted you to have the puppy, since you asked incessantly for one. And, since we knew you were going to be an only child at that point, we thought that you really did need a pal. That's when we went out and got Taffy from a breeder. You named her that after your favorite candy." Jacqueline chuckled. "Whenever you'd eat taffy, you'd stretch it so far apart with your little hands that the droop in the middle would touch the ground. You'd try to catch it with your mouth, but it would fall, nonetheless."

"We had so much fun together," Bryn said, gently outlining Taffy's ears with her finger. The memory of their softness returned. "Wow, all the times we'd play in the backyard. And, she'd even let me put bows in her hair and dress her up."

"I wasn't sure if you would still remember her, or if it would just be too painful to see the photo, given everything that's happened in the past few days."

"I can still remember her fur, and the way her tail would stand up and 'Poof,'" Bryn made a noise, her fingers splaying apart. "What a good girl," she repeated, slowly rubbing the side of the frame.

"Yes, you two were nearly inseparable."

"I just can't believe you still had this," Bryn repeated.

"I also wanted to say, I'm sorry about the way things ended with her. Your father and I thought it best to take care of Taffy while you were at college. She was slowing down, and then got sicker. It just wasn't fair to her."

"I know, Mom. I was upset before. But, not really much now." Bryn, still looking down at the picture, added, "Even though it was during finals."

"That's precisely why we didn't tell you right away, Brynnie. Don't you remember? You had had such a difficult semester, with an extremely heavy academic load. We wanted you to focus your attention on your studies," Jacqueline reminded her.

"Yeah, but—" Bryn looked up. "I only found out because I came home for Christmas. I mean—At Christmas. There was no way you could have told me sooner? I didn't even get a chance to say goodbye."

"But, again, Brynnie, she was very old and very sick. You wouldn't have wanted to remember her that way. Well, anyway, your father and I just thought—" Jacqueline looked down, tightening the side of her mouth. "Well, I'm truly sorry."

"It's OK," Bryn quickly waved her off. "It was really hard before, but it's been like what, ten, eleven years now?" Bryn's voice cracked, in an effort to convince herself.

"Anyway, I never really understood your relationship with Taffy until I found this along with it," Jacqueline said, presenting Bryn with another framed photograph.

"Who's this?"

Taking in a deep breath, Jacqueline said, "That's me."

"That's you?" Bryn responded incredulously.

"Yes. With my Ranger."

"You had a horse? Grandma and Grandpa actually let you have a horse?"

After Jacqueline recounted the story of Ranger and his demise, Bryn began to tear up. "Oh my gosh, Mom. That must have been so hard for you." Bryn's head cocked to the side. "Oh, so that's why I never got to go horseback riding—"

Jacqueline nodded. "Anyway, just wanted you to have Taffy's picture."

Bryn looked into her mother's eyes. They both saw pain, rivaled only by their shared grief at losing Edmond. Bryn leaned in and hugged her mother, then slightly pushed her back. The silence between them was thick with awkwardness, yet understanding.

Jacqueline gently set the picture of her and Ranger down on an entry-way table when Ethan ran into the foyer.

"Mommeee! What's that?" he said, grabbing and pulling the side of Taffy's frame so hard Bryn almost dropped the picture.

"Careful, bud. That's Mommy's dog she had when she was little," Bryn said, setting it down next to Ranger's picture on the table.

"Like Tucko?"

"Yeah, like Tucker."

Dragging her feet on the hardwood floor, Megan approached Bryn and pulled on her pant leg. "Mommmeeee, do we have to go?" Bryn smiled, since earlier Megan hadn't wanted to leave Bryn's side.

"Yes, it's time to go. Now go get your coats, please," Bryn said to her children, each tugging on one of her legs.

Megan and Ethan ran to the coat hooks in the foyer and returned, dragging their coats. As Bryn helped Ethan zip up his coat, Jacqueline said, "Anyway, Brynnie, I just wanted you to have the picture."

"Thanks, again, Mom." Bryn flashed a tiny smile to Jacqueline.

"Oooo, Mommeee. I remembered," Megan said. "My science project needs things. Like tomorrow. We need to go!"

"Oh, OK. Yes, sweetie, we're going now." Bryn leaned over and picked Ethan up.

"Talk to you later, Mom," Bryn said, walking out the door.

Standing still, Jacqueline blinked a few times and glanced down at the table.

"Don't forget the picture!" she yelled, running toward Bryn on the sidewalk.

Bryn, with Ethan in her arms, turned around. Jacqueline slipped the picture into Bryn's open fingers.

"Oh, yeah! Almost forgot. Thanks."

Walking back into the house, Jacqueline gently shut the front door. Her loud exhale echoed down the empty foyer and hallway.

"C'mon Meggie. Here's your backpack. And your lunch is in there," Bryn said. An unexpected chilliness in the air was more reminiscent of Christmas than Easter.

"But, I don't want to go," Megan moaned.

"But today is your Easter celebration at school! It should be so much fun!" Bryn cheered.

"Don't…..want….Easter….," Megan mumbled to herself, dragging her backpack decorated with frolicking kittens down the steps into the garage.

"Please pick it up. You're getting it all dirty. Where's your brother?"

Walking through the house and calling his name, Bryn stopped and looked out the kitchen window.

In the backyard, she saw Ethan kneeling at Tucker's grave.

"Oh, my gosh," Bryn said, running out to the backyard.

"C'mon, bud," Bryn loudly whispered, walking toward the grave site. She motioned to him on the morning-dewed grass.

"Wanna see Tucko," he said, standing with green-stained knees.

"We will later, OK? Right now we need to get to school."

She took his hand, and he snatched it away from her.

"Tucko lonely," he protested, remaining by the stone.

"C'mon, Ethan. It's time to go. We're late."

"No! No! No! Mommeeeee!" he shrieked. He arched his back, collapsed onto his knees and erupted into loud sobs.

Leaning over him, Bryn said, "OK, bud. It's OK," to a scrunched-faced Ethan.

Looking towards the grave, she said, "G'morning, Tucker."

"Love Tucko," Ethan said, kneeling on the grass, slowly rubbing the stone. "Miss Tucko."

"Yes we do. We do miss you, Tucker," Bryn said, "Thank you, Tucker, for being such a good boy. OK. We have to go now, bud." She picked up a noticeably calmer Ethan and walked back into the kitchen.

Megan ran out, "What are you doing, Mommy?"

"Just said good morning to Tucker," Bryn said.

"I want to, too!"

"Not now, Meggie. We're really late now."

She carried Ethan to the car with a vocal and protesting Megan following behind her. Bryn dropped Ethan off first because of the day's activities and Megan asked no less than four more times why she had to go to school before they arrived at Madeline's driveway.

"Hi, Allison. Hi, Madeline!" Bryn said.

"Bye, Maddie," Allison kissed her daughter's head, helping her into the backseat.

"How are you this fine morning?" Bryn asked, as Madeline climbed into the car.

"Good. Hi, Megan," Madeline said.

"Hi," Megan mumbled.

Madeline frowned.

"Aren't we going to have a great time at school today?" Bryn asked, fishing for excitement

"Have a great celebration!" Allison said, shutting the car door.

"Yes!" Madeline said, relieved that the tension had been broken. "My mom gave me lotsa things for the crafts."

"Oh, that will be great!" Bryn exclaimed. "That reminds me, I need to run to the store to get a few more things after I drop you two off. Aren't we going to have so much fun today, girls?"

In her rear view mirror, Bryn saw Megan staring out the window while Madeline nervously played with the pleats on her skirt.

After dropping the girls off at school, Bryn dashed to the store to get gluten-free cupcakes and more supplies for the craft tables.

Scurrying back to the car, she heard a familiar voice behind her. "Morning, Bryn!"

She turned and saw Reverend Owens walking behind her. A kind, welcoming man in his 40s, he had been Reverend at Woodhaven Run United Methodist for about five years.

"Oh! Good morning, Reverend Owens."

"Looks as though you have your hands full. Here, let me help you," he said, reaching for one of the bags.

"Oh, I'm fine," Bryn said, pulling the plastic bags away. "Thank you. Sorry to be in such a rush. But, Megan is having a celebration at school."

"Sure. I understand, but before you go, I'm so glad I ran into you. I wanted to be sure to thank you for organizing the Easter Celebration Program. I've heard nothing but good things from others, as well."

"Oh, that was no problem. I enjoyed it."

"OK, well then. We look forward to seeing you on Sunday," he smiled, heading towards his car.

Bryn opened the SUV's trunk. "See you then," she said, trying to rid herself of the bags that had dug into her hands.

Arriving at Megan's classroom, Bryn mouthed, 'How's she doing?" to Mrs. Sanner. Megan's teacher shook her head, slightly crinkling her nose.

"Hey, Meggie!" Bryn said. After spotting her, Megan ran over to her mother, throwing her arms around her legs. "Mommy! Where are you going?"

Bryn crouched down. "I'll be right over there helping with the Easter crosses."

"Oh, OK!" she squealed.

"But, you need to go over to Mrs. Meddaugh. She's going to read you the Easter Story."

Megan's smile disappeared. "But, I don't want to hear the Easter Story," she murmured.

"Go on. Go on over. Then, you can come over to my station."

Scuffing the toes of her new shoes, Megan plodded over to where Mrs. Meddaugh sat with other children. Plopping herself down, she crossed her arms.

Exchanging an apologetic look with Mrs. Meddaugh, Bryn said quietly to herself, "C'mon, Meggie. This will be fun."

The doorbell rang. "It's open, Laur," Bryn yelled from her kitchen. Lauren walked in, joining her.

"So glad you let me know you were going to be in town," she said, hugging Lauren tightly.

"Ummm, yeah! How could I and not tell my 'Kindergarten Buddy'? Hey, Acey. How are ya?" Lauren lightly touched Ace's head. The Boxer protectively held Tucker's squeaky Teddy clamped in his mouth, and he didn't jump up to greet her. "And, I know it's been a hard time for you. All of you, so it appears."

"Yeah, poor Acey has been so lethargic lately."

"So, I thought lunch, dinner, or whatever would be fun. I heard about a new place that has awesome salads that don't taste like rabbit food," Lauren suggested.

"Oh, definitely. I just need to run a few small errands, and then we can eat. What time do you have to head back?"

"I have a few hours. Just take your time."

Bryn ran into the other room. Lauren nearly tripped as she looked around the kitchen and saw dishes in the sink, various children's toys on the counter, and a week's worth of mail and newspapers piled up on the kitchen island and table, including the sympathy card from Dr. Carmichael's office. Hidden within the piles, Lauren's eyes fell upon the framed picture of Taffy.

"Oh my gosh—is this….? Taffy! Oh my gosh! I remember her! Where did you find this?" she asked, reaching for the picture.

"I know, right? Mom just gave it to me," Bryn said.

"Such a sweetie. I loved this dog."

"Yeah, I know. She was a great dog." Bryn hurried back into the kitchen and scanned the room. "Now where is—?"

Lauren chuckled. "Hey, remember when we were little, and we totally fed her our green beans! Thank God they were OK for her to eat. And also, that one time when we were dancing around in the house, knocked over and broke that—"

"Oh my gosh, my parents' vase!" Bryn added.

"Yeah, and we told them that Taffy was looking at a squirrel outside through the window and knocked it over."

"Yeah."

"Poor Taffy. She loved everyone, except that guy you dated. What was his name?"

"Bray...Brayton?" Bryn asked.

"Yeah, him. Brayton! What a dork. She really didn't like him. For good reason, come to find out," Lauren said. "Oh, and when we were in junior high and your parents had that huge party? Poor Taffy was so sick. We stayed with her in the basement all night."

"Yeah, that's right," Bryn said, flipping through her paper piles.

"She pulled through, though. Thank God. What a trooper. I always loved sleeping over at your house because she'd always sleep with us. And, she loved it when we would rest our heads on her belly." Lauren looked down and touched the picture. "Well, kinda like here. Loved that furry belly."

"Yeah. Good times," Bryn said, looking at her phone. "OK...let's see...now what did I forget? Go to the bank. Then pick up Megan's new dance costumes. After that, I can't forget to get Ethan's new piano music."

"Um, Bryn..."

"What?"

"Why don't you just—you know, just take it easy. Just slow down a bit."

"Would love to, Laur. But, lots to do," Bryn said, dancing around. "I need to get going before these places close. And I know you're only here a short bit."

"You sure you're OK?"

Bryn looked up at Lauren. "I'm fine. Don't worry."

"You haven't been jogging in weeks, and—Bryn?"

"Yeah?"

"You don't need to keep feeling guilty."

"What do you mean? Oh, there it is," Bryn leaned over to pick up a sheet of paper describing Megan's costumes.

"You know. Tucker," Lauren clarified.

Bryn looked over at Lauren, tightened her mouth, and walked past her into the other room. Ace trotted behind Bryn with Tucker's teddy still in his mouth.

"Sorry, Laur. But, I really don't feel like getting into this right now. I need to get to these places, and I want to spend time with you, and—"

"I know, but—"

"What?"

Lauren quickly exhaled. "You don't need to feel guilty."

"Thanks. I know. Now where is that other sheet about Meggie's dance…?" Bryn asked, skimming the living room. "Ah, here it is. You ready?' Bryn asked, returning to the kitchen.

Lauren gripped the picture of Taffy tighter, looking at her friend with understanding eyes.

Bryn froze, dropped her purse on the floor, and fell into the kitchen chair.

"We should have made that appointment sooner, Laur." Bryn rested her chin in her palm, elbows on the table.

Walking over to Bryn, Lauren set Taffy's picture down. Hugging her friend from the side, she pulled a chair next to Bryn and sat down. "I mean, it wasn't rocket science," Bryn continued. "He was in pain. Pooping and peeing everywhere. Could hardly move. And then…" Bryn looked over at the mudroom and burst into tears.

"He was all alone. I mean, when he took his last…. On the floor….," Bryn sobbed. "I just had to go to that stupid Spring Fling. Just can't believe I did that to him. After everything he did for us. And, for me."

Lauren gently tapped Bryn's forearm, "Yeah, but…"

"…Just couldn't have made the appointment sooner. Could I? And

Julian wouldn't. He told me. I mean, he literally said, 'Babe, I just can't do it.' So, what was I supposed to do?"

"Bryn, you had it all set. Tucker just, you know, died before you were ready," Lauren offered.

"He just kinda became like, I don't know, part of the scenery. In the background. I used to tell him to 'Move' all the time because he'd get right under me. But, the truth is, he just wanted to be near me. And then, when we started having the kids. It's like, he just became one more thing I needed to do." Bryn looked up at Lauren. "And now, he's gone."

Looking down and shaking her head again, Bryn asked, "How can I forgive myself? I mean, really? How could I do that to one of God's creatures? My sweet Tucker. How could I?"

Lauren paused. "Well…."

"I mean, the kids weren't even here. I was asleep. He was all alone…," Bryn's voice trailed off.

"Yeah, but—"

"Don't tell me I did right by him!" Bryn snapped. "Sorry."

"It's OK," Lauren said, tenderly. "You might just need to forgive yourself a little bit."

"I was supposed to take care of him. You know, like he took care of us."

"You did," Lauren consoled.

"Did I? Really? I mean, he was the *best* dog." Bryn's hands shot up, and she exhaled. "I failed him."

Lauren said, "You were so good to him, Bryn. The kids loved him. You loved him. Heck, even Julian liked him."

Bryn snorted, looking down at her crumpled Kleenex.

"And Tucker loved you," Lauren said. "We all do. And, did you ever think? Maybe Tucker didn't want to leave the house. Maybe he wanted to die here at home, not in some cold vet's office. Maybe this was supposed to happen."

"I guess," Bryn said.

"All I know is that the 'what-ifs' and 'woulda, shoulda, couldas' will eat you alive if you let them," Lauren asserted.

"I know. It's just, I know what it's like not to say goodbye," Bryn said, looking down at Taffy's picture. "And Tucker was basically my first child." She caught a glimpse of the time on her phone. "Oh, my gosh—the costume!"

"It'll just have to wait," Lauren said.

Bryn relented, sinking back into the chair. She said, "And, the kids too. They are having such a hard time. Ethan keeps having stomachaches and wetting the bed. Megan is just so whiny and clingy. Can hardly stand it. She hardly looks at Olaf, who is hiding much more these days, by the way." Bryn paused. "Megan talks about my dad a lot more now. Oh, and you've seen poor Ace. At least he's stopped walking from room to room, howling, looking for Tucker. But, poor guy. He doesn't know what's going on. None of us do. Oh, and Julian doesn't want to talk about it. Like, not at all. He says, 'Why bring up something you can't change'?"

"I know. It can be hard for guys," Lauren said.

"Well, it's no walk in the park for girls either!" Bryn retorted.

"I know. It stinks," Lauren paused. "Huh…just a question. Just asking because. Well, just wondering—"

"Yeah?" Bryn sniffed.

"Well, you know, when you had to tell the kids. What did you say exactly?"

"I said that Tucker passed away, and that God took Tucker. And, now he's in Heaven."

"Hm. OK."

"Why? *Now* what did I do wrong?" Bryn moaned.

"Nothing. Well, I mean. Actually, I read that it's good for kids to hear the word 'died' with the terms 'not coming back.' That way, they won't be waiting. Or, be mad at God."

"But they seemed OK," Bryn protested. "Well, at first, anyway."

"Yeah, but sometimes it can take a while," Lauren said.

"Wow, I can't seem to do anything right lately."

"That's not true," Lauren interjected. "Only reason I brought it up is because it's not too late. Kids are more resilient than we think." Lauren continued, "And, and I know this is a lot, but there are so many good books for kids. Like, *The Tenth Good Thing About Barney*. I mean, it's about a cat, but still. And, Mr. Rogers' *When A Pet Dies*. He's always good, sweaters and all. *Jasper's Day* is also a good one." Lauren paused. "But, I mean, only if you're interested."

Bryn exhaled. "Thanks, Laur. Can you text me those titles?"

"Absolutely. Glad I'm putting those psychology courses to good use. My parents would be so proud," Lauren chuckled.

Bryn grinned, making more thumb holes in the crumpled Kleenex.

"Another thing: I heard that there are groups and counselors that specialize in this. Not in Woodhaven Run, but—"

"Good grief," Bryn retorted. "There are counselors for everything now, aren't there?" She shook her head. "I don't know, Laur. I don't want to be like 'some people' we know."

"Well, did you put a half-page obituary in the paper like a certain older lady in Woodhaven Run we know? No. Plus, all your clothes match." Lauren said. They both smiled.

"Just gets to be a little much at times," Bryn said.

"I know. But do you remember after my Rufus died?" Lauren asked. "Oh my gosh. I was a wreck. Couldn't even jog or really do anything without my boy. It was horrible."

"Yeah, I remember that. Tucker missed his jogging buddy, too."

"And, well, unfortunately, I hate to say this, but…. well, the grief… never really completely goes away."

"Oh, great. Thanks," Bryn said.

"Sorry, but, it really doesn't. But, the good thing is…that… I don't know, that gut-wrenching guilt and grief don't strangle me anymore," Lauren said, curving her fingers to almost a fist.

"Well, I'll look forward to when that happens."

"Absolutely. Yeah, and another good thing is, as I said before, kids can bounce back from this. And, it might be easier for everyone.

Especially you."

Bryn smiled, wiping her eyes. "Tucker was just so pure, you know. Like, he didn't have any agenda. Just pure love. And, he loved everyone I loved. Actually, in some cases, even more."

Lauren nodded.

"You know, now that I'm thinking about it, the way he lived his life is really how we should be living our lives. You know. God wants us to live our lives. With love. I mean, God has truly blessed my life. Beautiful kids. This house. You. Mom. Friends. But, it's like, I forgot that Tucker is a part of those blessings as well."

"True. By the way, though, you are a very good mom," Lauren smiled. "Just remember: the kids will be OK with not having every single thing perfect for one day. They will live. I promise."

Bryn looked over at Lauren and gave her a hug, "What would I do without you, Kindergarten Buddy?"

"Well, you'll never have to worry about that! You've been there for me, too. Lots of times."

Bryn looked down at her phone. Stretching up, she said, "Well, since I'm not going to be able to do like, any of my errands today, you still want to get something to eat?"

"Sure," Lauren agreed.

Bryn fetched a bottle of wine and two glasses. Lauren grabbed two tubs of Ben & Jerry's ice-cream from the freezer and two spoons. They sat in the living room and put up their feet. Bryn turned on *Scandal*, and they both enjoyed their nutritious meal.

"Hey, Bryn. I'm leaving work now. Have a few books for you. Are you home?" Nivie texted.

"Yes. Come on over," Bryn texted back.

Arriving at Bryn's front door, Nivie was greeting by an excited Ace. "Well, hello, new puppy."

"That's Ace," Bryn said. "A Christmas gift from Santa a few months ago."

"I see. Well, you're a sweetie, too" Nivie said, petting his head as he snorted. "But, where's Tucker?"

"Oh, well. I didn't have a chance to tell you yet, but Tucker passed away about a week ago."

"*What?*" Nivie exclaimed. "Oh, no, Bryn!"

"Yeah. It's been tough for us."

"Oh, my god, Bryn. I'm so sorry. Poor guy."

"Thanks. He had been sick for a while. With osteosarcoma. Bone cancer."

"Oh, man. I had no idea."

"Yeah," Bryn continued. "Dr. Carmichael told us he only had a few months. We were going to take him in when...well, he passed away here."

"I'm sorry to hear that. That's really hard. Believe me, I know."

"Yeah, I know you do."

"So, how are *you*? And the kids? Speaking of whom, where are they?" Nivie asked, looking around.

"Oh, the kids are with Grandma Stanton," Bryn said. "I'm trying to get on top of some things, and Julian's still away on a business trip. But, we're all hanging in there."

"And how are the other furry ones taking it?"

"Well, they're doing OK."

"That's good, at least. So, you let them smell Tucker? You know, afterwards?" Nivie asked.

"No, why?"

"Well, I heard that helps them, you know, get through it."

"Hm."

"Yeah, like we need to see it with our eyes. They need to smell," Nivie clarified.

"Well, unfortunately it's too late for that."

"Well, maybe let them, you know, smell some of where Tucker was.

You know, afterwards. Just a thought. What can I do to help?" Nivie asked.

"Oh, we're going to be fine."

"Well, I'm not sure you would like what helped me. I eventually went to a pet loss group in Greenville."

"I heard they had that."

"And, I talked with a counselor, and other things," Nivie said. "Just hearing others' stories was really helpful. And, knowing others felt similar. Doesn't take away all the pain. But, it helped."

"Yeah, just don't know. Thanks, but I think we'll be fine."

"I also know there are places online. Like chat rooms you can go to for help. In case, you know, you don't want to go out—and, then there is the company that will make a stuffed animal clone of the pet that has died from a picture you send them."

"Well, we'll have to see," Bryn said.

"OK, well. Just a few options for ya. Anyway, here's a cookbook that I like. It has really good chicken recipes in it," Nivie said. "And, I know it's been a while, but this other book helped me when my dad died. I know you can get e-books from so many places. But, I like the feel of a real book. Plus, the backlights won't keep you up at night!" she chuckled, trying to lighten the mood.

"Thanks, Nivie."

"No problem. I'm here to help."

Returning home from Bryn's, Nivie walked into her kitchen and saw that food in the cats' dishes hadn't been touched. Sherlock was sitting at the window, chattering away at a bird while Watson was sleeping on the back of the couch.

"Hi, honey!" Alex said. "How was your day?"

"Hi, did you refill the boys' food?" Nivie asked.

"No, I thought you did."

"Uh, no. I'm just getting home! Did you see them eat today?"

"No, but I haven't been home very long."

"What about this morning?" Nivie pushed.

"Well, wasn't really paying attention."

"So, do you mean that they might have gone all day without eating?" Nivie's voice rose at the end.

"Well, I don't know, but—"

"Oh, my god, honey. Oh, my god, honey!" Nivie repeated, waving her hand back and forth, fanning herself.

"Now, Niv. I'm sure it will be fine," Alex said.

"You know cats can't go very long without food! They'll get that fatty liver stuff!"

"I'm sure it will be fine."

"We don't know that!" Nivie exclaimed.

"OK. Then, if they're not doing well, we take them in," Alex offered.

"Honey, I can't!" Nivie snapped. "I can't do that. I can't go back. All those damn needles and tubing. And the smells. Oh, my god."

"Honey, take a deep breath."

Without listening, Nivie yelled, "I just got back from Bryn's! And you know what she told me? Her dog Tucker died!"

"Oh, man."

"Yeah! I know. And, now I come home to this! Oh, my god, honey," Nivie shook her hands.

"Honey, take a deep breath." Nivie's arms wrapped around Alex, her sobs muffled in his chest. "C'mon now. I'm sure the kitties will be fine. Losing a pet is not like a virus. It's not like you're going to 'catch it' from someone you know who has lost their pet."

"I know," Nivie quieted herself and wiped her eyes. "I know. Damn, does this ever get any easier?"

"I don't know," Alex shook his head. "All I know is that I can't be here every time you freak out about this."

"I know." Nivie teared up again.

"But, let's just see how things go. It might blow over. We'll just wait and see. OK? Then, we'll go from there."

Sherlock left his perch after chattering at the bird from the living room window and joined them in the kitchen. Watson stretched as he sauntered next to Sherlock, rubbing his tail against his brother's face.

The next morning, Nivie sprinted downstairs. Seeing dips in the amount of food in their bowls, tears of relief trickled down her cheeks. She woke up a sleeping Watson on the back of the couch and said, "Thank you, big guy." Hearing his human talk, Sherlock jumped down from his perch at the window and rubbed up against Nivie's calf. "And thank you, little one," she said.

Arriving home from work later that day, she peeked through the window to see Sherlock and Watson eating at the food bowl, side by side. Their tails formed a heart, as they had many times as kittens.

Not realizing how dark it had gotten, Bryn jumped into the car after returning her library books. The cold spell at Easter reminded Woodhaven Run that winter hadn't finished its work yet by blanketing the town with seven inches of snow.

She turned down a dimly lit, yet well-plowed, two-lane road. Out of her left vision field, Bryn saw a squirrel scurry right in front of her car. She swerved to the right to avoid it, but the creature jumped to the right, directly under her tire. She felt and heard the stomach-turning thump.

She gasped. "Oh my gosh. No."

Pulling off to the side of the road, she stepped outside her car to check. Tears welled as she took in the grisly scene. Quickly hopping back in the car, she slumped.

"I am just so sorry. I am so sorry."

Each apology stuck deeper in her throat. Her grip on the

steering wheel tightened. Cars raced by, sounding as though they were underwater.

"I'm just so sorry.... I'm just so sorry."

She threw her head back onto the headrest. "Tucker. My boy. My first baby boy..."

Looking straight ahead she said, "And, Taffy....my girl.... You both passed away. Without me."

Staring off into the distance, she lost herself in her thoughts. With her hands still shaking, she struggled to put the car in drive, unaware of the songs playing on the radio or when she passed The Gardens.

Turning down her street, she saw three familiar cars in front of her house: Nate's, Michael's, and Sanjit's.

Parking the car in the garage, she walked into the kitchen, hearing muffled voices from downstairs. Her hands still shook as she set her purse down on the counter. Taking a deep breath, she opened the door to the basement. Ace's big brown eyes greeted her at the top step.

"Hey, Acey," she whispered, patting his head. He sprinted down the steps ahead of her, tail wagging. As she followed him down, the smell of beer, potato chips and pizza, as well as the noise of people cheering from the 60-inch TV, overtook her senses.

Julian and Michael sat on a leather couch, while Nate and Sanjit sat on leather recliners on either side.

"Hey, guys," she said, looking around the man cave to see empty pizza boxes, dirty paper plates, and a few empty beer bottles.

"Hey, babe!" Julian said, still looking at the screen.

"Hey, Bryn!" the other three yelled out. "The Tigers are up!"

"Oh. Good," she said, feigning interest.

"Can I get you something? Pizza, or breadsticks or—?" Sanjit asked.

"There's plenty of beer, too!" Nate added.

"Nah, I'm fine," Bryn crinkled her nose.

Loud whistles and cheering blared from the TV

"Oh, man! How could you drop it? The ball practically flew right to you!" Julian yelled, waving his arms at the screen.

"You know, if he keeps pulling this crap, this could be his last," Michael added. The other three nodded.

"I don't even know why he's still there," Nate said.

"So, um. Kids asleep?" Bryn asked.

"Oh, man! They just stole second base!" Michael roared.

"Yeah! What's that, babe?" Julian asked.

"Are the kids asleep?" she asked, more deliberately.

"Yeah, Eeth went down about, what would you say...?" looking around at the other guys. "I don't know, about an hour ago," he said, glancing at his phone.

"Yeah, I'd say about that," Sanjit agreed.

"And Meggie about, what? Maybe a half hour ago?" Julian said.

"Now, that's how it's done!" Nate and Michael roared, pumping their fists in the air.

"What? What'd I miss?" Julian quickly asked.

"He ran it in!" Nate said.

"No way! Yeah! They're coming back!" Julian rejoiced.

"Alright. Thanks," Bryn said, making her way back up the stairwell. "Have a good night, guys."

"Bye, babe!"

"Bye, Bryn!" The other three yelled in unison.

Ace followed her up the steps. "You stay down here," she whispered to him.

"Ace! Come back here!" Julian hollered from his leather chair.

"Come on, man. Everything is set for you guys. Let's do this!" Bryn heard from downstairs. As she shut the door, her eyes focused on Ace who was watching her from the steps, tail no longer wagging.

Making her way up to the bedrooms in the dim light, she saw a white puff on the steps. Olaf was lying on her back, a few steps down from the top. As Bryn ascended closer, Olaf drove her claws in the carpet, dragging her body along.

"Silly kitty," Bryn said, petting Olaf's head. She took a stride over the stair Olaf occupied, and a white paw reached up to swipe Bryn's foot. She missed.

Bryn walked past the guest room and play room to Megan's room. Her door was open a few inches. Bryn quietly watched her daughter's chest rise and fall. She knelt down and gently kissed Megan on the head.

"I'm so sorry," Bryn whispered.

Megan roused a bit, groaned, then returned to sleep.

She continued down the hall past her craft room to Ethan's room, still hearing muffled yells from the basement. Crouching next to his bed, she stroked Ethan's fine hair and kissed his head.

"I'm just so, so sorry. You guys both loved Tucker, too." Ethan made a little groan and took a deep breath.

"I am so sorry." She stood back up, looked at him a second, before shutting his door behind her.

Without turning on any lights, she walked straight through the master bedroom to the bathroom, locking the door behind her. The previously choked-back tears emerged. Sliding her back down the side of the bathroom wall, she landed on the cold, hard tile, sobbing as quietly as she could.

"Grandma Stanton and Megan Time" occurred as often as a Leap Year, but it was a joy for both of them when it did. After trying on some of Jacqueline's red hats in the living room, Megan reveled in sharing a genuine English afternoon tea with her Grandma.

They finished up a snack of tiny sandwiches, fruit, and tea, with Chloe at their feet, Lammikins in her grip.

"Gramma?" Megan asked.

"Yes, Megan? Oh, no elbows on the table."

Megan jerked her arms down. "Is Tucker with Gramp-E?"

Jacqueline stopped sipping her tea and set her cup down.

"Well, it's hard to say. But, yes. Yes, I believe that Grandpa Ed and

Tucker are up in Heaven together, enjoying each other's company."

"And, Tucker's playing with a squeaky Teddy from Heaven?" Megan asked, smiling.

"Yes, I believe he's playing with squeaky Teddy," Jacqueline affirmed.

"Um, Gramma?"

"Yes."

"Will they be back?"

"Well….. unfortunately…. They won't be back."

Megan's face fell. "Why not?"

"Well, that's how all this works. It is very sad, but we don't get to see them again. But, now we have two angels in Heaven."

Through a protruding bottom lip, Megan asked, "Are you going to go where Tucker and Gramp-E are? And Mommy? And Daddy?"

"Oh, honey," Jacqueline reassured. "Not for a long, long time. No reason to concern yourself with that."

Megan's face relaxed slightly.

"Yes. We're all going to be around for a long time. And, we all love you," Jacqueline quickly touched Megan's nose. Megan's looked down, bottom lip quivering.

"What's wrong, Meggie?"

"Well….Tucker…" Megan sniffed. "Tucker…went away…" She sniffed again. "Um….. after I…got mad at him…And…"

"…….And…?" Jacqueline asked, confused.

"And…I got mad at him…. And he went away…"

"Oh, Meggie. You don't think that you…."

"Sorry," Megan mumbled.

"Sorry about what?"

"Well, Tucker…car hit him…Brother…"

"What about Tucker and Ethan?"

"Mommy told me to hold Brother's hand. I didn't. Tucker got hurt."

"Oh. That wasn't your doing."

"Is God mad at me?" Megan looked around the room, using her shoulder to wipe her eyes.

"Meggie," Jacqueline reached over, bringing Megan onto her lap. Her granddaughter unleashed muffled sobs into Jacqueline's shoulder. "Oh, no. God's not mad at you. And, you didn't have anything to do with Ranger's, I mean, Tucker's death."

Jacqueline stopped.

Megan's arms dug deeper into Jacqueline's back, pulling her out of her new insight. "Oh, you've been holding onto that for so long."

Chloe stretched up on Jacqueline's lap. "Chloe, get down. It's all right," she whispered.

Stroking Megan's hair, Jacqueline said, "You know, we all have animals that...You know what? Look at me, Meggie. Did you know that when Gramma was a little girl, she used to have a horse?"

"Really?" Megan sniffed. "Mommy says they're dangerous."

Jacqueline sighed. "Not all of them."

"But, *I* love 'em," Meggie said, "They're pretty."

"Indeed they are. My horse's name was Ranger. I used to spend quite some time with him when I was little. He was my best friend. Come here. I want to show you something," Jacqueline said, lifting Megan off her lap and leading her to the bedroom. Jacqueline picked up the picture of her and Ranger, placing it in front of Megan.

"Wow, Gramma." Megan took the picture from her, tears still on her cheeks.

"Yes, that's my Ranger," Jacqueline's voice cracked. "Sometimes people and animals we love die. But, I believe we will see them again. Just not right away."

Jacqueline dabbed Megan's cheeks with a tissue, nudging her out of a deep thought.

"There. Do you feel a little better?"

Megan nodded after blowing her nose and handing the tissue back to Jacqueline.

"Would you like any more to eat? Or, more tea?"

"No, thank you, Gramma."

"Well, then, would you like to go outside now? Just for a minute?"

"Yes, please. Oh, can we make snow angels?" Megan asked, clasping her hands.

"Well, sure." Jacqueline hesitated.

Preparing to venture out into the snow took effort, as they both piled on layers upon layers with Jacqueline helping Megan into her snowsuit and boots. Jacqueline slid the glass door open to the backyard, and Chloe ran out to do her business.

Megan dashed into the snow and stopped. "C'mon, Gramma!" she yelled.

"I'm coming," Jacqueline said. Megan extended her arms, fell on her back, and swung her arms and legs back and forth. Jacqueline stood over her, watching and smiling.

"Now, you try it, Gramma!"

"No, that's OK. I just enjoy watching you."

"C'mon, Gramma!"

Jacqueline looked around sheepishly, smiled, and fell back. She heard the snow under her arms and legs crunch as she moved them around.

To her left, through a stream of giggles, Megan was busy making her own snow angel. Jacqueline delighted in this moment with her granddaughter.

Chloe sprinted up to Jacqueline, snorting and licking her cheek. "Oh, Chloe! We're OK! Really we are," Jacqueline laughed, pretending to block her face with her arm.

The Cocker Spaniel ran up to Megan, sniffing around her face. "Chloe, we're OK!" Megan repeated.

Chloe bolted, encircling them, barking. Her paws crunched the snow on her approach and got quieter as she ran the perimeter of the backyard. Each time Chloe returned to them, snow droplets flew off her paws and landed on their faces.

Jacqueline coughed. "Chloe, you're so silly!"

"Chloe, you're so silly!" Megan echoed.

After a few more Chloe circles, and a consistent litany of laughter from Jacqueline and Megan, Chloe stood directly over Jacqueline's face, releasing a large Cocker Spaniel sneeze that ended the moment.

"Yuck. All right. We'll get up," Jacqueline relented.

"Awww...OK," Megan said.

Jacqueline wiped Megan's back to remove the snow, and Megan attempted to do the same to her grandmother's back.

"Look Gramma! Your snow angel looks like it has two heads," Megan pointed to the ground.

"Why, it sure does."

"Maybe it's Gramp-E?"

"It could very well be," Jacqueline smiled.

Bryn had dreaded this night. Julian was gone on another business trip. Again. And, Megan was sleeping over at Madeline's. Bryn tried unsuccessfully to block the painful memories of what happened the last time Megan stayed over. Allison reassured Bryn that she would stay awake the whole night, if need be.

She's a better mother than I am.

Bryn was pleased that her mother called her to let her know about Megan's sorrow and grief, but she was saddened that even weeks after Tucker died, Megan was still struggling with his death. But, she could understand. The void Bryn felt without her dad seemed larger tonight, as she placed the grief book Nivie lent her down on her nightstand. Despite Ace's warm body curled next to hers and Olaf purring at her head, Bryn's feelings of loss seemed to increase, almost in lockstep with each passing year. She imagined her dad's arms cradling her. Would have felt nice.

She stretched to turn out the light and nestled her head into the pillow.

The possibility of Ethan's worsening night terrors returning seemed stronger. Terrifying to anyone else in the house, thankfully, they were not to him. Whenever Bryn ran from her room to console him, he was already fast asleep. Sometimes his sheets were wet from not making it to the bathroom in time. When she asked him about it the next morning, he would have no memory. Typical of night terrors, she read. Might be easier to just stay awake, so she wouldn't be startled.

Bryn first lay on her back.

That ceiling fan and light really need to be dusted.

Then, to her stomach.

Can hardly breathe. This hurts my back.

She flipped on her left side. The clock glared 2:16 am. Flipped to her other side.

I need to put that laundry away.

And, my bureau needs cleaning out.

And, my shoes need to be rearranged. Disasters.

She felt like a fish flopping on the ground.

When did this expensive king size mattress get so big and so uncomfortable?

A tear made its way across her nose and landed on her pillow. Ace stood up, snorted, licking her cheek. He curled his body back into another tight ball next to her leg. "Thanks, Acey."

Bryn finally found some comfort on her right side with a pillow between her knees.

As she and sleep almost reunited, she heard a tiny voice pierce the night.

"Mommy?"

Bryn sat straight up and saw the top of Ethan's head. The height of the bed dwarfed him. Ace jumped down to the floor to greet him, bottom wiggling. Olaf stretched out her body on the pillows.

"Oh, bud. Did you have another accident? Do you need to go to the bathroom?" Bryn asked.

"No. But. But, wiw big monsta go away?" His wet and wrinkled fingers muffled his words.

Bryn exhaled in relief, reaching out her arms to him. "Yes, the big monster is gone now. And, he won't be back."

She hoisted him onto the side of the bed. Pulling up his *Toy Story* pajama bottoms, she was relieved to feel they were dry.

Bryn adjusted her pillow under Ethan's head, bringing the pillow by her knees to under her head. Not one to be left out, Ace jumped back up on the bed to join his family.

Ethan exhaled and smiled. "Mommy?"

"Yes, bud."

"Wiw God? Wiw God give Tucko food and wowta?"

"Yes, God will give Tucker all the food and water he wants," she said, wrapping her arms around her little boy. Kissing the top of his head, she had forgotten how soft his fine hair was and enjoyed the calming fragrance from his shampoo.

"And, and, and, wiw God give him his squeaky Teddy? Squeaky Teddy sad."

Bryn smiled. "Yes. God will give him another squeaky Teddy from Heaven."

From the corner of her eye, Bryn saw the sides of Ethan's mouth rise up.

"In fact, God has even better squeaky toys than we have on Earth."

"Wiwwe?"

"Yeah, really."

"And... And... And, Mommy?"

"Yes?"

"Wiw God remembo? Give Tucko food and squeaky? No want Tucko be sad. He wiwee misses wiving in ow house."

"Yes, God will remember. We miss him living in our house, too," Bryn held him closer and began gently humming.

"Mommy?"

"Hmm...?"

"When God give Tucko back?"

Bryn stopped humming.

"You said: 'God needed him now'. But. But, when wiw he be back?"

"Well…" Bryn cleared her throat. "Bud, what Mommy meant to tell you is that Tucker died."

"Die?"

"Yeah, bud. Tucker died. That means…he won't be back."

"But. But, you said…." Ethan's face began to crinkle and tears welled up in his eyes.

"I know. I'm sorry."

"God gonna take Ace?" Ethan asked, pointing at the bottom of the bed, whimpering. "Don't want Him to take him."

"Oh, that will be a long time."

"Wong time?"

"Yes. But, guess what?"

"What?" Ethan sniffed.

"We can think about Tucker and remember him. We now have another guardian angel. And, God and Tucker are having a wonderful time together," Bryn assured.

"Wiwee?" Ethan asked, using the back of his hand to wipe both eyes.

"And, Tucker wants us to love Ace and Olaf and take care of them. And also, you know what?"

"What?"

"Tomorrow, when you wake up, we can draw a picture of Tucker. And we can pray and tell God that Tucker needs his toys."

Ethan smiled again, his soft arms wrapped around Bryn's neck. Then he furrowed his brow.

"Mommy?" he asked.

"Yeah?"

"I haffa go backa bed?"

Bryn sat up on her elbow and looked at his face. "No," she kissed his head again, appreciating his tiny forehead and fine hair even more. "No, you can stay here with me."

Ethan's face brightened, clapping his tiny hands above both of their heads.

"Mommy?"

"Yes."

"You mo nice when Daddy gone," Ethan said.

Bryn studied his face for a minute. "Love you, bud," she said, kissing his head again, hugging him tighter.

"Miss Tucko lots," Ethan yawned.

"I miss him too, bud. He was a very good dog." She cleared her throat. "So, let's sing our song about Tucker."

Bryn and Ethan sang, "Tucko…is bestest Tucko in the ho wide wod. He's bestest Tucko in ho wide wod…Bestest Tucko in ho…..wide…. wod." Ethan yawned again. "He….my… best ….fwuend…"

Ethan drifted off, finding Dreamland. Giving him a gentle squeeze, Bryn rolled her son over onto his belly. He slept through the night, which is more than she could say.

Before Ethan awoke the next morning, Bryn crept downstairs, with Ace and Olaf right behind, and opened the door to the mudroom. Instead of quickly shutting it, as she had in the past, she left it open. Ace wandered in, while Olaf stood at the doorframe, sniffing around. The Boxer smelled the floor, laid down and rolled around on the place his beloved friend took his last breath.

Bryn reached behind a pile of coats and brought Tucker's collar down for Olaf to smell. The kitten batted up at it, knocking it out of Bryn's hands. Clutching the collar between her front paws, she pulled it to her nose and rolled over it. Ace trotted over to Olaf and sniffed it; his exhales leaving tiny droplets on Olaf's back.

"You guys miss him, too. Sorry I kept you from your buddy so long."

Two days later, as soon as Bryn opened the door to the backyard, Ethan released his hand from his mom's grip.

"Hey, bud, wait up!" Bryn said, chasing after her son, making a direct line to where Tucker now resided.

"Can you get it, Meggie?" Bryn asked, turning around to look at Megan.

"Yeah, Mommy."

"OK, put it down right here."

Megan placed a gray, memorial stone that read, "Sadly missed. Our loving companion and friend."

"Such a good helper," Bryn said, side-hugging Megan. "Here are your bubbles, Meggie."

Megan twisted the top off and blew into the plastic wand. Iridescent soap spheres silently floated over Tucker's new headstone.

"Good morning, Tucker," Bryn said. "Meggie, what would you like to say to him?"

"Just that...Just that, I miss you." Megan bit her lip, in a failed attempt to prevent her tears from falling.

"I know." Bryn swallowed hard, hugging her daughter. "We all do."

Bryn held out Ethan's blue drawing of Tucker. "Did you want to show your picture, bud?" It was safe inside a Ziploc bag, preventing the elements from ruining it.

"Yeah. Here, Tucko. This is for you," Ethan said, placing the picture next to the headstone. Bryn found another stone nearby to hold the picture down.

"Do you want to read your letter, Meggie?"

"Yeah." Unfolding her letter, decorated with hand-drawn, colored dogs, Megan read:

> "Deer God,
> Tucker iz ther now with yoo. In Hevin. Pleeze dont forget his Tedy. It maks him hapy. He mite even smil.

We miss him. And Gramp-E to. He is a gud dog.
Tucker luvs bubles. He luvs hugs. But he luvs bubles
mor.

Luv, Megan Troxell

P.S. Iz ther watr in Hevin? He luvs watr to and when
yoo put yor hed on his bely. Don't wory, he likes it."

"That's beautiful, Meggie," Bryn said. "Why don't you sing your
song now, bud?"

"OK, Mommy," Ethan agreed. "Tucko is the bestest Tucko in the
ho wide wod. Ho wide wod. Ho wide wod. Tucko is the bestest Tucko
in the ho wide wod. He my best fwend," Ethan sang. On the second go
around, Bryn and Megan joined in, singing, holding hands and walking in a circle.

"Good job, kids!"

"Mommy? When Tucko done being dead, can we play?" Ethan
asked.

"Um, bud. Remember what Mommy said. We can't see Tucker
again. But, we can remember him. And, talk about him."

Ethan jutted out his bottom lip.

"So, what's one of your favorite memories of Tucker?" Bryn asked,
diverting his attention.

"Hmmm….when put my head on Tucko's belly," Ethan said.

"Yeah, that was fun, wasn't it?" Bryn said.

"I liked when we had Bubble Parades. And, when I got to hug him,"
Megan said.

"Me, too!" Ethan added.

"You can't like the same thing, Brother!"

"Uh, huh!"

"Nuh uh," Megan shot back.

"Uh, huh!"

"All right. It's OK," Bryn shushed, hugging Megan closer. "This is a time for appreciating Tucker. Mommy wants to share her favorite memory now. There was a time when we were all at the Lake Up North. You guys were tubing and Tucker was on the tube, too. He loved being on the water and loved you both so much." She paused. "Everyone was so happy." Pulling them closer, she said, "OK, let's say a prayer:"

Megan bowed her head, and folded her hands. Ethan, watching his sister, did the same.

"Dear God, we are thankful for Tucker," Bryn said, "We thank you for all the good memories we had with him. We miss him, but we thank you for letting him be an important part of our family. Amen."

"Amen."

Part Three: New Beginnings

"To live in hearts we leave behind is not to die."
~Thomas Campbell~

"The one best place to bury a good dog is in the heart of his master."
~Ben Hur Lampman~

"MOMMY, WHAT 'MOM-O-REAL DAY'?"

"What's that, bud?" Bryn looked down at a caped Ethan while dumping vegetables into a pan for dinner.

"What 'Mom-o-Real Day'?" he repeated.

"I don't know," she said, waiting for one of his usual punchlines. "What is 'Mom-O-Real Day'?"

"Mrs. Wusso said."

"Oh, when did Mrs. Russell say it?" Bryn asked.

"At schoo. On Wendsday. Is it for weal moms? Like yoo?"

"Oh! You mean Memorial Day!" Bryn said, rinsing her hands under the faucet.

"Yeah," Ethan said. "Mom-o-Real Day."

"Well, it's a day we remember the men and women who fought and died for our country. So you can have your freedom."

"Feedum?" Ethan asked. "What's feedum?"

"Freedom. Well, it's letting people do what they want."

He shook his head. "I no have feedum."

Bryn laughed. "So we remember them and also other people that are no longer with us."

"Like Gramp-E?"

"Yes. Like Gramp-E," she said, quietly. "Do you remember when you, me, Meggie, and Daddy went and saw the wall downtown? With all the people's names on it? And, benches and bushes around it?"

"Yeah."

"That's for them, the people who died in the wars," she said, checking the oven's temperature.

"Like cemotewee?"

"Yes, some have cemeteries. But, there are memorial parks for them, too."

He thought a moment, and asked, "Like Tucko?"

"What about Tucker, bud?"

Megan scampered into the kitchen with Olaf in her arms. Ace trotted behind.

"We membo him. He pawt Mom-o-Real Day?" Ethan asked.

"No, but we remember the doggies that served with the people."

Ethan furrowed his brow. "Need one for Tuckos. Go and membo them," he asserted.

"Good idea, bud," Bryn said, adding the chicken to the pan.

"Yeah, there should be! Not just in backyards!" Megan chimed in, dancing around the kitchen island, Olaf dangling from her arms. "For all doggies. And, kitties too!"

Ethan threw his arms around Ace, who licked his face. "'Cuz, Aces and Tuckos be memboed."

"Yeah, there really should be," Bryn said, placing the casserole in the oven.

Nivie and Alex gathered on the living room couch to eat dinner for Nivie's *Golden Girls* fix. Sherlock daintily walked over brown packing paper lying in the middle of the floor. Due to the crackle and popping, it was called his "crinkle-crisp." It wasn't completely flattened at this point but was on its way. Lying on the back of the couch, Watson watched his brother in fascination.

"Is it weird that when I hear the *Rocky* theme song I think about the movie *Mr. Mom,* instead of *Rocky?*" Nivie asked.

"Um, yeah," Alex chuckled.

"Hey, you know what your sweet little son Locky did today?" Nivie asked.

"You mean Sherlock?" Alex clarified.

"Yeah, Locky! Anyway, he was in the litterbox, covering up his 'deposit.' When he came out, he had a piece of litter on the end of his nose!"

Alex chuckled.

"And then Lotsa Watty Watson was like, 'hiding' behind the curtain, with everything showing except his face. It was like 'You can't see me!' Love our boys."

"They're so funny. Hey, Sherlock, when are you going to get a part-time job?" Alex asked.

"Yeah! Help pay for your food." Nivie joined in.

"And toys, too." They both laughed.

Sherlock stretched out on the floor, rolled over on his back, boldly showing his white belly and white-tufted arm pits. Watson stood up on the back of the couch, stretched, trembling with an arched back. He licked his back leg with his drumstick up in the air, then lay back down, one arm hugging either side of the couch. "Monorail Kitty."

"It's so funny, the two of 'em," Nivie commented.

"What do you mean?" Alex asked, setting his tray table to the side.

"Like, Locky loves his crinkle-crisp, but doesn't do 'Monorail Kitty.' And, Lotsa Watson loves his belly rubs, but he doesn't really like head-butts."

"Well, they do have their own personalities."

"They really do." Nivie looked down and tightened her mouth.

"Did Kimball ever do 'Monorail Kitty'?" she asked.

Alex furrowed his brow.

"And, what color were his ears?"

"What? His ears?" Alex asked.

"Yeah, I mean, Minerva's ears were all 'tortied' with different colors. I just can't remember."

Alex paused. "What's with all the random Kimball questions?"

Nivie sighed, "I don't know. Just seems as though all I can remember is, you know, the end. It's like all the other parts of him just fade away. God, I friggin' hate that."

"Well, we only had him a short time," Alex quietly added.

"Yeah. Too short." Nivie began playing with the tassels on the blanket.

"But, no. And, white," Alex said.

"What?" Nivie looked up at her husband.

"No, Kimball never did 'Monorail Kitty,' and his ears were white."

"Oh yeah! I didn't think he did. And, yeah, white ears." Nivie sighed.

Alex stretched out his hand to touch her arm. "And, remember when he would sit on your nightstand, and…"

"Oh, yeah!" Nivie said.

"He'd just bat his paw at things sitting there, watching gravity do its thing."

"Oh my god! I lost more pens that way!"

"And, he loved to be in empty boxes. Especially if they were too small!" Alex added.

"Yeah, he'd pour himself into it, with parts of his belly and butt hangin' over the side! And, of course, we can never forget…" Nivie tapped Alex's arm three times.

He reached his hand out to Nivie. She took it, gently squeezing it.

Sherlock darted through the living room, through the kitchen, down the hall, through the living room, and back through the kitchen again, emitting little warbles as he turned each corner. After a few rounds, he ran into the dining room, looked up at a point where the ceiling met the wall, and tried engaging it in conversation.

"We're in here, Locky!" Nivie yelled from the living room. "We haven't moved! We're still here!"

Completely awakened from his slumber, Watson jumped down from the back of the couch, stretching while simultaneously walking over to the food bowl. He picked up one kernel of food and carried it about three feet from the bowl to eat, repeating this maneuver a few more times.

Nivie giggled, carrying her plate from the living room to the kitchen.

"Hey, honey," Alex said, following her, his plate in hand.

"Yeah?"

"I was thinkin'. You really need to do it now."

"Really?" she asked, setting her plate down on the island.

"Yeah. Now. Now's the time for you to really move forward with your idea for an animal memorial park."

Nivie sighed deeply, trying to quiet all the doubts spinning in her mind.

"Love, we've talked about this. I don't know—"

"And, you know, I would help," he quickly added. "It's an awesome idea. And, I think people in Woodhaven Run would really appreciate it."

Nivie geared up to provide multiple reasons not to proceed. But, she looked at him and said, "You know what? You're right."

"Really?" Alex set his plate down.

"Yeah. Now is the time to start getting serious about this. No time like the present!" Nivie affirmed.

Alex smiled.

"How long have you been thinking about bringing the park idea up again?" Nivie asked.

"Since the last we talked about it."

She smiled. "I know I told you about the statues, flowers, benches and brick sidewalks that lead to the sanctuary, chapel area, the quiet area for adults, and not-as-much area for children," she said, surprised at how quickly the ideas flowed.

"Yeah."

"So, I was thinking inside the foyer of the enclosed area where the sanctuary is, or Chapel, whatever you want to call it, have a few touchscreens on the walls near the entrance to the sanctuary. Like maybe two of them," Nivie continued. "So people who contribute to the Park could submit pics about their pet. And, maybe even a one-or two-minute video."

"Awesome, honey! Love it."

"It could be like a virtual technological interaction for the person. And it would be available to anyone who wanted to see it." Nivie said.

"That's great! And I know, there are like, two guys at work that could help out, too. The ones that love animals. The ones that 'get it'."

"Yeah, I was just going to say we need to get others involved, too. Like, I know Dr. Carmichael would be great. And, I think Bryn would be too, 'cuz we can't do it all ourselves. Oh! And there will be a place where people could light a candle for them, too. I could even paint a mural!"

"Yeah!' Alex agreed. "So glad you're ready to finally move forward."

"Yeah, and there could be a place where, you know, the ashes could go. A place for interment," she said, looking over at the bookshelf where Kimball and Minerva's urns rested.

"Wow, yeah. That would be great," Alex slowly nodded his head.

Looking deeply at her husband, she said, "Thank you, honey. For all your ideas and support."

"Well, you know. For us. For Kimball. And, others, too," he said, embracing his wife.

"Hi, Dr. Carmichael," Nivie said. "Thanks for calling me back."

"Kelly gave me the message. Is everything OK with Sherlock and Watson?"

"Oh, yes. They're great," Nivie said, looking at Watson asleep on the back couch and Sherlock lying spread-eagled cleaning himself on the living room floor.

"Glad to hear," Dr. Carmichael said with relief.

"So, I'm calling because I've had this idea for a really long time. It's an idea for an animal memorial park in Woodhaven Run where people could go to honor their animals."

"You mean like a cemetery?"

"Well, sort of, but it will have much more. There'll be a chapel, or sanctuary for animal memorial services. And, an area just for children. And, then another place for the animals' ashes. And, people could purchase a personalized pathway brick as a fund-raiser."

"What a fantastic idea!" Dr. Carmichael said. "My fellow vets and I have talked about the need for something like this for a while. Just needed the right person to spearhead it."

"Thanks!"

"Be sure to let me know how we can help."

"Will do! Thanks so much!"

"No, thank you."

Nivie hung up the phone. She danced and hummed as Sherlock and Watson watched through half-opened eyes. "This is awesome, boys! I know just who I need to call next."

"Hey, Niv. What's up?" Bryn answered her phone from her backyard, dangling her feet in the kiddie pool. Megan and Ethan splashed around, squealing with glee.

"Bryn! I have. The. Most. Amazing idea that's been buried for a super long time. And, I wanted to talk with you about it."

"Ok," Bryn chuckled. "What is it?"

"Listen to this: We create a park somewhere in Woodhaven Run to commemorate the beloved animals we have lost."

"Wow." Bryn sat up in the Adirondack chair, plugging one ear with a finger to block out the kids' laughter and splashing.

"How great would that be? And, we can totally build it! I mean, not necessarily us. But, have it built. And people can come and visit to pay their respects, and there would be benches, and statues, and flowers, and brick sidewalks people could donate—"

"—That's so funny you bring this up. I was talking with the kids like, I don't know, a few weeks ago around Memorial Day and Ethan mentioned it. He was learning about Memorial Day at school."

"How awesome is that? Great minds think alike! Even if they're tiny and wee," Nivie laughed.

"We even put the stone on Tucker's grave in the backyard," Bryn said, looking over at it.

"Aww, so glad to hear. Tucker, sweetie." Nivie switched gears. "So, about the park. We could work on this together! Whaddya think?"

"You're serious?"

"Absolutely! We can do this. It would be awesome! And, other people will appreciate it too! Oh, and Dr. Carmichael is totally supportive, too."

"And, you're asking *me?*"

"Of course! Given that we talked about Kimball and Tucker, and our paths keep crossing at the pet store. I think we're of similar mindsets on similar paths. You're really a great mom, too. And, you're so organized!"

"Thanks, Nivie. I'm honored, and I do think it it's a great idea. But, you mean, actually build a park." Bryn paused. "Wow, that's a huge project, with land and permits."

"I know, but it just feels right, you know? And, I've started a list of other people who would love it and can help out, too. You could bring in Tucker to represent the dogs, and I'd have Minerva and Kimball for the kitties. We can *so* do this!"

Nivie heard the children yelling in the background. "Are those the kids?"

"Yeah."

"Hi, Meggie! Hi, Ethan!" Nivie yelled into the phone, forcing Bryn to yank it from her ear.

Nivie continued with increased enthusiasm. "Oh, yeah, and the kids can share their ideas, too. They have the most amazing insight into these types of things. Yeah, this is going to be awesome!"

"Wow, Niv." Bryn sighed. "That's going to take a lot of resources, financial and otherwise."

"Yeah, I know. But, we could have fundraisers. Ask people to contribute in different ways. Oh, we could crowdsource, too!"

"Wow. You've really given this a lot of thought," Bryn chuckled.

"Yeah, and I just have this feeling it will bring about good things. For everyone."

"OK. Well, let me think about this. Julian is out of town—"

"Of course."

"And, we're up to our ears with dance and piano lessons. But, I will get back to you this weekend."

"Yeah, OK," Nivie's voice dropped. "But, can I just say one more thing?"

"Sure," Bryn said, keeping an eye on the kids who had hauled Ace into the pool.

"Don't think about it too hard."

Bryn was silent, watching the kids with Ace.

"You have such a gift for organizing these types of things," Nivie continued. "And, the love you have for your children, as well as Tucker and Olaf and Ace, speaks volumes to what you'd bring. I've seen it in you. You'd be perfect."

"Thanks, Niv. I appreciate that. I really will give it some thought."

"You're welcome. Talk to you soon!" Nivie said, ending the call.

Bryn held onto her phone, watching her kids spin in circles on the grass while a wet Ace clumsily encircled them.

A few days later, Nivie turned on the television to watch *Big Bang Theory*, when her phone beeped.

Looking down, she read a text from Bryn: "OK—I'm in!"

"Yes!" Nivie said, pumping her fists in the air. Sherlock and Watson, asleep in the living room, opened their eyes to half-mast. After watching Nivie for a moment, they yawned, snuggled back down, and returned to their respective dreamlands.

"All right, boys. It's time to get moving on this," Nivie said, rubbing her hands together.

"What are you working on?" Jacqueline asked, on a quick visit to Bryn's house. She surveyed the various piles on her daughter's kitchen desk and table.

"Oh, it's something new. An interesting idea the kids brought up," Bryn said.

"Yes, they are certainly full of those," Jacqueline chuckled.

"Yeah. Well, we were talking about Memorial Day a few weeks ago, when they asked why there wasn't a park for the animals. Like, our pets. The little stone on Tucker's grave had a bigger impact on them than I thought."

"Oh," Jacqueline said, surprised. "A park? For our pets? My goodness. What a lofty idea."

"And I've been talking to—do you know Nivie Emerson?"

Jacqueline furrowed her brow.

"Nivie Emerson. Your friend, Ronni's niece?" Bryn prompted.

"Oh, Genevieve! Nivie. Why, yes."

"Well, she and I talked, and we are spearheading this. Actually, she was the one who set the whole idea in motion."

"Is that right? I haven't heard about Nivie in a long time. How is she?"

"Oh, she's doing well," Bryn said. "She's excited about the park. And she also said that Dr. Carmichael even supports it."

"I see. So, this park? Do you know how much it will run? That's quite an enormous undertaking."

"Yes, we understand it's going to be an expensive project. But, we are getting preliminary figures now and exploring fund-raising options," Bryn continued. "At the moment, we are trying to get different sponsors and volunteers to donate their time and energy. Maybe even online crowdsourcing."

"And, this park. Where would it be located?"

"Here. In Woodhaven Run."

"Yes, but, where, exactly?" Jacqueline asked.

"Well, actually, we thought near the Tridge would be the best of the central locations. There is quite a bit of space now because of the buildings that were demolished there."

"I see. Sounds as if you're determined to do this."

"Well, we'll see," Bryn shrugged.

"Don't misunderstand, Brynnie. I'm thrilled to see you so involved in a project, getting your energy back," Jacqueline squeezed Bryn's shoulder. "However, don't you think it might be too involved an undertaking for you?"

Bryn's head, and heart, sank.

Jacqueline continued: "Have you polled people or done a survey to consider what the citizens of Woodhaven Run want? Is there really a need or desire?"

"Based on the people we've talked to, veterinarians and pet owners, there definitely is an interest," Bryn responded flatly.

"Yes, interest is one thing. Need is another. And, have you given thought about marketing and promotion?"

"Yes, Mom. We know," Bryn sighed. "Those are things we're researching as well."

"I just think you might be biting off more than you can chew, Brynnie. This would be a colossal undertaking. You'd need to find land, as well as permission to build, and the needed permits—"

"—Yeah, Mom, we know," Bryn interrupted. "We're looking into all that."

Jacqueline looked at Bryn. "Isn't it hard enough when we lose them? Do we need to have a constant reminder of painful memories?"

Bryn looked down.

"It sounds like this is important to you. But, it would just break my heart if it didn't work out. Then you would have wasted all your time and energy, and frankly, money, for something that might never come into fruition."

"I know. But, I'm willing to take the risk," Bryn retorted, indignant.

Jacqueline cocked her head to the side. "Perhaps take a smaller risk at first. Then, build on that."

Bryn was silent.

"I just want to see you happy, Brynnie, and I'm not convinced this would do that for you."

"Ok, thanks, Mom."

"Tell you what? Let's all get together in Traverse City this weekend. Will Julian be here?" Jacqueline asked.

"Not this weekend."

"Well, then you and I and the kids can head up and enjoy the day there."

Bryn flashed a small smile. "We'll see."

"Well, then. Again, it's a unique idea. I just don't think it's good for you to do right now," Jacqueline said, giving a hug to her daughter. "Give my love to the kids," she said, closing the door behind her.

"Thanks, Mom. You too," Bryn said, choking back tears.

"Hey, Bryn!" Nivie said on the phone, "Were you able to gather that list of people who could donate to our silent auction?"

Bryn sighed. "Well, kinda. Niv, this is just so big."

"Yeah. What do you mean?"

"Well, my mom and I were talking the other day. She brought up some really good points. This really is a huge undertaking."

"I understand, but we already know that."

"It's just. It might be *too* big," Bryn said.

Nivie was silent for a moment. "Well, Bryn, what do *you* think? Do you like the idea of an animal memorial park?"

"I really do. Again, having the small service for Tucker really stuck with me. And, I know the kids would appreciate it, too. But, how can we, a stay-at-home mom and a teacher, do this on our own?" Bryn asked.

"Why not us?" Nivie said, "Plus, we're not doing this on our own. Others are contributing, too."

"I know, but—"

"Well, before you decide to back out of this, remember that you are 'The Organizing Queen'."

Bryn chuckled.

"I'm serious. You are great at planning and keeping things running. Those are true gifts."

"Well, thank you," Bryn said.

"And, can I say something else?"

"Sure."

"My Ma is one of the smartest, most intelligent women I know. But, she doesn't know everything."

"I know," Bryn sighed.

"Maybe your mom just doesn't want you to take on too much?" Nivie offered.

"Maybe. I just thought she'd understand. I just don't know…"

"Or, maybe Ranger's death still haunts her," Nivie hypothesized.

"You remember Ranger?" Bryn asked, surprised.

"Absolutely. When you told me about him, I never forgot it. And, I also remember your stories about Taffy, your dog growing up. I don't forget animals."

"Wow, Nivie. That means a lot," Bryn said. "But, I still just don't know."

"OK," Nivie's voice dropped. "But, can I just say another thing?"

"Yeah."

"This is an amazing opportunity to commemorate Tucker and Kimball and Minerva, and all the animals we've lost. They've given so much to our lives through their devotion and unconditional love. You would be helping so many others who feel the same way."

Bryn's throat tightened.

"And, I know that the kids would love to be a part of this, too. What a gift you could give them: working together on this. What a legacy. Regret is cancer on one's soul. And, now...we come back to your other gift again: organizing."

"Thanks, I really appreciate your kind words. I really do. But, I've never done anything this big before. Not even close."

"I know! Neither have I!" Nivie chuckled. "Just don't sell yourself short. You'll be great. We'll all be great!"

"Yes, we will. Thanks, Niv." Bryn ended the call, staring at the piles of documents on the table. Armed with a freshly poured cup of coffee and a newfound fire in her belly, she opened her laptop, organizing her possible contacts.

9

Washing their hands after their bike ride, Bryn said, "Meggie, Bud, come here. Mommy wants to talk to you."

"You OK, Mommy?" Megan asked.

"Yes," Bryn chuckled. "Do you remember the other day when you guys talked about a memorial park for animals?"

"For Tucko?" Ethan asked.

"Yes. You remember?"

"Yes," Megan said.

"Well, I like the idea so much that we are going to do it!"

"Yay!" Ethan jumped around.

"And, Daddy, too?" Megan asked.

"Well, probably not."

"Oh."

"But," Bryn side-hugged Megan. "You know who is going to help us? Mrs. Emerson!"

"Yay! I like Mrs. Emerson!" Megan clapped her hands together, and Ethan mimicked his sister.

"Yes. So, we need your help. We were thinking about having a kids' area in the park. Just for kids. Like you two."

"Can I put up my pictures?" Megan asked.

"And my doahing?" Ethan asked.

"Absolutely."

"We have to have a huge refrigerator," Megan said, extending her arms out on either side.

"Why?"

"For all the drawings to go on," Megan said.

In a failed attempt to contain their excitement, Megan and Ethan watched with wide eyes as Nivie unwrapped her sketches of the park on Bryn's kitchen table.

"We'll get official plans later, but this is to give you an idea of what I was thinking about."

"Wow, Niv. This looks great," Bryn said.

"So, the entrance of the Park is here. We walk over a small brick bridge which leads to the oval shaped park, lined with bushes and flowers. And, of course, Christmas lights on the bushes right after Thanksgiving! And, we could call it the HEAL Park! 'Honoring Every Animal's Legacy' Park!"

"Wow, great ideas," Bryn said.

"Heeo?" Ethan asked, looking at Ace near his feet.

"No," Nivie chuckled. "But, I can see why you'd think that! Heel, foot. Telling Ace to 'Heel.' All sorts of interpretations!"

Ethan smiled, still examining his foot.

"Anyhoo, just like The Gardens, I thought we could have one ginormous statue of our three different animals: Kimball, Tucker and Ranger at the entrance. Then, beyond that would be the walkway, a path of bricks with the donors' animals' names and a small sentiment engraved on them."

"Wow." Bryn's and the kid's eyes grew.

Olaf jumped up on the table, headed for the sketches. Bryn grabbed her in time.

"Here, let me hold her," Nivie said, cradling Olaf. She gave the white fluff a quick kiss on her forehead. Olaf threw open her front paws at Nivie in an attempt to grab her nose. The feline failed.

"So, I have some friends from Chicago who know an extremely talented sculptor," Nivie said, still laughing from Olaf's miss.

"There's Tucko!" Ethan cried out.

"You're right, Ethan. And standing behind Tucker is your Grandma's horse Ranger. Life-sized. And, lying down in front is my Kimball Kitty."

"You have a kitty?" Megan asked.

"Well, yes. Two. But, Kimball Kitty, no longer with us," Nivie said, pointing at the Kimball statue. "Like, Tucker is no longer with you guys. It's sad, but that's why we're creating this park."

"Pwingo sometimes thows up," Ethan said.

"Yeah, those are usually hairballs," Nivie chuckled.

"Olaf!" Megan yelled.

"Pwingo!"

"All right, kids," Bryn intervened.

"So, there would be a sanctuary or tiny chapel, here, for services, with benches and a table, altar-like chikawaka up front," Nivie said. "OK, now. I'll need to set you down, little one," Nivie said to Olaf, who had started to climb up her back. Bryn pulled Olaf off of Bryn's back and set her down. She scampered away into the other room.

"Next to the sanctuary could be a 'Zen Room' where adults could sit in silence and meditate, or pray, whichever, or both. There'd be a memory book, too. But, here's my favorite part I wanted to show you two. The kids' area, right here!" Nivie said, pointing to the other side of the sanctuary's doors.

"Yay! Lots of bubbles!" Megan rejoiced.

"Sure, why not?" Nivie said. Bryn nodded.

"And, doahing. And, cwayons," Ethan added. "And Teddy for Tucko."

"Well, not sure if we'll have dog toys there, bud," Bryn said.

"We could put Teddy Bears in the children's area," Nivie affirmed. "Oh, and other stuffed animals too! Excellent idea, Ethan."

He grinned, another thumb-filled smile.

"So, from the opening of the sanctuary, a smaller path to the right leads to an area of interment," Nivie said, pointing to the main entrance of the chapel. "And then, over here on the opposite side would be parking. Oh, and almost forgot. Bathrooms would be tucked between the sanctuary and children's area. Very important."

"Mommy, what about your dog?" Megan asked.

"You mean Taffy?"

"Yeah, is Taffy going to be here?

"Hmm...hadn't thought about it," Bryn thought. "Guess she could."

"Absolutely!" Nivie confirmed.

"Mommy, what about birds? Madeline has Fred," Megan said. "It's a cocka...cocka—"

"—tiel?" Nivie offered.

"Yeah, cockatiel—"

"—Yeah, he's gway. And, and his head gwows! Like this!" Ethan said, reaching for the ceiling.

"Brother! Stop! I want to tell them," Megan chastised. "Madeline got Fred when the old one flew away."

"He flew away?" Nivie asked, looking at Bryn, who tightened her face and slightly shook her head.

"Oh, I see," Nivie said. "But, that's a great idea, Meggie. Some people have their birds for years, even decades. They miss them when they're gone, too. We'll have to see how to include them. Great idea!" Nivie affirmed.

"Something to think about," Bryn said.

Megan smiled, standing on her chair, leaning on the table with her forearms. Bryn motioned for her to sit down.

"And, have you ever heard about the 'Blessing of the Animals'?" Nivie asked.

"Oh, yeah. Is that when they have the animals—?" Bryn asked.

"—Yeah, on October 4, St. Francis of Assisi Day, the church invites its members to bring in their animals. Like, to the actual church. Sometimes the service is held outside but sometimes it's even held *in* the church. Then, the priest or pastor, or whoever, blesses them. Doesn't even have to be Catholic. I love it!"

"Huh, I think that Reverend Owens does that at our church."

"Really? Do you think he'd be willing to spread the word about our Park?" Nivie asked.

"I'll ask."

"That would be great. The more help, the better!"

"Hm, I could even see if Father Kenneth would be interested, too." Bryn said.

"Who's he?" Nivie asked.

"He's the priest I grew up with when I was at St. Agnes."

"Yeah, ask if they are open to coming to the park dedication. And, also see if they can announce the park in the receipt, I mean bulletin, you get at the end of mass," Nivie laughed.

"I'll ask Mom about Fr. Kenneth. She sees him more than I do."

"That would be awesome! I haven't been connected to a church in a long time. But, it would be neat to include them. One of the things I liked about the 'Blessing of the Animals' is that it is inclusive," Nivie said. "And, apparently, Woodhaven Run is known for having 'more churches per square mile,' than many cities its size. So, let's see how we can make this work!"

"Definitely," Bryn said.

"And I was listening to *The Diane Rehm Show* on the way over here, and she was talking about her beloved dog. This touches many lives!"

"Wow, this looks great, Niv. It's a big undertaking," Bryn said, looking back down at the drawings, "but we can do this."

"Yes, we can. We're really doing this," Nivie said.

"We're all doing this!" Megan exclaimed.

Jacqueline loved the weekend in May when Woodhaven Run Blooms Garden Council sponsors the annual planting of the flowers along Main Street. The Chamber of Commerce bought flats of brightly colored red, white, and deep purple petunias to be planted by volunteers. Both Ronni and Donna had returned from their respective winter havens, Florida and Arizona, to participate. Since winter's ups and downs were more pronounced this year, Jacqueline enjoyed this time with her friends even more. After the planting, brunch was offered for the volunteers. Donna and her husband were unable to attend the brunch, but Ronni sat with Jacqueline.

"How are Bryn and the grandkids doing?" Ronni asked.

"They're doing well, but I'm afraid Bryn and the kids have this impossible idea—"

"—you mean the animal memorial park?" Ronni interrupted.

"Yes, that's it. How can she possibly take on such a project?" Jacqueline asked.

"Well, I know Niv has gone on and on about how wonderful Bryn is and the progress they're making."

"Really?"

"Yeah. I'm even donating a week at my Florida condo to the silent auction they're going to have."

"Silent auction? I hadn't realized they were that serious."

"Yeah, these youngsters—can't keep 'em down! Now, my breasts on the other hand," Ronni joked, clutching her chest. "Can't keep 'em up!"

"Ronni," Jacqueline shook her head, smiling.

"Listen, Jacquie," Ronni said, taking Jacqueline's hand. "I know my niece. This park is going to happen and that's a very good thing. Even among all the ladies here in Blooms. Many of them have talked about their animals and how much they miss them after they've passed. Not to mention in Book Club. It's been many years, but I still miss my boy, Riley. And, I don't even want to think about when my 'Queen Corky'—" Ronni quickly waved away her tears. "Anyhoo, it is a marvelous project. And, remember, you know this better than most: Life is short."

"Indeed. But, I don't know, Ronni. We'll see."

In an effort to recapture what previously brought her joy, and with the kids still in school, Bryn changed into her jogging clothes and slid her Ray Bans on. Ace popped his head up, forcing the napping Olaf to roll to her side away from the comfortable Ace pillow. After surveying the scene, Ace stood up and trotted over to Bryn. He stared at her, cocking his head, trying to ascertain if Bryn was indeed getting what he hoped she was getting from the kitchen drawer. Turning in circles, he snorted in celebration.

"C'mon, Acey," Bryn said, attaching the leash to his collar. Bryn took him to the backyard first, to take care of necessities. But instead of staying inside afterward, Bryn took him through the house and out the front door. He hopped up and down in anticipation of this new trip.

Walking faster than normal, Ace seemed a little confused, but he followed her. She quickened the pace and Ace sprinted in front of her. Her arm jerked around as if there were a large, thrashing fish on the end of it.

"No, Acey!" Bryn said, with her arm almost horizontal. "Stay here next to me."

Using all her might, she moved her hand to her abdomen and pulled back on the leash. Ace finally stopped, jumping up and barking in celebration of this new game. Bryn started walking again, slowly increasing her speed, but Ace zig-zagged in front, nearly tripping her.

"OK. We'll just take this slower," she said, trying to settle a leaping, enthusiastic Boxer.

———✦———

Climbing up a mountain, Jacqueline sees the trail in the woods where she once rode her bike. The plush trees are now a vibrant green. In the distance, she sees a horse galloping, and Edmond is standing off to the side. She hears a giggle. Looking down, she sees a baby in a carriage, extending her chubby arm with flowers in her hand to Jacqueline.

Jacqueline blinked her eyes open, hearing Chloe softly snoring at the end of the bed. Remnants of a memory evoked by the dream created an almost audible thud in her mind.

To avoid hearing her parents' incessant and now almost daily money arguments in the living room, nine-year-old Jacqueline crept out the back door and ran to the barn. Ranger was in his stall, resting his back hoof on his toe, bottom lip quivering. When he heard Jacqueline, his ears pricked forward. He gracefully turned his large body around stuck his head out of the stall door just as Jacqueline arrived.

"Hi, Ranger. How are ya today?" Jacqueline asked. She flattened her hand and placed a few carrot pieces in her palm. Ranger lowered his head, stretching out his muscular neck, contorting his lips to reach for the treat.

Jacqueline loved the sound he made when he ate and didn't mind the "Ranger residue" left on her hand. She stroked the side of his neck. Strands from his mane tickled her fingertips. Gently rubbing his velvety ears, she appreciated the tiny hairs inside. Ranger twitched his ear and shook his head. She also loved the feel of the sparse hairs on his velvety muzzle.

Accepting the bridle she put on him, Ranger began to chew on the bit. He willingly followed her out of the stable, reins dangling loose around his neck. Gripping some of his mane and taking the reins in her hand, Jacqueline pulled herself up on his back. Ranger stood patiently, though shifting his weight from side to side.

"C'mon Ranger," Jacqueline said, making a clicking noise and leading him to the forested trails behind their house. The sun filtered through the soaring pine and maple trees.

The trail was wide and seemed to welcome the girl and her horse. Ranger's four-beat walk rhythm lulled Jacqueline into a meditative state, as she took deep breaths in sync with his gait. The birds chirped in harmony.

Her beloved horse was the best gift any daughter could have received from her dad, she thought. Her dad said she earned Ranger for getting all As. Jacqueline's minimal understanding of horses derived from trial and error. However, after watching movies such as *Black Beauty* and *National Velvet*, as well as reading Walter Farley's *The Black Stallion* books, she felt more prepared. Today she wanted to try something new, so she squeezed her knees in tighter.

Ranger's head jerked up slightly in surprise, and he began trotting. She tightened her grip on his mane, and her body bounced up and down on his back, her arms flailing around.

"Whoa!" she said, pulling back on the reins.

Ranger slowed to a walk, but Jacqueline was determined. Squeezing her legs tighter, she made another clicking noise.

The trotting commenced, but increased in bumpiness and speed. Jacqueline's heart began to thump louder when she realized she was beginning to slip off of Ranger's back.

"Whoa!" she yelled again. Ranger snorted, slowing again to a walk.

This is not how Elizabeth Taylor did it.

She stroked the side of his neck, feeling his muscles under the fuzzy layer.

"Good boy. C'mon Ranger." Making forward movements with her body, she clicked again. His walk increased to a slow trot, quickly increasing to a fast trot. The insides of her legs ached. She hunkered down, grabbed the reins with some more strands of his mane, and squeezed her knees in tighter. At the moment when the bounce and speed of his trot became unbearable, Ranger stretched out his neck, breaking into a full gallop. His long legs dug into the earth and curled back up under his belly. His head moved in a rhythmic motion, as his long strides echoed thunderously through the woods.

"Weeeeeeeeeeee!" she squealed as Ranger settled into the gallop. His ears darted around in response to her proclamation.

Now she and Elizabeth Taylor had something in common.

Feeling the hair lift off the back of her neck, Jacqueline and Ranger were one entity, flying through the air. It was as though his hooves never touched the earth. All the worry, loneliness, and separateness she often felt at school and home dissipated. She and Ranger were connected in these liberating and powerful moments.

After a few minutes of flying, she pulled back on the reins. Ranger slowed.

"Oh, my gosh, Ranger! Thank you. Thank you. Thank you!" Once he came to a complete stop, she dropped the reins, leaned over, and whispered, "Thank you for being my best friend. I love you *so* much." Jacqueline wrapped her arms around Ranger's sweaty neck as he snorted.

She never felt more alive.

"Mom?" Bryn asked, the next day standing at own her front door. She held it open for Jacqueline. "Is everything alright?"

"Yes, everything's fine." Jacqueline said, walking in. Looking directly at Bryn, she said, "Brynnie, I owe you an apology."

Bryn stopped. "What? Why?"

"I've given it a great deal of thought. And," she drew in a deep breath. "And, I think what you, Nivie, and the kids are doing is remarkable."

"You do? Really?" Bryn asked.

"Yes, I really do."

"But, I thought that—"

"—Well, I was concerned for the wrong reasons," Jacqueline interrupted. "I was focusing on the pain of losing the pet instead of the love and joy they bring."

Bryn's face relaxed.

"And, if you are amenable, I would like to help in any way I can," Jacqueline said. "But, only with your permission, of course."

"Absolutely. Thanks, Mom."

"It's interesting that you and Nivie are working on this together," Jacqueline said. "From the bits and pieces I heard from Ronni over the years, I always knew Nivie would take on a leadership position of some sort."

"Yes, she's really amazing," Bryn said.

"But, don't forget. So are you," Jacqueline paused. "Your father would be so proud."

"Thanks," Bryn reached out and embraced her mom. "I miss him so much."

"He was always incredibly proud of you." Jacqueline cleared her throat. "I just have one request: Do you think that Ranger could be included in the park?"

Bryn smiled. "Of course, Mom. He was always going to be."

It was another frantic morning near the end of the school year when the minutes slipped away faster than Bryn could grasp.

"Where are your other special kitty socks? You know, the ones with the lace on them?" Bryn asked Megan.

"I don't know," she said.

"Third time this week," Bryn muttered. "Please go get another pair," she said, glancing down at her phone. "Oh my gosh! Time to get going. Meggie, do you have your lunch? Math homework?"

"Yeah."

"Bud, you have your book?"

Ethan nodded.

"All right. Let's get the show on the road."

"What does that mean?" Megan asked.

"Not today," Bryn replied, piling everyone into the car and, rushing so quickly she almost forgot to pick up Madeline.

Returning home from carpool, Bryn collapsed on the couch.

"Hey, Olaf," Bryn pulled out the fishing rod cat toy. Olaf swatted at it numerous times then grazed her tail against the jingly ball on the end. It was nice to see Olaf beginning to play again. The kitten's meandering and howling for weeks after Tucker died was almost too much to bear.

A pungent smell suddenly attacked Bryn's nose. She sat up, spotting two large piles of vomit on the floor.

"Good grief, Ace."

Looking over at his food, she noticed it hadn't really been touched. "You feeling OK?" The puppy blinked slowly with deep brown eyes.

"Wanna go outside?" Ace raised his head, his tail gently wagging.

She decided to ask the ultimate rhetorical question as a litmus test. "Do you want to go on a walk?" Ace struggled to get up. Standing anywhere near the leash drawer usually launched an earthquake. But, this time Ace only hopped up and down a few times. The usual springing and dancing were absent. Once outside, Ace stopped and squatted, only bringing forth a little diarrhea. Walking a few more steps, he stopped again, this time straining, without producing anything. After a few more unproductive stops, not far from the house, Bryn said, "All right, Acey. Let's go see Dr. Carmichael."

Bryn was directed to an examining room where Dr. Carmichael checked Ace over, saying she needed to take bloodwork and get an x-ray. She led the trembling puppy into the back of the clinic for tests, leaving Bryn alone in the room. The door shut loudly behind them.

In an attempt to avoid remembering the last time she was waiting for test results with Tucker, Bryn stood up, and studied the dog and cat posters splashed on the wall. Heartworm preventive. Flea and tick preventive. Breeds of dog poster.

Dr. Carmichael's entrance startled her. "Oh, sorry."

"That's OK. How is he?" Bryn asked.

"Well, we found out why Mr. Ace isn't feeling very well," Dr. Carmichael said, x-rays flopping in her hand.

"Yeah?" Bryn said, with increased heart rate.

Dr. Carmichael continued. "It looks as though our Ace has been eating things that don't provide much nutrition."

"The kitty litter?" Bryn asked.

"Well, yeah. That, too," Dr. Carmichael chuckled. "But, if you look here," she said, pointing to the x-ray, "it seems as though he's been snacking on socks."

"Socks?" Bryn repeated.

"Yes, from the looks of it, about two or three pair. Maybe children's socks."

"Oh, my gosh. So, that's where—"

"—They need to be removed right away."

"Absolutely. Whatever needs to be done."

"We were going to try use an endoscopy. But, since the socks are in his intestines, we'll have to do surgery."

"Oh, my gosh, Acey."

"It will be a few hours. But, we'll give you a call when we know more."

Bryn, collapsed on her living room couch again, and texted Julian. "Ace not feeling well. Took him to see vet. He ate kids' socks. As many as six."

"LOL. Time to get new socks! Great business trip. Love being in Texas!" Julian texted back.

Bryn's face and stomach fell. With a tight jaw, she texted back: "☺."

A few hours later, Dr. Carmichael called. "Looks like everything went well. He's stable now and should be able to go home tomorrow."

"Oh, thank you so, so much," Bryn said.

"You're welcome. I know it will be hard, but he'll need to stay quiet for a little while and get some rest. I'll send some pain meds home with you, but the little guy should be back on his feet again in no time."

"Oh, can we, I mean, the kids and I, see him today?"

"Sure. When they get home from school, come on over. He'll be glad to see everyone."

"Thanks again!" Bryn said. "I'm glad this time wasn't like last time. Sometimes it can be hard to, you know, go back."

Dr. Carmichael spoke in a lower voice. "I understand. You know, I was just thinking about Tucker. I'm sure you miss him."

"Thank you," Bryn sighed. "Yeah, we really do."

"We miss him here, too. They become part of our family, too. He was a really sweet dog."

"Thanks. I mean, Accy is a sweetie, too," Bryn said. "Except for, you know, when he's not eating things we put on our feet."

"But, he's not Tucker," Dr. Carmichael interjected.

"Yeah."

"I understand. I had a dog like Tucker too. Tally, my Shetland Sheepdog. She was incredible. These animals stay with you and become your 'Heart Animals.' She's probably why I became a vet." She cleared her throat. "Anyway, so, we'll see you soon."

"Um, Dr. Carmichael?" Bryn asked.

"Yes?"

"Um, we just wanted to thank you again for your support of the HEAL Park."

"Oh, yes! I think it's an incredible idea. I told Nivie to let me know how I could help," Dr. Carmichael said.

"Great. Thanks!"

Bryn texted Julian: "Ace pulled through surgery fine. Going to visit him this PM with kids." She didn't wait for a response and silenced her phone.

———❦———

Bryn stood at the end of the driveway awaiting Megan and Ethan's return from school.

"Thanks, Allison. I really appreciate your picking them both up today."

"No problem, Bryn. See you, kids!"

Waving goodbye to Allison, Bryn turned to the kids and said, "Let's go see Ace!"

"Why, Mommy?" Megan asked.

"We need to go see him. He's at the doctor's office. C'mon, let's get in the car."

"Doctor?" Megan asked, stopping in her tracks. "Is he sick?"

"Well, sort of. He ate your socks."

"He ate my socks?" Megan's eyes darted around. "He's not going to die, is he?"

"How taste?" Ethan asked, leaning over to see his wiggling toes.

"Is he going to die?" Megan repeated.

"No, he's OK, Meggie. We just need to—No, bud! Yucky!" Bryn said, watching Ethan sitting on the driveway curling his foot toward his open mouth.

"Don't do that. That'll give you worms."

"Ace has worms?' Megan asked, frightened.

"No, he had surgery because he ate your socks. C'mon kids, let's get in the car and go see him. Hurry! He's waiting for us."

When they arrived at the clinic, Dr. Carmichael escorted them to the recovery room. They found Ace curled up, resting in his cage. Hearing his humans' voices, he tried to lift his head. But, the e-collar cone hung heavy on his neck, appearing to weigh more than its plastic material.

"W' happen?" Ethan yelled, running up to Ace's bottom cage door, poking his fingers through the holes. "What that?"

"Shhhh, bud," Bryn said, looking around at the other dogs and cats who were recuperating.

"Hi, Ace. You have some people here to see you. Ethan, he has an e-collar on so he can't lick his incisions from the surgery," Dr. Carmichael said, cracking open Ace's cage door. Snorting and sniffing, Ace struggled to his feet. Regaining some balance, his backside wiggled.

"He's wearing that so he'll leave his belly stitches alone," Bryn translated.

"OK, take it easy now, Ace," Dr. Carmichael said, opening the door wider. "Don't overdo it."

"But. But, he's not going to die, right?" Megan asked again.

"No, his abdomen is sore, but he'll be OK," Dr. Carmichael said. "However, I can't stress enough the importance of keeping the places he goes free from things he could get into. Puppies really can get into and eat anything. Socks, rocks, Kleenex, coins, rubber ducks. I even had a puppy eat a fishing hook."

"Whoa!" Ethan yelled.

"Puppies can be like little goats," Dr. Carmichael continued. "That's why it's important to be careful and pick things up."

"Shh, bud. Yes, we'll be more careful," Bryn affirmed.

"Poor Ace," Megan said, moving her face close to his. "You're all right. You're not going to die."

"Ok, kids. You heard Dr. Carmichael," Bryn said. "When he comes home tomorrow, we'll need to be extra special and quiet around him. He's going to want to play, but we have to let him rest and get better."

"You gonna be OK." Ethan gently stroked the top of Ace's head.

Bryn knelt down and gently rubbed the side of his face. "Aww. Ace. You really are sweet. But, no more socks." Ace struggled in an attempt to lick Bryn's face. With his long tongue, he swiped the side of his own cheek instead.

The next day, Bryn and the kids brought their still-unsteady puppy home. In the kitchen, he turned left around the corner, scraping his e-collar cone on the side of the doorframe. Startled by his own movements, he overcorrected, scraping the other side of the doorframe. Backing up, he didn't realize Bryn was standing behind him and she felt his back nails scratch her foot.

"Mommy, he keeps running into the wall," Megan said.

"Yeah, that's going to happen."

Olaf, unsure of this new version of her buddy, watched the interactions unfold. As soon as Ace relaxed, he grunted, plopping himself down on the living room floor. Olaf crept toward him, extending her neck. Once Ace passed her "sniff test," Olaf touched her tiny nose to his flat face. She placed a front paw on Ace's ear, licking the side of his head. He leaned into it, groaning. After the grooming Olaf nestled inside the e-collar. The exhausted puppy hardly balked at the puffy, white body nuzzled on his head.

After a busy summer of working on the HEAL Park, in addition to summer's usual events, Bryn was grateful to see the fall arrive. Standing in her kitchen, she smeared the last of the frosting on Ethan's birthday cake when Megan marched in.

"Why can Brother have a big party?" she asked. "It's not even his birthday month."

Bryn sighed. "Because Daddy wanted it now. I mean, Daddy thought—whatever. Anyway, it will be fun! There will be a lot of fun things," Bryn said, spinning the cake to take a final look. "Let's see. There will be face painting. Big bubbles. Oh, and a bouncy house! You like bouncy houses."

"Yeah," Megan relented.

Bryn walked over to the cabinet, looking for candles. Speaking into the cabinet she continued, "There will be laser tag and—"

"—Laser tag?" Megan scrunched her nose.

Bryn added, "Yeah, OK. Probably not your favorite. But, there will also be balloon animals."

"Won't pop, will they?" Megan asked.

"Nah," Bryn hoped.

"Oh, will there be ponies?" Megan excitedly asked, clapping her hands.

Without thinking, Bryn answered, "No. Way, way too dangerous. Especially for little girls."

"But, Grandma had—"

"Yeah, I know, honey. But, they are so big, and so strong. And, what if they took off, and—"

Megan's head dropped.

"—No, there won't be any ponies," Bryn said, inserting the candles on top of the cake. "But there will be, let's see, there will also be a big slide."

Bryn took a step back, admiring her work, then looked at Megan, "Oh, I almost forgot, a big castle you can jump on. You can be the princess!"

"Yay!" Megan cheered. "I can be the princess!"

Crisis averted.

Carrying the last of the snack bowls to the tables on the lawn and driveway, Bryn pointed at each as she reviewed her mental checklist. "Cake. Check. Presents table. Check. Pop and water table. Check. Other food and goodies. Check. Think we're all set."

Bryn looked up at the sky and smiled. "Thank you, God, for this beautiful, sunny day."

Megan carried out the napkins, placing them on the table.

"Thank you, Megan," Bryn said. "You are such a good helper." Megan beamed. "Please go find your brother. He's probably with Daddy."

"OK, Mommy!" Megan skipped toward the bouncy house.

Ethan, sat atop Julian's shoulders sporting a huge grin and donning a crown that read, "King Ethan." With eagle-eye focus, Ethan watched and relished as each game being inflated.

Playing the hostess, Bryn and Megan greeted arriving guests. Megan enjoyed directing them to the food as well as where to place the gifts and cards. The guest list included Grandma Stanton, some of Ethan's classmates, his pre-school teachers, Mrs. Russell and Mrs. Hayes, and a few people from his soccer team. Allison, Madeline, Julian's supervisor and his wife, Doug and Janet, were also there, as well as Julian's friends, Nate, Sanjit, Mike, and their families. Bryn was disappointed neither Lauren nor Nivie could make it, but she was grateful they sent their gifts ahead of time. When she found out Julian's parents couldn't make it, Bryn secretly cheered. Looking out on the lawn, she saw Ethan running across with a crooked crown atop his head. He was having too much fun to care.

Turning on her heel, Bryn almost tripped over Megan, who was standing behind her, Olaf in her grasp.

"Mommy? Can we bring Olaf out? I wanna show everyone."

"Oh, Meggie. Olaf shouldn't be out here. Please put her back inside."

"Whiiiieeeee?" Megan protested.

"There are too many people, and...."

Suddenly, Ethan and his friends dashed by Megan, screaming, pretending to be knights. Olaf twitched her back, leaping out of Megan's arms. Her front paws landed on the birthday cake, and her back paws followed, leaving the frosting to read: "-appy Bi-thda- Eth--." Continuing her escape, Olaf jumped onto the snack table, sending chips and dips soaring through the air and splattering the ground.

"Olaf! Come back here!" Megan yelled, chasing after the escaped feline.

"Megan! Don't yell!" Bryn said, rushing after Megan.

Locating a solid crabapple tree trunk in the front yard, Olaf climbed up the trunk and out onto a branch. She stopped, looked down at the humans below, and mewed.

Hearing the commotion, Julian abruptly ended his conversation with Doug and Janet about Texas and ran across to Bryn. "What happened, babe?" With their curiosity piqued, Doug and Janet followed Julian to see if they could help.

"Oh my gosh, Megan brought Olaf out, and—"

"She what?"

"Anyway, doesn't matter! Olaf! In the tree!" Bryn pointed up. "Please go get her!"

Julian looked up. "Holy crap! Eh, just leave her. She'll jump down. Eventually. And if she doesn't, well...." Doug and Janet laughed.

Ethan and his entourage rushed to where Bryn was standing. "Pwingo in the tree!" He stomped up and down on the ground, laughing. His friends followed suit. "Pwingo in the tree!"

"Olaf!" Megan corrected her brother and his friends. "Daddy, can you get her?"

"Julian, please. Get your daughter's cat out of the tree," Bryn said.

"All right, all right. I liked my idea better. But..." Julian fetched a ladder from the garage and positioned it against the tree trunk. After gaining his balance, he took each step as quickly as he could.

Jacqueline ran outside from the kitchen to see a crowd of guests gathering on one small area of the lawn. Following everyone's sight line, she said, "Oh my goodness! Olaf!"

Bryn watched as Olaf walked further out onto the branch, mewing louder.

"C'mere," Julian commanded. The terrified kitten didn't budge except to look at Julian and mew. Reaching out toward Olaf, Julian wrapped his fingers around her frosting-laden body and began tugging. "Let....go! You ....stup....cat! Let go!" After a few concerted efforts, Julian pried her talons loose from the shaky branch. "Got her!" he yelled down.

Reacting to the spectators' cheering and applause, Olaf scrambled up Julian's shoulder. "Oh, no! This is *not* happening again." Keeping one hand over her body, and one hand on the ladder, Julian slowly climbed down, rung by rung. Olaf's body began to twitch in an attempt to jump, but he managed to thwart her efforts.

"Thanks, Daddy!" Megan hopped up and down a little, not paying attention to the tiny scratches she had sustained from Olaf's great escape.

Once both of Julian's feet were firmly on the ground, he gathered Olaf's white body in his hands. Smelling of crabapple, he had large chunks of white hair on his shoulder, in his hands, and in his mouth. Walking into the house, Julian plopped the cat down. The frightened feline ran and found refuge under the couch.

Bryn would have liked to join her.

A few hours later, after cleaning up the outdoor area and tucking the children into bed, Bryn walked into her bedroom. Julian was checking the residual claw marks on his shoulder in the bathroom mirror.

"The kids are in bed now. Megan has bandages on her little scratches," Bryn said. "Most of the cleanup is done. I'll just do the rest in the morning."

"Did you talk to her? Did you tell her never to do that again? Man, this was supposed to be Ethan's big day."

"Yeah, I know. But, Ethan seemed fine. Didn't seem to bother him in the least. After everything happened, he still had a great time," Bryn chuckled. "In fact, he—"

"—And, when will Ethan be able to speak properly? It's embarrassing. I thought you were taking him to that place."

"I am. It just takes time. They say that—"

"—And, why'd she bring that stupid cat outside anyway?" Julian interrupted. "Why did I ever let her have that thing?"

"She just wanted to show everyone," Bryn said, holding her pajamas in her hand. "Just, don't worry about it. Won't happen again. You took care of it. Everything's back to normal now."

"Well, not so sure."

"What do you mean?" Bryn asked.

"They offered me a transfer to Texas once the new building is finished there."

"What?" she exclaimed, looking at him in disbelief.

"And, I'm going to take it."

"Hey, Ms. Emerson!"

Nivie looked up from grading at her school desk to see her former student. "Hey, Chelsea! Good to see you. How are you?"

"Good. You're doing that animal park thingy, right?" Chelsea asked.

"Yeah, we are."

"Well...I mean, like, I guess I could help out, and stuff." She looked down, shrugging her shoulders and tightening the sides of her mouth.

"That would be great, Chelsea. Thanks so much!"

"Yeah, Mrs. Carlson asked a few of us in choir if we wanted to sing at the dedication. So, I thought it would be kinda fun."

"Awesome. So, what are you doing here after school?"

"Just wanted to tell you. And, also we bought a brick for Gracie. Can't believe my parents actually did that. And, one of the big ones, too. So, that was kinda cool."

"That is," Nivie smiled, nodding her head.

"Anyway, just wanted to let you know," Chelsea said, as she walked out the door.

"Thanks!" Nivie said, stunned as she looked around at the empty desks.

"Julian is being transferred." Bryn said, standing in her kitchen. "To Texas!"

"Oh, my goodness," Jacqueline said.

"Yeah, I just found out. He doesn't have a lot of details, but he'll be spending a lot of time visiting the area, house hunting. Yada, yada…"

"Oh, no," Jacqueline said, her voice falling. "I see, so…"

"—So, I thought you should know," Bryn interrupted.

"When was he thinking?"

"Again, he has to look into everything, but it might not be for several months until the new building is completed. Just have to see how things go. But, they gave him the offer and he's made up his mind."

"Oh, OK. We'll still have some time together then," Jacqueline said.

"I guess," Bryn sighed.

"Brynnie, what do you think about this move?"

"Well, I'm not so sure. I really don't want to leave Woodhaven Run. Or, you."

"Yes, it would be really difficult," Jacqueline said. "I sure would miss you and the kids."

"On the other hand, it would just be a great promotion for him." Bryn exhaled. "But, the reason I'm calling is we're looking at different venues to have our fundraiser for the Park," Bryn said, changing the subject. "Reverend Owens said we could have it at the church conference area. But, I would actually love to have it at a conference room in The Stadium."

"Yes, that would be a perfect venue. But—"

"—But, it's out of our range. And, well, we can't…we just can't seem to get connected to the right people."

"I see," Jacqueline thought. "I don't want to interfere, but perhaps I could look into it for you."

"Thanks, Mom. That would be great," Bryn said, after holding her breath.

"You're welcome, Brynnie," Jacqueline said, with a kernel of sadness about the move.

The next morning, after a walk with Chloe, Jacqueline stood in the kitchen, her phone in her grasp. She took a deep breath as Chloe looked up at her human with her head cocked quizzically.

"Hello, Bill? This is Jacqueline St—"

"Why, yes, Jacqueline! My goodness. How have you been?" Bill asked.

"I'm well. Thank you. How are you?"

"Just fine. What a pleasant surprise. It's great to hear your voice. To what do I owe this pleasure?"

"Yes. Well, I was hoping you could help us with a favor, or some ideas," Jacqueline said.

"Sure."

"Well, my daughter, Bryn, has been organizing a project and is currently looking for a place to host their function."

"Yes?"

"And, she was hoping to have it at The Stadium."

"Ahh, I see."

"I don't mean to put you on the spot, but—"

"Not at all. You're not at all. Has she tried reaching out to management?"

"She has tried to contact the person there, but without any luck," Jacqueline continued.

"And, you were thinking—"

"— I was hoping you might be able to help us."

"I'd be more than happy to see what I can do. What type of function was she planning?" Bill asked.

Jacqueline cleared her throat. "Well, it's a fundraiser to build an animal memorial park. To commemorate our animals, pets, who have passed away."

"Interesting idea," Bill said.

"She has garnered quite a bit of support. I hadn't realized the number of people in Woodhaven Run that would be interested in such a thing."

"It is a unique idea, and I'm learning new information about you, too," Bill pointed out.

"Yes?"

"I hadn't realized you held animals in such high esteem."

"Well, as you know, Chloe has been an angel for me," she said, petting Chloe on the head. "And, growing up, I, well, I had a horse named Ranger who was very special to me."

"Oh, you ride?" Bill asked.

"Well, I used to ride quite a bit as a young girl, but many years have passed since I last rode," Jacqueline chuckled. "However, recently I had considered getting back into it again."

"'Back in the saddle again'?" Bill joked.

"Yes, something to that effect."

"I have a buddy who runs an organization that uses horses to help children and adults. There are programs for all types of healing, such as multiple sclerosis and cerebral palsy, and autism and PTSD, as well."

"Sounds like a wonderful organization," Jacqueline said. "Horses certainly are healing."

"They really are, and he's a great person to talk to. For the park, and for work with horses. Perhaps I could introduce you to him."

"Perhaps," Jacqueline said. "But, The Stadium?"

"Oh, right. When was Bryn thinking of having the function?" Bill asked.

"Sometime later this year. Most likely in December. She spear-headed a college alumni event that was held there in the spring. It also holds special meaning for her since we used to go there as a family to watch games."

"I see. Well, I'd be happy to contact another buddy who works there, and we'll see what we can do."

"Thank you, Bill. She, I, we sincerely appreciate your willingness to help."

"I'm so glad you called, Jacquie."

"As am I. Thank you."

"Good bye. I'll be in touch," Bill said.

"Sounds good. Good bye, Bill." Jacqueline hung up. Grasping the phone, she exhaled.

"Babe! Guess who is in the running for 'Manager of the Year'?" Julian exclaimed, walking into the kitchen from work with a bouquet of roses in his hand. "Yours truly!"

"Oh, Jay!" Bryn said. "That's great! Wow! Thank you so much for these!" She brought the flowers to her nose to take in the fragrance. "My favorites."

"Yeah, no problem. There's going to be a big dinner and award ceremony and everything!"

"That's great! So, when is the big night?"

"December 2."

"Oh, no," Bryn's shoulders slumped. The bouquet turned upside down in her hand.

"What?"

"That's the date of our big fundraiser at The Stadium. I'm so grateful we got it. In fact, I was hoping you could come, too," Bryn quietly added.

"Man, Bryn, I need you at my dinner. Can't you change it?"

Bryn shook her head. "Sorry, Jay. I really can't."

Julian began shaking his head, massaging his forehead with tense fingers.

"Babe, Tucker was great and everything," he said, "but do you really have to have a shrine for dead pets? I mean, really."

"It's not a shrine. And, it took a lot to find the venue, settle on this date, advertise, send out the invites and everything." Bryn thought. "Well, maybe I can—"

Julian interrupted. "And, I know you're a big deal now and everything, but do you really have to be there?"

"I'm one of the founding members, Jay," Bryn hissed. "So, yes. I 'have to be there'."

Julian was silent.

"Anyway, what I was going to say is, maybe I can go to my fundraiser for alittle bit, and then join you at the ceremony later. Where is it going to be?"

"Just forget it. Better put those in water before they die," he said, pointing at the flowers as he stomped out of the kitchen, slamming the basement door behind him.

Nivie basked in the task of garnering fundraiser support. "This is like Christmas!" she exclaimed with each new contact. Meeting with others, visiting local businesses, and submitting an advertisement in *Woodhaven Run Daily News* energized her. She even slipped in a blurb in the daily school announcements with John's permission and contacted other schools, as well. Parents donated items, time, and treasure to the Park. When the Woodhaven Run Humane Society became a major supporter, all opportunities seemed possible.

The contact list grew longer and longer. Bryn kept all the fundraising items organized, updated social media, took pictures of silent auction items and posted them online. She also kept the contacts organized in a database. Whenever Nivie needed a name or number, Bryn was there.

The night was set and The Stadium's largest conference room was ready. During the fundraiser, Nivie flitted from person to person, relishing every moment. A buffet table, holding the hors d'oeuvres, was adjacent to the two silent auction tables, decorated with white tablecloths. Round tables in the middle of the room were covered in white cloth, with dark blue ribbons tied on the chair backs. Centerpieces comprised of a ceramic animal sitting on a mirror and a potted plant would go home with one lucky tablemate. The large, brick fireplace flickered as jazzy, relaxing music played in the background.

"Hey, Niv. I'm just finishing up the tables for the silent auction," Bryn said. "Did you bring the pencils and pads for the bidding?"

"Oh, my god! I totally forgot!"

"That's all right. I went ahead and got some," Bryn reassured.

"Oh, thanks so much, Bryn! You're the best!" Nivie said. "Hey, I enjoyed meeting your friend, Lauren, too. She's really helped a lot with this. It's awesome you guys have been friends so long. Really, since Kindergarten?"

"Yeah, she's like my sister. Just wish she could have stayed the whole evening."

"But, at least she was here. If only a short while," Nivie said. "I'm already thinking about the April fundraiser. I've got a couple good ideas brewing!" she grinned, looking around at a room filled with evening gowns and black ties. "Just still trying to find Marcia from the Humane Society. Have you seen her?"

"A few minutes ago. Last I saw her, she was near the silent auction tables," Bryn said, trying to block out any thoughts of their upcoming move.

"OK. I'll go back over there and see. Let me know if you need anything!"

Bryn looked over and saw Jacqueline walking in with Bill. She was dressed in her Neiman Marcus short-sleeved black dress; she finally got to wear it again.

"Wow, Mom. You look beautiful," Bryn said, leaning in to give her mom a hug.

"Doesn't she, though?" Bill asked.

"It's so nice to finally meet you, Mr. Langdon," Bryn said, extending her hand.

"Please, call me Bill. It's nice to finally meet you, too, Bryn," he said.

"I've heard so much about you," Bryn said, as Jacqueline blushed. "Thank you again for helping us to secure this venue."

"It was my pleasure," he said, smiling at Jacqueline.

"Well, if you please excuse me," Bryn said, motioning to the silent auction tables.

"Certainly, Brynnie. Do whatever you need to," Jacqueline said, smiling as Bryn walked away.

Jacqueline turned around and, behind Bill was an older woman with a cane slowly enter the entertaining area. She wore a multi-colored long-sleeved top with a calico kitten and a Bichon Frise puppy on the front. Her long black shirt almost hid her kitten and puppy socks. Almost.

"Ms. Paisley," Jacqueline said, walking up to her. "How nice to see you. It's been a while."

"Yes, quite. My, Jacqueline, dear. Don't you look lovely this evening?"

"Thank you. As do you."

"Thank you, dear."

Nivie approached them, almost skipping. "Hi, I'm Nivie Emerson. And you are…"

"Nivie Emerson, I'd like to introduce you to Ms. Gladys Paisley," Jacqueline said.

"Oh, Ms. Paisley! So nice to finally meet you!"

"Hello, dear," Gladys said, extending her hand, as her cat and dog charm bracelet jingled.

"Ms. Paisley has been a neighbor of mine for many years," Jacqueline said.

"That's great!" Nivie exclaimed.

"We're so pleased she could join us tonight," Jacqueline added. Bill gently touched her back. "Oh, if you will please excuse us."

"Of course, dear," Gladys said.

"I hope you enjoy your evening. Thank you again for coming." Jacqueline said, following Bill to meet his friend at the drink table.

"Glad you could come!" Nivie said to Gladys. "I love your shirt!"

"Thank you. Yes, well, I saw in the newspaper that —"

"—Oh, excuse me, Ms. Paisley," Nivie interrupted. "There's Marcia! I need to talk to—! Marcia!" she yelled, running after the contact person. Nivie glanced back. "So sorry, Ms. Paisley. Please, enjoy your evening!"

"—that you were having this marvelous fundraiser," Gladys finished, standing alone. Hearing the clinking of glasses and the hum of talking, she looked down and tightened her grasp on her cane.

The evening of laughing, music, and eating had ended. All the hard work paid off. After the patrons went home, Nivie suggested, "Let's do this every week!"

"Well, I'm not sure about every week." Bryn stood back and smiled. "But, it really came together."

"Did you have a good time?" Nivie asked, sitting down next to her to count up the numerous donations.

"I really did," Bryn said. "I'm just so grateful for everyone who came. It's amazing how many people are really committed to supporting The Park. And, it was nice to see Mom so...so...Well, it was just nice to see Mom smiling and looking so beautiful."

They were especially thrilled to see a $1,000 check from Bill. Then, Nivie picked up one check, and her jaw dropped. The check said $30,000.

"Who's it from?" Bryn asked.

"You're never gonna believe it!" Nivie exclaimed.

Arriving home after the fundraiser, Bryn set her purse down on the kitchen island. In the living room beyond, Olaf was licking Ace's ear; he leaned his head into her, groaning, "You two are so silly."

Bryn crept up the stairs and opened her bedroom door to a darkened room. Julian was under the covers with his back facing the door.

"How did it go tonight?" she whispered, sliding onto the bed on her hip, gently touching his back.

"I did it. I won."

"Oh, Jay, that's great!" Bryn exclaimed.

"Yeah. I know," he said, readjusting the sheets over him. "But, you should have been with me. I was left hanging there."

"I know, I'm so sorry, Jay. Just that, you know…."

"Yeah, I know. Anyway, tonight good?" he asked flatly.

"Well, it turned out to be really successful. Actually—"

"—How much money did you raise?" he asked, curtly.

"Well, um, we did really well. More people showed up than—"

"—Great," Julian interrupted, pulling the sheets and comforter tighter over him. "Just great." He yawned loudly. "Well, time to get to sleep. Long day tomorrow."

"Oh, OK. Sure." Bryn blinked quickly. "G'night, Jay," she said to her husband's back.

"'Night," he mumbled.

Jacqueline, Bryn, and Nivie stood on Gladys' front stoop. After ringing the the doorbell, they heard the clunk of a cane and footsteps on the other side of the door amidst two tenors of barking dogs. Gladys struggled to open the door in her terry-cloth robe.

"Good morning, Ms. Paisley," Jacqueline said.

"Oh, my goodness. Jacqueline, Bryn and Nivie, dears. What a pleasant surprise. Please, won't you come in?"

"We'd love to. Thank you," Jacqueline said.

"We were just watching *Animal Planet*," Gladys said, holding the storm door open. Behind her, the main door held an evergreen wreath decorated with cats and dogs in Santa hats.

"Jacqueline and Bryn, dear, I believe you know everyone. But, Nivie, dear, meet my Roosevelt. Piper and Petey are the two jumping balls of fluff. And, quiet Eleanor is asleep on her chair. We call it Eleanor's 'chat,' because it's cat chair" she giggled, pointing with her cane to a bleary-eyed long-haired black cat, unaffected by the barking dogs and new people.

"What beautiful animals you have, Ms. Paisley," Nivie said.

"Why thank you. They are my children," Gladys said, voice quivering more than usual. Her arms shook slightly from a perceptible tremor as she held onto her cane.

"I totally get that," Nivie agreed.

"How are your children Bryn, dear?"

"Oh, they are doing very well, Ms. Paisley. Thank you," Bryn said.

Gladys motioned them to the living room, where the fireplace mantle displayed urns and framed animal photographs highlighted by track lighting. The photographs included dogs, cats, a bird, and even a guinea pig. Photos continued along the walls in the living room and down the hall, alongside many framed obituaries from the *Woodhaven Run Daily News*.

"Would you care to sit down?" Gladys asked, slowly leaning over to turn off the television.

"Unfortunately, we aren't able to stay," Jacqueline said.

"Oh, I see." Gladys frowned.

"We don't want to keep you, but we wanted to stop by and personally thank you for your extraordinarily generous gift," Jacqueline said.

"Oh, it's the least I could do. Your Park is such a lovely idea. I couldn't be more pleased you dears are creating it." She took in a deep breath. "When do you suppose it will be completed?"

"We're still pushing for the end of this coming summer," Nivie said.

"Splendid," Gladys replied.

"Yes, and we wanted to talk with you about something else," Bryn said.

"Oh?"

"Yes. With your permission, we would like to dedicate an area in the park to you," Jacqueline said.

Gladys' took in a deep breath as her shaky hand gently cupped her cheek.

"We would call it 'Gladys' Glads'," Nivie said. "And then, we'd love for you to say something at the opening. What do you think?"

"Oh, dear. Oh, my goodness. How incredibly kind of you," Gladys said, her round rump slowly finding its way to her chair. She set the cane down next to her. "But, I couldn't possibly."

"It would really mean a lot to us if you would," Nivie added.

"How incredibly kind of you," Gladys repeated, "But—", she looked up at three eager women and sighed. "Thank you. That would mean the world to me."

"Wonderful," Jacqueline said. "We are delighted."

"And grateful," Nivie added.

"Did you hear that, Rosie? Did you hear that, little ones?" Gladys asked, voice cracking. "Oh, my goodness. Well, whatever shall I wear?" she asked, her hand shaking as she pulled at the decorative paw print sewn on her robe.

"Well, you have such a lovely collection from which to choose," Jacqueline sincerely added.

Gladys slowly stood up, balancing on her cane. She took Jacqueline's hand and looked at the three women standing in her living room. "You ladies are remarkable," she said, tears welling in her eyes. "I'm just terribly, terribly sorry that—" She paused. "At any rate, thank you for including me."

A heavy March snow had pummelled Woodhaven Run. The poor souls pushing their snow blowers transformed into walking snowmen from the snow's backdraft. Even with this dreadful inevitability, the envy of those who were forced to use a snow shovel was palpable.

Having been responsible for Gladys' snow removal and lawn for years, Kurt, Jacqueline's housekeeper, Shirley's son, and his business partner, Joe, pulled up to Gladys' house. She was last on their route, and they were ready to be done for the day.

"Oh, man. Go tell her to move her car into the garage. Ain't no way we can clear it off with her car in the way," Joe said.

They looked at each other.

"Man, I talked to her last time," Kurt said.

Joe tightened his lip. "All right. Rock, Paper, Scissors."

"1, 2, 3."

"Oh, man."

"Yep. Paper wins!" Kurt celebrated.

Joe reluctantly stepped out of the car and into the eight inches of freshly fallen snow. He adjusted his belt. Gladys usually greeted them at the front door in her terry cloth paw-printed robe and matching slippers, with the main door open and the storm door fogged with condensation.

After seeing the newspaper on the stoop, Joe rang the doorbell. No answer, except the sound of low hoarse barking mixed with high-pitched barking.

After a few seconds, Joe rang the doorbell again. The barking continued.

"Hey, Kurt!" Joe yelled with visible breath. "Roll down the window!" he motioned.

"What?" Kurt yelled from the car.

"She ain't answerin!"

"Heh?"

"No answer!" Joe said, pointing to the door.

"No answer?"

"Yeah!"

"Huh." Kurt opened the creaky truck door, slammed it shut, and zipped up his coat. Walking in Joe's foot prints, he joined him on the front stoop. Scratching his head, Kurt said, "Don't know. Give her a call. She might not be able to hear, ya know."

Joe pulled out his phone, craning his neck to look around the closed curtain in the front window. The phone rang and rang. Perplexed, Kurt walked to another front window and peeked through a gap where the curtains hadn't completely closed.

He saw Roosevelt barking at the front door and peeked down to see Petey and Piper barking as they twirled in circles.

"Hey, pooches. Where's Ms. Paisley?"

Kurt's eyes scanned the living room. They landed on Gladys lying motionless near her recliner chair and cane. She was face-down with her right arm stretched above her head toward her ringing phone.

"Oh, my god," he mumbled to himself, quickly motioning to Joe. "Hey, Joe! Get over here! Call 911!"

9

A bell jingled on the door. Two heads snapped around to look at Jacqueline as she walked into Chloe's groomers business.

"Hi, Mrs. Stanton. How are we today?" Cynthia, the friendly owner greeted Jacqueline. Another patron stood at the counter, checking out.

"Just fine. How are you?"

"Good. Good. Oh, how's the park coming along?" Cynthia asked.

"Very well, thank you. And, thank you again for your kind donation."

"Hey, no problem, no problem. I'll be able to help more when you break ground."

"We would appreciate that. Thank you," Jacqueline said.

"We'll get Miss Chloe to ya in a jiffy."

"Thank you," Jacqueline replied, placing her keys in her purse. She walked over to a chair facing the front counter, grabbed a *Dog Fancy* magazine, and sat down.

"Well, guess she won't be around here no more," the patron said to Cynthia, leaning her large belly on the front counter. Even speaking in a whisper, her raspy voice reverberated throughout the shop. "Heard they found her, ya know. Dead. Inside the house."

Cynthia's jaw dropped, as Jacqueline momentarily glanced up from her magazine.

"She was such a sweet, sweet lady," Cynthia said.

"Um, weird is more like it. I heard that they right away put her old dog to sleep."

Cynthia's eyebrows shot up. "Oh, no! Rosie? Why'd they do that?"

"Don't know." The woman shrugged her shoulders. Her voice increased in volume with the excitement of gossip. "I heard it was all wrote down ahead of time. Ya know, if she died first, that he was going with her type of thing."

Although Jacqueline's eyes were glued to the article, she focused on their conversation.

"And, I heard that when they cremated her, they mixed in her ashes with the dog's," the woman said, fumbling her hands over each other.

"Oh, my gosh."

"Yeah," the woman continued. "And, I heard that she was goin' to have those two little dogs put down, too. I seen them in here before. Forget their names…"

"Oh my gosh. Piper *and* Petey?"

"Yeah, them! They was goin' to be put down, too. But, they found someone that would take 'em 'cuz they was just babies."

Cynthia slowly shook her head.

"But, I guess that old dog. Jus' too old. But, he's with her now!" The woman guffawed, then coughed loudly.

"Poor Rosie. He came in from time to time for baths, ear cleaning, and such."

"Oh! And did you hear about her cat?" the woman asked.

"No. What about her cat?"

"They was going to put her down, too. But, I heard that she took off," she gestured with her hands. "Yep. Took off

like a shot when they was, you know, taking the old lady out of the house."

"Oh, my gosh."

"Yep, got out, and never looked back!"

"This is all just terrible," Cynthia said.

The woman slowly nodded her head, hiding what appeared to be a tiny smile.

"Mrs. Stanton?"

Jacqueline jumped a little.

"Yes?"

An assistant had Chloe on a leash, with a little red bow around her neck. Chloe's backside wiggled intensely.

"Oh, Chloe!" Jacqueline said, standing up. "Don't you look and smell so clean? Thank you, Cynthia. I'll see you next month."

Jacqueline stopped at the counter. "I couldn't help but overhear your conversation. I remember Ms. Paisley as a kind and lovely person deserving of our respect. We lost a lovely soul with her passing last week."

"Absolutely! Gonna miss her a lot," Cynthia added.

Jacqueline looked over at the other woman. The eye contact wasn't returned.

9

"I just still can't believe it. I mean, she's gone. Sweet Gladys is gone," Nivie said to Alex on the phone, leaning on the side of the kitchen island. "It's only been, like a week. But, I still can't wrap my mind around it."

"I know, Love," Alex said. "It's hard."

"I'm really glad we have the area in the park for her. But, what gets me is what they did to her dog Roosevelt. I mean, I don't think that we would do that. Would we?"

"Well…"

"Just doesn't seem right," Nivie said. "I mean, I know he was old and everything, but I'm sure *someone* could have adopted him. Silver whiskers, and all. But, she decided that ahead of time."

"I guess."

"And, it's sad, ya know. She didn't have any close friends or family to speak of. Or children."

"Honey, I know what you're thinking," Alex comforted. "That's not going to be you."

"I know, it's just…"

"Yeah, I know," Alex said. "Didn't realize it was getting to you again today."

"Well, it comes and goes. Good days and bad days." Nivie said, blowing her nose. "On top of these endless days of low-lying clouds and melting snow. Bleh."

"Well, just remember I love you. And, the boys do, too. They told me this morning."

"Thanks, Love."

"But, the reason I called is…Well, I have some good news," Alex said.

"Yeah?"

"But, you'll have to wait until I get home."

"Honey!"

Alex chuckled.

"Just finishing this update, and I'll be right home. Love you!" Alex said, quickly hanging up.

Nivie paced back and forth waiting for him to come home. Sherlock's and Watson's eyes followed her as though they were watching Wimbleton on television.

Seeing Alex's car pull into the driveway, she ran to the window, waving wildly. Sherlock and Watson scattered into opposite rooms. Nivie opened the door, barely letting her husband set his work bag down.

"So?" she asked.

"Soooooooo….," Alex drew out slowly. "I…I mean…we…"

"Honey, spit it out!" Nivie said, bouncing up and down.

"We have an opportunity to go to the Outer Banks in North Carolina for the weekend!"

"Really?"

"Yeah! Our department has a conference there. Someone couldn't go last minute, and they asked me if I could fill in. So, I thought you could come with."

"Oh, my god! The beach! You know I *love* the beach!" Nivie said.

"Yeah! And, like you were telling me last night. Everything is on track for the park. You guys found wonderful contractors, landscapers and builders. The statues will be here when they need to be. Everything's good. Plus, at the beach, we could…enjoy the warmer weather. And, maybe, could, you know." He smiled, pulling her closer, nibbling her ear.

She giggled before her smile disappeared. "But, what are we going to do with the babies?"

"I don't know. We'll put some food out for them. It'll only be for the weekend."

"Um. Yeah, that's *so* not going to work," Nivie said.

"We'll figure it out. But, the beach, honey! We can get a little sun. You know, enjoy ourselves!"

"Yeah." Nivie said, trying to feign excitement. "I mean, yeah!"

"What's wrong?"

"Just, you know. The last time we left…and then soon after we came home…"

"Honey, I know. But the boys are fine," Alex assured. "They're young—"

Nivie pursed her lips and twisted her jaw.

"I mean, they're fine," Alex corrected. "What about asking that girl who came over for the Kitten Bowl?"

"Megan?"

"Yeah, Megan. Can't we just ask her?"

Nivie furrowed her brow. "She's kinda young."

Alex shifted his weight, stepping back from Nivie. "Honey, it can't be that we can't ever go away again."

"I know, but—"

"Actually, weren't you around that age when you started taking care of others' cats when they went away?"

"Yeah…"

"So, I'm sure that her mom—"

"—Bryn," Nivie said.

"Yeah, Bryn wouldn't just leave her to do it on her own."

"I know."

"So, in a way, when you think about it, it's kind of like passing the torch."

"Wow. That's deep, honey," Nivie mocked.

"Just think about it."

Later that night, when Alex turned out the light, he rolled over in bed. Kissing Nivie on the head, he whispered, "G'night, honey."

"G'night."

Then from the silence came, "All right. I'll do it."

Alex lifted his head off the pillow. "Do what?"

"I'll ask Megan to take care of the boys while we're away."

Alex placed his head back down on the pillow. "Cool. Passing the torch."

"I know. You're right," Nivie relented. Not being right usually didn't feel good. This time was an exception.

9

Reaching into the mailbox, Jacqueline pulled out an envelope from Eastman Law Office. Her heart raced remembering the last time she received written correspondence from a lawyer.

Opening the letter, she focused on the words: "Ms. Gladys Paisley has named you a beneficiary in her will. Please contact us as soon as possible."

9

"C'mon, honey!" Nivie stood on the hotel bed, next to her reluctant husband. "You *know* I do this."

Alex gave her a look.

"C'mon—join me! The weather's better up here!"

She pulled on his arm to no avail. It flopped to his side.

"C'mon honey. We're on vacation!"

"Well, *you* are, anyway! Oh, all right," Alex said, taking off his shoes and stretching his toes.

"I just love this!" Nivie said, jumping up and down on the queen-sized bed.

When Alex stood up on the mattress, he smiled and, hunching over, tried to catch his bouncing bride.

"Oh, no you don't!" Nivie said, when she realized what he was about to do. Leaping across to the other queen-sized bed, she nearly missed her landing. Alex pounced over in hot pursuit. She jumped back to the first bed, contorting her body, avoiding Alex's reaching arms.

After a few passes back and forth, Nivie began losing steam. She laughed so hard, her attempts to talk turned to inarticulate mush.

"Gotcha!" Alex threw his arms around her, and together they fell on the bed, bouncing as they landed.

"I can hardly breathe!" Nivie laughed.

"I love hearing you laugh again. Seeing you *really* happy again," Alex said.

"It's been a long time."

"Too long," he said, stroking her hair.

The next morning, Nivie rose with the sun. With an easel tucked under her arm and painting supplies in hand, she located an open, quieter area in the sand within view of their hotel room. Flicking away some of the grass and sticks in the sand, she removed one new paint brush from its container. After running her fingers over the tip of the unused bristles, the same fingers automatically grasped the brush handle, as if no time had passed. She dipped the brush into the blue paint and placed it on the blank canvas. The brush moved around, seemingly independent of any conscious thought, as if it were guided by someone else. She squinted, focusing on the radiating, orangish-red disc that started to expand over the rhythmic waves. A few pelicans that had not made their annual trek to Florida flew in formation. A dog, with a stick in its mouth, waited for its owner to catch up. Splashing around, the surfers in the distance were merely dark, moving dots. The rolling water and the sea gulls' chattering lulled her into a meditative state.

Nivie took off her sandals allowing the moist sand slip in between her toes. She drew in a healing breath.

"Morning, honey!" Alex's voice made her jump.

"Oh. Hi, Love."

"You're painting again."

"Yeah, the sunrise was calling me."

"That is beautiful," he said, studying her painting. Kissing her head he added, "And, so are you."

"Thanks, Love."

"I gotta go. Look forward to seeing you after the conference."

"Me, too," Nivie said, smiling up at him.

"Have a good day, Love," he said, navigating through the deep, cool sand.

"Oh, my god!"

He turned around to see what happened. He smiled when he realized his wife squealed after seeing two magnificent pelicans fly overhead.

After the conference, Nivie and Alex rolled their pant legs knee-high and walked along the shoreline. Splashing each other a few times, Nivie squawked so loudly that the kids making sand castles nearby stopped to stare.

"Hey, if they can talk at over 100 decibels, so can I!"

Alex shook his head.

"Oh, honey. I feel so much at home here," Nivie said, holding onto Alex's hand as the waves gently lapped against their feet.

"Yeah?"

"Yeah. I feel, like, alive. Like really alive."

"Awesome," he said, kissing her head.

"I just feel as though this is what's been missing," Nivie continued. "Don't get me wrong, I love Woodhaven Run, but being here, I don't know, just lets me be me."

"What do you mean?"

"Well. What do you think about, you know, packing up the boys and…setting up shop here?"

"Wait, what? You mean *move* here?" Alex asked. "Here we go again."

"I know—but it's just, I don't know, magical."

"Man, Niv. First I can't get you to come, and now you want to—?"

"—I know."

"And, didn't you say this when we visited The Bay?" Alex asked.

"….well, yeah…."

"…and the desert? And…."

"…well, yeah…"

"…and the mountains? And, Mackinac Island?"

"OK. So, I might have mentioned this before."

"Yeah," Alex guffawed.

"But, I don't know. Honey, this time, it's different."

Alex studied her. "It does seem that way." He gave a quick shake of the head. "This is crazy. What about jobs? We can't live on puppy dog hugs and unicorn farts!"

Nivie chuckled. "Well, while you were at the conference, I poked around online a little."

"Uh, oh."

"And, there are some available positions down here. For both of us!" Nivie exclaimed.

Alex scratched the beard stubble on his cheek.

"Well, it's not to say that we'd get those, but it's nice to know there are options, at least," Nivie said.

"You know, you might lose the years you have toward your pension. Or, they might not honor the years of teaching you've accumulated. And, you might have to go through the annoying task of applying for your licensure down here," Alex pointed out.

"Bleh," she said.

"Yeah."

"I know. You're right, but they are little annoyances for a bigger gains," Nivie quipped.

"Maybe."

"And, you know, since it's just us and the boys. Well, one good thing is that we're more mobile," Nivie said. "Life is too short to spend in one spot."

"True," Alex pondered, watching a seagull soar overhead. "I just don't know, Niv. We'll see."

"Arg. I hate that! Anytime Ma said that, it meant 'No'."

"Not saying 'No.' We just need to look into it more. This is a huge decision, Niv."

"I know," she said, looking down, drawing in the sand with her toes.

"Just need to see if it works for me, too. Remember, it's my job that brought us down here."

"Well, maybe they have a branch down here?" Nivie asked with excitement.

"Maybe."

Nivie wrapped her arms around his waist and smiled. "So, you'll take it under consideration?"

"Yeah, I'll take it under consideration," Alex smirked. "But first, time for a nice bath!"

Despite her fervent smiling protests and flailing legs, Alex scoped Nivie up walked into the water and tossed her in.

Staggering out of the shallows, soaked, she spat out some water and pushed her drenched hair back.

"Still considering?" she inquired, little droplets of water flying from her mouth.

"Still considering," he replied, smiling.

After returning from their Beach weekend, Nivie stopped by Bryn's house. Standing in her foyer, Ace's backside wiggled as he snorted a greeting.

"Mrs. Emerson!" Megan said, running to Nivie, Ethan right behind her. "You're back!"

"Yes! We are," Nivie said, as Megan's arms wrapped around Nivie's legs. "You give the best hugs! I wanted to make sure that I thanked you in person for taking such good care of our boys. They seem happy and healthy. We appreciate the love you gave them. You did such an awesome job."

"Thank you," Megan said.

"Hi, Mrs. Emosin!" Ethan yelled.

"Hi, Ethan! Great to see you, too!"

"She had a really good time," Bryn said, stroking Megan's hair. "She scooped the food and changed the water."

"Yeah, I scooped the food and changed the water. Mommy did the litter, but I see how to do it now."

"Thank you," Nivie winked at Bryn.

"Ethan even knows how to do it now. Don't you, bud," Bryn said.

Ethan smiled. "Watson and Sholock are funny. But, Watson under couch. Sholock like food."

"Yeah, and they poop a lot! Like poop all over the place!" Megan said, stretching out her arms.

"Poop!" Ethan parroted, dancing around. "Poop!"

"All right, kids," Bryn said, tapping Megan on the arm.

"Yeah, there is more with two cats, isn't there?" Nivie said.

"Yeah! But, I love Sherlock and Watson," Megan said. "They are fun. But, Sherlock hurt my head when he hit me with his head," she said, pointing to her forehead. "And... And...Watson was on the back of the couch, like this." Megan said, rounding her arms in front of her.

"They are fun, aren't they?"

"Yeah."

"Meggie, why don't you and Brother take Ace out back to use the bathroom," Bryn said, pointing to the backyard.

"But, Mommy...."

"Mommy wants to talk to Mrs. Emerson."

"Ooookay," Megan quickly hugged Nivie and put her arm around Ethan. "C'mon, Brother! C'mon, Ace! Let's go!" Ace bounded after the two jumping kids, barking as they all went outside. "Bye, Mrs. Emerson!"

"Bye, kids!" Nivie said, turning to Bryn. "So, what's goin' on?"

"So, there was a bit of a snag this weekend," Bryn said.

"What do you mean, a 'snag'?" Nivie asked, with a tinge of worry.

"Well... so... well..."

"Spit it out," Nivie said.

"I took care of it, but it was uncertain if the statue was going to arrive here on time."

"Holy sh—! You mean the Taffy one?"

"No—"

"—Minerva? The bird statues in the foyer? The leaping foal by the children's area?" Nivie asked.

"No, not those either—"

"Oh, no. You mean the big one?"

"Yes, the one of Ranger, Tucker, and Kimball."

"Oh, my god," Nivie said, placing her hand on her temple. "What happened?"

"So, they said something about problems obtaining materials, and that it wouldn't be ready in time. But, I asked to talk to the manager and gave him the whole story. I also tol him about the opening of the Park and was able to talk to several different people to expedite the shipping to get it here on time."

"Oh, Bryn. You could have called me. You can always call me."

"But, I didn't see any point in ruining your vacation," Bryn said. "Anyway, everything is fine now."

"OK, so we're good now?"

"Yes. He said it would arrive on time," Bryn assured.

"All right, then. Whew. Good job, Bryn."

"Thanks."

"I must be relaxed because I'm not even freaking out about this!" Nivie chuckled.

Bryn smiled. "So, when do you think you can come over to iron out a few more things?"

"Actually, I can come tomorrow," Nivie said. "Took the day off from work."

"Perfect. Sans kids. So, when you are here, we can verify that everything is copacetic."

"That's the best word," Nivie said. "Thanks so much, Bryn. You're awesome!"

Bryn looked down, trying to hide her blushing face.

"Hello, Mrs. Stanton," the attorney said. "Please come in."

"Hello. This is quite a surprise," Jacqueline said, sitting down in an office chair.

"Yes. Thank you again for coming. Ms. Paisley wanted you to have this," the attorney said, handing her a folder.

Skimming the document inside, Jacqueline's eyes landed on the amount. She almost dropped the folder.

"Mrs. Stanton?"

"Yes, yes," Jacqueline waved her hand. "Oh, my goodness. How in the world did she—? Oh, my goodness."

"Ms. Paisley wanted to make sure you and the animal memorial park had what you needed. Not only now, but in perpetuity."

On the bottom of the document, Jacqueline read, "Please accept this token of my esteem. From the depths of my soul, my most sincere apologies for dear Tucker's accident and inury in the street. He was subjected to such pain and suffering by my hands. My heart is broken."

Jacqueline teared up and cleared her throat. "I cannot possibly fathom."

"There are many things we don't know about Ms. Gladys Paisley."

Jacqueline nodded, quickly blinking to prevent her welled tears from falling.

In contrast to Jacqueline's day, irritation fueled Nivie and Bryn as they both sat at Bryn's kitchen table.

"So, I heard back from the company again today, and they said there might be a tiny crack between Tucker and Kimball," Bryn said.

"Oh. My. God."

"But, that it wouldn't be visible. So, I told them that I wanted to check with you to see what you thought. But for now, I said that as long as the three animals could be set right next to each other, they don't need to be attached."

"Hmm…" Nivie thought. "Yeah, that should be OK."

"Oh, good," Bryn said.

"I mean, ideally they would all be connected on the same pedestal," Nivie added, "But, like you said, as long as they can be directly next to each other. Maybe even put some grass between and around them. Might make them look even more realistic. So, yeah, that should be fine."

"OK, good. I'll call and let them know that's what we'd like," Bryn said, standing up to retrieve her phone.

"I also heard from Dr. Carmichael," Bryn said, "She said she and her colleagues are still helping to spread the word, and will provide any necessary 'elbow grease.' Also, the son of my mom's housekeeper has a landscaping business—"

"—Awesome!"

"Yeah, so they can help, too," Bryn said. "Plus, the dozens of others who have signed up for working on the bushes, the paths with the bricks, building the sanctuary, including your principal—."

"John," Nivie said.

"Yeah."

"He's such a good guy. Whew...And, I'm glad we were able to secure reputable, reliable contractors to actually break ground and do the heavier lifting."

"Definitely. That was a huge load off," Bryn said. "So, we should be back on track now."

"Wow, Bryn. You've done so much. I don't know if it's my 'post-vacation blues' talking or the low-lying clouds, but it's just been harder to get movin' on things," Nivie said.

"Yeah, I understand that. But, you've done a lot already. You met with everyone and got the ball rolling. They're just following up with me. "

"Yeah, I know. Just feels like I need to kickstart myself," Nivie said.

"I've been there before," Bryn empathized.

"Yeah? It's hard. And, Ms. Paisley...It's just so sad."

"I know. Such a sweet woman. Kinda felt sorry for her," Bryn said, quietly.

"Yeah, me too. And, really misunderstood," Nivie said, taking in a deep breath. "And, on top of all this, Alex and I were discussing the possibility of moving. Like, to a different city. Out of Woodhaven Run."

"Oh, my gosh. Wow," Bryn said, setting down her phone. "When?"

"Oh, don't worry! Only after the opening of the park."

"Oh, OK. Do you know where?"

"Actually, we were looking at the Outer Banks in North Carolina, where we just were. But, again, don't worry. *If* it happens it would be after the opening of the park."

Bryn's face relaxed.

"Yeah, no way. This park means the world to me. And after all the hard work we've done, I wouldn't skip out before the opening and just leave you holding the bag."

"Wow," Bryn said, trying to collect her thoughts.

"Yeah, but not even sure if it'll really happen. Just wanted to let you know. And, I really don't want anything mentioned to the kids because again, I'm not even sure what's going on."

"No, I wouldn't say anything to them," Bryn said.

"Yeah. It sure would be hard. But, who knows. May not even happen. Anyhoo, didn't mean to have that come out of left field and scare you. Just wanted to let you know."

Nivie looked at Bryn. "You OK?" Nivie asked.

"Yeah. Well, actually, we found out that Julian is being transferred to Texas."

"Wait. What?" Nivie asked.

"Yeah."

"Oh, my god," Nivie said. "So—"

"—So, it's an excellent opportunity for Julian. It would be an incredible promotion. But, I don't know, Niv."

"What do you mean?"

"Well, it's just...the timing of everything," Bryn said. "There's just so much. Just not sure. And, our lives are here now. The kids' and mine. Are here."

Nivie studied her face. "Gotcha."

"Anyway, just wanted you to know since—"

"—Yeah. Well, who knows what the future will hold!" Nivie said. "For both of us!"

"But, for now..." Bryn said.

"Yeah, back to the park," Nivie cleared her throat. "So, now that the 'statue crisis' is over, what do we need to focus on for the spring fundraiser?"

"We have a majority of everything ready. I'm so glad we will be at The Stadium again."

"Yeah! And, I know that place holds special meaning for you, too." Nivie said.

Bryn's phone rang. She looked down to see Jacqueline's name on the screen.

"Mom?.....Everything OK?...Yeah, Nivie I and are here hammering out details for the spring fundraiser."

"Tell her I say 'Hi!'" Nivie said, waving her hand

"Yeah...Oh, really?" Bryn said. "Wow. We were just talking about her...You went today? Yes, I'm sitting down....She what?" Bryn placed her left hand over her mouth. "Oh, my gosh. Oh, my gosh."

"What?" Nivie asked.

"Yeah, of course. We'll be here."

"What'd she say?" Nivie asked again.

"See you soon!"

"What? What?"

Bryn cupped her hand over the bottom of the phone. "I don't think we'll need to worry about the spring fundraiser results after all."

The April fundraiser was an even greater success, bringing the community of Woodhaven Run closer together. Volunteers had worked fervently to ensure an early September dedication day.

"Still considering?" Nivie asked Alex one July night after dinner.

"Still considering," he said, smiling.

"All right. So, the chikawaka for the touchscreens," Nivie said.

Alex furrowed his brow.

"You know, the software program," Nivie clarified. "For the park touchscreens in the foyer attached to the chapel. How's it goin'?"

"Oh, yeah. It's goin'. Slower than I had hoped, but we're making progress."

"OK, because you know everything has to be up and running by the middle of next month."

"You mean the *end* of next month."

"No. I mean by the *middle* of next month," Nivie said.

"I thought you said—"

"No! I said *middle* because the builder guys have to make sure everything is built correctly and works in the foyer. The only time they can do it is...Remember when we were in the kitchen and I said—"

"Oh, my god. Totally heard you wrong."

"C'mon, you're kidding me. Right?"

"Dammit. So sorry."

"Oh, my god! Alex! Oh, my god. First the statue, now this? If this doesn't get done, then it might not be ready for the opening!"

"OK," Alex muttered. "We can fix this. This can be fixed."

"Oh, my god," Nivie whimpered.

"It's OK. It's OK," Alex repeated, convincing himself. "I'll just stay later and work on it myself. Whatever it takes, I'll haul ass and get it done."

"Is that even possible for one person to do? I thought you needed your work buddies' help," Nivie said.

"It'll get done. I'll get it fixed. It'll be OK."

"God, I hope so."

Ace accompanied Bryn as she made her way to the leash drawer. He knew what this signaled. Luckily, all of Bryn's efforts in the preceding weeks had turned Ace into a true jogging companion.

Although Ace moved at a faster pace than Tucker had, Bryn was able to keep up as they jogged to Jacqueline's house. She was grateful he finally learned to stay next to her side. Not too far ahead, or behind. Right at her heel.

Bryn and Ace were greeted by Jacqueline and Chloe at her front door. Upon seeing Ace, with her new Lammikins in tow, Chloe widened her stance. Ace snorted around her, trying to befriend this determined Spaniel. Chloe's tiny lip raised up as a small growl was emitted. He looked at her, then turned in circles back to Bryn's side.

"Haven't seen you in a while, Chloe," Bryn said. "How's she doing, Mom?"

"She's doing much better. Dr. Carmichael says her thyroid was off. But, I think we finally got her meds right."

"Oh, good."

"It was touch and go there for a while," Jacqueline added. "And, it was so sweet of the kids to call and check on her."

"Thanks. We were all very concerned. Megan kept asking if she was going to die."

"No, she's fine now," Jacqueline said. "Thank you for coming over. I wanted to discuss something with you. I've been giving a great deal of thought about getting a vacation house Up North. What do you think?"

"Wow, Mom, that would be great," Bryn said, a large grin spreading across her face.

"You might remember that your father and I had discussed buying a property there. I know how much you always wanted a cottage, or lakehouse. And, I know you love going to Barbara and Lawrence's."

Bryn cringed and said, "Well, I love being on the water, anyway."

"I thought it would be nice for all of us to be able to spend time together there when you come back to visit from Texas. We can spend a weekend there. What do you think?" Jacqueline asked.

"Texas…yeah," Bryn's voice dropped momentarily. "Well, I think having a vacation cottage Up North would be really good. For all of us," she added, with more excitement.

"I'm so glad to hear," Jacqueline said, and paused. "I wanted to check with you first. Looking back, I know that many choices, some rather consequential, were made for you, instead of allowing you to give input into your own life. So, before I pursued this, I wanted to be sure it was something you really wanted."

Bryn swallowed the lump in her throat. "That really means a lot, Mom."

"It would to me, too, Brynnie," Jacqueline said, hugging her daughter.

Nivie, deep in thought as she put the finishing touches on her painting from the Beach, felt Alex's kiss on her neck. "Well, I'm done considering. I think we should do this," he said. "You're right: Life is short. I think we should move."

"But, there's so much," Nivie said. "The opening dedication of the park is—and, the software program. You're still working on that, right?"

"Yeah. Don't worry. It's coming together."

"Really?" Nivie asked, raising an eyebrow.

"Yeah."

"Not just blowing smoke?" she said, setting down her brush.

"No," Alex chuckled. "It'll be ready to go. Actually, a few days before to test it."

"OK. Because you know that we don't have a lot of time, here. And, if it's not done, then—"

"—I know, Love. It'll be ready to go."

"OK. If you say so," she said, grinning with narrowed eyes. "But, moving…You really think so?" Nivie smiled as her question ended in up talk.

"Yeah. After the opening, of course. So, you'll be there for your fall semester."

"Yay!" Nivie jumped up and down, quietly clapping.

"Yeah, I poked around, too," Alex said. "And I talked to some of the guys at work. It would be a long commute, but there is a slight possibility of tele-commuting."

"And I just looked again today. The position is still open," Nivie slyly added.

"We should do this," Alex confirmed. Nivie leapt around the kitchen and wrapped her arms around her husband.

They both glanced down at Sherlock and Watson who were lying in the middle of the kitchen, unaware of the upcoming disruptions to their feline lives.

"Uh, oh. Who's going to tell them?" Nivie asked.

Jacqueline climbs up a steep mountain. She takes a step off and flies high above the forests below. She looks down to see power lines dwarfed from her vantage point. When she lands on the ground, she sees a child, extending her tiny arm to Jacqueline with flowers in her hand. She moves closer. Jacqueline sees it is her when she was a little girl.

"So, tomorrow's the big day?" Donna asked Jacqueline, who was gathering last-minute items for the Park opening and placing them on her kitchen counter. Chloe, with her pal Lammikins, was at her side. "I'm looking forward to being there with Ronni. How are things coming together?"

"Really well. It's remarkable how the people of Woodhaven Run have gathered together and contributed to the project."

"Fantastic," Donna said. "And, how are you?"

"I'm doing well, thanks. Would you care for some tea?"

"Yes, please. But, Jacquie. How are *you*?" Donna repeated.

"For a moment I almost forgot with whom I was speaking," Jacqueline said, sitting down into her chair, motioning to Donna to sit. "I wish he were here," Jacqueline said, pouring tea into Donna's and then her teacup. "I really miss him. Especially now. But, I am doing better."

"With your permission, I'm going to put on my 'therapist hat.'"

Jacqueline smiled. "Sure."

"It's important to remember that although everyone grieves in their own way, it's never really done. One is never completely 'over' it. Just hurts less. Or, less often."

"I've found that to be true," Jacqueline affirmed.

"In fact, closure is one of my least favorite words when talking about grief work," Donna added.

"It certainly is work."

"Indeed. People 'close' on a house, not on grief," Donna continued. "The healing process allows people to find a place in their hearts for their beloved, allowing room for joy to return."

"I understand. As I look back, the first year was the hardest. All the birthdays and holidays. Anniversaries, too," Jacqueline said.

"Those can be particularly difficult. Anniversaries, of any sort."

"Yes, holding your breath until the next milestone event passes. I would think: 'I made it through. One more down.' But, sometimes grief can sneak up on you when you least expect it," Jacqueline said.

"Very true. Have you found that your grief has seemed to return since working on the HEAL Park?" Donna asked.

"Yes, and I keep thinking that it should be gone by now. But, as you said, it's never completely gone."

"Unfortunately, grief is rarely linear and there is no timetable. It's important to be gentle with ourselves, but grief will just sit and wait," Donna said. "Plus, the loss of Edmond and Ranger is a lot for anyone to bear. It can be compounded."

Jacqueline nodded.

"Ranger was a lifeline for you during an extremely lonely time in your life. It was painful for you to lose your best friend. Many times, a child's first experience with death is after a beloved animal dies. And, it can be extremely traumatic, as you well know."

"You are so right. It is very hard, especially as a child," Jacqueline said. "But, I'm grateful the good days have become more frequent."

"I'm so glad to hear," Donna said. "And, you're better able to talk about it now."

"Yes, sometimes simply finding words for one's grief can be nearly impossible," Jacqueline said. "Especially in the beginning."

"Indeed," Donna said. "But one thing is for sure: it's very healthy to channel one's grief into doing something. Because of your involvement with the park, you're using your pain to help others, by providing a safe place, inclusive of various faiths, to heal from their grief. So, it's not only a gift to yourself, but a gift to others, as well."

"Thank you, Donna," Jacqueline said. "You have been so helpful and supportive. Not only in contributing to the park, but in so many other ways. The friendship you and Ronni have shared with me has meant the world."

Donna smiled, gently tapping Jacqueline's hand on the table. "Well, we're only giving back what we've received from you."

Jacqueline smiled. "Oh! And, you'll be pleased to know that I'm looking at vacation lake houses Up North," she added.

"That's fantastic, Jacquie!" Donna clapped. "I'm curious, what prompted you to do this now?"

"Well, as you know, Edmond and I talked about it before he died. And, when Brynnie was young, she always wanted a consistent place we could go to get away. Even though our lives took different paths than what we originally imagined, I'm so pleased that she is excited about this." Jacqueline looked down. "I will miss them terribly when they move to Texas."

Donna leaned over and gave Jacqueline a hug.

"I did want to mention, however, that my dreams have been really bizarre," Jacqueline said.

"Really? You remember some?" Donna asked.

"A few. They have changed over the years. They started out as peculiar and have morphed to almost serene."

"So glad to hear you are tuned in," Donna said. "Was Edmond in any of them?"

"One," Jacqueline replied. "But, he was really a part of all of them. It just took a while to realize that." Donna raised her teacup to clink hers with Jacqueline's.

The night before the Park opening, Nivie and Alex taped a few more packed containers shut, adding to the array of box piles in the living room. Sherlock had inspected every bin, box, and package by shoving his grey nose into any open crevice. Jumping into the open box added an extra level of examination, even if it meant he and a knick-knack from the living room were the only items in the box. Watson curled up under the dining room table, as he had done the first night, allowing ample space from all the ruckus his humans were creating.

"That's going down last," Nivie said, pointing to the Christmas tree in the corner of the living room that had stayed up all year.

"I figured," Alex smiled.

"So many memories here," Nivie said, scanning the room, choking back a few tears.

"Yeah."

"Good and bad."

"Yeah. But, on a different note, everything really came together," Alex asserted.

"Yeah," Nivie said, hands on her hips, looking around the discombobulated living room.

"And, I told you I could do it."

"What do you mean?"

"The park..."

"Oh, you mean the software program," Nivie clarified. "Um, yeah, OK. But, we didn't get *two* touchscreens like I hoped. Just one. And, I was a 'Work Widow' for a while there!"

"But, it's done," Alex said.

"Yeah. That's just not the way I like to work," Nivie reiterated.

"Good thing I love ya so much!" she said, sending him an air kiss. "Well, ready to take a break?"

"Sure," he said, wiping the sweat from his forehead.

"So, honey. Do you want to...do it? Might be one of the last times in this house," Nivie pointed out.

"Sure," Alex said, grinning.

Upon his approval, Nivie ran to the refrigerator and grabbed a few blueberries. "Blueberry Time" commenced one last time. In this house.

Bryn knew the question was coming. All the prior discussions she had with Julian where she smiled and nodded saying, "We'll see" and "That's something to think about" were merely a dress rehearsal for this moment. Climbing into bed, she pulled the comforter over her, leaving just her head exposed.

"Well, babe, I need to let Doug know," Julian said, turning off the bathroom light. "I'm leaving tomorrow for Texas to house-hunt, and maybe sign a contract on that one house I showed you online. When are you guys coming down?"

Her mouth tensed. She looked up to see Julian towering over her.

"Not sure. But, I don't think right away," she whispered.

"What are you talking about?" Julian's look of astonishment surprised her.

She pulled her arms out from beneath the comforter. "Don't you think it would ultimately be better if the kids stay here? You know, start the school year here?"

"No. Like I've told you many times before. It's better for them to go down now, get settled in, and get used to the area right away," Julian declared. "We've already discussed this."

Bryn paused, then almost whispered, "I'm considering applying for a job at the Chamber of Commerce."

Julian grunted.

"And, my mom's here."

"You hardly ever see her!" Julian snapped.

"Well, I'd kinda like to see her more. And the kids would, too."

"That's a change," Julian hissed. "Why is this coming up now? Is it because of that chick that keeps coming over here?"

"You mean Nivie?"

"Yeah. Her."

"No, it has nothing to do with Nivie."

"Whatever. So, what then? You're just not coming?" Julian yelled.

"Well, I just think it would be best for m—for all of us, if we left it open for now," Bryn replied, motioning to him to quiet his voice.

"'Left it open'? What are you talking about? We've been over this many times. I need to know now when you're coming."

"I mean, just not sure about this," Bryn shrugged.

Quickly looking around the room, Julian shifted his weight with his hands on his hips. His eyes glared down at Bryn. "So, tell me. When will it be 'convenient' for you? When will you know?"

Bryn swallowed hard. "Probably not for a while."

"Wow. OK," he chuckled, angrily. "Well, then. You just let me know when it would be good for you— I mean all of you. All right? *Babe*?"

He flung his body into bed, yanking the comforter over him and slightly off of Byrn. She hardly slept a wink.

9

The rising sun reflected against the dewed September grass. Alex, John and Bill finished setting up the sound system and lectern. Shirley and her sons sprinkled some last minute mulch around the bushes and flowers Jacqueline and Woodhaven Run Blooms had planted. At the entrance, a wooden sign that John carved read, "Welcome to Woodhaven Run HEAL Park."

Nivie's heart leapt watching fellow animal lovers and their animals pour in. Rejoicing in the moment, she looked down to see who had texted her. It was from her sister, Siobhan: "So excited for you! ☺ U did it! Kimball Kitty is grateful 2. Thank U 4 B so good 2 & 4 him. Love you, Niv!"

Nivie also saw she had a voicemail from Ma. "Sorry can't be there today, Nivie. Yeah, I said 'Nivie!' I am very proud of ya. Love ya, *a leanbh!*"

Bryn received a text from Julian that morning: "Good luck today, babe." She didn't respond back. The kids wanted their father to be there, but Bryn told them they could video chat with him later that night.

Overseen by Jacqueline and Woodhaven Bloom volunteers, the oval shaped HEAL Park was surrounded by bushes of red tip photinia and Korean or wintergreen boxwoods. Butterfly bushes and burning bushes peppered the periphery. Near the parking lot, an eight-foot long by eight-foot wide flagstone bridge was erected over a man-made brook. The moving water would be disconnected once the colder weather came, but dogs would lap it up during the warmer days of summer.

Beyond the welcoming bridge, surrounded by green pachysandra, the large statues of Ranger, Tucker, and Kimball Kitty stood. A brick pathway on the left led to a plaque reading "Gladys' Glads." The adjacent bench provided rest where the red, pink, orange, yellow, white, multicolored gladiolus flourished through the late summer into the fall. Continuing along the path, to the left was the interment area. Encircling that area were flagstones around a sleeping Minerva statue. Walking back onto the main path led to the main doors of the chapel-sanctuary and its inside foyer. Nivie's murals highlighted each foyer wall, including the one with the mounted touchscreen. The chapel entrance itself down the hall was flanked by two perched bird sculptures and the restrooms were tucked behind the chapel. The solid doors to the chapel itself opened to an area where animal memorial services could be held. Inside the chapel, rows of benches were separated by an aisle, that lead to a table-clothed altar, and the stone floor allowed for leashed or contained animals to be welcomed. Along the right wall was an area for flameless flickering tea light candles to commemorate any lost or missing animals. Out the chapel's double-doors to the right was the Zen room, a quiet, soft-lit area, only for adults. It housed a memorial book, comfy chairs, and was accessible from the main hallway.

Across from the Zen room was a foal statue prancing in front of the Kids' area. The door opened to a large corkboard covering the far wall dedicated to children's artwork. The various drawings and poems to their beloved animals were heartwarming. Drawers of paper, markers, pens, and pencils were housed to the side, and primary-colored plastic tables and chairs sat in the middle of the room. Dog, cat, horse, and bird stuffed animals rested on built-in benches on both sides of the room. Ethan's drawing and Megan's letter to God were pinned up within arm's reach of a small container of bubbles.

All the last minute details were ironed out and the crowd gathered near the entrance to the park. Opening the dedication ceremony, Father Kenneth and Reverend Owens each gave blessings, supported by various leaders from local places of worship.

Jacqueline approached the lectern, located at the beginning of the welcoming bridge. Behind her, Ranger's life-sized statue, emphasizing his head and neck were visible. "Good morning, everyone," she said.

"Good morning," the crowd responded.

"Thank you for coming. My name is Jacqueline Stanton, and it is a true privilege to be with you today," she said, smiling at Donna and Ronni in the crowd. "The Woodhaven Run HEAL Park would not have been possible without all of your support," she added, smiling over at Bill. "In addition, I want to mention the extraordinary efforts of Mrs. Genevieve Emerson and Mrs. Bryn Troxell. These two remarkable women spearheaded and developed the park, from start to finish. And, I'm proud to call one of them my daughter," she said, smiling at Bryn. "My cocker spaniel, Chloe, is still at home. This would not have fit into her schedule," Jacqueline joked.

The crowd chuckled.

"We would also like to express our deep appreciation to Ms. Gladys Paisley," Jacqueline continued. "Her open spirit, respect, and devotion to animals was unparalleled. And, due to her extraordinary generosity, she created an endowment so that the HEAL Park will be cherished for years to come. In honor of her, please visit the area of Gladys' Glads to the right of me," she said, pointing.

"Growing up in the country, as I did, visitors were rare. But, my beloved horse, Ranger, was my true friend and companion," she said, motioning to the noble horse statue behind her. "I understand that when a horse is buried, they often will bury the head, hooves and heart. Although Ranger isn't buried here, all of him is still with me. I also want to mention my husband, Edmond. Although he isn't physically here today, his memory is still a big part of my heart." Clearing her throat, she said, "At this time, I would like to introduce my daughter, Bryn Troxell, and my two favorite grandchildren, Megan and Ethan."

The crowd applauded as Bryn approached the lectern and Jacqueline hugged her daughter. "Good morning. Thank you again for coming." Her nerves were quelled when she saw Lauren standing in the crowd, smiling. "Tucker, our dog, was really our first child and when we had our children, he helped me to connect to them," she said, motioning behind her. "To me, Tucker was an illustration of how God wants us to be: showing unconditional love and sacrifice," she nodded to Reverend Owens and Father Kenneth. "This love was also shown to me as I was growing up. Since I did not have any siblings either, my dog Taffy was my 'sister.' Her statue is near Gladys' Glads area because the park is for her, too. I would also like to acknowledge our kitty, Olaf, and our Boxer, Ace. They continue to keep me on my toes but do it all with pure hearts. Lastly, working on the park with my mom was an amazing experience. I really wish my dad were here, but I believe that he and Tucker are together in Heaven."

The crowd clapped, and she smiled at Lauren again. "My daughter, Megan, wants to honor Tucker in her own way."

Megan waved to her friend Madeline and Allison in the crowd

before taking the microphone. Bryn stepped back with Ethan firmly affixed to her leg.

"I love Tucker and the way he always jumped at bubbles," Megan said. "I have my bubbles here because he would always jump at bubbles." Volunteers stood ready with trays of mini bubbles and passed them throughout the crowd. Megan struggled to twist open the cap of the bubble container and Bryn reached out to help her.

"I got it, Mommy," Megan said, turning her back to Bryn.

Bryn smiled and stepped back again. Megan removed the three-circle plastic wand and blew into it, creating several bubbles of various sizes. "Tucker would jump at them, like this," she said, springing into the air as the crowds' bubbles floated by her. "When I was young, I brushed Tucker and his soft fur. I love Tucker. I miss Tucker," she said, jutting out her bottom lip. "But, Tucker is with Gramp-E in Heaven. So, he'll be OK. Now, my brother is coming. His name is Ethan Troxell. Brother?"

Megan handed the microphone to a caped Ethan. He shook his head vehemently. "Come here, Brother," Megan motioned him to her. "Come closer to me."

The crowd chuckled.

Slowly uncurling his arm from Bryn's leg and holding Tucker's old squeaky Teddy toy, Ethan's wide eyes scanned the audience as he joined his sister. Taking the microphone from her, he exhaled loudly creating a blaring high-pitched feedback noise. He shielded his ears from the screech and the microphone and Teddy toy smacked to the ground.

Bryn grabbed the Teddy toy and Megan picked up the microphone. She said, "Here, let me hold it, Brother," as her voice loudly echoed.

Looking straight at the tip of the microphone, Ethan quietly said, "I miss Tucko. He was my best fwend."

"Sing your song, Brother," Megan coaxed.

"He was the bestest Tucko in the ho wide wod," Ethan quietly sang. "He was the bestest Tucko in the ho wide wod."

Ethan turned around to look for Bryn. "Mommy?"

The audience responded with, "Awwww," clapping in support.

Bryn knelt beside Ethan, clutching him. "I'm right here, bud." Megan leaned over on her mom, too, passing the microphone to her. Bryn nodded to the choir, maintaining her balance with the kids and holding the mic in the other. "Some members of the Woodhaven Run High School choir are going to sing for us, under the direction of Mrs. Anna Carlson. This is *Wind Beneath My Wings*." The song transported Nivie. She smiled at Chelsea who was belting the soprano part.

After the song, the audience applauded and Nivie approached the lectern.

"Good morning! Man, that song always gets me," she said. "Thank you to these members of the Woodhaven Run High School choir. And, in case we haven't said it already, thank you all for coming!" she laughed. She found great strength in seeing Brad and Esteban standing in the crowd. She smiled and waved back. "My name is Nivie Emerson. I first want to thank Alex, my husband, my rock and companion for believing in me," she said, turning to face him standing slightly behind her. "I, too, am grateful for the hard work, creativity, commitment, and determination of Bryn Troxell and Jacqueline Stanton. These two women are simply fantastic people. I also want to give a shout out to Ms. Paisley and her amazing devotion to our park. And, I would be remiss if I didn't acknowledge our two boys, kitties Sherlock and Watson, who are, even as we speak, busy sleeping at home. But, despite their lack of waking hours, their lives have shown me unconditional love and the compassion we all cherish in our animals.

"This park has been a dream of mine for a very long time. Words simply can't do justice to how much it warms my heart as I look out and see so many people who feel the same way. You, the community of Woodhaven Run, created this," she said, opening her arms wide, "by sharing your love, time, energy, and treasure of animals. I see the dedication of people who understand the important role that animals play in their lives and in their families.

"So, in saying all that: let's talk about our animals. What can I say about these fabulous, sentient creatures? I am eternally grateful to my two kitties who are no longer here, tiny Mini, or Minerva, who is sleeping near the interment area. And, Kimball, the one sleeping over there," she said, motioning over to the trio of statues. "There should have been a statue of a lap nearby because that was Kimball's favorite place: sleeping right next to you, through joyous and painful times. Although he was only on Earth a short time, he taught me every day is a gift. Tomorrow isn't promised to us. And, although it took me a while to see it, he taught me to open my heart to future animals.

"One of the things that makes difficult after we lose them is that it's as though we've lost that part of our lives, too. Like with Minerva, she represented my college years and my 20s, and then the time when I met my husband. It's like she became a warehouse of memories of that time in my life. When we lost her, it was like someone closed a chapter in my life that I wasn't ready to say 'Good bye' to yet.

"Even though our animals may frustrate, surprise, and worry us, through it all, they love us unconditionally, each demonstrating in their unique way what that means. Our lives aren't the same without them, and they leave their paw prints on our hearts. We know that the grief never completely goes away, but our intention is that HEAL Park will be a special place for healing and celebrating their lives.

"Alex and I are leaving Woodhaven Run, but perhaps we can start more HEAL Parks so that other communities can honor their beloved animals in a similar way. I could not be happier knowing our HEAL Park will be left in such capable and loving hands.

"I believe some angels have paws, hooves and feathers. They heal hearts, mend fences, build bridges; and now build parks. These angels connect us to one another and they are our companions on Life's journey. Although their ashes may be here, our memories of them will always be buried deep in our hearts. For all the animals who have touched our lives and have crossed the Rainbow Bridge, this is for you."

"Look!" Someone yelled from the crowd. Casting their eyes to the sky, the crowd saw it dotted with two hot air balloons. A few seconds later, two more appeared, and then two more, until the sky appeared bursting with them. The occasional burner sound triggered some of the dogs to bark and pull on their leashes. Nonetheless, Nivie's heart grew warm. She smiled at Bryn: their idea of coordinating the Hot Air Balloon weekend with the opening of the HEAL Park had worked.

Barking pierced the air, as one of the dogs jumped into the brook behind the lectern, lapping up some water.

His visibly shaken owner said, "I am so, so sorry."

"Oh, no problem. That's what it's for," Nivie chuckled, turning around.

"Tucker liked water, too!" Megan said from the side.

"Yeah, Tucko wato!" Ethan parroted.

"That's right, Megan," Nivie agreed. "So, enjoy yourself, pup!"

She turned back to the audience. "So, without further ado. Welcome!" Nivie said, as she cut the ribbon.

Visitors streamed in to enjoy the new addition to Woodhaven Run.

"Hi, Nivie."

"Oh! Hi, Dr. Carmichael," Nivie said, looking down at two yipping dogs on leashes. "Well, Piper and Petey! So good to see you! How are ya guys?"

"I'm not sure how much walking they did before, but it sure forces them to think!" Dr. Carmichael joked. "They tend to quiet down a little when they have to focus more intently."

"Not always a bad thing!" Nivie joked. "Thanks again for coming, and for everything."

"And, thank you for spearheading this. Absolutely wonderful," Dr. Carmichael said, walking across the bridge.

Nivie talked with and hugged a few more Woodhaven Run residents before she, too, walked over the bridge. She looked down at the path. Single and double bricks read: "Tucker, Our Wonder Dog" and "Ranger: You Taught Me Love." Her throat tightened reading the adjacent brick: "Kimball Kitty, Gone Too Soon" and "Minerva: Our Loving

Matriarch." With each step, Nivie read the cornucopia of names who had touched peoples' hearts: "Roosevelt, Tally, Rufus, Trixie, Gracie, Kano, Velma, Riley," and countless other animals' names she didn't recognize. "Katie, Fezzick, Jelly Bean, Lucky, Puppsie, Sasha, Ebony, Jubilee, Timmy, Cocoa, Angel, Lance, Smokey, Jessie, Charlie, Dumbo, Scruffy, Spunky, Gopika, Blossom, Nota, Kadison, Leroie, Little Box, Buffy, Sam, Shiloh, Mckinzie, Max, Theo." Just to name a few.

Approaching the large wooden door to the Chapel Sanctuary, her footsteps clicked on the foyer's stone floor. Nivie took a quick peek inside, marveling at how well it came together. She turned back around into the foyer and walked up to the touchscreen on the wall. She touched the screen and a menu displayed many beloved animals. Touching Tucker's name led her to a video of him frolicking on the boat at the Lake, posing at Christmas, running around in the back-yard, and sleeping with Megan and Ethan. Nivie touched on Ranger and smiled, looking at a younger Jacqueline with the few stunning pictures of Ranger.

Her finger quivered as she reached to touch Kimball's name.

"This is quite a memorial."

Nivie turned around and saw a tall, large man with a scruffy white and peppered beard leaning on a walking cane.

"Oh, thanks. And, thank you for coming," Nivie said.

"Yeah, I know in North Carolina they have a memorial park honoring military dogs and their service."

"Oh, cool," Nivie said. "I'll actually be moving there soon."

"Well, when you get settled, go and visit. Pay your respects. You won't be sorry you did."

"I will. Thank you, Mr.—"

"Steele. Stan Steele."

"Thanks again for coming, Mr. Steele."

"Sure thing. And, thanks again for doing this," he said, sniffing. "Our animals. Well, they're somethin' special."

Nivie saw Chelsea walking through the double doors toward her.

"Hey! Ms. Emerson!" Chelsea said.

"Hey, Chelsea! How are ya?" Turning back to finish her previous conversation, Nivie said, "Thanks again for coming, Mr. Steele!"

He nodded, hobbling away on his cane.

"Hey, Ms. Emerson."

"How are ya?"

"Outstanding," Chelsea said, walking toward Nivie.

"You guys sounded great," Nivie said.

"Yeah, it was fun."

"Hey, Love," Alex said, returning from surveying the park and mixing with the crowd.

"Hey, honey. Alex, this is Chelsea, a former student of mine," Nivie said.

"Nice to meet you, Chelsea."

"Hi, Mr. Emerson," Chelsea said, giving a quick wave to Alex.

"We had quite a time together, but we worked it out," Nivie said, winking at Chelsea.

"Yeah," she slowly nodded.

"Thanks again for all your help," Nivie said.

"Nah, no prob," Chelsea said. "Actually, kinda glad to help. Ya know, be a part of it. And, ya know, Gracie's ashes are here now. And, she has a brick, too. So, pretty cool."

"Yeah, it is. And this is going to help a lot of people," Nivie said.

Nodding, Chelsea said, "That's the plan. So, I have to go, but have a blast at the beach!"

"Oh, definitely."

"You're so lucky." Chelsea said, leaning in to give Nivie a quick hug. "See ya, Ms. Emerson. Nice to meet you Mr. Emerson!"

"Bye, Chelsea," Nivie said, with a little surprise at the hug and sadness.

Nivie turned back around to the touchscreen. Glancing at Alex, she touched Kimball Kitty's name. Watching the video of Kimball fetching, Alex hugged his wife as she choked back tears.

After the crowds thinned, Nivie and Alex walked toward Jacqueline and Bill who were admiring Gladys' Glads. Bryn stood nearby and pointed to one, describing it to an eager Megan and Ethan.

"Hello, fellow creators!" Nivie said.

"Mrs. Emerson!" Megan and Ethan ran to her. "I haven't seen you in forever!" Megan said, hugging nivie around the waist.

"Look what you did!" Nivie said, pointing out at the park. "Isn't this amazing that we all created this?" she said, continuing toward the adults at Gladys' area.

"Yeah, we hepped Tucko!" Ethan said.

"We sure did. We sure did," Nivie said. "Where's Tucker's Teddy toy?"

"Mommy has it," Ethan said.

"Ms. Emerson, guess what?" Megan said.

"What?"

"Mommy said I can go horseback riding!" Megan exclaimed. "With Grandma!"

"Oh, that'll be awesome!" Nivie said.

"It sure will," Jacqueline said, holding onto Bill's hand.

"And, I'm pwaying peeano mo!" Ethan said.

"You're playing piano even more? That's awesome, too!" Nivie said. "And, I hear you'll be staying in Woodhaven Run for a while."

"Yes, we are," Bryn said. She exchanged smiles with Jacqueline.

"Mommy said we can video chat with Daddy all the time!" Megan added.

"So much fun! Oh, and I know that school is starting very soon," Nivie continued. "How exciting!"

"Yeah!" the kids shouted.

"Ethan will have Mrs. Brooks for his next level of preschool. Megan will have Mrs. Gardner for second grade," Bryn said.

"Oh, you guys will have so much fun," Nivie said.

"And, how are your moving plans coming along?" Jacqueline asked.

"Well, they're comin' along."

"How long can you stay?" Jacqueline asked.

"Well, the movers are here Monday, and then we're outta here Wednesday. We'll get there just in time to begin the new school year," Nivie said.

"Yeah, and I'll start my job then, too," Alex said.

"Don't want you to go," Megan said, clinging tighter to Nivie.

"I know. I'm going to miss you, too, Meggie. But, you need to stay here to take care of the HEAL Park."

Megan's lip jut out. "Gonna miss you and Sherlock. And, Watson."

"I'm going to miss you, too. But, we can also video chat. And, don't forget: Blueberry Time for Olaf!" Nivie added.

"Yeah." Megan hugged Nivie tighter.

"Yep, ready for new adventures at the beach." Looking around at the Park, she added, "But, we did pretty well here, I'd say."

"We really did," Bryn smiled, gently taking Ethan's hand in hers.

"Nivie, it's been such a pleasure to work with you, as an adult," Jacqueline said.

"Yeah, life is funny, isn't it? Who would have thought I would be creating an animal park with one of my aunt's closest friends?" Nivie chuckled.

"Indeed! And, we'd love for both of you to join us all for lunch," Jacqueline said, looking at Nivie and Alex. "We're going to celebrate at Timbers Restaurant."

"That sounds awesome. Thank you," Nivie said. "But, just go ahead. I'll meet up with you guys soon."

"Come now, Megan. Ethan," Jacqueline said, holding out her hand. "Mrs. Emerson will be joining us shortly."

"Yeah, c'mon kids," Bryn said, as Megan slid away from Nivie. Megan took her grandmother's hand, and Ethan grabbed Bryn's hand.

"Bye, Mrs. Emerson!" Megan said.

"Bye, Ms. Emosin!" Ethan added.

"Here, Brother. Hold my hand," Megan said, taking Ethan's hand.

"See you soon, kids!"

"You sure?" Alex asked Nivie.

"Yeah, yeah. I'll be fine, Honey. I'll be right there."

Alex leaned over, kissing her head.

Nivie watched them all walk back over the bridge. Jacqueline and Bryn swung the kids between them, creating a link between the generations. Bill and Alex talked, following the familial chain. All six of them passed the majestic Ranger, Tucker, and Kimball statues, turned a hard left, and disappeared.

Ambling back to the interment area, Nivie crouched down and touched the Minerva statue. "Well, kiddie kitties, this is it. Thanks. For everything," she said, her tears nourishing the earth. "Man, this is harder than I thought it'd be. But, you have to watch over Tucker and Ranger. And the others that'll join you."

Standing up, Nivie wiped her tears and pulled Kimball's collar and Minerva's paw print tin out of her pocket. "Thanks for being my angels. See you both at the beach."

On her stroll back to the entrance, a bluebird soared in front of her, resting on top of Ranger's head.

She smiled.

Resources

Websites

www.AnimalsConnectUs.com
www.aplb.org: The Association for Pet Loss and Bereavement
www.RainbowsBridge.com
www.Pet-Loss.net
www.PetLoss.com

Colorado State University Veterinary Teaching Hospital:
http://csu-cvmbs.colostate.edu/vth/diagnostic-and-support/argus/Pages/default.aspx

Cornell University College of Veterinary Medicine:
http://www.vet.cornell.edu/Org/PetLoss/

Michigan State University Veterinary Medical Center:
http://cvm.msu.edu/hospital/services/social-work/pet-loss-support-hotline

North Carolina State University Veterinary Hospital:
http://www.ncstatevets.org/owners/counsel/

Ohio State University Veterinary Medical Center:
http://vet.osu.edu/vmc/companion/our-services/honoring-bond-support-animal-owners/online-support-resources

<u>Tufts University Cummings School of Veterinary Medicine</u>:
http://vet.tufts.edu/petloss/

<u>University of Tennessee-Knoxville Veterinary Social Work</u>:
http://vetsocialwork.utk.edu/grief.php

<u>University of Minnesota Veterinary Medical Center</u>:
http://www.cvm.umn.edu/vmc/specialties/social-services/
grief-loss/

<u>Washington State University College of Veterinary Medicine</u>:
http://www.vetmed.wsu.edu/outreach/pet-loss-hotline/
grieving-process

Books

A Big Little Life by Dean Koontz
Angel Animals: Exploring Our Spiritual Connection with Animals by Allen and Linda Anderson
Blessing The Bridge: What Animals Teach Us About Death, Dying, and Beyond by Rita Reynolds & Gary Kowalski
Coping With Sorrow on the Loss of Your Pet by Moira Anderson
Dogs That Know When Their Owners Are Coming Home and Other Unexplained Powers of Animals by Rupert Sheldrake
Grieving the Death of A Pet by Betty Carmack
Goodbye, Friend by Gary Kowalski
Kindred Spirits by Allen Schoen
My Angels Wear Fur by Devon O'Day
Pet Loss: A Thoughtful Guide for Adults and Children by Herbert Nieburg
The Soul of Animals by Gary Kowalski
The Loss of a Pet by Wallace Sife
What Animals Can Teach Us About Spirituality by Diana Guerrero
When Your Pet Dies by Alan Wolfelt

Books for Children

Jasper's Day by Marjorie Blain Parker

Jungle Journey by Barbara Betker McIntyre

The Tenth Good Thing About Barney by Judith Viorst

When a Pet Dies by Fred Rogers

When Kitty Passed Away by Linda Makkay

Reflective Discussion Questions

(These questions contain spoilers)

1. What life lessons have you learned from your animals? Nivie said that Kimball showed her that "Every day is a gift and tomorrow is not promised to us." What do each of the characters learn from their beloved animals? What have you learned from yours? Sometimes having an animal and then losing them can be the impetus to start something new, such as a new relationship or a new job. Have you ever had this experience?

2. Jacqueline's experience with Ranger affected how Bryn dealt with Tucker's death. What experiences did you have as a child with animals and their deaths? How do you think that shaped your understanding of animal loss? Donna said that many times the death of an animal is the first experience a child has with death. Was this your experience?

3. Brad and Esteban, Nivie's friends, got their cat, Roxie, soon after their beloved cat, Velma, died. Nivie, however, initially didn't want to ever have another animal after Kimball died. How would each of these approaches feel "comfortable" at first? What are the benefits and challenges of each approach?

4. Sometimes it is not just the loss of the animal himself, but the agony of having to make the dreaded euthanasia decision, as with Nivie and Kimball. Then, after the animal dies, it can be painful to see others grieve as well, as with Bryn seeing Olaf and Ace, and Nivie seeing Alex. How have you made the decision to euthanize? What experiences have you had with others' grief?

5. How is the loss of a beloved human similar to losing a beloved animal? How are they different?

6. What role do friends play in grief? (Ronni, Donna, Bill, Lauren, Brad and Esteban)

7. In looking at Alex's reaction to Kimball's death: Do you think it's different for a boy or man to grieve over the loss of an animal than it is for a girl or woman? If so, why?

8. Many times in life, people experience compounded grief (i.e.) Nivie not being able to have children, Jacqueline's loss of her husband and Ranger. How does this impact the experience of grief?

9. Do you believe that Bryn "waited too long" for Tucker, or do you think he preferred to die at home, as Lauren suggested? Bryn and Lauren discuss guilt in animal loss. How much does guilt play in the grief over the loss of an animal?

10. After Kimball dies, Nivie initially says she doesn't want any more animals, partly because she only "remembers the end." One of Jacqueline's initial reasons for not supporting the HEAL Park is also, in part, due to the same reason. Have you had this experience?

11. Various ways of dealing with grief were outlined in the book: Tucker's memorial service; Megan's letter to God; Ethan's drawing; Gladys's full-page obituaries; framed pictures and urns on display; creating the HEAL park. Do you agree when Donna says that "… it's very healthy to channel one's grief into doing something."?

12. After Tucker's death, Megan eventually shares with Jacqueline that she feels guilty about being angry at Tucker. Ethan responds to Tucker's death by bedwetting and having nightmares and night terrors. How have you seen the children in your own life (your children, nieces, nephews, children of friends, grandchildren, etc.) react when a beloved animal died? Did they respond in the same way as Megan and Ethan or differently?

13. For teachers/educators: how might you help a student who is dealing with the loss of an animal either at Ethan, Megan or Chelsea's (Nivie's student) age?

14. How unusual do you think Gladys' behavior toward animals is? What are your thoughts about her wishes for her dog Roosevelt after she died?

15. Discuss the role of religion and spirituality in healing from grief.

16. Donna asked about Jacqueline's dreams. Have you ever examined your dreams during a time of grief for guidance or information? If so, did you find any relief from them?

17. Discuss how different people process grief. Bryn pushes grief aside, doesn't take help from others, keeps busy, and won't allow others to grieve, including Olaf and Ace. Nivie had an outburst, retreats into herself, avoids animals, and is easily triggered. Jacqueline avoids discussing horses, doesn't allow her daughter and grand-daughter to go horseback riding, even demonizes horses, and tries to get rid of Chloe, a reminder of Edmond. Do you see yourself in these women?

18. Do you agree with Donna when she says grief "sits and waits."? Sometimes it can come on like a watershed moment, like with Bryn's incident with the squirrel. Have you had an experience like this?

19. Do you think that Bryn should have stayed in Woodhaven Run or joined Julian in Texas? Should Nivie and Alex have stayed in Woodhaven Run?

20. Discuss the different implications of the title *Buried Deep in our Hearts.*

21. How will the children likely change their viewpoint about animal loss from participating in the HEAL Park?

22. Would your community be open to having an animal memorial park, like a HEAL Park? How would it benefit and, on the other hand, where might the resistance be?

23. Many resources are available now to help with the loss of an animal: for example, individual counseling, hotlines, support groups, and animal communicators? Have you ever, or would you consider, participating in any of them?

Made in the USA
San Bernardino, CA
10 February 2017